GATHER THE FORTUNES

GATHER THE FORTUNES

BRYAN CAMP

A John Joseph Adams Book

HOUGHTON MIFFLIN HARCOURT
Boston   New York
2019

For information about permission to reproduce selections from this book,
write to trade.permissions@hmhco.com or to Permissions,
Houghton Mifflin Harcourt Publishing Company,
3 Park Avenue, 19th Floor, New York, New York 10016.

hmhco.com

Library of Congress Cataloging-in-Publication Data
Names: Camp, Bryan, author.
Title: Gather the fortunes / Bryan Camp.
Description: Boston ; New York : Houghton Mifflin Harcourt, 2019. |
Series: A Crescent City novel ; 2 | "A John Joseph Adams book."
Identifiers: LCCN 2018043604 (print) | LCCN 2018044778 (ebook) |
ISBN 9781328876744 (ebook) | ISBN 9781328876713 (hardback)
Subjects: | BISAC: FICTION / Fantasy / Contemporary. |
FICTION / Fantasy / Urban Life. | FICTION / Ghost. |
FICTION / Fairy Tales, Folk Tales, Legends & Mythology. | GSAFD: Fantasy fiction.
Classification: LCC PS3603.A4557 (ebook) | LCC PS3603.A4557 G38 2019 (print) |
DDC 813/.6—dc23
LC record available at https://lccn.loc.gov/2018043604

Book design by David Futato

Printed in the United States of America
DOC 10 9 8 7 6 5 4 3 2 1

For Harold H., Gwen S., Michael, Richard, and Betty B.,
Richard C., Bruce I., Mary R., Judy O.,
and all the others who have made the journey ahead of us

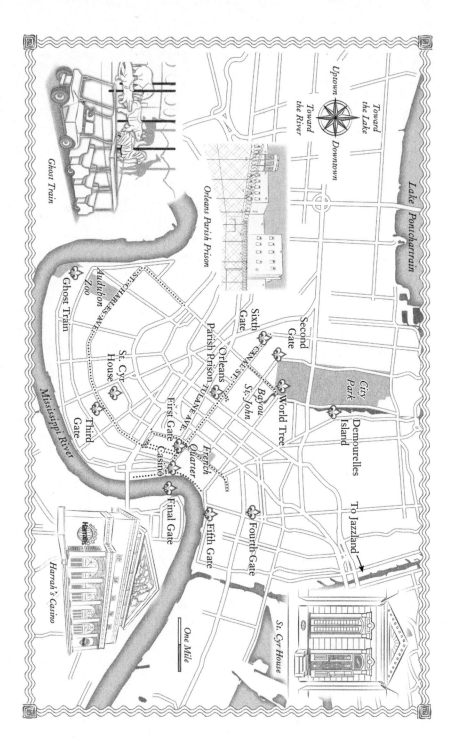

Lake Ponchartrain

Toward the Lake

Uptown · Downtown

Toward the River

Ghost Train

Orleans Parish Prison

City Park

Demourelles Island

Second Gate

Sixth Gate

World Tree

Bayou St. John

CANAL ST.

French Quarter

Orleans Parish Prison

TULANE AVE.

First Gate

Fourth Gate

Fifth Gate

Final Gate

Casino

To Jazzland

St. Cyr House

St. Cyr House

Harrah's Casino

Mississippi River

Ghost Train

Audubon Zoo

ST. CHARLES AVE.

Third Gate

One Mile

PART ONE

THIS WORLD

CHAPTER ONE

WHEN DEATH COMES, he carries a tool for harvesting grain slung over his shoulder, his skeletal form swallowed by a billowing black cloak. And she descends from the heavens astride a magnificent horse, blood-flecked armor glinting in the light of a battlefield sunset, to carry a fallen warrior away to an everlasting feast. And he leads the way to the Scales of Judgment with his human arms stretched wide in welcome, while his scavenger's eyes stare down the length of his jackal's muzzle, weighing and hungry. And she waits—either hideously ugly or unspeakably beautiful depending on the way you lived your life—on the far side of a bridge that is either a rainbow or the Milky Way or both, a span that is either treacherous and thin as a single plank of wood, or wide and sturdy and safe, whichever you have earned. They are sparrows and owls, dolphins and bees, dogs and ravens and whippoorwills. They are the familiar faces of ancestors who have gone before, they are luminous beings of impossible description, and they are the random firings of synapses as the fragile spark of life fades to nothing. He is a moment all must experience. She is a figure to be both feared and embraced. They are the concept that rules all others; a constant, like entropy, like the speed of light. Death is both an end and a transition. Simultaneously a crossing over and the guide on that journey, one that is unique to each individual and yet the same for all. Death is able to be every one of these and more—all at once without conflict or contradiction—because death is the end of all conflicts, is beyond contradictions. Both nothing and everything.

The only thing Death has never been is lonely.

⧖

One of those many contradictions, a young woman named Renaissance Raines, waited for death in a neighborhood dive bar named Pal's, scratching the label off a warm half-finished bottle of Abita with her thumbnail, unnoticed and sober and bored. She sat in one of the high-backed swivel chairs at the long bar that took up most of the main room, facing a back-lit altar of liquor bottles that glowed beneath a couple of flat-screen TVs and the chalkboards advertising drink specials. The wall behind her held a few small, two-person tables that were empty in the early afternoon but wouldn't stay that way for much longer. Bright blue walls rose to a high orange ceiling illuminated by lights that tapered down to points in a way that reminded Renai of spinning tops. The life of the bar shifted around her—the electronic jingle and chirp of the digital jukebox in the corner, the brash, too-loud laughter coming from the handful of mostly white college kids playing air hockey in the back, the warmer, subdued conversation between a quartet of locals, an older black couple, a white woman holding a tiny, trembling dog, and a middle-aged Native American guy bellied up to the bar, a swirl of cigarette smoke in the air, the soft whir of ceiling fans overhead—and though breath filled her lungs and blood pulsed in her veins, she was as a ghost to all of it. She spoke to no one, shared no one's companionable silence, sent no texts to check on anyone's arrival, made no attempts to catch a stranger's eye. If anyone looked at Renai long enough to really see her—her dark brown skin taut with youth and free of laugh or frown lines, her full cheeks that dimpled with the slightest of smiles, her loose coils of hair, usually allowed to hang down along her jawline but today pulled and wound into a bun on each side of her head, her slender runner's frame lost in the depths of a thick leather jacket despite the heat that still hadn't relaxed its grip even in late October—they'd wonder if she was old enough to drink the beer in her hand. She knew nobody would, though.

Most people didn't really seem to notice her at all these days. She hadn't gotten carded when she came in, no one had stopped her when she'd slipped behind the counter and taken a beer from the cooler. If she took her hand off the bottle and left it on the counter, the bartender would scoop it up and drop it in the trash. If she switched chairs to sit right next to the locals — or even leaned in between them — so long as she didn't touch them, they'd keep talking as if she wasn't there. If she interrupted, if she tapped someone on the shoulder, if she shattered one of the TVs with a thrown glass and shrieked with all her might, they'd see her, briefly, giving her the unfocused, confused look of a person shaken awake. If she stopped talking or touching them, though, they'd turn back to whatever they were doing, unsettled, maybe, but with Renai already on her way to being forgotten.

Life just wasn't the same since her resurrection.

The details of her untimely end and her unusual return were still frustratingly hazy for her, even though she'd had years to try and remember. She had only a scatter of disconnected, vivid, and hard-to-trust flashes of memory to try to piece together. A moment of violence in a familiar room. A difficult journey across a place that was somehow both New Orleans and somewhere else. An eerie black streetcar that didn't exist in the living world. A moment of choice — though not the specifics of the choice she'd made — in front of a pair of huge empty chairs: the Thrones that embodied Death. Rising again in a concrete tomb with another voice in her head: that of a Trickster named Jude. His body hanging upside down in a tree in Audubon Park. A Red Door that filled her with dread. None of it fit together into a narrative that made any sense to her.

What she knew for sure was that she'd died late one night in August 2011 and woke up some random morning that September in a bed not her own with the feeling that many days had passed without her knowing, like she'd fought through an intense illness whose fever had just broken. Over the days and weeks and months and years that followed, she'd discovered that her new existence carried consequences: what she'd come to think of as the aura of disinterest that surrounded her, these snapshots of her experiences in the Underworld burned into her memory, and a strange, profound distance from the world around her. She hadn't been dead long, less than a week, but that was enough to destroy everything she had been. Family and friends had buried her. Certificates had been signed. Mourners had mourned. And then, before she had a chance to return to it, her world had moved on.

She'd been brought back to life, just not to her own.

Renai gulped down a couple of mouthfuls of Abita as if her thoughts had left a bad taste in her mouth. She grimaced at the lukewarm beer and considered swiping a cold one. What she really wanted, she realized, was heat. Coffee, tea, lit gasoline; anything that might ease the chill that had burrowed deep within her since her resurrection.

"Least she got some kind of justice," the Native American guy said, with a hint of an accent Renai couldn't place, just enough to guess he wasn't from here. "Too little, too late, but better than nothing."

For a moment Renai thought he was talking about her, but of course he couldn't be. He didn't even know she was in the room. She'd been half listening to their conversation while she brooded, though, so it didn't take long for her to realize that they were still talking about the young woman who'd been murdered in this very bar a few years ago whose killer had just been convicted. Their maudlin discussion turned to the dead girl's last words, and Renai spun her chair to face away from them. She didn't need to listen to the rest of it to know what they'd say. The final sounds that passed across most people's lips were either a plea for more time, or a question they'd never hear answered.

Renai had heard plenty of both in the past five years.

When she was just about to leave some cash for her beer—she had no fear of being caught, but her momma hadn't raised no thief—and make her way across town to what she was in this bar avoiding, the door to the men's room swung open, and one of the college guys came barreling out. "Brah," he shouted to his friends, "you gotta check this shit out! There's, like, seventies porn all over the walls!"

"Wait till your ol' lady meets Burt in the little girl's room," Renai muttered, referring to the picture of a nude Burt Reynolds reclining on a bearskin rug that hung over the bathroom sink.

As though in response to her words, Renai heard a man's chuckle come from behind the bar. She glanced over and saw a brown-skinned older man who was, simply put, unfortunate-looking. He had a large, bulbous nose that looked like it had been broken twice as often as it had been set, and an obnoxious set of ears, too wide, too long, and oddly flat at the top. His eyes were either too small for his face or just dwarfed by the combination of the nose and ears. He wore a dark blue button-down work shirt with the name SETH embroidered over his chest pocket in gold thread. He twisted a washrag inside a pint glass with the deft, unconscious motions of someone who'd done it for years.

To her surprise, he seemed to actually see her, grinned at her, even. "Yeah you right," he said, all one word like he was born here. "Mr. Reynolds done made more than one lady question her choice of companion over the years." He set the glass down and rested his hands on the bar, leaning in closer to make his next statement quiet and conspiratorial. "Though a pretty young thing like you might just convince him to hop down off that wall and buy you a drink."

Renai opened her mouth to answer, but something made her hesitate. He felt off somehow. Wrong. Not girl-grab-your-shit-and-run bad, but definitely worth choosing her words with care. It could be the fact that he'd noticed her at all that set her spidey sense tingling, but she *had* spoken. He might just have really sensitive hearing. Death had rendered her hard to notice, not completely undetectable. Nor was it the creepy thing he'd said, though gross bartender pickup lines were always cause for concern. As were the scattered designs inked across his taut forearms, which had the simple line-drawing look of prison tattoos. No, Renai realized, following the stretch of his arms down to the bar, it was his hands that had thrown her off.

Seth's hands were *filthy*.

He had dirty shadows beneath his too-long nails, and some red substance was crusted into his cuticles and packed into the folds of skin at his knuckles. Renai's heart clenched at the sight of it, her thoughts leaping to images of Seth wrist-deep in a pool of blood—but no, she reminded herself, blood dried a darker, browner shade than what stained Seth's hands. This was soil: thick red clay. Her imagination shifted her horror-movie scenario to one of Seth burrowing down into the earth.

Or out of a grave.

That, coupled with his ability to see her at all, made her think that Seth was more than he appeared. "What are you?" she asked. It wasn't a polite question to ask in the world of myths and gods that she'd been resurrected into, but she had places to be and no time for games. Besides, if he didn't want rude, he shouldn't have called her a "thing."

"As you can see here," he said, tapping a sharp fingernail against the name on his shirt, "they call me Seth."

She raised an eyebrow into an imperious arch, a feed-me-none-of-your-bullshit gesture. "I can read, boo, but I guess you can't hear too good." She let a little Ninth Ward creep into her voice, knowing people tended to underestimate you if your dialect sounded a certain way. "Code switching," the

Internet called it. "Cooning," her mother would have said, after kissing her teeth. "With them filthy hands of yours, I think we both know you ain't no bartender, and since nobody in here seen us talking, I guess you ain't exactly human, neither. So what are you? Psychopomp? Zombie? Jiang Shi? You here on your own, or did the Thrones send you?"

Seth smiled, his teeth crowded and uneven, and all pretense of humanity slid away from him. He didn't have a vampire's fangs or a ghoul's obscene tongue or a wendigo's fetid breath. His smile wasn't even threatening. But in Seth's sly, effortless conviction, Renai saw the kind of knowledge and power no mortal could possess.

"You," he said, "are exactly the person I was led to believe you would be." His voice had changed, too, the drawl of a local's accent replaced by the clipped non-accent of someone so profoundly educated that regional markers had been bleached from his vowels.

See what happens when you try and play a player, she thought.

He reached into the chest pocket of his work shirt and pulled out a long, thin strip of paper, curled in on itself like it had once been rolled into a tight little cylinder. He set it on the bar next to her beer bottle, but kept it pinned beneath his soiled finger. "I'm going to request a favor of you now."

That word, *favor,* resonated in her chest in a way that made her hold her next breath. In this new reality in which she'd found herself, one where myths walked the streets of New Orleans and magic was possible, Renai had learned that things like wealth and power had little to do with the accumulation of material possessions or hoarding of currency, and far more to do with will — with one's ability to impact the world. Trading one action for another was the coin of the realm. The fact that he just assumed that she would want what he was offering told her she wasn't dealing with some pitiful undead who had scraped up just enough magic to be able to resist death's grip. No, she got the feeling that Seth was talking about *divine* favor.

Because whatever he called himself, Renai was pretty sure that this ugly, grimy-handed bartender was a god.

Renai chewed at her lip until she realized she was doing it and made herself stop. "I'm listening," she said.

"This is the name," Seth said, "of someone whose well-being I consider significant, someone who will soon come into your realm of influence."

"I don't have the authority to let—"

Seth cut her off before she could finish by closing his eyes and shaking his head slowly, his mouth compressed to a thin line. She couldn't read the gesture well enough to tell if he was disappointed in the conclusion she'd leapt to, or if she'd offended him simply by interrupting, but she could tell she'd misstepped somehow and it stole the voice from her.

When he opened his eyes, he had the squeezed, horizontal-slitted pupils of a goat.

"If I thought you might neglect your duty in pursuit of personal gain, I wouldn't have approached you. I'm merely asking that you give the situation careful consideration and do your best to see that he is well-cared-for. Nothing more."

Renai tried to swallow, her mouth suddenly dry. She was caught, she realized, between not trusting Seth's cryptic proposition and not wanting to deny any god, especially not one who'd gone to the trouble of finding her. And also, whispered a voice she tried to deny, it would be pretty fucking sweet to have a literal deus ex machina in her back pocket. There were about a dozen questions whirling in her mind, but only two of desperate significance, and only one she had the courage to ask.

"Why me?"

Seth frowned, like the answer should be obvious. "Because Renai—if I may call you Renai—out of all your associates, you alone have a unique perspective." He'd pronounced her nickname correctly, like it had two *ee*'s at the end, which made her think that he'd heard her name out loud, not read it. Most people saw that *ai* in her name and acted like it added a couple more syllables. Made her wonder who'd spoken her name to him and what else they'd had to say.

"You retain," he continued, "the ability to question orders. You are still capable of compassion. Simply put, I'm speaking to you because, of all the others I might have asked, you alone are still alive."

Oh, Renai thought, *so when you said I was the person you thought I would be, what you meant to say was that I'm Death's Little Mistake.* A flash of annoyance sparked within her, prompting her to ask the question she didn't really want to ask.

"And if, after careful review of my options, I still make a choice you don't like?"

Seth's frown deepened, but he nodded, as if this, at last, was the question she ought to be asking. "Then you will have done me no favors, and so I will owe you none in return. I may offer some small token of gratitude for your time, if I believe your consideration was genuine, but I assure you that I won't hold a grudge. I recognize that you are under obligations of your own."

Wonder how small a token we're talking about, she thought, and then heard, in her grandmother's voice: *Always free cheese in a mousetrap, but I ain't never seen a mouse happy he found it.* She looked down at his hand, as if she could read the name through the paper, as if it would matter either way if she could. Seth had the five dots of a quincunx inked in the place where his thumb joined his hand: four bluish pinpricks arranged in a square, a fifth in the center. Another jail tattoo, the dot in the center representing the prisoner surrounded by four walls. She couldn't decide if the tattoos were part of the mask Seth wore to disguise his true form, or if they represented something profound about him. Couldn't say which she thought would be worse. What choice did she really have, though?

Putting her hand close to his soiled skin made every muscle in her abdomen clench, but she reached out and took the slip of paper from him anyway. He made her tug it out from beneath his finger, keeping just enough pressure on the paper that if she pulled too fast it would tear. "I'm not saying yes," she said, "and I'm not saying no. I'm just saying I'll consider it."

The ugly god smiled, warm and cheerful and genuine. "Excellent! I'm sure that when you see . . ." He trailed off, raising a hand as if to ward off what he'd intended to say. "No, I've spoken my piece. The decision must be yours."

On the bar where she'd left it, her phone lit up and trilled, the alarm she'd set to remind herself when it was time to leave. When she looked up, Seth was gone. The paper remained in her hand, though: RAMSES ST. CYR. The name tickled at her, like it was one she should recognize. She silenced the alarm and slid her phone and the slip of paper into her jacket pocket, deciding to file this whole conversation under "shit to deal with later."

Death waited for no one, after all.

Outside, her noble steed waited on the curb, black and gleaming and powerful. Murder and resurrection had stolen just about everything from Renai, but sometimes when the gods took with one hand, they gave with the other. The Thrones did, at least; they'd given her the leather jacket she wore—far more than the simple garment it appeared to be—and after she'd found that buses passed her by if she was the only one at the stop, they'd also given her a ride. Not a "steed" in the truest sense of the word—even Renai's difficulty at being noticed probably wouldn't hide a horse galloping through city streets—the Thrones' gift had taken the shape of a motorcycle: a Honda Valkyrie. Unlike an actual motorcycle, though, this bike rumbled to life as soon as Renai swung a leg onto her, always seemed to know exactly where Renai wanted to go when she gripped the handlebars, and never ran out of gas. Renai called her Kyrie. She didn't know how intelligent Kyrie was, or if she had an actual name of her own, or why the motorcycle felt so strongly like a "she." She also chose not to think about what sort of fuel powered a motorcycle from the Underworld.

As Kyrie sped away from Pal's with a roar that could only be called eager, it occurred to Renai that she avoided thinking about a lot these days. Her old life; her duties in this new one. The dead and the Thrones and the other gods she'd met, however briefly. The changes she'd endured since her resurrection. She'd made a habit of pushing it all down deep into the cold, empty well in the center of her, far enough from her present moment that she hardly thought about anything at all, letting one day bleed unexamined into the next. Years had gone by like this, with her learning almost nothing new about the world she'd found herself in, just doing as she was told. Following the rules she'd been given.

She leaned into the slide as Kyrie turned from Orleans onto Broad, leaving behind the green sprawling canopy of the live oaks growing in the neutral ground for a wide stretch of asphalt open to the afternoon sky. She patted her jacket pocket absently, making sure that she still had the slip of paper Seth had given her.

He had described a much different person than the one Renai saw in the mirror. Seemed to think she was capable of defiance when she didn't even bother to question. But was it apathy that dictated her actions? Or fear?

Kyrie's tires thumped and bucked over the streetcar tracks running down Canal, shaking away Renai's thoughts. Those bumps meant she was almost there, so it was time to get her game face on. She unzipped a small pocket on the front of her jacket that she never used—small and awkwardly placed, probably for a cell phone—and pushed the little scroll of paper inside, zipping it back up, knowing she didn't want to lose it, knowing she'd get distracted by it if it wasn't somewhere secure.

She did her best to clear her mind of doubt and questions, of everything but her only true purpose in this world of hers. A few minutes later, Kyrie swung past Tulane and Broad, turned and bumped up onto the sidewalk on Gravier across the street from a squat, ugly cinder block of a building, her engine grumbling to a stop. Renai kissed her fingertips and tapped them against Kyrie's chassis as she swung her leg off the bike. The metal was cold to the touch despite running full throttle in the late October warmth. Something else she and the bike shared. The building was yet one more thought she'd been avoiding, a task she chose to think of in the abstract until the moment came. Hands clenched into fists in her jacket pockets, Renai forced herself to look across the street.

In its distinct lack of personality, the building that Renai didn't want to think about could have been a cheaply designed office complex or a parking garage, if it weren't for the half-sized windows and the coils of razor wire woven through the surrounding fence, but when she allowed herself more than a glance, it looked exactly like what it was.

The place Kyrie had brought her was Orleans Parish Prison, and Renai had come here to take a man's life.

CHAPTER TWO

HALF AN HOUR later Renai paced up and down the sidewalk across from OPP, bored and pissed and starting to wonder if she'd gotten the time wrong. In her earbuds Destiny's Child sang that they'd been through the storm and the rain, that they were survivors. Since the dead didn't really respond to texts, music was about the only use she got out of her phone, smart as it claimed to be. She'd programmed a bunch of numbers into it back when she'd first gotten it—the hospital where her mom worked, her cousin's place in Houston, the house Uptown she still thought of as home—but had deleted all of them after she'd almost called her mom once. She still couldn't be sure if she'd really pressed the CALL button by accident or if it had been subconscious desire, but forcing herself to hang up had been harder than the first time she'd taken a life. She didn't know if she had it in her to resist the temptation to hear her mother's voice again.

At the thought of taking lives, her attention wandered back to the building across the street, and then flicked away again, back to her sneakers and the unexpectedly smooth sidewalk beneath them. Her pacing resumed. An NOPD cruiser pulled up to the curb, so close that she could feel its engine rumbling. Renai felt a nervous, obsequious smile stretch across her face, immediately pissed she'd done it and then remembering it wouldn't matter, that the white cop behind the wheel wouldn't notice her any more than the drinkers in Pal's had, that she was the next best thing to invisible. Sure enough, he studied the computer screen built into his passenger seat as if she weren't there at all. She'd never thought she'd be free of the second look, the immediate suspicion that the color of her skin elicited, but now that it was gone, she found it strangely unnerving. She was pretty sure there was a French word for it, something about the feeling of being in a foreign country.

Girl, Renai heard her mother say, *you always could find shade on a sunny day.* Turned out she didn't need a phone call to speak to her mother after all.

Just as "Survivor" ended and Lorde said she'd never seen a diamond in the flesh, a raven swooped out of the sky—framed by the glowing red letters of the Falstaff tower—and landed with a little hop on the top of the police cruiser's light bar. *About time,* Renai thought, shutting the music off and tugging out her earbuds.

"You're here early," the raven said, tilting his head to the side, "you got a hot date or something?"

Renai raised an eyebrow. "I ain't so much early as you are barely on time, *Salvatore.*" And there was Renai's mother again, in the yes-I-did-just-use-your-full-name sound of her own voice.

The bird dipped his head and raised his beak, a gesture that made Renai think of someone rolling their eyes. "Barely is still on time in my book, *Renaissance.*" The raven had an accent that was halfway between old New Orleans and some Brooklyn gangster on TV, an accent that came from Chalmette—one of those places on the outskirts of New Orleans that wasn't exactly in the city, wasn't quite a neighborhood, and wasn't quite its own town—not far from the Bywater neighborhood where Renai's extended family was from. What Sal and Renai shared was that they were both psychopomps, guides who led the dead to their just reward.

That was where the similarity ended. Sal was, like every other psychopomp Renai had ever met, a spirit stuffed into a temporary physical body. In that, he had more in common with her motorcycle than with her. Renai, on the other hand, was a living, breathing human who taken on the role of a psychopomp after her resurrection. What was a definition for Sal was merely a title for her. As far as she knew, she was the only one of her kind. Some might say that made her unique. Others would call her a mistake.

"Besides," Sal continued, "it ain't like he's exactly goin' nowhere." He dug beneath his wing, nipping at a feather. "Not on his own, anyway," he muttered.

Renai sighed and held out her arm, inviting the raven to perch there. A rustle of feathers and a clench of talons later, and his weight settled onto her shoulder, far more than even a bird as big as Sal ought to weigh. She didn't know if he was a once-human soul wearing a raven's shape or an animal's soul who had learned human speech or if he was something even stranger, but he'd taught her all she knew about being a psychopomp, and in this strange new life of hers, he was her closest friend. So she didn't much care what he was, so long as he kept showing up.

"You got the name?" Sal asked, not lowering his voice even though he was right next to her ear.

"Miguel Flores," Renai said. "5:12 p.m." She knew more: his location in the prison, the circumstances of his end, and all the other details she'd need to be able to find him, but all Sal ever seemed to need was a name.

He aimed a wing in the direction of the prison. "Then let's hop to it, Raines."

The cop turned his engine off and got out of his cruiser, talking into the handset on his shoulder. Despite the fact that Renai had to step out of his way as he walked past her and up the stairs leading to the NOPD office building, he didn't spare a glance for either of them. Usually, when Renai went out on a collection, she could depend on what she'd come to think of as her personal aura of disinterest to move around undetected. She'd stood in hospital rooms next to grieving loved ones, in bedrooms next to sleeping spouses, in nursing homes next to hospice nurses, and on roadsides next to paramedics, as unnoticed as she'd been in Pal's. Walking into a prison, though, would take a little more effort.

She pulled up the jersey hood of her jacket and spoke the word the Thrones had taught her when they gave the jacket to her, a difficult-to-comprehend collection of hissing syllables. It meant a lot of things all at once: *unseen, unheard, unknown, untouched.* Renai had come to call it "the ghost word." She hated using it.

As soon as the magic took hold, all the color went out of her vision, shifting into varying shades of a dark, shadowy purple. Her skin felt too tight and impossibly sensitive, all the intensity of a tab of molly with none of the euphoria. The air around her grew chilly, then full-on cold, as if the well of emptiness inside her leached warmth from her surroundings. A whine began just at the edge of hearing, like tinnitus or the antique computer monitors at her old elementary school. The power lines overhead glowed, incandescent as a lightbulb, crackling and popping like an open flame. Sal's oil-black feathers turned white as bone.

Grinding her molars against the assault on her senses, Renai hurried across the street and the small, almost-empty visitor's parking lot, right up to the razor-wire and chain-link fence. Hands deep in her jacket pockets so Sal wouldn't see them clenched into fists, head down so the hood would hide her purse-lipped squint, Renai stepped through the metal.

Once, on a dare, Renai had touched the tip of her tongue to the two prongs of a nine-volt battery. The pain that resulted was brief, potent, and numbing. The jacket's magic, activated by the ghost word, allowed her to move through physical objects as though they'd become fog, but doing so felt like the whole world was made of batteries and she was all tongue. The fence left stinging lines hatched across her body. Walls and doors would be worse. She forced herself to breathe and kept moving.

For a brief moment when she first entered the prison, a strong stink of antiseptic cleaner and body odor overwhelmed the pain of piercing its outer wall. She soon grew accustomed to the smell, though, and the hurt returned to the forefront of her focus. Thankfully, the dull roar of hundreds of people talking and stomping and arguing and bullshitting drowned out the insistent whine plaguing her ears. With a clenching of claws and a pointed beak, Sal guided her forward. Every person she saw—white, black, or brown; guard or prisoner, teenager or elderly—glowed with the fire, the life, that burned within them. Renai knew from experience to keep her distance, did everything she could to make sure she didn't even come close to touching any of them.

By the time she followed Sal's directions through two cinder-block walls, up a flight of stairs, and through enough steel security doors that she lost count, the pain of slipping through so much solid matter compounded until Renai's breath came in heaves and tears leaked from the corners of her eyes. If the raven felt any discomfort at all, he gave no sign. *Is that because he's a death spirit and I'm still alive,* she thought, *or because I've only done this for five years and he's older than the dirt in God's garden?*

Two inmates, one a younger black guy with his hair done up in twists and the other an older white man with a weak chin that made him look like a turtle, stood in the middle of the hallway with a couple of janitorial carts, one for collecting trash and the other for mopping floors. They were too close to-gether for Renai to be sure she wouldn't brush up against one of them if she tried to slip past, so she stopped, chewing at her lip, fighting the urge to leap out a window, to break the spell and reveal herself, anything to make the ex-perience of using the ghost word end.

"Didn't you use to have dreads?" Sal asked.

"What?" It just spit out of her before she could figure out what he meant, incredulous and hurt and confused all at once.

Sal aimed his beak at the janitors. "Like him. Don't get me wrong, I like your hair fine the way it is now. Suits you. Just never got around to askin' why you cut the dreads off."

Renai wondered if he'd hit the wall if she threw him at it or just pass through it. "You really think this is the best time to be asking me about my hair?"

"Ain't like they're gonna hear us," he said. "I'm just makin' polite con-versation is all."

What you're doing, Renai thought, *is trying to distract me so I'll keep calm.* It was sweet, in a dumb, insensitive kind of way. "New Orleans is technically a city, but really it's a small town," she said. "I figured I was bound to run into somebody who knew Renaissance Raines. More importantly, someone who knew she's supposed to be dead. Thought it might be best if I looked like someone different." Which was true, but also a lie. She'd cut her locks off herself and dealt with the funky, unevenly tangled mess that followed until her hair grew out into something she could manage on her own because she couldn't stand the idea of going to a different hairdresser than the one she'd known her whole life. Not that Sal ever needed to know that.

He let out a playful little snort. "People need to notice you to recog-nize you."

She allowed herself a grin. "You're real good at sharing information I al-ready know, bird. Where were you with those gems when I first came back?" She shrugged the shoulder Sal perched on, giving him a playful nudge. Be-fore she could tease him more, the men finished their discussion and moved in opposite directions. Renai backed against—and partly through—the hall-way wall to let the white guy pass. It felt like falling backwards into a pool of fire ant bites. She really couldn't take much more of this.

"Almost there," Sal said, once she was moving again.

"So we talked about my hair, what's next, girlfriend, my love life?"

"You got enough of one to discuss?" He indicated a left turn at the end of the hall by pointing with his beak.

"Not even enough of one to lie about."

"That's too bad," Sal said. "I always expected you to end up with our old pal Jude."

At the thought of Jude Dubuisson, Renai's stomach did a pleasant little clench, and some of the chill went out of the air. No matter how hazy her memories from her time on the other side, there was no forgetting how fine that man looked. She laughed and shook her head. "Like that could've gone somewhere good. You ever meet a Trickster you could bring home to . . ."

She trailed off when she saw the crowded room through the reinforced Plexiglas window of the next door. A common room two stories tall with a row of cells along the back walls, a handful of round tables and seats bolted to the ground, and a flight of stairs leading up to a second-floor landing and another set of cells. Televisions hung on the wall far out of reach, humming and crackling with a light that was painfully bright to Renai's ghost-word-touched eyes. The iron-barred doors of all the cells stood open, their occupants spilling out into the common area, seated on the tables with their feet on the seats, leaning against cell doors with their arms folded, pacing or standing in small clusters, staring up at the televisions or talking or both. A soft, welcoming glow emanated from one of the cells on the upper tier: Miguel Flores.

"I can't do this," she said, not realizing she'd spoken out loud until Sal clicked his tongue in disagreement.

"Sure you can," he said, "it's his time."

"Not that." She waved a hand in the direction of all the men in between her and the stairs. "How am I supposed to get up there? We don't all have wings, Sal."

"I got faith in you. Just be quick. It's almost time." And with that, he launched from her shoulder, swooping up to the second-floor railing with a few flaps of his wings.

So much for sweet, Renai thought. She took a deep breath and studied the area, trying to concentrate despite the ringing in her ears and the magic stretching and scraping against her skin, hoping she'd discover a path she could slip through without touching anybody. It shouldn't be this hard to cross a room. Under normal circumstances, people moved out of your way, even if they weren't really paying attention. It had taken more than a couple of bruised toes before Renai learned that that rule didn't apply to her any-more. Under the influence of the ghost word, it would be worse.

Much worse.

Renai let out a disgusted huff. "Hell with it," she said. She cracked her knuckles, shook her arms and legs limber. "Don't think about it, girl, just *move*." She hit the door at a quick walk—popping through in a burst of pain—and kept moving. Unlike everything else in the world when she was un-der the shroud of the ghost word, living people weren't cold, they were bon-fires, so the common room air hit her like the gust from an open oven. She managed to dance around the group closest to the entrance with no trouble, but that took her too close to an older black man telling a story to another handful of inmates, his hands waving around as he added details to his nar-rative. She did her best—turning sideways and straightening her spine—but his hand swept through her stomach. Warmth filled her, starting in her core and racing through her veins like a shot of strong liquor. That was the worst part; it felt amazing.

The older man shivered visibly and grinned at his spectators. "Whoa," he said, "somebody musta walked over my grave."

That's closer to the truth than you know, Renai thought.

When she brushed up against another inmate after another couple of timid steps, heat flooding into her from the contact, she gave it up as a lost cause and broke into a run, tearing through the crowd of unsuspecting men like a sudden draft, siphoning away minutes or hours or days from their life span with every touch. She reached the stairway a few seconds later, full of energy and sick to her stomach at the same time. Sal started to say something when she got to the top of the stairs, but stopped when he caught the side-eye she shot him. Head hanging a little, he hopped from the railing back onto her shoulder. Renai followed the glow to Miguel's cell, readying herself for what came next.

⧗

Laying on a thin cot built into the wall, his breath coming in shallow, whis-tling gasps, Miguel Flores was dying.

Miguel was a short, compactly built young man, with light brown skin and thick black hair slicked down with sweat. He clutched a woolen blanket to his chest, ink swirling and sketched across his arms, both the smooth, delicate lines of professional tattoos and the rougher, simpler designs of prison ink. No one lay in the bunk above him. "My man's got a private room," Sal said as they entered, "lucky break, right?"

Renai frowned. "No one should have to die alone, Sal."

"No, I just mean you won't have to worry about bumping into nobody else in here is all." He hopped from her shoulder onto the top bunk, an involuntary squawk coming out of him, like an old man groaning when he stood up too fast. "Besides, he ain't alone. *We're* here."

Like the others, Miguel radiated heat, but his fire burned low, his life span down to nothing but smoldering embers. He shined instead, a beacon to anyone with the eyes for it that he wasn't long for this world. Renai leaned down to him, smiling in case he could see her despite the jacket's magic. The dying could, sometimes. He whispered something she couldn't quite catch, a word in Spanish maybe, and then, "Katrina." Oddly, he grinned a little when he said it.

"No," she said, "that was years ago. This moment is just for you." She hated the way her voice sounded to her own ears, harsh and cold. She had to be this way in this moment, though. If she let herself care, let herself feel, there was no way she'd be able to do what needed to be done.

Miguel's eyes went wide with fear, and even with the asthma filling his lungs full of gunk and squeezing the breath out of him, he managed to suck in enough air to speak four words in English. "Don't want," he said, gasping, "to die."

Renai tried to keep her face impassive, but a frown tucked at the corners of her mouth. "Nobody does," she said, "but everybody's got to." And then she reached inside of him and ripped his soul out.

OFTEN THEY ARE fields of untamed nature: Aaru, the peaceful land of reeds and plentiful hunting believed to be the soul of the Nile; Elysium, the always sun-kissed valley of unending bliss, and Asphodel, the merely pleasant meadow of unrelenting banality; Fólkvangr, where the slain warriors chosen by Freya feast and fight amid their stone ships and wait for Ragnarok. And sometimes they are gardens: Eden and Firdaws and Fiddler's Green and the orchard where the Jade Emperor's peaches grow. It is a euphoric tunnel made of light created by hyperactivity in the brain due to blood loss. They are the lands on and above Mount Meru where the virtuous await their next chance to attain moksha. It is the island of Magh Meall, the Summerland, the House of Song. Heaven. Paradise. A place of reward for living a righteous life.

It is not the end that awaits us all.

⧗

One of the first misconceptions about humanity and life that Renai had to let go of once she'd taken on the role of psychopomp was the idea that the human soul was a single object. Since she was a child watching cartoons, she'd been taught that when a person died, a glowing, incorporeal version of that person rose out of the body, usually crowned with a halo and clutching a harp. As she grew older, movies and depictions of Heaven had reinforced this concept until she'd come to believe that a soul was just a person-shaped light trapped inside the body in the same way she believed that her tongue had different spots for sweet and salty, or that bulls hated the color red: never considered, never questioned, and completely wrong.

Beneath her, the dying man let out one last truncated exhale and went still. What Renai held in her grip was a braided coil of light and quicksilver and shadow, the sum total of everything that made Miguel Flores unique: his identity, his destiny from his birth to this moment, his ability to influence the world around him. A whole human life in her hands.

It was her job to tear it apart.

As she worked at unbraiding the soul, she was struck by the memory of Sal teaching her to do this, his words so clear in her mind that she had to glance up at him to make sure he wasn't repeating his instructions yet again.

You start, Sal said, *with the most crucial part of your dead, their Fortune.* She gripped the strand of Miguel's soul that was composed of light between her thumb and forefinger and unwound it from the other two, the rest of the braid going awkwardly slack in her fist when the first piece slipped loose. When it came free, it stretched and oozed, like warm taffy. Renai gathered it up into the palm of her hand, tugging it up and rolling it into a ball, her fingers moving quick and sure in an upsettingly accurate impression of a spider's legs looping webbing around its prey. When she had all of it gathered into a golden sphere about the size of a fist, she set it to the side.

You get the dead's Fortune into the Underworld, Sal had repeated many, many times, *no matter what. That's Rule Number 1.*

Next came the person's ability to influence the world around them. There were many names for this capacity: ka, spirit, medicine, juju. Sal called it Voice. She unwound the shadowy and the silvery strands away from each other, letting the shadow-thread drop in a coil on Miguel's stomach, gathering the liquid silver of his Voice into a pool cupped in her two hands. *None of this shit gets into the Underworld. Not one bit. That's Rule Number 2.* Miguel's Voice rippled and swirled in her palms, pulling into a tight bead like a giant drop of mercury, growing more solid as she watched. It shifted colors and forms, first a bunch of grapes, then an apple, and finally settling into the shape of a peach. She bit into it, and her mouth flooded with tart and syrupy-sweet juice and a rush like a spike of adrenaline. The same sensation of warmth and vitality she'd siphoned away from the inmates she'd brushed against downstairs filled her when she swallowed. In the past she'd offered some to Sal, but he always flicked his beak away in a raven's version of a head shake and told her that if he was meant to eat it, the Voice would have taken on a shape he could stomach.

Renai devoured the rest of the peach in a few eager, slurping bites, so full of energy when she finished that she half expected her skin to glow. She wiped her mouth on her sleeve, a little chagrined at her enthusiasm. Voice was the part of the soul that let a person, if they had the training or the will or the faith, perform magic, so if the dead were allowed to bring even a fraction of what they possessed in life into the Underworld, they might find their way back to life. She reached down and placed the peach pit—fighting the urge to lick the last droplets of dew from its rough pockmarked surface—in the hollow of Miguel's throat. A tiny portion of Voice was always left with the body, to fuel those little magics of memory and nostalgia, those whispers of guidance and support, all the subtle ways that the dead still influenced the world once they were gone. Whenever she'd asked Sal why they ate most of the Voice instead of leaving it all with the body, he'd only tell her, *There's two kinds of shit that would happen if we didn't: bad and ugly.*

The part of a person that most people would think of as their soul: their identity, their mind—what Sal called Essence—was what remained after death. That's what psychopomps guided to the Underworld. Renai bit her lip, waiting. This part didn't always go the way she wanted it to. Sometimes, the dead were just . . . dead.

After a tense moment, the shadowy thread on Miguel's stomach rose, wavering like a plume of smoke. It grew bulging, too-large eyes, a face that only vaguely resembled the man he had once been, and long, spindly arms capped by massive hands. The rest remained a wisp, dwindling into a thread-thin tendril that vanished into Miguel's abdomen. Renai plucked the golden sphere of Miguel's destiny from the cot where she'd left it and squashed it between her palms until it formed a flat, round disk. When she held it up to the light, it had become a coin. Miguel would use it to pay his way through to the other side.

If you ever have to choose, Sal said, *between the Fortune and the Essence, you pick the Fortune every time. Call that Rule Number 3.*

"Not bad," Sal said, in the present now and not just a voice in her memories. "Few more decades of practice and you'll be good enough to start collecting the dead on your own." His beak gaped open in a raven's version of a grin. "Course, then you won't get to see my pretty self all the time."

Renai laughed. "Too pretty for prison anyway," she said. "Let's get the hell out of here."

Rather than facing the gauntlet of the crowd below her, Renai went out through the prison wall, a sharp splash of pain and a quick drop that left her buried up to her thighs in the basketball court below. After a few more minutes of hurt and irritation, she made it out of the prison entirely, and could finally pull her jacket's hood from her head, breaking the ghost word's spell and returning her to the world of natural light and physical objects and the ambient sounds of traffic. The relief made her groan aloud. Once again perched on her shoulder, Sal shot her a look but said nothing.

The streetlights flickered to life above her; twilight had fallen while she navigated her way through the prison and collected her dead. She crossed to the side of the street where she'd left Kyrie parked, leading the Essence of Miguel by one hand and holding the coin of his Fortune in the other. Miguel had taken on a little more definition, his torso filling out, his face smoothing into a fuller, healthier version of the man she'd seen in the cell. He now wore a dark blue dress shirt with the buttons done all the way up his neck, the collar ironed to sharp points. At the waist he tapered off into a smoky wisp like a cartoon genie. That smoke thinned down into a hair-thin thread that vanished back the way they'd come. She tucked Miguel's coin into a jacket pocket and straddled Kyrie, coaxing Miguel into a position that more or less approximated sitting in front of her.

At first, she'd spoken to her dead in a constant, soothing litany at this stage of their journey, worried that they were terrified, panicked. She'd come to find that it was a waste of her breath, since they were always like Miguel, drifting along beside her with a placid, dreamy expression. That slender thread connected Miguel to his body, allowing him to claim the parts of himself that he wanted to keep: his looks, his fond memories, his sense of humor if he had one, and let him leave behind the burdens he didn't: his perpetually overreacting lungs, his regrets, whatever crimes he may have committed. Without fail, every one of her dead had chosen to leave behind their last moments. The nicest thing about death, she'd found, was that you didn't remember it.

She envied that luxury.

Standing there with both feet on the pavement and Kyrie still sleeping beneath her, it all came rushing back. One of the things she found it hardest to reconcile about her new life was why, out of all the memories she'd lost, she'd kept these. She'd been closing up at the store—a tourist-trap voodoo shop in the Quarter that her aunt had owned—when she'd felt the sudden, frightening realization that she wasn't alone. One moment she'd smelled cinnamon, and the next she'd been knocked to the floor. A sudden line of ice at her throat, a blade so sharp it didn't hurt when it cut. Fear, and then panic, and then the struggle to breathe and—

"Hey, Raines, you forget something?" Sal asked, overly loud, like he was repeating himself.

Renai realized that she'd just been staring, her chest tight with held breath, her pulse pounding. She dropped into Kyrie's seat with all her weight at once, the kickstand popping up and almost ditching the bike. She recovered and grabbed the handlebars, the motorcycle coming to life with a comforting rumble, like the purr of a massive cat. Sal's talons clutched at her shoulder to stay upright. She kicked off and let Kyrie carry her away with a roar.

"You okay?" Sal asked after a minute, raising his voice to be heard over the wind.

She made him say it again, like she couldn't quite hear him. "Long day," she yelled back.

Except that wasn't really true, either. With the potency of Miguel's Voice flowing in her veins, she felt like she could sprint for miles without slowing, without even breaking a sweat. But as much as she wanted answers about her missing time, she wanted to talk about her own death even less. So she ignored the throbbing of her heart, her every instinct screaming, *run-run-run*, and forced herself to drive slow, keeping Kyrie under the speed limit and obeying traffic lights, even though she usually didn't. This part of the trip was more about giving the dead time to acclimate, to come to the realization that all of this was really happening. She couldn't rush it just because she had a bunch of bad juju in her head.

Glancing down, she saw that Miguel had formed legs, like a tadpole abandoning his tail. His head swiveled back and forth as he watched the city roll by, and it looked to her like his vacant expression had been replaced by one more aware of his surroundings. He'd probably be wondering how he'd gotten out of jail, would be just coming to the realization that this wasn't some strange dream.

"Soon," she said to him, making sure she had a firm grip on his ghostly hand, "we'll be there soon."

A few minutes later, they turned off of Canal and onto Basin Street, riding along the edge of the Quarter. Renai did her best to guide Kyrie around the jagged cracks in the asphalt and the abrupt holes that pockmarked the streets, even though the bike had handled everything New Orleans's disregard for infrastructure had thrown at her so far. Miguel shifted around in his seat, getting agitated now. She could feel the weight in the air of something unspoken, but she'd consumed his capacity for speech back in OPP.

"Relax, chico," Sal said, when they eased to a stop at a red light, "you'll get all the answers you want, I promise."

"Careful, Sal," Renai said, giving the raven a poke that earned her a pecked knuckle. "You don't want to be making promises you can't keep."

Before Sal could reply, they were rolling again. Kyrie carried them past the eerily quiet Iberville Projects—closed since the storm and in the process of being torn down—and then hopped over the short curb of the neutral ground when they reached St. Louis Cemetery No. 1, idling to a stop on the recently cut grass. The high brick wall facing Rampart Street was coated in cracked white plaster, with the boxy aboveground tombs common to older New Orleans burial sites peeking over the top. The trees growing in the cemetery swayed in the breeze. A wrought-iron gate barred the entrance, topped by a filigreed cross. Miguel went tense—or as tense as an incorporeal spirit could get—at the sight of it, but he was far from the first of her dead to show reticence once their destination became clear. She pulled him off the bike and led him forward, as gentle as she was implacable.

A young brown-skinned man wearing a do-rag the light purple of an almost-healed bruise sat slumped against the wall to the side of the entrance, his head nodding on an unsteady neck, a bottle of white rum nestled in his lap. He wore a leather jacket the same color as his do-rag, the sleeves patterned with white crosses. Renai cleared her throat, and when that didn't work, she kicked him in the side of his thigh, nearly toppling him over.

"The fuck?" His words came out in a sleepy slur, more the tone of a child asking for a few minutes more sleep than any real anger. He squinted up at them, taking in Renai and the raven on her shoulder and the dead man next to her one at a time. "Masaka's on duty now," he said. "They'll let you in."

Renai kissed her teeth. "Your twin watches the Gate during the day, Oussou."

The drunk on the sidewalk grinned up at her. "If we're twins, how you so sure I'm who you say I am?"

Renai smirked and started to answer, but Sal cursed under his breath and spoke over her.

"Because you're the only one who's piss-drunk enough to wear that ugly-ass jacket," he said, way more bitter than he ever was with her. "Quit being a dick and do your job."

Oussou's grin didn't fade like Renai expected but widened. "That you, Salutation?" he asked. He rose to his feet in a series of lurching movements that were always one precarious second away from being a fall, groaning and spilling rum and farting. When he was more or less upright, he swilled from his rum bottle in greedy gulps before glaring at Sal through one blood-shot eye. "Didn't recognize you wearing a shape that can't lick his own balls. What happened? The Thrones make you turn in that dog-skin so they could beat the fleas out of it?"

"I wear this skin at night because the dog can't stand the stink of you," Sal said, an indignant squawk finding its way into his voice. "Why's the Gate still locked? You trade your key for a cheap bottle of booze again?"

"Traded it away, he says," Oussou muttered, digging in his jacket pocket with the hand that wasn't holding his rum. "I got your key right here, see?" He pulled out his hand, his middle finger thrust up toward the sky.

"Children!" Renai yelled, loud enough that a couple walking halfway up the block turned to look at her. Both the psychopomp on her shoulder and the loa in front of her went quiet. She reached into her own pocket and pulled out the coin of Miguel's destiny. "We're kind of in the middle of something here, Oussou. You mind?" She smiled at him, feeling her face take the shape of her mother's, that smile that said: *If this is the game you want to play, let me go ahead and teach you the rules.*

Oussou frowned but nodded. He moved his bottle into his other hand and—still giving Sal the finger with the hand that held the bottle—reached into his pocket and took out an antique key made of black iron. It was cast in the shape of the veve for the Marassa twins: three circles laid out in a line, each with four different ornate and symmetrical spokes poking out, like three conjoined compasses. Glaring at Sal the whole time, Oussou reached behind him, pressed his key into the plaster wall of the cemetery, and turned it.

A single vertical crack shot up the wall and into the night sky, a line of brilliant light three stories tall. Oussou pressed a hand to the wall and pushed, and all of it—cemetery wall and the palm tree rising above it and the few stars visible through the light pollution of downtown New Orleans and the night sky itself—swung open on a smooth hinge, revealing a sky obscured by fog and bright green grass and a warm, sweet breeze. Light seemed to come from everywhere. Beside her, Miguel's mouth was open in naked astonishment.

The first look into the next world never failed to impress.

CHAPTER FOUR

THE WORLD ON the other side of the Gate wasn't quite New Orleans, and it wasn't quite the afterlife, either. The cemetery's tombs were still there in various stages of repair: some the reddish brown of crumbling, exposed brick, others the solid, almost-gleaming white of freshly applied plaster. Thick fog curled overhead, obscuring the source of light and turning the sky into the ceiling of a great cavern. In the world of the living, the cemetery's ground was almost entirely paved, but in that place a lush green carpet of dew-kissed grass covered the earth.

A still and profound silence hung in the air. New Orleans sang every hour of every day with the cacophony of traffic and trills of birdsong and with shouts both joyous and angry and with the throaty wails of brass instruments and the thunderous pounding of bass speakers. In that place, in the Underworld, no one spoke, no one sang, no one breathed. That silence called to Renai, promising a rest she hadn't been able to find in the living world.

Once and only once had she summoned the courage to cross over, but found the threshold of the Gate was as diffuse to her living body as dust motes dancing in a sunbeam. She had slipped through into the cemetery in the living world without touching the Gate at all, as though it were merely an image, a hologram. She sometimes wondered if the ghost word would let her cross over to the other side, but—as Sal would say—hadn't yet found the stones to test that theory. She didn't fear death, knowing what she did about what came next, but every living cell of her craved life. Staring into what waited on the other side of the Gate was like looking out over the edge of a tall, tall building: toes curling in her sneakers for a better grip, stomach muscles clenched tight in recoil, thoughts dizzy with vertigo, and a quiet voice underneath it all that whispered, *Jump.*

Sal hopped from her shoulder to Miguel's, and even though he didn't actually have a body for the raven to perch on, the psychopomp's claws gripped his spirit as tightly as they had her leather jacket. Miguel didn't seem to notice, couldn't tear his attention away from the Gate. It always took a while for anyone to get over their first sight of the other side. Part of it, Renai imagined, was that this was usually the point in their journey where the dead really seemed to *get* that they had died. That particular pot needed a little while to simmer, no matter who it was doing the cooking.

It wasn't fear that the dead experienced in this moment. Awe and confusion? Epiphany or cosmic insignificance? Those were all possible. But they couldn't really be afraid. True fear was a product of chemical reactions produced by a part of the brain that rotted in the body the dead had left behind. The newly dead were usually as incapable of being afraid as they were unable to speak. Sometimes they carried with them the *memory* of fear, though, and staring into the proverbial abyss could cause them to recall that sensation just enough to try something stupid. That's why Renai kept Miguel's spirit hand clasped firmly in her own.

You never could tell who would try to run.

The other part of it—whatever particular flavor of "it" that was taking up Miguel's thoughts just then—was that the other side didn't look the same to the dead as it did to psychopomps like her and Sal. According to the raven, it didn't even look the same from one dead to the next. What looked to psychopomps like a gray, peaceful limbo of "not-here" but "not-there," the dead saw as a series of trials, each Gate an obstacle or challenge that they had to overcome in order to complete their journey to their just reward. Whatever they'd believed in life, the gods they'd worshiped—with their hearts and actions, if not with their tongues—their deeds and regrets and sins, all of that determined what kinds of challenges they'd have to face. Lakes of fire, knife-thin bridges over deep chasms, rivers full of blood or scorpions or lost souls. That sort of thing. Oussou and Masaka's Gate was the first of seven.

Renai couldn't remember what she'd seen on the other side when she'd died, what she'd faced, one of the few mercies of her own death and resurrection. She did know she'd triumphed over her trials, knew she'd stood in judgment before the Thrones. She remembered a cold, dark place, her dress a bloody ruin where her heart had been torn from her chest, an obsidian mirror in her hands enabling her to look on the dual faces of the god who sat in the Thrones, to hear their voice. She tried not to think about it. She'd see it all again one day, after all.

Sal cleared his throat, yanking her back to the present. The raven shot her a glance that conveyed both impatience and a distinct lack of confidence in her. Pretty impressive really, considering he only had one solid, dark eye aimed at her. *Goddamn, girl,* she thought, *handle your shit.* Without saying a word, she held out the coin of Miguel's Fortune to him, which he took with his beak and tucked away beneath a glossy black wing.

Miguel's eyes caught hers, his face full of questions and trust and an earnestness that she had to harden her heart against. "This is as far as I go," she said. "I only show you the Gate. It's up to you to walk through." The dead man's full lips compressed into a tight, grim line. He looked back toward whatever he saw on the other side, and though he had neither lungs nor a need for air, he took a deep breath.

"Let's go, chief," Sal said, tapping his foot twice on the spirit's shoulder, "no time like the present." He launched himself into the air and swooped in a graceful arc through the Gate.

Miguel tightened his grip on Renai, but she pulled away, his spiritual hand like smoke against her flesh when she wasn't holding on to him. "Go on now," she said. "You've been on this path your whole life. This is just the next step." Renai made herself watch while he crossed over and, in case he looked back, forced herself to keep a calm expression on her face. Serene, like she had all the answers. She didn't, of course; for all she knew, Miguel wouldn't even make it as far as the next Gate, much less all seven of them. Or he'd be found unworthy to pass into the next life, and his Essence would be devoured. She never knew if she was leading her dead to eternal bliss or oblivion.

Judging was somebody else's job. She was just the guide.

A gloom descended when Oussou swung the Gate shut and locked it, like a cloud had passed in front of the sun. He gave Renai a squinty-eyed appraisal, like he'd noticed her for the first time, like this wasn't part of the routine they'd established. "You wanna stick around and have a drink?" he asked.

"Looks like you've had enough for the both of us," Renai said over her shoulder as she walked back to her bike. She couldn't quite make out what he said in response, but she let him have the last word. She considered, very briefly, taking him up on his real offer. He was good-looking, in a mistake-she'd-enjoy-regretting kind of way, and she'd eaten enough of Miguel's Voice that she still thrummed with energy like a plucked guitar string.

If she brought him home, it wouldn't be the first time she'd gotten laid right after delivering a soul to the Gates. Oussou surely didn't seem like the type to get possessive once the deed was done like some of the guys she'd slept with before she'd died, nor would he forget her as soon as he left her bed like the mortal men she'd been with since her resurrection. His ability to remember her when most everyone couldn't was why, appealing as the prospect was, Oussou had no chance with her. Because he wasn't a psycho-pomp like Sal or a living human man, even though he looked like one. Oussou and his twin were loa of the Ghede family, voodoo ancestor spirits who presided over the realm of the dead. Gods, more or less. So even if he was sober enough to handle his business, looked like Will Smith—lanky early '90s *Fresh Prince* Will, not buff action-movie Will—and was her last option on this Earth, she'd have still turned him down; Renai knew better than to be fucking around with gods.

Besides, what would happen to the dead if Oussou wasn't there to open the Gate?

That thought followed Renai as she rode Kyrie back to her new place, an all-but-empty one-bedroom apartment on the edge of the Garden District in a building that had once been a school and was now full of condos. It nagged at her as she changed out of her clothes and into track shorts and a long-sleeved Saints T-shirt and a pair of Nikes. It nipped at her heels as she ran down to Audubon Park and back—a four-mile circuit along the wide, grassy stretch of St. Charles's neutral ground that housed the street-car tracks—which she did without stopping for rest, lungs seared as she sucked in the cold air. It weighed on her as she did push-ups and crunches and pull-ups in the apartment when the run didn't burn off enough of her excess energy, muscles straining and aching. It haunted her during her brief but intensely hot shower and joined her on her bare-mattress-on-the-floor version of a bed, where she burrowed under the blankets and lay staring up into the dark.

Renai knew, of course, that not everyone who died made it through all seven of the Gates. During her brief glimpses through the First Gate, she could sometimes see them wandering through the fog of that in-between place, and there had been others that Sal implied weren't just lost but *gone*. It also happened that once in a very rare while a person would refuse to enter the First Gate at all, either too attached to this world to move on, or simply unable to believe that they'd actually died. She'd seen her share of those walking the streets of New Orleans since she'd returned, though they usually fled once they realized what she was. Ultimately, though, what happened to a single identity didn't matter much to the overall system. It was the coin of Fortune that she couldn't stop thinking about.

Voice, life, magic—whatever you wanted to call it—the part of the soul that psychopomps consumed when a person died was a renewable resource. It grew inside everything that lived, restored itself from the tiniest amount if it was drained, and its absence on the other side was part of what *defined* the other side. If human souls were only that one thing, nothing would change if the Gates no longer opened. But destiny—that coin of Fortune—was another thing entirely. Your luck could run out. Your fate was sealed. Like the first law of thermodynamics, destiny could neither be created nor destroyed, and that made it precious. No matter what happened to a person's Voice and Essence, their Fortune *had* to get to the other side of the Gates so it could be reused. Carrying that coin was the psychopomp's true purpose. Sal had told her that bad things would happen if they didn't consume the dead's leftover Voice, but what if they couldn't get the Fortune to where it was supposed to go? Would newborns start their lives with no fate? Would the whole cycle of death and life grind to a halt?

She couldn't decide which was worse.

These thoughts wouldn't torture her so much if she weren't a psychopomp now. A normal human could detach herself from these greater concerns, but devotion to the cycle of life and death had been hardwired into her when she'd been resurrected, instinctive as a migratory urge. Which was why, as she spiraled down into sleep, the god who called himself Seth and his strange request were pushed from her mind by an almost-pathological anxiety about the First Gate. By the time she woke the next morning, she'd forgotten all about the red-handed god.

🔲

There were times where Renai felt—with the tingling ache of a phantom limb—that she could envision the Underworld as surely and as clearly as if she had spent the past five years there instead of in the world of the living. These moments were always fleeting: a flicker of memory just before the oblivion of sleep or a scrap of dream left over just upon waking, a tickle of scent from a passerby, a misheard line from a song just at the edge of hearing.

She knew, from her glimpses through the First Gate, that the Underworld was a shadowed, muted version of a New Orleans shrouded in fog. What she couldn't know, but still believed to be true, was that in that place, pine and oak and magnolia grew thick and towering, the spirits of the trees that had been cleared away to make room for the grids and snarls of city streets. The Underworld had no parking lots or sidewalks underfoot, no cell towers or power lines overhead. The homes and the restaurants, bars and shops and high-rises—those remained, their doors unlocked, their rooms empty of all but dust and memories.

She could picture that other Renai, too, hair still twisted into long dreads, still dressed in the lace-laden white graduation dress that she'd been buried in, barefoot and hovering in midair, like a ghost. Or an angel.

Since St. Louis No. 1 had once stood at the outermost edge of the city, in order to get to the Second Gate, that other Renai had to lead Miguel through the duckweed-coated waterways and the fetid, squelching muck of the swamp that had been drained as New Orleans grew. The path changed with every soul. Some meandered past landmarks personal and historic; some followed a course as straight and precise as if it had been laid out with a ruler and compass. Some paths were solid wooden walkways of fresh-cut pine and taut rope guidelines, while others were all slick, weathered cobblestones spread a full stride apart. It all depended on what the soul believed they deserved.

If Miguel strayed from his appointed path, all his personality and individuality would fade, his Essence dimming into a mere reflection of personality. That other Renai walked through the Underworld burdened by an unshakable paranoia, haunted by the constant attention of these lost souls, these shades.

When the knowledge and sensations of the Underworld overshadowed

Renai's mind, it was always an unsettling feeling, like déjà vu or vertigo. Always a sensation of sadness and loss. For the next day or two, she'd catch herself studying her face in mirrors as if checking that her reflection was still her own, found that she struggled to fall asleep, unsure that she'd still be herself when she woke.

Afraid that when she closed her eyes, it would be for the last time.

⧗

The next span of days passed in the blur of uniformity that had occupied her life for years. She woke to her cell phone's alarm at the same ass-crack of dawn, stumbled the same groaning path from mattress to bathroom to kitchen, drank the same black coffee from the same WELCOME TO THE BIG EASY ceramic mug, pulled on the same leather jacket, no matter whether the temperature demanded it or not. Within an hour she was gone from the empty apartment, killing time until that day's collection in coffee shops and libraries, laundromats and bars, anywhere she could eavesdrop on conversations and interact with the living in the superficial ways still available to her. She always met Sal at that day's deathbed, gathered up the coin of Fortune, ate the Voice in whatever form it took, and led the Essence to the First Gate. Any time after sunset Oussou was there to unlock the Gate, fight with Sal, and flirt ineffectually with her. During the day his twin, Masaka, held the key. They were a mirror image of their twin: sober and alert, dressed all in white like a Santeria iyawo except they had lavender crosses on their jacket where Oussou had white ones. Masaka was always polite in a detached sort of way that Renai found insincere, though that might have more to do with the high school she'd attended than any insight into Masaka's personality.

Day or night, Masaka or Oussou, once the Gate opened, Sal took the coin and guided the dead through to the other side, while she remained behind to occupy herself however she could in this half-life of hers. She exercised her body to exhaustion or read one of the battered Anne Rice paperbacks she'd taken from the free pile outside a used bookstore or found a willing one-night stand down in the Quarter — one of the only benefits of her aura of disinterest being the ease with which she could ditch the inevitable creeps when they turned dangerous or needy or gross — only to find herself once again within these same four walls, wrapped in the same sheets, waiting for sleep to carry her into the same absence of dreams.

And she woke, always alone, to do it all again.

It certainly wasn't the life she'd envisioned for herself before she'd died, but at least it was life. She knew firsthand how uncertain the alternative could be. The hope that carried her from day to identical day was that her time with Sal was preparing her for something more, some greater assumption of the psychopomp's role. It was the kind of hope that shared a place in her heart with anxiety, with despair. She never asked Salvatore straight out what her future held for fear of his answer. She didn't examine too closely the uniqueness of her circumstances out of worry of what she might realize. Ignorance was far from bliss, but when the truth might literally destroy her, it would do.

Renai couldn't be sure how much time went by in this way before she remembered her conversation with Seth; two days, three, maybe as much as a week passed without her paying any attention. The routine made everything bleed together. It wasn't like death got weekends off. When the situation changed, the morning didn't begin any differently than the ones before it. In fact, she almost missed it. She leaned against the faux marble counter in the empty kitchen in the empty apartment, humming to herself while her coffee brewed. The only things in the kitchen were a sleek new coffee machine and an ancient radio, and she couldn't function without both of them. The former because if she didn't get a couple of cups of steaming hot, chicory-bitter coffee in her first thing in the morning she might as well still be in her grave. The latter because it gave her access to the Deadline.

Growing up in New Orleans, she couldn't say when she'd first listened to the Livewire — the local independent radio station's listing of that week's music performances that played at the top of every odd hour — it had just been something she picked up in the tap water, like the words to "Iko Iko" and the "Who Dat?" chant or knowing when hurricane season started. The Deadline, though, she'd only discovered once she'd become a psychopomp. It wouldn't play on WWOZ's internet feed or any radio modern enough to have digital tuning. You had to be able to twist the knob just the slightest bit off, so that the signal got a little funky with static, but not so far that you lost the music entirely. There, amid the hiss of white noise, a voice read off the names, times, locations, and manner of every death that would occur in the next twenty-four hours. Each morning, before she'd even brushed her teeth, Renai would sip her first of the day and listen to the list, choosing a life to take. If asked, she wouldn't be able to explain the criteria behind her choices. Some deaths just *felt* right, like she'd heard their names before, like she'd once known their whole life story and they'd simply drifted apart.

That morning, just a few days before Halloween, she was trying to decide between an old lady in the Poydras Home assisted living community and a homeless man beneath the Calliope overpass when the staticky voice of the Deadline said, "Ramses St. Cyr, gunshot wound," followed by an address on Washington Avenue and a time later that afternoon. Renai swallowed her coffee so fast it nearly scalded her throat on the way down. She snatched her leather jacket off the counter and dug through the pockets, pulling out a crumpled little slip of paper that could have been a receipt or a fortune cookie's message or just a balled-up straw wrapper, but when she pulled it open, the words RAMSES ST. CYR stared back at her. Her meeting with Seth, his odd request to consider her options, all of it came sweeping back in a how-could-I-have-possibly-forgotten-this rush, like walking into class and seeing everyone else last-minute cramming for a test.

She smoothed the little slip of paper out so that it lay mostly flat on the counter and picked up her mug. She raised it to her lips but didn't drink, chewing her lip instead. She set the cup back down. "Ain't this some shit," she said, to no one in particular.

She could, of course, just pretend that none of this had happened. She could toss this scrap of paper in the trash on her way out the door to collect one of those other deaths, and nothing would change. Seth had made it clear that neither of them would owe the other anything unless she did . . . whatever he thought she'd do once she saw Ramses' circumstances for herself. As if she had the authority to do anything but collect him and lead him to the Gates once his name was read on the Deadline. Really, she couldn't do anything unless Salvatore said she could, and she hadn't even mentioned meeting the ugly god to him, much less gotten permission to color outside the lines. She knew exactly how the psychopomp would react if she told him *now*, especially since—according to the Deadline—Ramses' death would be a violent one.

Gotta crawl before you can fly, Raines, he'd say, and send her off to collect some other dead. Then she'd turn around and another year would have gone by just like the one before. Shady as this whole situation felt, at least it was something new. She couldn't ignore that part of the temptation. If that was all it was, though, some desire for a break in the monotony, she probably wouldn't have considered it this seriously. But the name on the paper kept nudging at her, some memory from her old life just out of reach, maddening as an elusive word escaping the tip of her tongue. She could remember a woman she'd called "Miss St. Cyr," but not how she'd known her. Couldn't have been too close, if she hadn't been "Aunt" something or other. Just someone she'd see out on the parade route or while making groceries or—

Or on Grandma Raines's front porch at the house on Washington Avenue.

And just like that, she made her decision. She dressed quickly, tugging on a pair of jeans and yanking the tag off a bright yellow top before she pulled it on. Her recollection of events was a pretty thin thread to use to tie everything together, she had to admit. For all she knew, the Ramses on the Deadline could be some distant cousin of the Miss St. Cyr she remembered, if they were even related at all. She could be confused about the name of the woman from her childhood. The memory from her grandmother's porch might be no more than wishful thinking. Nor was she blinded by the blank-check nature of Seth's offer. A favor for a promise? That was the kind of shit they said when they thought you were too stupid to read the fine print.

No, the real reason Renai decided to see where this name led was because she'd realized that for the first time in a long time, she'd been weighing her options based on her past instead of her present. That she'd been thinking like Renaissance Raines, instead of the psychopomp who wore her face.

CHAPTER FIVE

THE FIRST MURDERER, punished with a mark that assured that none would give him shelter, or salve his suffering, or release him from his isolation by ending his life. An unbeatable warrior, refusing to restrain the mighty weapon he had summoned from a blade of grass, his mystic gem torn from his forehead and exiled to the wilds, his pus-filled wounds unhealing, his cries for death unanswered. A powerful wizard, whose magics came from his demonic parentage, trapped in a tree by the student whom he lusted after, doomed to be evergreen and everlasting. A desperate king, sacrificing son after son after son to his one-eyed god in order to gain another span of years; so feeble at the end that he fed by sucking milk from a horn's tip like an infant. The consort of the dawn, prince and poet both, whose lover was arrogant enough to demand eternity but not wise enough to plead for vitality, forcing him to endure an undying senescence. The shoemaker who mocked the condemned man—a healer and a teacher and a child of God—by telling him to hurry on his way to his own death, who was commanded in turn to wander without rest until the end of days. Again and again, immunity from the grave is not a gift to be granted but a sentence to be carried out. Not a blessing, but a curse.

⧗

Renai killed time for the majority of the day—an expression she found especially apt these days—breakfast in a kitschy local chain coffee shop on the corner of Magazine, a movie she didn't have to pay for because no one noticed her when she walked in, a beer in a crowded Uptown bar where the fountain outside was made out of beer taps.

She didn't need to eat these days, since the Voices she consumed sustained her far better than any mortal food, but she found that the simple act of having a meal could make her feel human when the weirder parts of her life got overwhelming. What little cash she needed to move through the world in this way she got from the pockets of her dead, which she took without shame or second thought. It wasn't like they needed it where she was leading them.

Twilight had wrapped itself around the city by the time she eased Kyrie into a parking spot on Washington, an easing off of heat that wasn't yet the relief of fall, a gloom descending that wasn't quite enough to spark the streetlights into life. Renai sat astride her rumbling bike, trying to decide if she really wanted to go behind Sal's back like this; after all, the foul-mouthed psychopomp was the closest thing she had to a friend.

She checked the time on her phone. *Early yet,* she thought, *still plenty of time to talk myself out of this.*

As if sensing Renai's indecision, Kyrie sputtered and stilled, ending the debate.

When Renai got off of Kyrie and looked up and down the two-block stretch of Washington where Ramses St. Cyr was destined to die, it seemed like the perfect metaphor for the line between life and death she had tightroped since her resurrection. One side of the street held the quintessential New Orleans neighborhood: sprawling oaks and small front yards overgrown with clover and a row of shotgun houses—only one room wide but stretching four rooms back, the porch leading to the living room to the bedroom to the kitchen and then out again—built half a step away from one another. Many were shotgun doubles, one building split down the center into a duplex with a separate door for each residence. Most homes actually had two front doors: a wooden one that swung in, and a wrought iron security gate decorated with whorls and fleurs-de-lis that swung out.

Two cemeteries took up a block each of the other side of the street: St. Joseph and Lafayette No. 2. The closest one, St. Joseph, held plaster tombs above paved concrete much like St. Louis No. 1, though unlike the cemetery on the edge of the Quarter, here only a chain-link fence separated the quick and the dead. Lafayette No. 2 looked more like a combination of a park and a burial site, with grass covering the ground and growing over some of the flat plots that interspersed the more common tombs. A much sturdier fence of slender, upright iron bars with sharpened tips wrapped around the block.

And right in the middle, belonging to neither world, was Renai.

She didn't quite remember where on Washington her grandmother had lived before the storm, but she was pretty sure it was deeper into the Central City neighborhood than this. Maybe her memory of "Miss St. Cyr" was wrong after all. She walked down Washington until she stood at the corner of Loyola, the street that separated St. Joseph from Lafayette No. 2. The absence of streetlights over the two cemeteries made them pockets of night in the deepening twilight, ominous even to her.

Renai ought to be finding her way to Ramses' deathbed, but instead she stood staring into the dark spaces, wondering if any of her dead had been laid to rest here, if that simple padlocked gate might hide another of the Seven Gates. She even imagined something moving in the depths of St. Joseph, some dark shape that moved low to the ground and darted from one shadow to another.

Get it together, girl, she thought, *you got shit to tend to,* but then she saw it again, moving closer this time, and she tracked its progress to the base of a tomb just on the other side of the chain-link fence. One breath, another, and then a passing car's headlights lit a pair of eyes an eerie, predatory green. Everything in her clenched, coiled tight in case she had to spring quickly away. Most people would tell themselves that they were seeing nothing more than a feral cat, but Renai knew better.

Renai knew monsters were real.

She doubted she could fight it, whatever it was. Her best bet was escape, but Kyrie was too far away given how fast she'd seen that thing move. She pulled the hood of her jacket over her head, shifted her weight onto the balls of her feet. If it came for her, she decided, she'd call on the ghost word and sprint for the nearest house. If the iron gate and solid wood door didn't keep it out, maybe she could find something she could use as a weapon. Flight if she could, fight if she had to, die if she was wrong. Would they have said her name on the Deadline if this was her end? Or was she a special case?

Maybe there was another way. "I'm under the protection of the Thrones," she called across the street, "so unless you wanna answer to them, you better just go back the way you came."

At first, her only answer was a low growl that made her blood run cold. And then a voice she recognized said, "The fuck you are." It should have been a relief to see Sal—now wearing the shaggy-furred and long-eared dog-skin he sometimes used—leap over the fence and into the light, but as he crossed the street, she could see fury in the lay of his ears, in the stretch of his tail. He didn't even wait until he reached the sidewalk before he started berating her. "At *this* moment, in *this* place?—you're under the protection of Jack Shit and Fuck All. That's the kinda help you can expect when this shit goes tits-up, which it will."

Renai tried to answer, but all she got out was his name before the psychopomp made a noise that was part yawn and part sneeze, a huff of indignation where a human would have held up a hand for silence. Somewhere in the distance, a siren wailed. "You don't get to talk yet," he said. "I don't know what bug crawled up your ass lately, but you gotta tighten up." He plopped down on his haunches and glared up at her. "You don't get to choose when you follow the rules, Raines. That's what makes 'em *rules*. Your ass shouldn't be anywhere near a violent death like this one. You ain't got the juice." A city bus came toward them down Loyola, groaning to a stop at the corner of Washington. Sal started to say more, but the pneumatic hiss of the bus's air brakes startled him and made him whip his head around.

"It's just the bus, Sal," she said. The doors swished open and a handful of teenagers swung out, laughing and giving each other shit. The driver watched them cross the street before making its wide turn onto Washington, the bus's PA system announcing its next stop. Renai got a close look at the teenagers as they walked in front of her; none of them pulled at her the way Miguel Flores had in the moments before his death. Down the block, a dark SUV pulled out into the street, bass beat thumping. The driver forgot to turn the headlights on. Sal still stared off in the direction of the cemetery, ears flat against his head. "What's got you so jumpy?" she asked.

"Nothing," he snapped. Then he turned his mournful, doggie eyes at her and gave his lips a quick lick. "Sorry. It's just . . . this shit we do? I know it's easy to get lost in the day-to-day, but this isn't just life and death, Raines. It's eternity and oblivion."

Renai didn't hear what Sal said next, couldn't focus on anything but the fact that the dark SUV still hadn't turned on its lights, that it slowed when it got alongside the group of teenagers on the sidewalk. Renai was running before her thoughts caught up to what her instincts knew was happening. The window slid down, DJ Khaled's "I Wish You Would" blaring from inside, and a puffy jacket sleeve stretched out, a gun clutched in a side grip.

Renai—stretched out to put as much of her body in front of the teenagers on the sidewalk as she could—couldn't see any faces in the darkened interior of the SUV, the night going purple as the ghost word took hold, her skin drawing tight and ephemeral. The shooter yelled something angry and vulgar that was drowned out by the music and the sharp *pop, pop-pop, pop* of his shots. She felt the sting of each bullet passing harmlessly through her, a pinprick of pain quick and immediate as a mosquito's bite. The SUV's engine roared and the back tire chirped against the concrete when it clipped against a curb as it vanished around the corner.

She looked down at the group of kids, who had fallen to the ground, didn't remember turning toward them, didn't remember running beside them, the adrenaline surging through her system chopping time into disconnected film frames.

There were five of them, three boys and two girls. One of the girls was Latina; the rest were black. "Are you okay?" she asked, realizing too late that she was shouting. Lowering her voice, she said, "Anyone hurt?" They were all muttering to each other and starting to sit up, one girl wiping tears from her eyes, another girl rocking back and forth and unable to stop crying, the first one in the group to hit the ground—a lanky boy in pants a couple of sizes too big—still lay with his hands covering his head until one of his friends shook him by the shoulder. Renai opened her mouth to say something else, and then realized that they couldn't hear her, since the ghost word had rendered her invisible, intangible, and silent. In the shock of the moment, it didn't occur to her that she hadn't spoken the ghost word at all. She raised her hands to pull off the hood and break the spell but hesitated when Sal cleared his throat. She turned to find him standing beside her, his attention fixed on her and not the kids.

"You gotta start thinking like a 'pomp, Raines. Don't *ask* these kids if they're okay. *Look*."

Her jaw clenched, but when she turned back to the group, she understood what he meant. None of them had the smoldering-embers glow of a life on the cusp of ending. Each of them burned with health, with vitality. One of the girls, in fact, had a second flame kindled in her belly. Renai knew right away what that meant. She wondered if the girl knew yet.

She took a couple of deep breaths, tried to still her shaking hands. The teenagers were already on their feet, phones out and texting, eyes scanning the street with every other step. Shaken and crying and anxious to be gone, to be home. By the sound of their conversation, they had a good idea who the shooter was, knew it had something to do with one of the three boys—the tallest and oldest of the three with a head full of twists—and some "ratchet-ass ho" at their school. Renai found it hard to hear them past the roaring rising in her ears. *Not now,* she thought, *not again.*

Something moved within her that was more than just adrenaline. Something dark and cold. It wasn't anger, that would have burned through her in a hot wave, and it wasn't fear, that was a chill that raced across her skin and raised the hair on her flesh. It wasn't an emotion, wasn't a part of her at all. This was a fierce, frigid wind, a tightening coil of intent. A storm with a mind of its own.

She didn't know exactly what this entity was or where it had come from, but she knew it didn't belong inside of her. She'd had no magic of her own before her death, and being a vessel for a living storm wasn't any part of being a psychopomp that Sal had told her about. It might be some miasma of the Underworld that had infected her, some unexplained "gift" from the Thrones, or some strange consequence of her unusual resurrection, but— unsure of its origins—Renai had kept its existence to herself. Whatever it was, it came and went without warning, roused by her anger and whispering promises of power in her mind. She knew she controlled it just based on the simple fact that it wanted to be released. Each moment it whirled within her, it begged for freedom, needing only once for her litany of *no, no, no* to be broken with a *yes.* Needing only her permission, a simple exhalation, for its mere anarchy to be loosed upon the world.

She knew it was her rage that had woken the storm. These five were just kids. Still in high school, based on the flashes of school uniforms she'd noticed. Caterpillars still in the chrysalis. Buds on the vine that had yet to bloom.

At least, they ought to be. The law said they weren't yet responsible enough to drink or buy cigarettes. Or marry. Or vote. But nobody seemed to have a problem with them getting shot at. They were adult enough to have their lives snatched away without warning or reason. Adult enough that they were hurrying away in case someone called to report the gunshots, in case the cops actually showed. Adult enough to be startled, to be scared, to be relieved, and to not be surprised. The relentless, roaring whirl within her made it hard to breathe, and she recognized it for what it was: hatred.

She hated everything about this, from the idiot who wanted to solve his problems with a gun, to his targets who knew his name but wouldn't snitch, to the city that tutted and fretted and turned a blind eye to it so long as it didn't happen in the nice neighborhoods, to the industries that profited off of the myths of the gangsta and the hustle and the game, to the nation founded on the bones of slavery and bigotry, a nation that left its people impoverished and uneducated and addicted and hopeless in order to fuel decades of war and feed a bottomless greed. Hate rose within her so powerfully that it filled her lungs and coated her tongue. Hate tasted like the oil-slick, dead-leaves rot of floodwaters. It howled with a hurricane's fury.

Hate seared her lungs like gasoline and a struck match, and the tempest within her stretched up to greet it.

She held the storm in, both doubting that she'd be able to restrain it again if she ever released it and fearing its intentions. Would it seek out the shooter and snatch his life away as easily as she'd taken Miguel's? Would it stop there? *Could* it stop? Or would it grow? Scouring the flesh from his bones with the force of its winds, swallowing even the memory of him in its flood? What would sate this hate inside her? His home? The block? The city? What would be enough?

Renai felt a cold, wet nose press into her palm, and remembered where she was. She pushed the hate back down into the icy, empty place in the center of her where it lived, forced herself to take one deep breath, and then another. Clenched shut her eyes and imagined her mother's kitchen: the gentle breeze of the ceiling fan swinging overhead and warm sunlight through the open curtains and the rich, buttery scent of a roux just before the trinity went in. The slow, hypnotic scrape of a wooden spoon against cast iron as her mother stirred and stirred and stirred.

Gradually, sullenly, the tempest retreated deep enough that Renai was able to release her breath. She opened her eyes to find that the teenagers had made their way out of sight, and Sal looking at her with his head cocked to the side. He didn't ask; he didn't have to. She could read the concern and the confusion and the question all over his doggie frown.

"You told me to look so I looked," she said. "Don't give me any shit about what I found."

Sal's ears twitched back, and he made an exasperated sound in his throat, but all he said was "Fair enough."

Renai gestured down at the grass where the teenagers had thrown themselves. "So what now?" she asked. "If none of them was destined to get shot—"

Sal tilted his head at the house behind him, the one the teenagers had been standing in front of when the shots were fired. "These drive-by assholes always got shitty aim. I'm betting our boy is in there."

It took a moment for Renai to catch the nuance of what he'd said. "Wait, 'our' boy?"

Sal pulled one of his hind legs up to scratch behind his ear. "Aww, hell," he said, "if I'm gonna get my ass chewed out, you might as well learn something out of it. You stick by me, you don't touch *nothin'*, and you save your questions for later, we clear?"

She dropped to one knee and hugged the psychopomp around his thin dog shoulders. A little girlish squeak came out of her before she could stop it. She knew she was at least as elated by the fact that he hadn't made her talk about the weird shit going on with her as she was about getting to see some new side of being a psychopomp, but that didn't diminish her joy in the slightest. These days she took her good moments whenever she got them.

"Aww-right, aww-right," Sal said, pulling away from her as though he hadn't draped a paw around her shoulder when she hugged him. "Don't go fallin' in love with me. I ain't crowned you Queen of the Underworld or nothin'. You're still just a punk kid who don't know shit from Shenandoah."

Renai stood, the world still tight and painted in shades of purple with the ghost word's power. She couldn't tell if she was growing more accustomed to its effects, or if the storm within her had numbed her, but it didn't seem to irritate her as much as it had before. She followed the psychopomp down the brief path to the front door, in search of the dead boy that Seth had sent her after. "And I'm not a kid," she said. "You have to stop treating me like a child."

"Sure," Sal said, "soon as you quit acting like one." But he leaned his weight against her leg to take the sting out of his words, just before the actual hurt of pushing through the iron gate and the wooden door slapped against her skin. She might be growing used to the word's discomfort, but moving through physical objects still hurt like hell.

Though none of the lights were on in the room beyond, the ghost word's influence infused the darkness with a subtle lavender glow. This first room looked to be both dining room and living room, with a round table large enough for four on one side of the room, and a small worn beige sofa, an ancient pleather recliner, and a flat-screen TV on the other. School textbooks were strewn across the surface of the dining room table, and family photographs adorned the walls. Since someone over the years had taken out most of the far wall, Renai could see into the kitchen from the front door: countertops and a gas stove from the '70s, a humming, rattling fridge from the '90s, and linoleum floors that gleamed as though they'd been scrubbed that morning. Sal had his nose to the floor, sniffling like he had a cold.

"Something wrong?" she asked.

"Something . . . weird," he said. "See what the rest of this place is like."

Renai gave the kitchen a glance as she moved through it but found nothing unexpected. Glass-fronted cupboards showed plates and spices and cereal boxes. A cast-iron skillet had place of honor on the stove, probably one of the first things to get packed in the hurricane box. Ramses' report card from a charter school down in the Bywater hung on the fridge by a magnet, more A's than B's. A note signed MOMMA said she'd picked up an extra shift and would be home late. A short hallway separated the kitchen and the first bedroom, with a small bathroom off to the side. The first bedroom obviously belonged to an adolescent boy: unmade bed, school uniform polo shirt and khaki pants hanging out of a wicker laundry hamper, Reggie Bush and Jimmy Graham posters on the wall.

The last room in the house was another bedroom, this one belonging to Ramses' mother—Juliette, according to the name tag Renai found on the vanity. That might have been the name of the Miss St. Cyr she remembered from her childhood, but she couldn't be sure. Juliette's room was as neat as the kitchen, the paisley bedspread made with military precision, the romance novels on the nightstand lined up in order instead of thrown into a stack. Renai turned to go when a photograph on the far wall caught her eye. The laughing young black woman in the picture had her arm thrown around the neck of a skinny preteen with a troubled expression on his face, an exaggerated scowl that he was hamming up for the camera. Next to them stood a black man in a white tank top, his crisp hat brim turned just so, a sweet and mild caught in his pursed lips. On the man's shoulders sat a boy who couldn't have been more than five or six, his grin wide and bright.

Renai was the one who had taken the picture.

It was 2006, the Carnival after the storm. She couldn't remember much from that time, just that people hadn't been sure they'd even have a Mardi Gras that year. She'd only been fourteen, not much older than Zeke, the frowning boy in the photograph. All of it came rushing back. Miss St. Cyr —Juliette—had swaggered up to Renai's family's spot on the parade route with her man and her boys and a giant daiquiri that she'd obviously already had plenty of. She'd made a couple of jokes about Renai—who she'd called "Nay-nay"—hooking up with Zeke, which was why he was pulling that face in the picture. She'd loved to give people those repeating nicknames, had called her younger son "Ki-ki." When Renai had asked her mother later that day why Miss St. Cyr had given her son the kind of name you'd give a panda, Renai's father had thrown his head back and laughed.

It's just a nickname, baby, her mother had said, *because he's got the name of a king, just like Zeke.*

So Renai had known Ramses, or at least her family knew his family, though she'd only ever heard him called Ki-ki or "Lil' King," if his dad was talking to him. Was that connection why Seth had thought she'd spare his life? Or was it just a matter of time before she'd collected the soul of someone she'd known, given how small a city New Orleans was?

Sal called her from the front of the house, interrupting her thoughts. She hurried to him, found him sitting on top of the dining room table, his ears laying flat against his scalp. "What is it? What's wrong?"

"Check the window," he said. It only took her a minute to see what he wanted her to notice, the irregular, dime-sized hole in the glass surrounded by a spider's web of cracks. "Now follow the path," he said. She put her face close to the glass, careful not to slip through it, and moved only her eyes, sighting along her outstretched arm.

"There," she said, pointing to right where Sal was sitting.

"Right. Now come look at this."

She went over to the table, where Sal aimed his snout at the chair directly across from the window. The topmost plank of wood was likewise punctured and splintered where the bullet had torn through. Without needing to be prompted, she let her hand travel the rest of the imagined path across the room, to where she found the hateful slug of metal buried in the Sheetrock. She went back to the chair, imagining how it would have happened. Ramses sitting at the table, doing his homework like he did every night, and then the shots—except there was no blood on the chair or the floor. Certainly no

Ramses St. Cyr gasping his last breaths. *Must have been one of the other shots,* she thought, but then she noticed that the air around the chair seemed to ripple, like the shimmer in the air on an especially hot day. It felt wrong, hurt her eyes and churned her stomach and *hurt* somehow just at the edge her perception, like a wound in the world. By the expression in Sal's eyes, he saw the same thing she did. It was then that she understood. This was it. This was the time and the place and bullet that was supposed to end a life.

Except it hadn't.

Somehow, Ramses St. Cyr had escaped the death that the Thrones had planned for him.

The thought of Ramses adrift somewhere between the worlds of the living and the dead gave Renai a chill, not just of fear or revulsion, but of recognition, too. She was overcome by one of those moments of memory or imagination or prophecy, and saw herself guiding the Essence of Miguel Flores through the Second Gate.

Holt Cemetery had originally been a potter's field—a burial ground for those who could afford nothing better—and it was one of the few cemeteries in New Orleans where the dead were laid to rest in the earth. In the world of the living, it was sad and gray: a few struggling patches of brown grass, a sprawl of crowded plots with leaning or broken headstones—sometimes no stone at all, just a wooden cross with a hand-lettered name—all tucked behind the fence of a community college's baseball field. In the land of the dead, Holt cemetery flourished: every plot covered with vibrant flower beds growing over and into one another, a striking, vibrant riot of color, like a garden planted by Jackson Pollock. At its center a gigantic oak towered over the whole seven acres, and at the base of that oak waited the Gatekeeper, Nibo.

Like Oussou and Masaka, Nibo was a loa of the Ghede family. Renai pictured him as having dark brown skin and a long, lean frame wrapped in a tailor-cut three-piece suit: dark pants, a cream-colored waistcoat, and a light blue jacket covered with a pattern that belonged on an old white lady's sofa: flowers in blooms of long thin petals in pastel shades of red, orange, and yellow and pale green vines snaking all over. In Renai's mind, Nibo made every inch of that jacket work, a confident slouch to the way he leaned against the giant oak, like everyone who saw him in it owed him money for the privilege.

Nibo's domain was of the unburied, the unremembered dead. They found a place here, tending Nibo's gardens and resting and drinking the Ghede's obnoxiously spicy rum. Some souls had nowhere else to go. Some were given the choice to remain here or to press on in search of greater reward. Miguel Flores, Renai knew, would make it through Nibo's Gate and down into the next level of the Underworld.

But Ramses St. Cyr wouldn't make it even that far if Renai couldn't find him.

CHAPTER SIX

RENAI STARED AT the place where the dead boy should be, trying to process her reaction. On the one hand, a senseless death, a life ended far too soon, had been avoided. Ramses had managed to sidestep a fate he didn't deserve. She ought to feel good about that. Overjoyed, even. Wasn't this the definition of a miracle? Why, then, did she feel so disgusted? Now that she realized what the empty chair meant, she had to force herself to endure its presence, the trembling of the air reminiscent of an insect's quivering mouthparts, an aftertaste in her mouth like weeks-rancid milk. She choked back a gag.

"My thoughts exactly," Sal said, breaking the silence. He hopped down from the table and started pacing the other side of the room, his nails clicking on the hardwood floor. She was only too happy to follow him away from that part of the house.

"Does this—"

"Happen a lot? No. This kinda shit simply does *not* happen." She couldn't tell if the tone in his voice was angry or confused or nervous, but Ramses' absence had definitely agitated him. She chewed her lip. The tension of the ghost word against her skin finally tipped over from dripping-faucet annoying to nails-on-the-chalkboard unpleasant, so Renai pulled off the hood and broke the spell. Night crowded in and the pressure abated. She waited for her eyes to adjust to the darkness and then sank into the comfort of the old recliner, worn and accepting as a pair of old jeans. She tucked her hands into her jacket pockets.

"I'm not sure I get what's going on here," she said. "Is something wrong?"

Sal paused midstep, placing his paw slowly onto the floor and easing down until he sat on his haunches. When he spoke, he seemed to be choosing his words carefully. "Does it not feel wrong to you?"

"Yeah, no," she said, "it totally does. Just looking at"—she waved in the general direction of the chair—"is, like, *ugh.*" She didn't know why she'd fallen into the cadence of an inarticulate teenager, why she felt the need to distance herself from Sal. To make herself seem not just innocent but too vapid to be anything else. She'd never felt the need to play a role for him before. But then, the psychopomp had never been cautious with his words before, either. "I just mean, like, shouldn't we be happy for him? 'Innocent bystander in a drive-by' is such a bullshit cliché way for a young black kid to die. Shouldn't we be glad he gets a chance at something more?" Some part of her, she realized, was hoping for just that. Hoping that she could convince Sal to walk away, to forget that this death had been avoided, wrong as the whole situation felt. That Ramses could be allowed to escape. *Is this why Seth wanted me here?* she thought. *Am I just a puppet dancing to his tune?*

Sal's long, pointed ears flicked, as if shooing away a fly. "What makes you say the dead we're here for is black?"

Renai rolled her eyes. Even though the gesture made her feel like a teenager, she couldn't stop herself. "There's pictures of Ramses all over this house."

Sal tilted his head to the side and watched her, long enough for the silence to become uncomfortable. Renai almost spoke but got the impression that's what he was waiting for. "Maybe," he said at last, "we should talk about why you came here in the first place."

Since the moment Sal had caught her at a death where she didn't belong, Renai had been building an answer to this very question in the back of her mind. She'd woven a hopefully convincing lie around an initial knot of truth, planning to say that she'd simply gotten tired of the monotony and had chosen to collect a violent death just to experience something new, the rules be damned. It wasn't *entirely* untrue—it just wasn't the *whole* truth. But when she opened her mouth to let the lie unravel, it occurred to her that Sal was both a full-fledged psychopomp—which meant she had no idea what he was truly capable of—and her only friend in this life—which meant if she couldn't trust him, she was well and truly alone. Not to mention the fact that if they had any chance of figuring out what was going on with that hole in reality where Ramses' death should be, Sal would need to know the whole truth.

So she gave it to him, all of it. Her meeting with Seth, his unusual offer, her boredom and frustration and confusion, the tickle of familiarity that came with the name St. Cyr and how she and the dead—or at least, the supposed-to-be-dead—were connected. "And I don't know why he wanted me here," she said, feeling a little off balance, as if she'd been carrying this secret around for way longer than a few days, "that's the truth. I don't know if he thought I'd convince you to let Ramses live, or if my being here is what changed things—"

"Ah, you ain't done a damn thing wrong," Sal said, more weary than angry, though not without a certain measure of pissed off. "I mean, you let some shit-for-brains deity lead you into the briar patch and then thanked him for the fuckin' thorns, but you ain't had nothin' to do with that." He nodded toward the empty chair, then wrinkled his upper lip, as if he smelled something foul. "C'mon, let's get outta here. This is beyond my jurisdictional parlay, if you know what I mean."

I think you mean purview, Renai thought, but didn't say anything other than the ghost word so she could slip through the door as he led her back out onto the street. She pulled the hood off as soon as they were outside, and her sudden return to visibility spooked a large bird perched in the oak overhead. Renai caught a glimpse of wide pale wings as it took flight. A prickle that had nothing to do with the jacket's magic ran along her flesh, unpleasant and cold. A wisp of memory flickered in her mind like a single frame of one movie spliced into the film of another. *The thing that killed me had wings,* she thought.

She didn't have long to dwell on this memory, though, since Sal hadn't stopped walking, hadn't even seemed to notice the startled bird. Renai caught up to him just as he reached the stretch of sidewalk where Kyrie leaned on her kickstand. "I'm gonna need to bum a ride from you," he said, "unless you got some other plans."

"I'm free as a bird," she said, easing onto her seat on Kyrie.

Sal made a noise that was half grunt and half chuckle. "Speaking of which . . ." He hunched down on all fours and gagged, jaws gaping wide and fur rippling like a dog about to vomit up some grass. Starting at his back hips, the psychopomp's flesh sagged and went limp, as though the bones and meat within had simply vanished. A dark and glistening shape wriggled in his throat and stretched down the pink curl of his tongue. Bit by bit, Sal's dog-skin collapsed in on itself until nothing was left, nothing but the raven that strained and clawed and cursed his way out of the dog's mouth to stand spit-soaked and black-winged on the grass.

"Where are we headed?" Renai asked.

Before he answered, Sal spread his wings and wiped the saliva from his feathers on the rapidly decaying fur that had once been his dog-shape. "Can't believe I'm saying this, but we gotta visit that piss-blind drunk at the First Gate, see if anybody brought in our lost soul by mistake."

Renai let out a huff of breath. "Sal, be straight with me. How bad is this? What's going to happen to Ramses?"

Sal launched off the lawn with a flutter, staggering through the air to clutch at a perch on her shoulder. He shuffled around until he found a position he liked. Once he settled in, Kyrie rumbled to life, her headlight piercing the darkness. Renai pushed off and they rolled into the street, making a slow turn on Washington and heading back down the way they came.

"The kid who was supposed to die?" Sal asked, his voice raised over the growl of Kyrie's engine. "Ain't no question. He's gonna die, if he ain't dead already." Renai turned her head to look at him, and he dipped his beak down in his raven's shrug. "It's us and taxes, Raines. What can I say?" Renai guided Kyrie into a turn onto St. Charles. "It's this Seth character that's a concern to me."

And then, when Kyrie kicked it up a couple of gears and really got roaring, Sal muttered to himself, maybe thinking Renai wouldn't hear or maybe not caring, "Fuckin' Hallows caca starts earlier every year."

Though she'd been kept at arm's length from the Hallows over the years, Renai didn't have to ask Sal what he meant. They were the days when the physical world of the living and the many worlds of the dead and the spirits overlapped. This stretch of time went by different names: Samhain, the Parentalia, the Zhongyuan Festival, Día de Muertos, Allhallowtide. Different cultures celebrated or revered these days at different parts of the year and for varying lengths of time. In New Orleans, the Hallows lasted for the three days starting with Halloween and ending on All Souls' Day. The dead visited the living, the living honored their dead, and sometimes those on the edges of things used the blurred lines of an otherwise rigid system for their own ends.

It was a busy time for psychopomps.

She did wonder why Sal had jumped to the conclusion that Seth had anything to do with the Hallows, since it didn't start until Halloween, a couple of days away. As far as she knew, the boundaries between worlds were as impenetrable as always. Could Ramses' disappearance be a part of some larger plot? Did Sal know Seth's true identity? She chewed on these questions as she rode Kyrie down the wide stretch of St. Charles that ran through the Garden District, past the columned entrances of mansions-turned-into-hotels and the neon lights of bars and restaurants, around the tight loop of Lee Circle and its hateful Confederate shadow, through the looming high-rises of the CBD — that congested, snarled area of the city full of office complexes and condos — and out across the noise and hustle and blaring lights of Canal Street. No matter how she turned the situation around in her mind, the only thing that mattered was finding Ramses. *That's my true North,* she thought, waiting for the light to turn so she could cross Canal, *whether he's alive or dead, in this world or the next, I'm going to find Ramses.*

"I'd appreciate it if you did the talking," Sal said, while she was waiting for a break in traffic to be able to cross the street. She turned to him and raised an eyebrow. "Just ask him to tell you about the 'pomps he's let through recently," Sal said. "I'll track 'em down on the other side."

"So this is why you had to 'bum a ride' even though you got wings," Renai said. "You need Oussou's help, but the way you treat him, you know he wouldn't piss on you if you were on fire. Is that it?"

"Be like gasoline, much as he drinks," Sal muttered, just as the light changed.

Renai laughed and guided Kyrie across the streetcar tracks. "You see? It's shit like that. What's he done to you to make you hate him so bad?"

"Long story. Will you help or not?"

"Yeah, I'll talk to him. But you owe me one."

Sal didn't answer her. Nor did he say a word when she parked the bike, just hopped down to Kyrie's handlebars and left her to cross Rampart alone. She practically had to jog across the street to keep from getting clipped by some asshole cabbie going at least ten miles an hour over the speed limit. Oussou took one look at her and grinned. "Decided to come visit without that shit-bird shepherd of yours, huh?" he asked.

"He's, uh, occupied. With something else." *Nice recovery, Raines,* she thought, in Sal's droll voice.

Oussou was too busy hauling his drunken self to his feet to notice her lack of composure, though. He pulled his cuffs straight and ran a hand along his do-rag, making sure it lay smooth. It was then that Renai realized what this must look like, what he must think she'd come here for. She considered playing into it, flirting a little and playing coy until he'd tell her anything she wanted. *How far you really gonna take that, though,* her mother asked, and the disappointment Renai imagined in her tone was all the answer she needed. Besides, he was Ghede and she was a psychopomp. She shouldn't have to play games to get the information she needed.

And loa or not, god or not, sparing his fragile male ego wasn't in her damn job description.

When Oussou turned his eyes to her appraisal, Renai kissed her teeth. "You kick that game at somebody who's got time for it," she said, fighting the smile that teased at the corners of her mouth when the expression on the loa's face shifted from pimp to punk. "You know damn well I ain't here for all that."

"Damn, it's like that?" Oussou jerked his head away and muttered some curse, but when he looked back at her, his mouth was twisted in wry amusement. "So what you want if you ain't buyin' what I'm sellin'? You need me to open the Gate?"

"No. I just need to know who you let through already. Sal's got me checking up on something."

Oussou nodded to himself, his attention now on the cars passing by on Basin and the bottle he raised to his lips. "Wasn't many," he said. He scratched his chin with his thumb and then counted them off on his fingers as he named them. "Link. Azreal. Dar. Howl. Flyboy. Lil' Tee. Big Riley."

Renai nodded as he said each name, though she didn't know if these were nicknames or true ones. She hadn't met many psychopomps other than Sal, and most of them seemed either unwilling or unable to speak to her. Some death spirits, Sal had told her, had about as much personality as those suckerfish on the inside of aquariums. They just traveled back and forth, performing their function without question or thought. "And the dead they were guiding?" she asked when he finished his list. "What do you remember about them?"

He shrugged, cleaning off a tooth with the tip of his tongue before answering. "You know how it is," he said, "after a while, the dead all kinda look the same, you feel me?"

Renai didn't. Not at all. She could remember her dead distinctly, their names and their faces when they'd died and the faces they'd chosen when they'd stood at the First Gate. Maybe things would be different if she'd seen as many dead as the loa must have seen. She doubted it. Instead of calling him out, though, she said her goodbyes and left, waiting until she was in Kyrie's seat and rolling away before she said anything to Sal. She repeated Oussou's list, then asked, "That all you need?"

"Yeah," he said. "Thanks. I'm gonna head over to the other side and look up these 'pomps. See if they know what's what." They rode in silence for a moment, Renai heading back to her empty apartment out of habit. She knew what she wanted him to say next, but she didn't want to ask. Knew she'd go behind his back again if she had to. "If you don't hear from me by tomorrow, why don't you try to track down this kid topside? Might be he's still alive."

Renai was so relieved that she decided not to give Sal any more grief about his inability to get along with the rest of the Underworld. She didn't have to sneak around, didn't have to lie again. By doing what Sal had told her to do, she'd be doing what she'd intended to do anyway. She'd worry about the decisions she'd have to make if she found him alive when she came to that particular bridge.

"Ramses," she said. "His name is Ramses St. Cyr."

"I know," Sal said. "I ain't forgot." And then, in a pounding of wings, he was gone, and Renai was alone once more.

⧗

Later, back in the apartment where she slept, she realized that, for the first time in a long time, the place seemed emptier than just its lack of furniture. She felt cut-off, unnatural. Maybe it had something to do with the crawling sensation she got whenever she pictured the empty space where Ramses was supposed to die. Or maybe it was the presence living inside her, that storm surge of hate and rage that had almost broken loose; she always had a kind of hangover when she had to wrestle the flood back into its cage. Maybe it was as simple as her role as a psychopomp finally touching a remnant, however insignificant, of the life she'd once had, forcing her to take a good long look at the hollow shell of a life she'd curled up in. Whatever the reason, that night as she lay awake waiting for sleep, Renai once again felt that strange, tenuous connection to the Underworld.

Laying there in the dark timelessness on the edge of sleep, Renai saw the Third Gate as a cemetery filled with bookshelves. The cemetery itself wasn't one that she recognized; for all she knew it was an imagined combination of Holt and St. Louis No. 1, with the expected aboveground tombs of brick and mortar and plaster along with a handful of concrete slabs about half a foot tall that marked belowground burials. The shelves—identical towers of smooth, white-washed wood ten feet tall and only a few feet wide—seemed designed for the books they held: a uniform collection of volumes thick and tall and bound in brown leather, with gold lettering on the spine indicating a year and a span of letters, like encyclopedias or dictionaries.

At the center of this eerie archive of the dead, behind a massive lectern that looked like it belonged in a Gothic cathedral, sat the Gatekeeper of the Third Gate, an angel named Plumaj. Their task was to collect the Name of the recently departed so that the soul could move on with all their deeds recorded. The angel was also, Renai knew, the voice on the other end of the Deadline. *If only I could cross over like Sal,* she thought, *Plumaj might know why Ramses' death went so wrong.*

For some reason, though, the thought of actually speaking to Plumaj filled Renai with a panicky, fluttering dread. She'd flirted with gods and bargained with Death, but picturing an angel made her want to crawl out of her own skin, and she had no idea why.

Dying, it turned out, really fucked you up.

It took her almost an hour to calm down enough to slide into sleep. When she woke the next morning and turned the radio on, more out of routine than actually seeking a soul to collect, the Deadline played nothing but hissing dead air.

CHAPTER SEVEN

ASERIES OF PLAYING cards, the symbols and values assigned esoteric meanings, shuffled into randomness and drawn in ignorance, arranged into a pattern and interpreted. A shape seen in the billowing clouds, in the erratic flames, in the sprawl of stars across the night sky. Questions answered by stalks of yarrow and animal bones, by coins and cowrie shells, by graven stones and sticks of bamboo, tossed into a bowl or scattered in a circle or dropped onto a white cloth or spilled from a cup. Mirrors and numbers and the letters in the Name of God. Decisions made by an animal's feeding habits, or flocking patterns, or by the entrails ripped from its flesh. Identity confirmed by the creases in one's palm, by the shape of one's skull, by the ridges on the tips of one's fingers. Fear in a handful of dust; truth in a spray of blood. Cartomancy and forensics, astrology and meteorology and Ifá: all are just nonsense unless one has the ability to read the signs. Just chaos, unless one has the eyes to see.

Renai leaned against one of the palm trees that grew in the neutral ground across Basin Street from St. Louis Cemetery No. 1, hands stuffed down in the pockets of her leather jacket, chilly even though the temperature would hit the seventies by noon, humming along with the music bumping in her earbuds. André 3000 told her that she didn't need to panic even though the sky was falling.

Kyrie sat parked a little ways away, but Renai couldn't decide if she should wait or leave. Part of her wondered how far the bike would carry her, if they could escape this city entirely. It's not like she would starve. Between her aura of disinterest and the ghost word, she could take anything she needed. Anything she wanted, really. Of course, that was assuming the jacket's powers would work if she abandoned the duties the Thrones had given her. But given the general trajectory of the last couple of days, it might be a risk she had to consider.

First, Seth had appeared out of nowhere to offer her some cryptic deal. Then, someone slipped free of their destined death, which she hadn't even known was *possible*. Then the Deadline went silent. Now this: even though she'd been watching for almost half an hour, Masaka wasn't in their spot at the First Gate.

"Ain't no time to panic, my ass," she said, not realizing she'd spoken aloud until she heard a woman's laughter, high and tittering, louder than her music. Renai pulled out one of her earbuds just in time to hear the voice speak.

"No moment like this moment," the voice said. "It's a gift. That's why they call it the present." Renai looked around but saw no one, certainly no one close enough to be able to hear her. A trilling, two-note whistle, off to her right, and then the voice said, "Over here." The first thing Renai saw was a bronze statue of a clean-shaven man, one hand holding the wrist of the other, which held a rolled-up scroll of paper. Shit had gotten just weird enough that she was willing to believe that the statue had spoken, but then she saw the small bird standing on the black pedestal, next to the statue's feet. "Hi there," the bird said. "I'm Cordelia. You must be Renaissance."

Renai paused the music and tucked the earbuds into her pocket. "You can call me Renai."

Cordelia was a small brown bird with a long tail of coarse feathers, stripes of darker brown running down her wings, a white underbelly, and a short beak that curved down to a sharp point. A spiky crest of reddish-brown feathers bristled atop her head like the crest on a Spartan helmet. She had the faintest hint of Victorian aloofness in her voice, like she wished she'd been born British, but not enough to fake the accent. "Nice to meet you, Renai," she said. "You can call me Cordelia." She hopped to the edge of the pedestal in a couple of quick, jerky movements. "Apparently you need a little help locating a certain lost someone?"

"Great," Renai muttered, "another 'pomp. Did Sal send you?"

She tilted her head to the side in a bird's version of a furrowed brow. "A 'pomp . . . oh, yes, I like that. Fits what we do very nicely, don't you think? Just a bunch of pomp and circumstance." She spread her wings and hopped off the pedestal, swooping through the air and mimicking the trumpeting song that played at every graduation, sweeping past Renai and landing on Kyrie's handlebars. "Of course, you've found yourself in quite a different kind of circumstance, haven't you?" There was a hint of a grin in her tone, a kind of polite mischievousness, as if she were laughing, if not *at* you, then certainly at a joke you probably wouldn't get. She had the easy confidence of a person who took what they wanted and set fire to the rest, who took zero bullshit but dished theirs out with both hands.

Renai liked her right from the start.

"So you're here to help me find Ramses?"

The little bird tilted her head to the side. "'Help' is not the word I would use. 'Evaluate'? 'Assess'? These are better terms for what I am here to do."

Renai clenched her jaw. The Thrones did love to pass judgment. She and Sal must have really fucked up. She hoped the grumpy old dog was okay, wherever he was. She let out a long, slow breath and forced herself to relax. *Nobody never fixed nothin' by frettin' 'bout it*, her grandmother would have said. "Can you at least tell me what's going on there?" Renai asked, aiming her thumb at the abandoned First Gate.

Cordelia angled a single yellow eye in that direction. "You mean the Gate? Or the Underworld?"

"I mean the fact that there's no one there to open it."

Cordelia made a sound halfway between a chirp and a giggle. "Oh, *that*," she said, wiggling her flight feathers at the Gate in a disconcertingly human gesture. "The Thrones are having themselves a bit of an identity crisis. Way above your pay grade, not to worry. Mine too, frankly. They'll work it out before the Hallows, I'm sure. At any rate, to the task at hand." She gave a little come-hither wave with one of her wings. "You know this lost boy better than I do. Where should we start?"

Hands still tucked into her jacket pocket, Renai rolled the tiny slip of paper Seth had given her between her thumb and index finger. She'd caught herself doing that all morning, as if the little scroll had some kind of talismanic power, as if it could show her the way. It must be made of something more durable than modern paper, though, because it hadn't torn no matter how much she worried at it. Cordelia's explanation about Masaka's absence didn't exactly put her at ease. It didn't even really count as an explanation. In her experience, "Don't worry about it" belonged on the same list as "It won't hurt much" and "I'm doing this for your own good" and "Trust me."

Even though she didn't entirely trust the psychopomp, Renai knew she wouldn't learn anything new by staring at a cemetery wall all day. *Besides,* she thought, *Cordelia looks about as threatening as a hummingbird, even with that punk rock frill. Let her try something. I wish she would.* "I drove over to the St. Cyr house first thing this morning," she said, pushing away from the trunk of the palm tree and crossing over to where Kyrie and Cordelia waited. "I figured that just because he didn't die at his appointed time didn't mean he wouldn't go home. I mean, he probably doesn't know he's supposed to be dead, right?"

"Smart," Cordelia said. Renai lifted an eyebrow, but if the little bird was mocking her, she couldn't tell. "But if you've found our lost lamb already, I have to say, you really hid the rose among the brambles."

It took Renai a second for the context clues to catch up with that expression, but she didn't waste time asking about it. "He wasn't there this morning," she said, "but I'm pretty sure he went home last night because the bullet hole in the window had a piece of cardboard taped over it, and his mom was asleep in her bed."

Cordelia nuzzled at an errant feather on her wing, absently it seemed, like a person chewing their nail. "Why does the one lead to the other?"

"You know any mother in the history of *ever* who would stretch out for a good night's rest after her house got shot up if her baby wasn't sleeping right where she could watch him breathe?" She pursed her lips and leaned in, as if waiting for a rebuttal. "Yeah, me neither. And on top of that, his textbooks were all over the dining room table last night, but this morning they were gone." She swung a leg over Kyrie, tilting the handlebars and making Cordelia shift over to stay level. "Which means," she continued, "that I know where he went when he left the house."

The psychopomp might be in a tiny little bird form, but she was sharp. It only took her a second to get it. "Ah," she said. "School."

"School," Renai repeated, making a kick-starting gesture with her leg as Kyrie's engine roared to life.

⧗

Between his report card and his uniform, Renai knew that Ramses went to a charter school out in the Bywater, which wasn't surprising. These days, it seemed like just about all the schools in the city that weren't private—which, aside from a couple of exceptions that proved the rule, meant Catholic— were charter schools of one form or another. Seemed like after the storm, everybody and their grandmother figured that they knew how to fix what was wrong with education in this city. Some of them were one-off local start-ups; some were part of larger out-of-state organizations. Ramses had gone to one of the latter, a national group that called itself EITA—which was an acronym for something Renai couldn't remember—that sometimes gave its individual schools a single inspiring noun for a name, unlike the saints and saviors of the parochial schools. Ramses went to EITA: Empower, and from the look of his grades, he went often enough to do well. As a young black woman, Renai had some opinions about a national chain coming into the in- ner city to educate the poor urban community, but as a good Catholic girl whose middle-class parents had the means to send her to one of those private schools in explicit avoidance of the public school system in New Orleans, she figured her opinions might ring pretty hollow and so kept them to herself.

Cordelia had struggled to remain perched on Renai's shoulder as Kyrie prowled down the edge of the Quarter on Rampart and then shifted over onto St. Claude out toward the Bywater, eventually giving up and burrowing into the cloth hood of her jacket. Renai didn't mind. It freed her from hav- ing to make small talk, from having to decide whether she wanted to question the psychopomp's motives or trust her at face value. She'd grown weary of thinking these past few days, of the constant litany of doubt and evaluation that had invaded her spartan predictable life of routine. The tempest within her stretched and moved, aching to move, to act.

The predictable, tourist-friendly antiquity of the Quarter fell away as they crossed Esplanade and headed toward the Upper Ninth Ward, becom- ing a murky mix of entropy and gentrification that had invaded pockets of the city since the storm. Buildings here and there were tagged with graffiti —sometimes they were homes left vacant for years; sometimes they were food co-ops and reclaimed building material thrift stores. One block might have a handful of black men in plain white tees gathered around one front stoop, while the next would have a trio of bike-riding white folk with their hair in grungy, pocket-lint dreads. Some parts of the city weren't segregated so much as they were striated, like two or three disparate neighborhoods squeezed together until they occupied the same space.

She picked up details here and there out of the blur of Kyrie's rush down St. Claude: a house decorated with a glittering mosaic mandala made out of broken chrome and polished glass and reflective tile, a corner store turned daiquiri shop, a place that advertised AFRICAN HAIR BRAIDING with pictures taped to the plate glass to show what styles a customer might choose, so faded they'd might've been there since before the storm. And then Kyrie slowed and leaned to the side and rolled up onto the gravel shoulder. The bike came to rest in front of a three-story building with wide cement steps leading to three narrow glass doors, above which hung a banner that read: EITA: EM- POWER HIGH SCHOOL — EDUCATION IS THE ANSWER.

So that's *what it stands for,* Renai thought, as Kyrie's engine eased silent and Cordelia poked her head out of Renai's hood. "Wake up, buttercup," Renai said, "we're here."

Renai had expected that Ramses' school would be different from her own, but the metal detectors at the door still surprised her. The three narrow doors at the front seemed designed with them in mind, creating a space where — when the students crowded in at the beginning of the day — three single-file lines would form, pass through the elongated empty door frames of the detectors, and then diffuse into the halls. She told herself that if they had them, they were probably necessary, but that thought started the flood of anger swirl- ing inside of her. She made herself take a deep breath, pushed it back down.

The building that EITA had taken over had been a school when it was built in the '40s, had remained a school even after the storm, though it had hardly been a place of education then. Her father would bring it up whenever she'd brought home a grade lower than a B, that school back in the Ninth Ward where they set trash cans on fire. The bones of the place persisted even after all those years and EITA's renovations, high ceilings and creaking hard- wood floors and wide, sturdy staircases at the end of the long hallway. Come name changes and hurricanes and metal detectors all, this place was built to last.

"So we're here," Cordelia said from Renai's shoulder, "where's the boy?"

"Can you, I don't know, sense him?" Renai asked, thinking of the way Sal zeroed in on his dead like a homing pigeon.

Cordelia made an exasperated cough in the back of her throat. "If I could find him, why would I need—"

She was interrupted by a set of ancient bells *briiinnng*ing into life and the hallway exploding with teenagers and noise. It felt both eerily familiar and somehow alien as well. For one, it was strange to see boys as students. Her four years in halls like these had been at an all-girls school, so seeing the antics of boys posturing and insulting and braying that Renai had only ever seen at dances and parties made the whole scene feel oddly false, like she'd wandered onto a movie set. She also realized, after a moment, that almost every single student was black. Her school had been predominately white, and though she'd never been the only black student in her classes, there had been a couple of times where she'd been one of just two. She'd had classmates who were Latina, who were of Vietnamese descent, and a couple of girls from Middle Eastern families who wore hijabs along with their plaid skirts and white blouses. Here though, aside from a couple of white teachers, every person Renai could see had dark skin.

She couldn't quite process how she felt about all of it—the de facto segregation and the privilege and cultural gaps—couldn't decide what it meant about her and her perspective on the world and the life she might've lived if she hadn't died, so she pushed it to the side and focused on the details. These kids all wore uniforms just like the ones Renai had seen scattered across Ramses' bedroom: white polo shirts with a shield on the chest and dark blue or khaki pants—even the girls, an option Renai, who had been forced into four years of plaid skirts, envied. She smiled a little, remembering how teenager-in-skirts Renai had obsessed about how ashy her knees would get.

These kids didn't wear name tags like she'd had to, so she couldn't just wander the halls and classrooms looking for Ramses. She hadn't really considered how she'd find him, she realized, had just assumed that Cordelia would share Sal's unerring sense of their quarry.

"Sal always just knew," she said over the noise. "I figured you would too. Didn't know if it was a psychopomp thing or a bird thing or—"

"Whatever talent he possessed, I do not," Cordelia said. "Not one of these mortals looks any closer to death than the next one, to my eyes."

The crowd jostled and swarmed past Renai, ignoring her as the living always did. She kept having to sway and shift out of people's path, otherwise they'd walk right over her. At least she never had to worry about doing that awkward back-and-forth synchronized dance of avoidance people did when both were polite enough to move out of the other's way. It was harder to stay still than to flow with the crowd, so Renai just picked a direction and started moving. The momentum carried her along, almost as though the students as a collective were leading her toward Ramses, and that thought gave her an idea. She pulled her cell phone out of her pocket and scrolled through the pictures she'd taken at the St. Cyr house that morning, searching for the report card on the fridge.

She leaned over to the person next to her, a tall light-skinned girl with long relaxed hair, and said, in a kind of oh-shit-I'm-totally-lost voice, "Do you know what period this is?" The girl looked at her with the startled double take that Renai had come to the expect, the almost-comical mixture of surprise, confusion, and immediate acceptance that came with her sudden intrusion into their awareness. "I'm new here," Renai continued, not having to stretch very hard for a memory of being overwhelmed by everything and everyone around her, "and I don't know where I'm going and I lost the girl who was supposed to help and I don't even know what *period* it is and—"

"Third period," the girl said, half her attention on Renai and half on where she was going. "That your schedule?" she asked, dipping her chin at the phone in Renai's hand. When Renai nodded, the girl just waited with an expectant expression on her face.

"Oh, right," Renai said, "uh, Brennan, 208."

"Ms. B on the second floor," the girl said, "up them stairs and two rooms down. She cool, don't even stress." She started to turn away, Renai already dismissed from her attention, but she looked back. "She catch you with that phone, though, you gonna lose it. She cool, but she don't play, neither." And then the girl was gone, slipping out of the rush and into the open door of a classroom with ease.

"That was easy," Cordelia said.

Too easy, Renai thought, but kept it to herself. Her heart rate increased the closer they got to room 208. What happened when they found him? Would Cordelia insist on taking his life right there, in front of his classmates and teacher? Or did he have to die in the right place in order to close off that wound his escape had left behind? Could she convince the psychopomp to let him live? Could she convince the *Thrones* to spare him?

And if trying to save Ramses meant Renai failed Cordelia's "evaluation," what would the Thrones do to *her*?

She got to the classroom just as the bell rang again, alongside another student who grinned as he walked in like he timed it that way every day. Renai scanned the students who were already seated in their desks, but couldn't see them well enough from the back of the room to be able to tell one way or the other if any of them were Ramses. Renai leaned against a table in the far corner that held handouts and college application flyers. Before she could say anything to Cordelia, the teacher—a short, middle-aged white woman she assumed was Ms. Brennan—projected her voice over the collective murmur of her students.

"Okay, my lovelies, you know the routine. Your bell-ringer is on the board, a short-response question that you should put in your Social Justice notebooks, which I will remind you is part of your Force for Change assignment. Which is due . . . ?" A mumbled chorus of voices replied that it was due at the end of the nine weeks. "It is indeed, and that day is fast approaching." Her gaze swept the room, making sure that everyone did as she said, and for a moment Renai thought the teacher looked right at her, even raised an eyebrow. She couldn't be sure, as the woman wore thick glasses that gave her an owlish expression.

The teacher stepped over to her desk and scribbled something on a piece of paper, and then began reading off the names of her students, getting mostly "here," in reply, though one boy said, "present" in the exaggerated, nasally voice of a stereotypical white person, which earned a couple of snickers, and another girl who—without taking her eyes off her paper—threw up a fist and sang out, "A-hey, yo-ya-ya-yooo," which must have been a reference Renai didn't get, because half the class laughed and even the teacher crooked an indulgent smile.

When she asked for Ramses St. Cyr, her only answer was silence.

Once she finished with the roll, she did something at her computer—presumably entering attendance, since she stayed standing while she did it—then walked up and down the aisles of the classroom, glancing down at her students' work. When she got to the end of the row closest to Renai, she kept walking, looking straight at her and, saying nothing, handed her a sheet of paper folded in half.

MEET ME OUTSIDE AFTER CLASS, the note read. AND YOUR LITTLE BIRD, TOO.

⧗

About an hour later, Renai sat on the steps out front watching the traffic pass by, M.I.A. in her ears telling her to live fast and die young, and images of the Fourth Gate—where the Essence of a soul was separated from its opposite, Shadow self—on her mind. Ramses' teacher came around the corner of the building and waved at her, urgently, to follow. Renai plucked her earbuds out and rose to her feet only to find that the woman had already vanished back the way she'd come. Cordelia fluttered up onto Renai's shoulder from the low stone wall she'd been pacing along. "Be wary," the psychopomp said in her ear, "this one sees more than she should."

Renai didn't know what she expected to discover when she followed the teacher, but finding her smoking a cigarette, leaning against the railing that led up to a side door, wasn't one of the possibilities she'd imagined.

The woman wore a loose black skirt that fell past her knees and a dark blue, almost denim shirt with the collar unbuttoned and the sleeves rolled up her strong, wiry forearms. Her glasses were tucked up on top of her head, holding back stray strands of her salt-and-pepper hair. Hints of tattooed rose vines on each pale white arm peeked out beneath the sleeves. She breathed out a thin plume of smoke as Renai walked up. She didn't turn to greet them, seemed lost in contemplation of the house across the street. Her cheerful, exuberant demeanor had vanished. When she spoke, it was as if she were talking to herself. To anyone else, Renai realized, that's exactly what it would look like.

"Couple, three months ago," she said, "one of my students was implicated in a shooting. Good kid, momma raised him to say 'yes, ma'am, no ma'am,' came to school on the regular, the whole deal. The police learned he was diligent in his attendance and showed up to my classroom to arrest him. I stood in the door and told them that if they thought they were stepping foot in my room, they better plan on putting cuffs on me, too." She took a drag of her cigarette, held it, blew it out through her nose. "Now, I'm no fool. Just because he's sweet as sugar in my class doesn't mean he didn't have a part in some bad thing. All the bad shit in this world was done by someone who was a good kid once upon a time." She flicked ash off the tip of her ciga-rette, watched it go spiraling away into nothing. "And I'm not some 'eff the po-leese' cop hater, either. My uncle was a cop. You do what you do, you pay the price. They picked Deke up after school and booked his ass. But that's not the point." She glanced down at her watch, frowned. "The point is, school should be a safe place for everyone. Period." She shifted her whole body around to face Renai, her gray eyes angry and hard.

"Which means you two, whoever the fuck you are, have found yourselves on my shit list for strolling into my classroom like it belongs to you. Please feel free to explain. And quickly, too. I got sub duty in, like, fifteen minutes."

Cordelia started to say something, but Renai spoke over her. "We're looking for someone," she said. "One of your students. We think he's in dan-ger." It wasn't a lie, she told herself. They did, after all, genuinely want to help him. The fact that they also might have to end his life was simply a mat-ter of perspective.

"Ramses," the teacher said, not exactly a question, but her tone was look-ing for confirmation. When Renai nodded, she did too, but slower, like she was accepting more than agreeing. "Okay," she said after a moment, "okay." She stuck the cigarette in between her lips and reached down to take Renai's hand. Her grip was strong and warm. "Name's Opal. Opal Brennan."

"I'm Renai."

"I kinda figured you two were here about him," Opal said.

"What makes you say that?" Renai asked, at the same time that Cordelia said, "How can you see us?"

Opal laugh-coughed out a puff of smoke. "So the bird talks too, huh? Sure, why not." She rubbed at her eyes like she was trying to wipe away a headache. "I say that because he's the only student I've got that's, you know" —she waved the hand holding the cigarette in a way that included both Re-nai and Cordelia—"special. Like y'all. And I can see you because I can see *everything*. It's my 'gift.'"

Opal made little air quotes with her fingers when she said the word *gift*, pronounced it like it was a curse word. "I used to be a card reader in the Quarter. I was good at it. Real good. And then I helped out a friend who turned out to be an honest-to-goddess magician. Come to find out I was good at reading the cards because my spiritual sight or whatever you wanna call it was half-open. But then my friend opened it up all the way for me."

She chuckled and took one last drag off her cigarette before she crushed it out on the metal railing and, making sure it had been extinguished, tucked the butt away in a pocket. "That was the end of fortunetelling for me. You'd think being able to clearly and accurately see someone's past, present, and future would be lucrative, but actually it just weirds folks out in a get-the-torches-and-pitchforks kinda way. So here I am, finally using the Tulane history degree my daddy bought me and trying to change some lives."

"What does 'special like us' mean?" Renai asked.

A flash of Opal's earlier suspicion wrinkled the flesh around the woman's eyes. "You know, otherworldly. Mythic." She let out an annoyed huff. "You really gonna make me say the word? He was *magic*, all right? That's something else I can see, now, too. Auras, if you wanna get all New Agey about it. How do you think I knew you weren't just some spooky-looking girl with a bird on her shoulder when you walked in my room? Miss Feathers there shifts and glows like a lava lamp, and you're always standing in shadow. Ramses is magic, just like the two of you."

Before Renai could wrap her head around what that might mean—both in terms of what she knew about herself and how it might impact her search for the missing boy—the bells rang, faintly, in the building behind Opal. The seer frowned.

"Crap," Opal said. "I really gotta go now. Give me your number and I'll call you later on. I'll ask around, see if anybody knows where he's been the past few days. I'll get Tameka to check his Facebook and Twitter and whatnot; that sneaky little shit has always got her phone on her. Don't need to be a prophet to see that." As they exchanged numbers, Renai's mind spun, trying to think of something she could ask that might tell her where to look next, but when Opal pulled open the thick metal door and waved an absentminded goodbye, it was Cordelia who spoke.

"What did you see when you looked at the boy?" the 'pomp asked. Opal froze, didn't leave, but didn't answer, either. "You see something different for each of us, you said. What's his aura?"

"He looked like fire," Opal said, after a long, uncomfortable silence. "From head to toe and in his smile and in his eyes, Ramses *burns*."

CHAPTER EIGHT

A **FTER THEY LEFT** Ramses' school, Renai and Cordelia spent the rest of the morning and the early part of the afternoon bouncing across the city, chasing Renai's memories of the few times she'd skipped school when she was Ramses' age. They lurked in shopping mall food courts and greasy spoon diners, stalked up and down the darkened aisles of movie theaters while superheroes battled onscreen, hunted among the sprawling oaks of City Park, the jogging and bike paths of Audubon Park, the sweating, hustling bodies on the fenced-in basketball court behind the Second District Police Station. Renai had never really thought of New Orleans as a big city, certainly not in comparison with a place like New York or Chicago, but she quickly realized it was plenty big enough to get lost in.

It didn't help that she couldn't seem to shake her uneasy recollections of the Fourth Gate, where the Gatekeeper, a red-haired white woman named Bridgette, forced the dead to examine themselves in her mirror and — if they could stand the truth that was revealed there — cut away their Shadow before letting them pass. It felt like her own mind was trying to tell her something important about Ramses, about the true version of him that Opal had seen. Something she'd once known and forgotten.

Just randomly stumbling across Ramses' path — a needle in a whole field full of haystacks—would take, as her grandmother would have said, the dev-il's own luck. But with Cordelia letting Renai take the lead and Sal MIA, she had to turn over the stones she could reach. She had hoped that Ramses' presence would give off that same sense of wrongness as the wound he'd left in the world, that he'd carve a wake through the living world that she and Cordelia would be able to smell and see and feel. But in all their search-ing, Renai didn't sense anything out of the ordinary, and if Cordelia caught any such scent, she gave no sign—content to ride in a quiet little bundle of feathers on Renai's shoulder and answering all her questions with a negative monosyllabic grunt.

All Renai found was a growing unease, a fear that Ramses' disappearance was bigger than Sal had told her, that the missing boy—though according to Opal, he wasn't *just* a boy—and the locked Gates and the silent Deadline and her mentor's absence were all connected somehow, that she was in the mid-dle of something she didn't yet entirely understand. So once the afternoon turned to evening, she rolled past the St. Cyr house once more in hopes that the boy had gone home, and if not, that she might find some clue there about where he could be.

Instead, she found an NOPD cruiser parked at the curb.

Using the ghost word just long enough to get inside, Renai walked into the middle of a conversation between Juliette St. Cyr and a white lady cop that had been going on for at least a few minutes before she got there. Long enough that they were past the introductions and the please-have-a-seat parts of the discussion. The police officer—short for a cop but average height for a woman, dark red hair pulled back into a tight ponytail, her intent eyes study-ing Juliette's face without looking down to write on the pad in her hands —sat in the old pleather recliner, perched on the edge of it like a spring, compressed and tense. Her thigh muscles bulged in her uniform pants; Re-nai recognized a fellow runner when she saw one. She wondered if the offi-cer knew she sat in the "good" chair, if she'd been offered that seat out of re-spect, or if she'd just taken it.

"—know I'm supposed to wait twenty-four hours before y'all say he missing," Juliette was saying as Renai walked in, the older woman's voice raw as if she'd been crying, "but I'm tellin' you, my Ki—my Ramses ain't the kind to go runnin' them streets. He ain't never cut school before, neither."

"That twenty-four-hour thing is just something they say on TV, Mrs. St.

Cyr," the cop said, drawing out her vowels in a not-from-New-Orleans sort of accent. "You did right to call us. You say he skipped school today?"

Juliette, a decade older than the memory Renai had been picturing, nodded. She'd always been a very pretty woman, and age had merely drawn her tighter, her cheekbones more pronounced, her hands more knuckle and bone than in her youth. She had dark purple extensions in her long, straightened hair and was also wearing a uniform: the burgundy jacket of a clerk at one of the fancy hotels in the Quarter. "They called while I was at work this afternoon. They say he ain't been all week, but that don't make no sense. I got him up and out the house same time as always, this mornin' even. He carried his books with him and everything."

The cop, Officer Coughlin according to her name tag, fought a smirk. "Whenever I used to cut class—not that I made a habit of it, you understand—I always brought my school stuff when I left the house. Added authenticity."

"Yeah?" Juliette asked, sniffling into a handful of tissues. "What high school you went to?"

To her credit, Coughlin smiled like she knew what Juliette was *really* asking, what anybody in the city meant by that question. "I stay in the Irish Channel," she said, sidestepping the issue pretty deftly. She took her eyes off of Juliette for the first time and nodded in the direction of one of the photographs on the wall. "You think we oughta speak to his dad?"

"Ramses' daddy?" Juliette got a far-off look on her face that Renai caught but Coughlin—unless the NOPD had a much more mystically sensitive training program than Renai assumed—probably misread. When you encountered the supernatural on a regular basis, your worldview shifted to accommodate the impossible as simply factual. So talking to a demigod or summoning a spirit or witnessing a miracle became just a thing that happened to you. Remembering one of these events might be profound or alarming or confusing, but only in the way that recalling a car accident or the birth of a child might be impactful. Things were different when the divine touched your life only once. Assuming you didn't just deny it, didn't push the moment down into a locked box that your memory never opened, that experience became fundamental to the way you saw things, the pivot that your world spun around. For Renai, a god showing up was a hassle. For most people, it would be an epiphany.

And whenever someone with only a single connection to the magical re-membered that pivotal, miraculous moment, they couldn't stop themselves from pulling the same dreamy, half-stoned face that Juliette St. Cyr wore when she thought of Ramses' father.

Cordelia, who hadn't said more than half a dozen words since they'd spo-ken to the teacher, chuckled from Renai's shoulder. "Oh my," she said, "you naughty kitten. Whose cream have you—" Renai jerked her arm and made a shushing noise. The little psychopomp huffed and settled her weight in a way that felt like turning her back, but at least she stayed quiet.

When Coughlin cleared her throat and said Juliette's name, the woman blinked and seemed to remember where she was. "No," she said, "Dom stay in Houston now."

"Dom?" Coughlin asked, lifting her pad and pen slightly to finish the question.

"Dominic St. Cyr." She peered at the cop's notepad when Coughlin wrote down the name as if she were checking the spelling. "He found good work out there after the storm and just kinda stayed. We talked about all of us going out there, but I got a good thing at the hotel, and he ain't making *that* good a money." She shrugged. "You know how it go."

Coughlin nodded as if she knew exactly how it went. "You think Ramses might have gone to Houston to see his father? Wouldn't be the first time a young man—"

"Nah, Ki-ki wouldn't do that just to see Dom. We was gon' spend Thanksgiving with him, and they on that FaceTime once a week. I'm telling you, my boy got *took*."

Renai couldn't quite pin down exactly what changed about the police of-ficer—she still sat just as straight-backed and still on the edge of the reclin-er's seat, still watched Juliette with those intense eyes, but all of a sudden she went from being a coiled spring to a plucked guitar string, not just tense, but vibrating. "Do you know someone who might want to abduct your son, Mrs. St. Cyr?" Renai bet Coughlin sounded exactly the same when she recited Mi-randa rights.

"Sex traffickers!" Juliette snapped, like she'd been holding it back the whole time the cop had been in her home. "They told us all about 'em in church. I know you think they only go after pretty little white girls, but Ramses is different. He special."

Renai felt as deflated as Coughlin looked. It wasn't that Juliette's theory was impossible, but it just wasn't the solid lead that it had seemed. From Renai's perspective, it was even more unlikely. No mere human would have the capacity to deny Ramses his fate, no matter how malevolent they might be. She'd heard enough. She flipped her hood up and used the ghost word to slip outside.

"Don't you want to hear the rest?" Cordelia asked on the way out.

"Juliette doesn't know anything we don't already know," Renai said. "She probably doesn't even know who Ramses' real father is. Not his real name, anyway."

"You caught that too, did you? I suppose that accounts for what the teacher saw in his aura. There's no end of fire deities, I'm afraid."

But that wasn't what had Renai's mind whirling. The identity of Ramses St. Cyr's father, the source of the boy's power, didn't matter to her as much as Juliette's conviction that her son had been taken. Renai had collected enough sick children—had seen enough mothers awaken with the knowledge of their child's death already in their eyes—to know that maternal instinct was real and powerful, if not exact. She'd assumed that Ramses' absence from his own death had been a kind of cosmic accident, worried that her presence had somehow thrown things out of balance. But what if Ramses hadn't simply missed his own death?

What if he'd been *abducted* from it?

Despite these suspicions, she needed to follow through on the more simple explanations before she could turn toward the more supernatural side of things. And since it was now clear that Ramses wasn't just missing from his moment of death but from his everyday life as well, she would need to start checking the hospitals and morgues.

Settling onto Kyrie's seat, Renai turned the bike around in the street and headed for the closest one: Touro Infirmary. Cordelia curled into a quiet ball of feathers once more. Renai couldn't tell if the little psychopomp was up in her feelings about something Renai had done, giving her the silent treatment as part of her "evaluation," or just so bored that she'd fallen asleep.

As an emissary of Death, Renai had become familiar with the labyrinthine back halls and the convoluted bureaucracy that surrounded the process of dying in the twenty-first century. Sal often grumbled about how "fuckin' complicated and sterile" dying had become, and—even without a frame of reference to judge against—Renai had to agree. People used to die at home, used to be cleaned and prepared for burial by the family. Now, unless you were in the room when it happened, death was like a disappearing trick on a magician's stage. Now you see 'em, now you don't. In a way, the morticians and coroners and hospice nurses she'd come across in her collections were all doing the same job as she was: easing an individual's transition from one world to the next while keeping the lines between the living and the dead defined and inviolable.

Her aura of indifference allowed her to slip past the ordinary barriers of EMPLOYEES ONLY signs and let her peek over nurses' shoulders when they logged into their patients' records—which made searching the database for Ramses St. Cyr and John Doe as simple as it was illegal—and the ghost word gave her access to the more secure areas like the ICU and the cold chambers of the morgue without needing a magnetized ID badge. Just like her earlier search, Renai wandered the hospital's halls in a growing fog of frustration and doubt. It wasn't until they'd gotten to the morgue at the depths of Touro's labyrinth, that Cordelia finally broke her silence.

"What song is that?" she asked.

Renai had grown so used to the psychopomp's quiet, still presence that she'd almost forgotten the little bird was there. And it wasn't until Cordelia pointed it out that Renai realized she'd been humming. She knew the song, though, the same one that had been stuck in her head the whole time she'd been wandering up and down the identical taupe-walled, fluorescent-lit hospital hallways and inspecting the variations on the theme of antiseptic-stinking, frigid-aired autopsy rooms. "'St. James Infirmary,'" she said.

"You say that like I should know it," Cordelia said.

Renai made a noise in the back of her throat. "Made famous by Louis Armstrong? Then sung by basically every New Orleans musician ever?" She half sung, half muttered the first couple of lines. "*I went down to St. James Infirmary. Saw my baby there, she was stretched out on a long white table. So cold, so sweet, so fair.* Nothing?"

"Can't say it's a path I've walked."

"Girl. Where have you been 'pomping all this time? Baton Rouge?" Renai dug in her pocket for her phone. "We have to remedy this right quick so we can stay friends." When Renai unlocked her phone, she saw a notification she didn't recognize. After a minute of swiping through menus, she realized that it indicated a voicemail, the first she'd ever gotten on this phone. She knew without checking that it had to be from Opal, since the prophet was the only person—living or dead—who knew her number. "Hang on," she said to Cordelia. "Opal called. Must not have heard it because we were on the bike." Renai set her phone down on a steel instrument tray next to a bone saw, pushed the SPEAKER button, and started the message, the song she'd been about to play already forgotten.

"Spooky Girl and Miss Feathers," Opal said over the cacophony of shouts and laughter and traffic and PA announcements that Renai recognized as the end of a school day. "So bad news first, social media was a bust. Looks like his moms was real paranoid about cyberbullying and knew his passwords, so most of his feeds are just videos of people falling down. I do have a little something for you, though. Probably nothing, but it doesn't hurt to check. Last time anybody heard from our boy, he was supposed to meet up with some friends to ride the Ghost Train. They went in a big group, so no one can say for sure if he was there or not. Maybe you can pick up his trail there. I'll keep asking around, and if I find out anything else I'll let you know. Give me a call either way. Ramses is a good kid and I want to help find him."

When the message finished, Renai slipped the phone back into the pocket of her jeans, disappointed but not surprised. After the conversation she'd overheard—okay, spied on—at the St. Cyr house, she'd all but given up any hope that Ramses would be found by conventional means. Still, she was running out of time. The Hallows began at midnight the following night, whether she'd found Ramses or not. She couldn't decide whether she should even bother with the long shot of picking up his trail at the Ghost Train. He sure as hell wasn't in this morgue.

She poked her finger at her shoulder to give Cordelia something to perch on and—once she felt the little bird's claws get a good grip—held her out at arm's length so they could talk face-to-beak. "So look, tell me straight. If Ramses did ride the Ghost Train, can you track him down? Will you even be able to tell he was there?"

Before Cordelia could answer, the electronic locks behind Renai beeped and clunked, the double-wide door swinging open on smooth hydraulic hinges. A red-haired white woman in hospital scrubs pushed a gurney through the doorway, the shape of a body zipped up within the thick white envelope of a body bag.

The nurse had a phone trapped between her shoulder and her ear, talking into it in a tired, detached voice. "—asphyxiation due to strangulation.

His folks gave us the OK for organ donation, so I'm wheeling him into the morgue now. I figure Dr. Carlie will wanna come right down and start with the corneas."

The woman wheeled the gurney into the room and set it into position next to the instrument table, right in front of Renai. As she locked the wheels with her sneaker's toe, the nurse nodded and made a couple of affirmative noises to whomever she was talking to. "Call me when she's on her way, will ya? I ain't had a smoke all shift. Thanks." She hung up the phone and dropped it into the apron pocket on the bottom of her shirt. She looked down at the body bag for a long moment, her face expressionless. Then she frowned. "What the fuck, man?" she said, though it wasn't clear to Renai if she spoke to the body or to herself, or to someone who wasn't there. "Just. Fuck." And then she turned and left, already tapping a cigarette out of the packet she pulled from her pocket.

Given the luck Renai had had the past couple of days, she felt no surprise at all when—smooth as a hydraulic hinge and with the crinkling rustle of plastic and fabric—the corpse on the gurney sat up.

CHAPTER NINE

THE SILENCE OF the grave is not always peaceful. For some—those who drowned, or who took their own lives, or who died with some crucial task left unfinished, or who were killed by a spirit alone in the wilderness—a single ember of quickness remains with the corpse even after the rest of the soul has departed. What is left is remnant of life given teeth and claws and a familiar face. A puppet of necrotic flesh gyrating to a danse macabre; a hollow automaton clinging to the basest instincts of humanity, driven by the machinery of lust and hunger and rage. When they rise and walk again among us, we call them draugr and Widergänger. When they are still bound within their shrouds and stagger ungainly with one-footed leaps, we know them as pocong, as Jiang Shi. Nachzerer. Revenant. Ghoul. They are relentless and violent and unreasonable and invulnerable, but their true horror lies in their humanity. In the fact that they were once one of us. A reminder that the "requiescat in pace" we put on tombstones is not a promise.

It is a prayer.

It said a lot about the life Renai had been living the past few years that she barely flinched when the dead body on the gurney sat up within its shroud of thick plastic. She reacted, of course—a step back and a clench of the eyes and a frustrated, disgusted shake of her arms that went from her shoulders to her fingertips—but it was an involuntary, instinctive thing. More akin to the little gasp of revulsion wrung from someone confronted by one of New Orleans's huge roaches skittering across a kitchen floor than the panicked shriek or the terrified paralysis that one expected from horror movies.

Cordelia, shaken from her perch on Renai's finger, fluttered in the air a moment before coming to rest on a countertop. They waited for a long, tense moment and—when the corpse made no other move—Renai let out a brief, anxious chuckle.

"This amuses you?" Cordelia asked.

"Just didn't think this would be part of my day when I woke up this morning, I guess. You ever see anything like this?"

"I've seen more than one kind of un-death."

Renai felt what was left of a smile slide off of her face. "The Gates," she said.

"What about them?"

"If they're still locked, then psychopomps can't get over to this side to do their jobs, and souls can't cross over to the other side either."

"I assure you, the Gates will reopen once the Hallows begin. Until then . . ."

Renai turned to the little bird, a frown twisting one side of her mouth. "Until then *what?*"

"Until then, there is at least one psychopomp remaining in this place who can still fulfill their role."

"Yeah, I figured that's what you meant," she said. She took a long breath and blew it out, surprised at her reluctance. She did this literally each day of her life. Somehow, though, there was a difference between taking a life and handling the dead. One felt natural, the other taboo. She gave herself a moment to consider her state of mind—nervousness that this new aspect of being a psychopomp was beyond her, fear of desecration or contamination, frustration that yet another thing had stepped between her and Ramses St. Cyr—accepted all of her frailty and shortcomings, pushed them all to the back of her head, and then did what she'd been taught to do her whole life: she did the work.

Unzipping the body bag was like unwrapping the worst Christmas present ever.

She peeled the crinkly plastic shroud back just enough to reveal the head and torso of a skinny dead white boy. His face was puffy and distended, and skin was already starting to purple and bruise in the places where his blood had pooled when his pulse quieted. She couldn't really put an age to him with the way death had twisted and distorted his features, but he couldn't be out of his teens.

Once Renai looked away from his face and saw the marks on his face, she understood why the nurse had been so affected by this boy's death. The raw, angry gashes of ligature marks made tracks across his neck, telling her not just how he'd died, but that he'd taken his own life. Mingled amid the scents of bodily excretions that came with death and the antiseptic cleaners that the hospital used against them, Renai could smell the shampoo that lingered in the boy's hair.

She knew she should feel something profound in this moment, remembered how much death had pained her back when she'd been alive, but now the only thing the dead boy awoke in her was a fierce sense of purpose. Renai flipped up the hood of her jacket and spoke the ghost word, braced for the slap of tightness against her skin, for the monochromatic shift of her vision.

She was unprepared for how strange the dead boy would appear.

The flame of life was entirely absent in him, not even the banked-coals glow of someone on the cusp of death, which made sense, since he was already dead, not dying. Instead of merely lacking any sort of life, he seemed to emanate dimness, projecting shadow like the antithesis of a flame. In the same way a cloud occluding the sun could leave part of the world in daylight and part in twilight, this boy's presence sucked the light from the room.

Worse than that was the way the parts of his soul had come unbraided and dangled obscenely from his flesh. The golden coil of his Fortune spilled out onto the gurney next to him like a loop of intestine, tarnished and weathered, its usual gleam now a brassy fatigue. The shadowy strand of his Essence—difficult to see within the corona of shadow the dead boy emitted—stretched out taut from his back and though the door, tattered as a pair of ruined nylon stockings and leading off to wherever this boy's spirit wandered, lost and alone. Renai couldn't see the quicksilver sprawl of his Voice, imagined it must still be somewhere inside his body. Cordelia kept any comments she had about the dead boy's appearance to herself.

That's right, Renai heard, in her father's voice, *only people entitled to opinions are the folks getting their hands dirty.*

Renai reached for the dead boy's Fortune first, though she couldn't say whether she chose it as a woman examining her options, or as a psychopomp whose whole existence depended on getting every scrap of Fortune back into the Underworld unharmed. She couldn't be sure, but she thought she saw something shift in the dead boy's face when she tore his Fortune loose—a grimace maybe, or a narrowing of the eyes—but when she stopped to study him, he didn't move again, if he'd moved at all.

Turning to the Fortune in her hands, she found it harder to manipulate than she was used to, tacky and resistant, like wax that had cooled and hardened. After a few moments of effort, she managed to squeeze and stretch it enough that the Fortune could be molded and flattened into a coin. She slipped it into the same pocket of her jacket that held the scrap of paper she'd gotten from Seth.

Finding her rhythm now, she plunged her hands into the dead boy's belly, seeking out his Voice. She found nothing. At first, she thought that her hands had merely been numbed by the sting of her ghostly flesh penetrating his physical corpse, but as she sought around within him like some grotesque version of the game of Operation, she realized that something else had already consumed the dead boy's Voice—had scooped him out like an avocado and left the rind behind. She wasn't dealing with a creepy side effect of his death not being properly collected by a psychopomp. This was something else.

This was a ghoul.

She was just about to pull her hands free when she brushed up against something inside of the corpse, something that went skittering away from her touch. She had time to let out an involuntary grunt of surprise before the ghoul's hands latched onto her forearms with an implacable grip so icy-cold that it burned. She threw her weight back, trying to yank free, but the dead boy's hands had clamped on her like manacles. Even as she fought against the restraint, she struggled to accept the fact that the ghoul could touch her despite the ghost word's magic. The swollen face and unseeing eyes turned, straining against rigor mortis, to look right into her own. A hoarse whisper came from the corpse's open, unmoving lips, echoing and far away. "We have a message for you," someone said.

Despite the shock, despite the pain in her arms, Renai stopped fighting. Could this—creepy as shit though it was—be Sal reaching out to her from the other side of the locked Gates? Or maybe the Thrones? Until the possibility was in front of her, she hadn't realized how desperately she wanted some authority figure to step in and take control.

Before she could say anything in response, a brown-feathered, shrieking blur swept in between her and the corpse; Cordelia buffeting at the dead boy's face with her tiny wings and scratching at him with her ineffectual claws.

The ghoul forced her palms together and shifted so that it held both her wrists in one hand. The other dead hand reached up and snatched Cordelia out of the air, squeezing her so tightly that the bird let out a pitiful little squeak. She'd scratched the corpse across the eyes, leaving bloodless furrows gashed into its waxy skin. The ghoul moved with the unconscious, disaffected gestures of a puppet, had seized Cordelia without shifting focus of those unseeing eyes away from Renai. She felt her small measure of hope trickle away.

"We have a message for you," the whisper deep inside the corpse repeated.

Renai had never wanted to hit someone so badly in her life. Either of her lives, come to that. She allowed herself a brief, glorious vision of driving her forehead into the dead boy's nose, of finding whatever animated this corpse and destroying it. Yet she knew it was a fantasy, knew she dealt with something that didn't feel pain, even as tears leaked from her eyes from the icy burn of the ghoul's fingers on her wrists, the electric crackle against her ephemeral flesh buried within the dead boy's solid guts. "I'm listening," she said.

"Cease."

It took a moment for Renai to realize that the one word was all the ghoul —or, more accurately, whatever drove the ghoul—intended to say. "Cease what?" she asked, though she had a sinking feeling that she already knew.

"Cease your search."

Shit.

Every curious impulse, every desire to find Ramses St. Cyr, everything but the need to escape washed away.

Renai struggled against the ghoul's grip, even though she knew it wouldn't do any good. Her mind raced. She couldn't overpower the ghoul, and she couldn't use the ghost word to slip away. She considered throwing her head back—dislodging the hood and breaking the spell and returning to solidity —but her ghostly hands were still inside the dead boy. Two objects suddenly occupying the same space might throw them violently apart and free her, or it might fuse her flesh with the corpse's and ruin her hands.

Cordelia struggled as well, twisting her tiny body and stabbing at the ghoul's fingers with her sharp beak. It was a futile, pitiful gesture that reached past the barrier of Renai's fear and woke the spirit within her, set its winds howling.

Release me, whispered the presence as it probed against Renai's restraint. Its voice was halfway between a gasp and a groan. *Promise to free me, and I will give you the power to free yourself.* In her near-panic, Renai nearly agreed without thinking, but its power frightened her almost as much as the ghoul did. She refused the temptation, straining against the ghoul's grip with all her might. It was just as futile as the struggle of a tiny bird in a monster's hand.

Another sound came from the depths of the ghoul's open mouth. Not another message, not even words, but a hissing noise, sharp and abrupt and harsh. Laughter, she realized. Whatever drove this ghoul was fucking *laughing* at them.

Power, whispered the storm, *if you promise.*

She had only the space of a breath to decide. If she let the spirit loose, it would lash out and destroy all that it could. She was certain of that. Storms could only do what was in their nature. Images of flooded streets and people clinging to makeshift rafts and houses flattened by implacable winds and piles of debris left in the aftermath flashed through her mind, but if this corpse killed her here, the spirit would likely slip free anyway, and there would be no one there to stop it. So her choice wasn't much of a choice at all.

Yes, Renai thought, *I promise.*

The tempest stretched free of its cage, and Renai swelled suddenly with its presence, an uncomfortable, bloated feeling, her limbs numb and stiff. Her guts twisted, tighter and tighter, first merely hunger pangs, then period cramps, then an excruciating clench that made her vision waver. She'd expected the storm would increase her strength or that it would beat the ghoul away with a fierce wind.

You promised to help! Renai thought.

Yes, said the spirit, its moaning voice filled with a dark kind of glee. *YES.*

What kind of power is this?

The power of the flood, the storm spirit replied.

She could taste it as much as smell it, that brackish, rotten, oily reek of floodwaters, of rain constant and incessant and deadly. It seeped through her pores like sweat, spilled like tears from her eyes. Brown water puddled at her feet. She could hear the voice inside the ghoul hissing something, Cordelia's twittering reply, but any meaning was drowned out by the torrential downpour roaring in her mind. Renai clenched her hands into fists, imagined that they were levees, felt the flood within her beat in time with her heartbeat against her palms, her knuckles, the bones of her hand. Whatever happened next, she knew, was going to hurt like a motherfucker.

Still, she smiled.

And opened her fists, releasing her floodwaters inside the flesh of the ghoul.

The waters burned like acid, filled with household cleaning chemicals and gasoline and factory-strength solvents, the flood ripped her palms and fingers and bones open and apart over and over again as it tore through the breach of her hands. It was agony, a torture of destruction that would have pulverized her flesh if it weren't also a thing of magic. It was a greater pain than anything she'd ever felt before—but it was nothing she couldn't endure.

At first, nothing happened. There was room inside the body, gaps and crevices for water to flow and seep and pool. When that filled, the release valves of his orifices began to leak, streams of dirty water oozing from his nostrils, his ears, between his lips. Renai clenched her teeth against the torment in her hands, straining to force the flood to even greater heights. The ghoul's distended belly, flesh slack and pliant in death, bulged and stretched and rippled. The hand holding Cordelia released her and grabbed Renai by the back of the head, pulling her into a gruesome embrace, dragging her face toward its own. Toward its mouth. Its teeth.

The ghoul opened its jaws and lunged at her, but the flood burst out of it, a vomit of viscera and water and oil and rotting leaves that flowed through Renai without touching her, thanks to the ghost word, and knocked the corpse onto its back instead. It thrashed there for a moment and then went limp. As soon as Renai's hands were free, she pulled back the flood, fighting to control its torrent just as hard as she'd been fighting to urge it on a moment before.

Remember, the storm moaned, twisting and writhing in Renai's mental grip, *you promised.*

When the tempest was once more just a quiet churning in her belly, she pulled off her hood and returned to the physical world, amazed to find that her hands were fine, if aching and raw, instead of the gaping wounds she'd expected.

Cordelia hopped among the clogged-catch-basin junk the ghoul had spewed all over the morgue floor, searching among the leaves and brambles and empty potato chip bags and cigarette butts and chunks of flesh in her intent birdlike way. One eye on the ghoul, Renai watched her, not wanting to disturb whatever the little psychopomp was hunting. When she found it, Cordelia pounced, beak stabbing down to seize a target that Renai only caught a glimpse of, twitching stick legs and a fat insectile body, before it was snatched down Cordelia's gullet and gone. Whatever it had been, Renai had seen enough of it to recognize that though it was tarnished—by the floodwaters or whatever power had animated the ghoul, Renai couldn't be sure—the bug Cordelia ate had the same quicksilver appearance of a person's Voice.

Renai, who hadn't consumed any Voice of her own in going on two days now, felt a pang of hunger and then an immediate shudder of revulsion.

"Sorry," Cordelia said. "Should we have split that?"

"Not at all," Renai said, remembering what Sal had told her. "If it was meant for me, it would have been a shape I could eat." She looked down at her ruined shoes and, even though none of the floodwaters had actually touched her, felt filthy and tired and drained. "Let's get out of here before that nurse comes back and makes me mop this shit up."

⧗

After a long, hot shower that left her skin feeling clean once more but did nothing for the cold hollow in her chest, Renai put on a pair of running shorts and an old Jazz Fest T-shirt and went into her all-but-empty kitchen to make coffee, knowing that she wouldn't be getting much sleep for the second night in a row, certain she'd see the ghoul's cloudy, rotting eyes every time she closed her own. She was surprised, at first, to find Cordelia perched on her counter, head buried beneath a wing in sleep, but then, with the Gates locked tight, it wasn't like the 'pomp could go back to the Underworld where she belonged.

There was a place, deep in the Underworld, where Renai had once thought she belonged. The Fifth Gate, kept by a loa named Babaco, was a never-ending party in a mansion at the foot of Elysian Fields, a waiting place where the souls who weren't ready to cross over into the afterlife—whichever one they might deserve—could pass their time in revelry. She didn't remember much from her time there, couldn't be sure that her memories were real, in fact, but she knew that it hadn't truly satisfied her. Like most places in the Underworld, the revels at the Fifth Gate were a shadow of true enjoyment, a mere reflection. Come to think of it, so were most of the denizens of the Underworld, too. The loa and the Gatekeepers and Sal were vibrant, potent exceptions to the rule that said that most beings on the other side were dismal shades. Most psychopomps, too.

Renai still wasn't quite sure which category Cordelia fell into.

Maybe it was unkind, but Cordelia's presence didn't inspire much confidence in Renai. In truth, without Sal guiding her, Renai had no idea what to do next. Every thought, every option felt leaden, purposeless. After her nightmares the night before had made sleep impossible, she'd lain awake in her empty apartment, staring at the ceiling and putting together a plan for how this day would go. She'd listen to the Deadline, meet up with Sal, they'd track down Ramses, and she'd somehow find a solution to the wound he'd left in the world that didn't require his death. She'd been wrong about every single thing, and no one would give her a straight answer. Nobody was where they were supposed to be or *who* they were supposed to be, and she was just some cosmic accident who should have died years ago.

What hope did she have of changing anything?

Once she'd taken a few sips of coffee, she found her cell phone and played the message from Opal once more. The call reminded Renai that she'd asked the little psychopomp a question in the morgue, and that they'd been interrupted before she'd had a chance to answer. So after the voicemail finished playing, she cleared her throat, and when that didn't work, reached out and nudged the little bird with a finger. Cordelia ruffled her feathers when she pulled her head out from beneath her wing, and Renai couldn't read the bird's body language well enough to tell if she was sleepy or irritated, or something else entirely.

She didn't much care, either.

"Listen to this," she said. She played the message again. When it finished, she set down her mug and leaned onto the counter so that she and the little bird were eye-to-eye. "You never answered my question before. If I get you to the Ghost Train, can you tell if Ramses was there? Can you track him?"

"Ghost Train? I've never heard of such a thing," Cordelia said, a note of prim injury in her voice. "This mortal seems incredibly well-informed, to know about an aspect of the Underworld of which even I am unaware. Are you sure she can be trusted?"

"It's not—" She took a deep breath and a sip of her coffee before answering. "The Ghost Train is made-up. It's a Halloween thing, like trick-or-treating or . . ." She trailed off, faced with Cordelia's blank stare. It occurred to her that Cordelia was either incredibly uninformed about the modern living world, or she was fucking with her. Renai was starting to lean toward the latter. "It's like a play," she said. "A scary play that they put on every year for Halloween. Get it?"

"Ah, yes, I see," Cordelia said. "In that case, the answer is no."

"To what part?"

"To all of it. I am neither specially attuned to this boy nor able to follow his spoor like some woodsman stalking game."

Renai's eyes narrowed. "Weird. Because that's just how Sal would do it."

Cordelia clicked her tongue. "And what makes you think he and I have anything in common?"

"Um, you're both psychopomps?"

Tittering, condescending laughter. "That is a role, not a denomination." Renai spun her finger in a circle, a keep-on-going gesture. "There is more variation in the cosmos than merely gods and men," Cordelia said. "There are spirits and demons, kami and geniuses and djinn. Some psychopomps are full deities who have been worshiped for millennia; others are mere scraps of magic, alive only so long as they fulfill the purpose for which they have been created." Her head tilted to the side and studied Renai. "Did your mentor truly explain none of this?"

"He never explained anything!" The words burst out of her throat far more angrily than she'd intended, the darkness within her rising in response to her anger. She didn't even really believe what she'd said. Sal had taught her how to use the ghost word, how to collect the dead and lead them to the First Gate. But nothing about the world in which she'd found herself.

Nothing about how to survive without him.

"And why do you think that is?" the little bird said, her voice quiet and measured, as if she were trying to calm a child throwing a temper tantrum. It only made Renai even more pissed off. She paced across the apartment, clenching and unclenching her fists. She tried to calm herself, tried to remember if she and Sal had ever had a conversation like this, but all she really wanted to do right then was break something.

"I'm starting to think," she said, "that no one really has any idea what's going on, all the way up to and including the Thrones, but nobody wants to admit it. Mortals, spirits, psychopomps, gods. Everybody's clueless. We're up here chasing our tails, and we can't talk to the mysterious, all-knowing Thrones. Do they decide who gets to live and who has to die, or don't they?

There's some weird shit going on, but don't bother the Thrones, they need a little 'me time.' The Hallows start tomorrow at midnight and we're all on our own. Isn't there supposed to be some kind of harmonious balance? Isn't somebody supposed to be in goddamn *charge?* What's the point of all this if not even Death has their shit together?"

Cordelia merely stared at her with her unblinking bird's eye, but Renai got the impression that the psychopomp was trying to hide a smile.

"Feel free to jump in with an idea whenever you feel the urge," Renai said, "because to tell you the truth, I'm pretty sick of being the only one who seems to give half a shit about what's happening here."

"It seems to me," Cordelia said, "that if you can't get the answers you want by following the rules, perhaps you ought to try talking to those who have broken them."

A strange frisson ran up Renai's spine at Cordelia's words, a sensation that was both invigorating and transgressive. "Do you know anyone like that?"

"Oh, yes," the psychopomp said, delight evident in her voice. "One or two."

CHAPTER TEN

THE NEXT MORNING, Renai went about her routine the same as always, though Cordelia's presence and the still-silent Deadline left her feeling irritable and out of place, like she didn't quite fit in her skin. She dressed in a pair of jeans with torn knees and an old Audubon Zoo T-shirt, from which she'd cut the sleeves and the elastic collar in a style her friends had called "gutter-punk chic," which had struck her as both accurate and classist as hell.

As she laced up a pair of black combat boots with thick soles that added a few inches to her height, she told herself that her sartorial choices had nothing to do with the possibility of having to flood out another ghoul before the day was done. She pulled her hair back into a tight bun that would be hard for anyone to grab, and touched, absently, the bare skin along her collarbone, not realizing that she'd reached for the St. Christopher medal her mother had given her, the one blessed by a voodoo priestess named Celeste.

Everything felt off and out of control, but in a way that was more familiar than the fog of routine that had shrouded her mornings for longer than she could recall. Sure of nothing—not even her place in this world—except for the fact that she needed to find Ramses St. Cyr, she slipped into the leather jacket the Thrones had given her despite the high of eighty degrees that the weather app predicted, despite the fact that she swore she could still smell guts and floodwater on it even though none of it had touched her, even though she'd scrubbed the leather until her arms were sore.

She had to come correct for Halloween, after all.

Downstairs, Renai found Cordelia on Kyrie's handlebars, speaking quietly to the bike, who already rumbled with life. Renai climbed on, the little bird launching into the air instead of swooping to her shoulder as she'd expected, and as soon as Renai had a grip on the handlebars, the motorcycle surged into the street in a spray of gravel and exhaust.

Ignoring red lights and swerving around a truck idling its way through the intersection, Kyrie squealed around a turn and headed through the Uptown streets all the way to Canal, where she made a tight left turn and headed toward the lake. Any remaining doubt Renai might have had about Kyrie's intelligence vanished as the bike wove through midmorning traffic and tore down side streets with an abandon she had never displayed when she was following Renai's guidance. Renai had always found Kyrie's easy, casual glide to be relaxing, a chance to gather her thoughts and consider her next move, but this scorching, reckless path across the city forced everything from her mind other than phrases like "breakneck speed" and "whiplash." She clutched the handlebars and squeezed the bike with her thighs and, for the first time, wished she'd worn a helmet.

When they dashed beneath the I-10 overpass and continued down Canal without slowing, Renai figured they were heading for the cemeteries at the foot of Canal Street, but Kyrie braked hard when they passed RTA headquarters—a massive four-story edifice where the streetcars were housed—went *thump-thump-thump*ing over the crisscrossing streetcar tracks, and made an illegal turn across the three oncoming lanes of Canal, to come skidding to a stop at the corner beneath a skeletal oak, engine idling and then sputtering out, leaving Renai facing a DO NOT ENTER sign.

Hope that's not a hint, Renai thought. She slid off the bike, a little wobbly-legged from the intensity of the ride. A yoga studio sat on the other side of the street, but she imagined the place she'd been sent to was the derelict building in front of her.

It rose three stories high, with sheets of weathered plywood covering the windows on the first two floors, cut so that they fit flush inside in a way that made Renai think that once, many years ago, someone thought they would be unshuttered again before long. A stratum of fallen leaves covered the brick steps that led from the front walk to a small landing that had once sheltered a garden, and now held only the desiccated remains of ferns and weeds that hadn't lived long enough to grow over the cement railing that edged the landing. The front door was grandiose, with a boarded-up arch that stretched to the second floor and a small balcony above that, with a coat of arms embellishment in between. A diagonal slash with a stilted *A* on either side. The entire front of the building had been whitewashed to cover up graffiti and had then been tagged once more.

It was a sadly familiar sight: a building that had the desolation of a decade's vacancy, which had been built so well that it might stand vacant for another century if no one tore it down to build condos that wouldn't survive a hurricane with half Katrina's strength.

"Welcome," Cordelia said from the branches above, startling Renai so much that she had to stifle a surprised yelp. If the psychopomp noticed, she didn't mention it. She glided down to the stone railing and settled in, as if she were laying in a nest.

"Where are we, exactly?"

"An abandoned building, same as any other. This one just happens to be the refuge of a handful of the dead who chose to stay on this side of things rather than find their rest. Salvatore never told you about this place?" When Renai shook her head, Cordelia *tsk*ed to herself. "He seems to have neglected much in your upbringing. Well, denying the thunder won't halt the lightning. Do you have any questions before you go in?"

"Don't you mean 'we'?"

Cordelia tittered, a sound halfway between a human's giggle and a bird's whistle and entirely forced. "Those are the fugitive dead in there, Renaissance. They'd flee the moment I entered." Renai started to protest that she was as much a psychopomp as Cordelia, but the bird held up a wing and kept talking. "You aren't steeped in the aroma of the Underworld as I am; they won't know what to make of you." She preened beneath a wing with the fastidiousness of a person checking their fingernails after a manicure. "Unless you'd prefer to wait for the Gates to reopen. Perhaps Salvatore will return with instructions from the Thrones."

The thought of sitting on her hands and waiting made Renai grind her molars together. "No," she said. "We're here, might as well see what we can find out." She pulled the hood over her head, shutting out the noise of traffic, the glare of the morning sun. She flexed her fingers and bounced on her toes,

like some part of her expected she'd have to chase one of these fugitive dead
—or flee from them. "Any advice?"

"Just remember that you are an emissary of Death, and these dead are under your authority. Respect is not given. It is compelled."

"Got it. R-E-S-P-E-C-T, just like Aretha taught us." Before she could
lose her nerve, Renai spoke the ghost word, braced herself for the electric
sting of passing through a physical object, and walked through the front door
into the derelict building.

The wrongness of the place pressed in on her from every direction, the
stench and the whine and the waver of the wound that Ramses' escape had
left in his living room, but less intense and spread all over the place, the way
her uncle's aftershave had lingered, faintly, throughout the whole house
hours after he'd left.

Though the influence of the ghost word illuminated the darkness in shades
of purple, Renai still had trouble picking out the details of the room she'd entered because of the destruction within. It looked like fire and transients and
time had all taken their turn giving this place their undivided attention.

She stood in a large open foyer whose walls stretched up all the way to
the second floor, an ancient rusty chain dangling—pathetic in its uselessness,
whatever chandelier or fixture long since looted—from the ceiling. A staircase ran along one wall and led up to a second-floor balcony along the back
wall of the foyer, its banister splintered and fallen. Opposite the stairs stood
a long half-wall that could have been a speakeasy's bar or a hotel's front desk
or just a dividing wall that had partially collapsed. She couldn't be sure if the
dust and mildew savaging her sinuses was purely from the house itself, or if
it was merely adding to the spoiled-milk stink she'd come to associate with
a death avoided.

That sense of wrongness was the only thing that told her that the fugitive
dead Cordelia had told her about might actually be here, because her eyes
told her that she was alone. She pulled off the hood, hoping that might ease
the stood-too-close-to-the-speakers-at-a-concert whine in her ears, but her
return to solidity only robbed her of sight.

In the darkness, though, she noticed something: the whine she heard felt
off. Not just its fundamental wrongness, but also distorted somehow, out of
tune. She imagined a dial, like the old-fashioned radio she used to listen to
the Deadline, and with the ringing in her ears as a guide, slowly adjusted it,
as if seeking the right station. The noise warped and trebled and then, with a

soft *pop* that felt like plucking cotton out of her ears, the whine was replaced by conversation and laughter and ice tinkling in glasses and the lights came on, blinding her.

When her eyes adjusted, Renai's first thought was that she'd wandered into a saloon from one of the Westerns her grandfather had loved.

Tinkling, twangy music came from a piano on the far side of the room, in a style that Renai had no name for other than "old timey," played by a balding black man whose back was to her. A short middle-aged white man with slicked-back hair and an impressive mustache stood behind the bar — restored to solidity and fully stocked and polished to a gleaming shine — wearing a stiff white dress shirt, a bolo tie, and cords tied around his elbows. The ornate and intricate wheel of the chandelier hanging overhead illuminated the room with dozens of burning candles. She couldn't decide if she'd stepped out of time or if she was merely seeing something that had happened long ago, when a pink-haired young white woman in acid-washed jeans and a Cyndi Lauper T-shirt walked in front of her and headed toward the bar.

Once she stopped thinking of her surroundings as belonging somewhere in the 1800s, she was able to recognize that the handful of figures in the room — sprawled out on velvet couches or huddled around a poker table or leaning on a barstool — came from all over the span of New Orleans's three hundred years. Fedoras and flapper dresses, plaid suit jackets and mom jeans, grunge flannel and petticoats and crushed velvet leisure suits.

In just a few moments of watching the dead, Renai noticed a few things. First, that the crowd had more men than women, and far more white people than any other race, which, after a little thought, made sense. You had to have had a pretty privileged life to assume that no afterlife could be a step up from what you'd had on Earth, and you had to be pretty arrogant to tell Death that you were better off considering your options instead of crossing over. Second, these dead weren't impacted by her aura of disinterest like the living. She kept locking eyes with someone whose gaze would dart away, kept seeing heads turn away from her with feigned nonchalance. The third thing she'd noticed was that although she'd been expecting the ghostly forms of the dead she'd led to the First Gate, these spirits weren't just ethereal, they were also strangely flat, like a series of two-dimensional images superimposed onto the real world. They were just wisps of Essence. Remnants. A deck of playing cards killing time until the end of days.

Is this the part where I'm supposed to say "curiouser and curiouser"? she thought.

Though her heart pounded in her chest and her skin crawled with the weight of scrutiny falling on her for the first time in years, Renai reminded herself of what Cordelia had told her. *Respect.* She cleared her throat and breathed in deep and—nearly shouting to ensure she could be heard over the piano—said, "I'm looking for a lost boy named Ramses St. Cyr."

A couple of discordant notes, a few furtive glances, and a brief lull in the conversation was the only response she got. All the tension spilled out of her, replaced by a sudden flush of heat across her face and chest. Suddenly she was invisible again, but unlike the aura of disinterest that had surrounded her since her resurrection, this felt familiar. This was the involuntary vanishing act that black women were made to perform whenever it came time for promotions. Or opinions.

Or respect.

She felt the cold, furious wind of hate rise within her demanding release, and—since it had given her the flood in the morgue, since she'd promised, since she was so very tired of fighting—she let it come. Let it come for every white doctor at the hospital where her mother worked as a nurse who treated her like she worked for them. Let it come for every man who asked her aunt why, with a body like hers, she was wasting her time in college. Let it come for every person who assumed she was her older sister's daughter, when they were only ten years apart. For the country that once made her grandmother drink from separate fountains from white people, use different bathrooms, attend different schools. For every slap, every suspicious look, every "Where are you supposed to be?" and every "Do you work here?" and every "I bet you'd be real pretty if you smiled more." For every use of the word that turned a person into a thing. Let it come for every time this world turned a black woman's skin into glass: fragile, brittle, transparent.

Let it come.

When she finally let the destructive, impulsive presence living inside of her slip free of her restraint, it seeped out from every pore of her skin. The sensation was one of expansion, as though she grew to fill the room with her influence. It began as a breeze, hardly more than if she'd simply puffed up her cheeks and blew, but definitely noticeable in the stagnant air in this place. She pushed, and the wind grew stronger. And stronger. Every eye turned toward her now, but she'd lost interest in merely being seen. The woman in her had taken all she could take, and the psychopomp in her couldn't stand the presence of these spirits in the living world.

Time for these death-defying fucks to reap the whirlwind they'd sown.

Her awareness spun around the room along with the storm winds she'd freed, so she saw the moment each pair of eyes shifted from scorn or amusement or interest into fear.

Good, she thought, *these dead have remembered what being afraid feels like. That will make this easier.*

The chandelier creaked and spun overhead. The dead didn't allow the wind to ruffle their clothes or tousle their hair, but it bent them, forced them to lean in order to stay upright. Another push and her presence became a gale, more than these weak shades could withstand. They flopped to the ground and went whisking through the air and smacked against walls, pinned and unharmed, but entirely at her mercy.

Even though the tempest inside of her had stretched to fill the room, it remained tethered to her body, so when she spoke, it was not with her own voice, but with the storm's eerie tornado howl. "I'm here for a lost boy named Ramses St. Cyr," she said, and the walls groaned under the onslaught of her will.

He ain't here, the bartender said in that whispery non-voice of the dead, flickering in and out of visibility from where he'd caught edgewise between two bottles of liquor. *We know every soul ever entered this place, and we ain't never heard no one of that name.* A chorus of agreement came murmuring from every corner of the room.

"Then help me find him," she said. "He's hiding from Death, just like you."

We can't. Another whisper barely audible over the roaring wind, this one from the pink-haired girl from the '80s, pressed against the staircase banister and half-hidden by a thin man who'd covered his face with his bowler hat. *We can't leave. We're too weak.*

"This is what happens when you avoid your fate," she said. "Some of you should have crossed over centuries ago."

We were waiting, someone said, and Renai scanned the room twice for the speaker before she realized that it was all of them speaking in unison, that they'd always been speaking with one voice.

"Waiting for what?"

For someone to help us leave. Every eye turned her way had a hungry, manic gleam to it. Every mouth twisted into a rictus grimace of a smile. *For someone to carry us.* And then each of the flattened remnants of Essence let go of whatever they'd been holding, slapping against the walls or the floors or the ceiling. Lying flush, where her winds, no matter how powerful they were, roared right over them. They stretched toward her like shadows, arms extended. Supplicating. Eager. Demanding.

If one of them touched her, slicing her flesh with an impossibly thin blade of a finger, slipping inside to mingle with the Essence of her own soul, to press their memories and thoughts and desires alongside her own, she could handle the intrusion. They were only slivers of a whole soul, after all. A fraction of an identity. She'd feel a strange impulse from time to time. A memory that didn't belong, a snatch of song she couldn't forget. Just another touch of haunting to go along with the spirit already living inside of her.

But there were dozens and dozens of shadows reaching for her.

No, Renai thought. *You can't have me.*

The presence within her shifted in response, became a kind of disturbance she'd never experienced before. Renai knew the rumble of a lazy summer thunderstorm and the abrupt violence of a tornado and the hurricanes that blew in from the Gulf: fierce, powerful behemoths that stomped and roared and flattened everything in their path. But the presence within her knew of other places, other kinds of destruction. There were storms of the deep desert that carried within their tempests grains of fine sand: immense, relentless things that hissed and scoured and destroyed by wearing away.

It was that kind of wind that tore through the room, abrading the shadows wherever they lay, peeling them from the floors and the walls, casting them once more into the air. Once they were caught up in this whirlwind, however, the spirits weren't merely shaken up and thrown around.

They were unmade.

Renai let it happen. She couldn't be sure where her will ended and the storm's began, but she knew that it was responding to her wishes. Knew that she could restrain this power if she chose to. Knew that even though the tempest had a mind of its own, she was responsible for whatever it did, whatever it destroyed. In moments, the crowd of renegade dead had been reduced to Shadows, wisps of magic and substance. Hers, like the storm, to command.

She thought of the image she'd had of them when she first entered this place, and sent her wind forth again, to unmake these Shadows, shaping them with her will into a form she could carry, could conceal. One by one the Shadows collapsed and squared off and wrote designs on themselves, hearts and clubs, diamonds and spades. She held out her hand and unmade a haunted house into a deck of cards: solid black when held one way, but flickering into a specific card when tilted toward the light. When the lost scraps of spirit and memory had all been reduced to a handful of cards, she tucked them into an empty card box she found on the table, which she slipped into her pocket, her wind still whirling around her.

She felt no pity for the Shadows she'd destroyed, no guilt for what she'd done. They weren't alive, she reminded herself, weren't even aware the way a person's full Essence was. They'd been little more than the shapes of the people they'd once been, only able to function as a collective, and even then nothing more than a Venus flytrap that remembered human language. Just like Cordelia said, more than just gods and men moved in this world, and in the hierarchy of reality, those barely coherent shades were as far away from a recently collected dead soul as she was from her own shadow. Besides, they hadn't gotten trapped here by accident.

They'd run.

And collecting souls, in whatever ragged form they took, was a psychopomp's job.

Now came the hard part. Now that the spirit was free — more unrestrained than it had ever been — it wanted to spread. It had a list, this power that lived within her, statues to tear down, institutions to sweep away, people who deserved to feel the floodwaters rising over their heads. And why not? Weren't hurricanes natural? Wasn't the city brightest right after the wind and rain had washed the streets clean? That was the scariest thing about this power within her. Not that it had desires and a voice not her own, though that was terrifying enough. No, the most terrible thing was that its argument was almost convincing.

It might have even worked, if she hadn't seen for herself what all storms really desired. Their destruction was indeterminate, punishing sinner and saint alike. It preyed on the hatred that felt like righteousness to her, but it had the capacity to despise the whole world.

Renai reached out and — with the same unnamed part of her that had pushed the winds into greater fervor — she *pulled*. The winds fought back, lashing against her body and soul, but Renai held on. It hurt, bone deep and ruthless, but nevertheless she persisted. She gritted her teeth and clenched her fists and, inch by agonizing inch, pulled the winds back inside.

It took time, though she couldn't say how long, to still the desire that raged within her, to calm the tempest, to coax it back inside of her. When she was done, her breath came in ragged gasps, and she knelt amid the ruins of years of abandonment that she'd seen when she first used the ghost word to enter the building. She ached all over, but the storm was restrained. For now.

She rose to her feet, unsteady but feeling more in control than she had in days and — using the ghost word — walked back into the afternoon light. She was no closer to finding Ramses, but she had, at least, another source of magic. A whole box of aces she could hide up her sleeve. Cordelia stared at her from her perch on the railing, her tiny beak gaped open in some form of amusement. Renai didn't know exactly what Cordelia's game was, but she wasn't going to let the little bird know how tense things had gotten in there.

Never let 'em see you sweat, she heard her mother say, and Renai let herself grin at the realization that, storm or no storm, Shadows or no Shadows, she was already plenty haunted by voices from the past. "So," she said to the 'pomp, "you got any other bright ideas?"

CHAPTER ELEVEN

IN PURSUIT OF it, emperors have poisoned themselves with po-
tions of quicksilver and of cinnabar and of arsenic. Herodotus thought
it came from a naturally occurring fountain, whose waters moved like
oil and smelled of violets. Others sought this same fountain in Persia, calling it the Aab-i-Hayat, or in a mythical land called Bimini in Spanish Flor-
ida. In the deserts of the southwestern U.S., it was the red sap of a particular kind of frankincense tree, believed to heal all wounds. It can be found in
a variety of cups: the chalice that caught the water that spilled from Christ's
side on the cross, or a cup of seven rings whose contents could reflect a vision of anywhere in the cosmos along with conveying longevity with a single sip. Some seek it still, in treatments and in surgeries and in vials of en-
zymes meant to lengthen their telomeres. Others believe that, while it could
be persuaded to become liquid, its natural form was solid and everlasting
as the earth itself. Water or oil or stone, generation after generation sought
the substance that could transmute lead into gold, which could melt flawed
diamonds and re-form them into a perfect gem, which could purge the im-
purities of age and return one's lost vitality. A potion, a fountain, an amu-
let, a powder, an al-iksir, an elixir. We hunt anything that might grant youth

and health and freedom from disease or infirmity or age. We all crave a little piece of eternity.

⧗

Demourelles Island — a three-and-a-half-acre stretch of land hugging the edge of the Bayou St. John that held a single upper-class neighborhood — was formed when the natural curve of the bayou proved too narrow and too prone to blockage and the current straight channel was dredged. Renai knew it, as most locals did, as Park Island, made famous by the presence of "the ashtray house," a former mayor's notoriously ugly and expensive home, so named because of the line of brown glass ashtrays adorning the lintel of the house. So when Renai had forced Cordelia to tell her, and not Kyrie, their next destination, it only took a few minutes of discussion before she knew where to go. It shouldn't be hard to find, she'd thought, since Park Island only had a single loop of a street, a short bridge the only entrance and exit that didn't require a swim.

"The farthest house on the island from the bridge," Cordelia had told her back at the formerly haunted house before winging away, "the tip of the island."

So it surprised Renai when — despite forcing Kyrie to drive slow enough that she could check house numbers — she found herself back at the bridge that led off the island without having seen anywhere to turn off of Park Island Drive, and it frustrated her when she passed in front of the ashtray house a second time, looping back around to the bridge once more. Kyrie seemed confused too, bucking beneath Renai as if she was slipping out of gear. Renai patted Kyrie's side. "I'll figure this out," she said. "You wait here." Kyrie's engine revved once and then stilled. Renai couldn't tell if that meant annoyance or gratitude, or if she had started to read personality in the bike's behavior where there was only reaction. *Strange,* she thought, leaving Kyrie behind and continuing down the sidewalk, *all this time and I really don't know anything about her. I used to question everything.*

She thought about this as she walked in and out of the dappled shadows cast on the sidewalk by the oaks overhead, past the manicured lawns of modest homes that could have belonged in any suburb in America and the more opulent foliage of the gardens and hedges that preceded the larger sprawling buildings twice the size of their neighbors. She didn't know if it was the peculiarity of Ramses' collection, or if it had to do with the fact that she hadn't consumed any Voice in days, or if it was the way Cordelia seemed to be pushing her when Sal had always tended to shelter her, but she was examining herself in ways that she hadn't in years.

When Renai had been alive, she'd had a friend who had moved to the Northshore for college, and sometimes when driving across Lake Pontchartrain, Renai had just gone on autopilot—the long, long stretch of the Causeway across the featureless mirror of the lake requiring only a fraction of her attention—until a car changed lanes unexpectedly or she saw a speeder pulled over into one of the crossovers, and she'd fall back into full awareness like she'd been startled out of a daydream. The more she thought about it, the more she realized that the years since her resurrection had passed in a blur, like mile after mile of driving in a straight line with still water below and cloudless sky above and her mind wandering in aimless digressions, quickly and easily forgotten.

And just like that, she came to the end of the sidewalk. A thin iron fence ran alongside her, half-hidden by overgrown grass and palm fronds and the roots of a giant oak stretching up from the ground and sprouting their own branches like saplings. Across a short stretch of asphalt, the sidewalk resumed, curving back around the way she'd come amid flowerpots and ferns and a two-car driveway littered with fallen leaves. The air across the road glistened, transparent and iridescent at the same time, like a soap bubble had been hung between the lamppost and the DEAD END sign in front of her. This strangely empty place didn't repulse her like the quivering quality of the wound left behind by Ramses' escape; instead, it felt slick to both her mind and her vision, her attention sliding away from it whenever she tried to focus on it. So she closed her eyes and walked forward blindly.

When she crossed the boundary, it stretched across her face and clung —unpleasantly reminiscent of a spider's web—before it tore and let her through. She opened her eyes to the house she'd been unable to see from the road: an open gate and a long gravel driveway through high, thick hedges leading to a thick tower of a structure, twice as tall as it was wide and painted a deep, rich green. *Come out, come out, wherever you are,* she thought. A spiraling staircase rose to the first floor, which was raised up an entire story— the space beneath just an empty concrete driveway with a shining, antique convertible parked in it. Cordelia perched on one of the iron gate spikes and raised her tail in greeting when she saw Renai.

"Is this all some kind of test?" Renai asked.

"Why, whatever do you mean?" Cordelia said, in a mocking tone that said she knew exactly what Renai meant.

"You could have warned me about what I was walking into back there, just like you could have told me about the magic hiding this place. Once is an accident. Twice is some bullshit. I'm not really sure who you think you're playing, but I am not the one. I—"

"Yes," the little bird said, cutting Renai off. Cordelia tilted her head all the way to the side. Renai realized her mouth was hanging open and closed it with as much dignity as she could muster. "I'm sorry," Cordelia continued, "did you expect me to lie about it? Would you rather I kept you in a gilded cage like that pathetic excuse of a psychopomp you've been following around? The answer is yes, on top of what the Thrones sent me for, I am testing you."

"Why?" she asked. "Why are you doing this to me?"

"Because wolves howl in the darkness, Renaissance. Because the ground shifts underfoot. Because the sun grows dark at midday. You can feel it as well as I can. You know that this boy's disappearance is ill-omened, and that the Gates being abandoned is worse. Simply put, I am testing you because I need your help, and, based on your loss of a freshly deceased soul, I'm not certain that you will measure up to the task. If that's the case, I'd prefer to find out now, instead of when the Hallows begin." Before Renai could ask any of the questions that fought for prominence on her tongue, the little bird hopped off the spike and, with a snap of her wings, glided to Renai's shoulder. Then, whispering in her ear—in that voice that sounded like she was hiding a smile—Cordelia said, "Since we're being honest, I have to admit that I didn't expect you to make it this far."

Neither did I, Renai thought.

As she made her way up the spiraling stairs, her footsteps clanging on the metal despite her attempts to move quietly, the wind picked up, driving away some of the day's warmth. The temperature would drop pretty sharply once the sun went down, enough that she'd stop sweating in her jacket, at least.

When she reached the small balcony at the top, even though she was only a single story off the ground, in a place as flat as New Orleans, the change in elevation meant a change in perspective. She could see down a stretch of Bayou St. John, able to make out two of the many bridges that crossed its brief span, the cars flashing by. It wasn't much compared to the lake that it fed into, or the Mississippi that held the whole city in its crescent, but the bayou had been wider once, had stretched many fingers throughout the city instead of the one channel it was allowed now. But it still ran deep enough to kill. Just a few years back, a schoolteacher's car had been pulled from its quiet waters, her body inside. Renai had known before the news reported it, naturally. She'd heard the woman's name and the cause of death on the Deadline. Sal, of course, hadn't let her do the collection.

She was starting to wonder what else he'd denied her over the years.

Renai turned her attention to the door she'd climbed to, weathered and paint-stripped with age. A bronze door knocker in the shape of a fist hung in its center, and based on the patina rippling across the metal, it was just as old. The black globe of a security camera tucked away beneath an eave looked impressively modern in contrast to the rest of the place. Renai reached for the door knocker, only to pull back, startled by Cordelia's clicked tongue.

"All that prattle about not having the knowledge you require, and here you are, a bull with horns lowered." Cordelia flapped up off of her shoulder and onto the rain gutter overhead. "Have you no questions about who awaits you inside?"

Guess that means I'll be going in alone here, too, Renai thought. She couldn't help but notice that Cordelia's new position also took her out of sight of the camera. "How about a name?"

Cordelia did that giggling-and-chirping thing again. "He calls himself Jack Elderflower, but I'm sure I needn't tell you that this is not the name he came into this world with. I'm afraid his true name is his own secret, however, not mine."

"And he's another rule-breaker? Like those souls back on Canal Street who refused to cross over?"

"Ah, no. His continued existence flies in the face of the natural order, this is true, but Jack is no wandering shade. Death holds no sway over him."

For a psychopomp, Renai thought, *Cordelia sure does have a hard-on for people who defy the Thrones.* She managed, somehow, to keep the smirk that threatened to spill across her face from making itself known. A little of her irritation slipped free instead. "So making sense of all these vague hints is my next test? Do I need to figure out who this Jack fool really is to get his help?"

"I am no sphinx," Cordelia said, "and Jack is no riddle. He will aid us because his skills are for hire. The challenge you face is whether you will be capable of paying his price. Not everyone deals in favors, after all."

Renai's skin prickled with gooseflesh, thanks to both the ominous tone Cordelia used when she said "price" and her implication that she knew about Renai's conversation with Seth and his offer of a "favor." The only person she'd told about her "deal" with the dirty-handed god—whether she'd fulfilled her side of that bargain was a worry for another day—was Sal. Had he, in turn, told Cordelia? Or did she have some other source of information she hadn't shared? Just what kind of 'pomp *was* Cordelia? Cop? Spy? Rebel? Whatever her story, Renai knew one thing for sure: the little bird hadn't given her the whole truth.

Renai hoped her doubts didn't show on her face. Like it or not, Cordelia was the only help she had right now. So she pushed her growing suspicions to the side—promising herself that she'd circle back around to them as soon as she could spend the time to really think things through—and smiled up at the little bird like her subtle innuendo had been *too* subtle. "I hear you," she said. "Not even talk is cheap." She squinted up at Cordelia. "What kind of skills are we talking about?"

"Jack is quite adept at finding things that would prefer to stay hidden."

All of a sudden, a different kind of shiver swept through Renai, as a bunch of pieces fell into place in her mind: a man who defied death, who had talents for sale, and who hid his home in a cloak of anonymity. She'd known someone who fit that description once, and though her time with him had gotten all jumbled together in her mind, her few clear memories of Jude Dubuisson were damn good ones. He was a mess of trouble with the devil's smile and a bag of tricks that never turned up empty. He'd played a part in her resurrection; a demigod back then and—if she remembered right—a full-on god now.

And like this "Jack Elderflower," Jude had always had an affinity for lost things.

A confident smile spread across her face. For the first time in days, she felt the clouds part and let a little sunshine through. She reached up for the door knocker, but the click and harsh buzzing sound of an electric lock disengaging told her that "Jack" already knew they were here. She wondered, as she pushed the door open and slipped inside, whether Jude would recognize her. She'd seen some shit since the last time they'd met. Done some shit, too; the kind that left a mark. Maybe that was the real reason people didn't notice her anymore.

The room she entered was as dark and as hot as an attic in the depth of summer, the air so thick it took an effort to breathe. Blinded by the sudden gloom, she could only rely on her ears, which were full of whirring and ticking and a vibration underneath it all so potent she thought for a second that the ghost word had taken hold. As her vision adjusted, she could make out the uniform shelves of server racks, stacked high and tight throughout the room, cables snaking and twisting their way across the floor. Her stomach sank. The Jude she remembered had barely known how to operate a cell phone, much less a setup like this.

She let out a huff and wiped away the sweat tickling her brow. Whether Cordelia had brought her to Jude or to Jack, it didn't change anything. The only thing that truly mattered was finding Ramses.

A line of small lights came to life on the floor, not powerful enough to illuminate anything on their own, but as a collective marking a direction, a path, and then a series of stairs and landings along the outer wall that curved around out of sight. "Sure," she said, muttering under her breath, "just go alone up the dark stairs with the creepy lights. Like this ain't the beginning of a damn horror movie." Despite her desire to get out of the heat, she crossed her arms and cocked her hip. Raising her voice, she said, "You can quit with all this 'come into my parlor' spider-and-fly business right now. I know you got better lights than this, and I know you can hear me, too."

Lights snapped on, some dying with a flash and a pop, but enough flickered to life that she could make out the room clearly, the servers and the stairs curving around to another door two floors up and the thick braid of cable that fed into the ceiling.

"That's more like it," she said. Allowing herself a hint of a smirk, she made her way up to the door, which unlocked with a buzz as she approached.

Inside, a blast of much cooler air, and a single-room apartment, sumptuous, decadent, and brimming with technology. Flat-screens hung on each of the four walls, each playing a documentary that depicted a different ecosystem: the dark blues and sweeping glides of an ocean, the rich greens of a swamp's duckweed and hanging moss, the more muted tones of a forest viewed from high above, the brownish reds of the wind blowing across a dune in the desert.

The furniture—a single wide bookshelf crammed tight with books, a massive desk crowded with computer monitors, a high-backed chair, a four-poster bed tucked into its own niche and half-hidden by a curtain, an empty leather armchair—was too uniform to not be of a set, and too well-made to have been mass-produced: the wood an elegant eggshell white, deliberately distressed like a pair of designer jeans, the leather brown and thick and luxurious. The carpet was lush and pristine, with one of those vacuuming robots in each corner. The monitors, crowded together in a jigsaw's jumble, showed a map of New Orleans stretched across all of them as if they were one giant screen.

From the chair, its back to her and hiding the speaker, a soft, aristocratic voice recited, "'Will you walk into my parlour?' said the Spider to the Fly. ''Tis the prettiest little parlour that ever you did spy; / The way into my parlour is up a winding stair, / And I've a many curious things to show when you are there.'"

Renai kissed her teeth. "I'm supposed to believe you just know that off the top of your head, I guess?"

A chuckle, warmer and more genuine than she'd expected. "Not at all. I googled it after you mentioned it." And then the chair swung around and revealed the man who called himself Jack Elderflower.

And he was definitely *not* Jude Dubuisson.

He was a thin, broad-shouldered white man with wispy light brown hair that might have been receding, or he might have just been cursed with that large forehead his whole life. Shadow ran along his square jaw and cleft chin, the kind of stubble that was meant to look carefree and ended up appearing manicured. He wore a T-shirt with a comic book character's symbol on the chest and faded jeans that—judging by the rest of the room—probably cost as much as Renai's whole wardrobe. Elderflower smiled when he saw her, a wide stretch of bright teeth that was either so practiced it seemed almost honest or so genuine it felt like he was mugging for a camera. Jack was so normal—so disarmingly, unthreateningly normal—that the last thing Renai noticed about him was the colorless irises of his eyes.

Since becoming a psychopomp, one of the senses Renai had gained that she'd never been able to fully understand was that when she met the gaze of anyone—whether they were god, spirit, or mortal—she had felt a connection, had sensed some aspect of their existence that she'd never been able to name or even describe, in the same way that the sensation of being watched or the awareness of time passing was more ephemeral than something as concrete as sound or smell.

Until she looked into Jack's unusual eyes, she'd had no idea what it was that she'd sensed as a constant in the world around her. It was only in its absence that she was able to put a name to it: whoever or whatever else he claimed to be, the man who called himself Jack Elderflower completely and utterly lacked a soul.

CHAPTER TWELVE

WOULD YOU LIKE to have a seat?" Jack asked, his voice turning serious even though he spoke through that hundred-watt smile. He gestured over to the leather armchair. "I'd offer you a drink, but I'm afraid all I have is suited only to my unique palate."

The hell is that supposed to mean, she thought, unable to tell by his tone whether he meant it as an insult or was merely referring to his supernatural nature. Still, she raised an eyebrow and tucked her hands into her jacket's pockets. "I'll stand, thanks," she said, "and it's a little early for me to start drinking. You do you, though."

Jack's face fell, his chagrin as borderline insincere as his mirth. "My apologies for the theatrics," he said. He had a buttery purr of a voice with hints of old money New Orleans, genteel and confident as an NPR podcast. "I don't get many visitors these days."

Renai didn't know whether it was his lack of a soul or his "theatrics," as he called them, or just the fact that he wasn't Jude, but everything Jack said grated on her nerves. She made her disdain known with a sharp grunt of a laugh. "I feel you. Gotta put out the good plates when company comes, right?"

Jack's brow crinkled, and then he chuckled. "No, nothing like that," he said. "I've just found that unless I force them to focus, most people look right through me."

An unpleasant frisson raced across Renai's scalp and down her spine. Jack had just described her aura of disinterest pretty much perfectly. She looked at herself in the mirror every morning when she brushed her teeth and did up her face — grumbling the whole time that she'd been so conditioned by patriarchal bullshit that she still wore makeup even though most people didn't notice her — so she knew that her eyes were the same light brown they'd always been, save for those ill-advised six months as a sixteen-year-old when she'd worn green contacts. If she could see herself with the same clarity that she saw Jack, though, would her irises be as bleached as his? Was she as soulless as he was?

She took a deep breath and filed that away with all the other shit she'd decided to worry about later.

"Little hint?" Renai said. "If you want people to see you, it helps to turn on the lights."

Jack's answering chuckle was a little more hearty than her joke deserved. "I'll remember that. What can I do for you, Miss . . ." He trailed off, giving her an opportunity to fill in her name.

"Rain," she said, deciding in the last second that she didn't want this weird-eyed grinning creep with a national space program's worth of processing power downstairs to know her real name, even if it would only lead him to a dead girl. "You can leave out that Miss/Missus mess, too. It's just Rain. Only man in my life you need to concern yourself with is the one I want you to find."

To his credit, Jack didn't even blink, just gave a brief nod and waved for her to come closer, swinging his chair back to face his monitors. "So you're looking for a person," he said. "You have a name?"

"Ramses St. Cyr," she said, moving close enough to see the screens over his shoulder, but staying a lunging arm's length away from him. She watched as he typed the name into a search engine that was only a text box on a blank page. It whirled for a few seconds and pulled up a page in French. He leaned forward, humming a song that she recognized, after a few notes, as "When the Saints Go Marching In." Renai bit her bottom lip. He hadn't mentioned a price so far, but then he hadn't found anything yet, either.

His humming paused. "Don't suppose he's a real estate company in France, by any chance?"

"Wow," she said, deadpan. "You're a genius. Can you find Tupac next?" She bit the inside of her cheek, told herself if she didn't hide some of her irritation, she'd never get the help she'd come here for.

"You'd be surprised how often it's that simple," he said, "people these days hide *nothing*. Secrets used to be a challenge."

These days? Renai thought. *My dude looks about thirty.* Of course, appearances didn't mean much in her world. She herself looked like she was the same age she'd been on the day she died. Her lips compressed to a tight line, and she turned her mind away from any thoughts that found similarities between her and the soulless Jack Elderflower.

Jack's fingers were busy on the keyboard, filling a different screen— which was solid black with green text—with Ramses' name over and over, interspersed with the numbers and punctuation marks of computer code and, occasionally, symbols that looked more like zodiac signs than letters in any language she could recognize. He raised his hand dramatically, a conductor lifting his baton, and then stabbed it down on the ENTER key. Immediately, windows popped open on his other screens: a scan of a birth certificate, a student information page with the EITA logo and Ramses St. Cyr's school photo, an NOPD database file from something called Palantir, half a dozen social media pages, an Amazon wish list, two separate browser histories—one free of porn, one practically all there was—a Spotify profile, a cell phone bill.

In a matter of seconds, Jack had Ramses' whole young life splayed out on his screens, cold and invasive as an autopsy.

"Voilà!" Jack shouted, throwing his fists up, triumphant, as though he hadn't just done something horrible. "My demons will never be denied." He bent back over the keys, pointing up at the picture of Ramses without looking at him. "This our boy?"

"That's him," Renai said. "And I'm sorry, but did you say 'demons' just now?"

His fingers froze in their dance for a fraction of an instant, just long enough for Renai to notice, and to know that the next thing he said would be a lie. "Figure of speech," he said. He resumed his humming perusal of Ramses' information. "Our boy has been naughty, hasn't been to school all week."

"Knew that already," Renai said.

"Gunshots reported on his block, no known casualties."

"Knew that, too. Can't you just, you know . . ." She waved her hand at the ceiling, a half-dozen terms from cop shows and spy movies on her tongue, things like "ping" and "triangulate." "Can't you track his phone or something?"

"First thing I tried," Jack said, paying more attention to the screen than his explanation. "Thought he just had his GPS turned off, but when I tried calling him to get a hit off the nearest tower, I got nothing. So he's either got the data switched off or the whole device is dead." Renai winced at that last word. "I've got a de— um, a bot dialing him every thirty seconds, so as soon as he's back on the network, I should know about it." He swiveled his chair to face her, and when she met his eyes, she took an involuntary step back.

"So that's it? You're done now?"

"No," he said, cracking one knuckle after another, slow and methodical. "Now is when we talk about payment."

"Payment? For what? You haven't told me anything I don't already know."

Again that hundred-watt smile, though this time there was something sly in it. "Not true. Now you know exactly how hard it will be to find him without me. *That*, I'll show you for free. If you want me to show you where he *is*, though, *that* will cost you."

"If he's so completely vanished, what makes you so sure you can find him?"

"If the one-eyed man is king in the land of the blind, the man with a video camera would be their god."

She kissed her teeth. "That supposed to be convincing?"

"It's just facts. Question isn't if I can do it, question is whether you can pay. You take your time thinking it over." He swung back around to his desk, sweeping all of Ramses' pictures and data onto one small screen, the rest returning to the broken-up map of the city they'd displayed when she'd come in.

Much as she wanted to punch him right in his perfect teeth, his confidence gave her some hope for the first time in days. Maybe she could find Ramses before the Hallows started after all. She had no money, no valuable possessions to barter—save the jacket, and he could kick rocks if he thought she was giving that up. No real power of her own to make a favor worth anything. When she tried to decide which bank vault she could offer to empty out using the jacket's ghost word, she realized she'd already decided to pay his price. "How much?" she asked.

"Just a single coin," Jack said, half turning back to face her. "One of those golden coins that you take when you reap the dead."

Renai's surprise yanked a bark of a laugh out of her, cut short by the expression on Jack's face. "You're serious? What makes you think—"

"I've lived long enough," he said, cutting her off, "to recognize a psychopomp when I see one, 'Rain.'" He actually did the little air quotes when he said it, just to get the full smug-asshole effect. "And we both know that once the Hallows start, no one will notice if a single coin goes missing."

The coin in her pocket suddenly felt dense with all the weight of her trying not to think about it. A half-dozen responses came to Renai—doubt and denial, questions and curses—but she dismissed them all. She'd come this far. Might as well see it through to the end. "Show me," she said. "Show me what you can do that's worth a person's destiny."

In reply, Jack stood, nudging his chair out of his way with the back of his legs. He slid open a desk drawer and took out a pair of brown work gloves with coils of brass wound around each of the fingers and the wrists, bent into odd glyphs on the palms and the backs of the hand. Sparks arced off of them when he pulled them on. The floor began to vibrate, a rhythmic pounding like an approaching marching band during a Mardi Gras parade. Renai thought at first that this rumbling came from Jack, but as it grew stronger, she realized that she was feeling the computer equipment downstairs coming to life. Jack reached out to the assorted monitors on his desk and, gesturing like the air in front of him was a touchscreen, manipulated the displayed map of New Orleans, zooming in on the Central City neighborhood, then a handful of blocks, then a single street, and then centered on a single house, which Renai recognized as the St. Cyr home by the two cemeteries across the street.

Renai opened her mouth, intending to congratulate Jack on inventing Google Maps, when he reached out, made a grabbing gesture, and pulled the image off the screens and held it in midair.

She'd seen holograms before, ephemeral creations of light, but this was something else. The disc of the city floating in front of Jack's outstretched hands was more vivid than any projection and was solid as the floor she stood on. Nor was it simply a re-creation of the architecture and streets and green spaces; Renai saw cars on the streets and birds in the sky and people everywhere, all captured in a single moment. No mere computer could do this, no matter how advanced. This was a marriage of magic and technology that made Renai's stomach flutter. Before she could articulate any of the questions she wanted to ask, Jack moved his hands again, and the city swooped and tilted until they were at ground level, looking at the St. Cyr's front door. Renai had an impulsive desire to see what happened if she tried to touch the city, but then balled her hands into fists, immediately recoiling from the thought.

"Pretty impressive, no? I call him Maxwell. Now watch this." His hands now cupped like he held a bowl in his palms, Jack slid one hand in a counterclockwise motion. Instead of spinning, like she thought it would, the frozen city began to move, cars flickering by, shadows lengthening and shifting, people on the sidewalk moving in lurching backwards steps like a video rewinding. Night rose on this city and day fell, again and again, and then Jack slowed his hands, stopping at a single moment.

Ramses St. Cyr stood at his front door in his school uniform with his backpack slung over his shoulder.

"Do you know when this was — uh — taken, I guess?"

"This is the last day he went to school," Jack said without turning away from the city, as though his attention helped sustain whatever magic he had wrought. "Five days ago."

So three days before he was supposed to die, Renai thought. *Where the hell have you been, kid?* "Now what? Can you track him with this?"

"Yes and no," Jack said. "I can't just skip ahead to where he is right now. But I can follow him, see?" He moved his hands to demonstrate, and the image leapt forward to hover just over Ramses' shoulder, keeping pace with him as he walked to the corner, dapped another teenager wearing the same uniform, waited for a yellow bus to pull up, and climbed aboard. Jack pressed his palms together, and the perspective shot back up, so high that it took in the whole city once again. For just a moment, before it went static and fell flat and confined to the screens once more, Renai saw a cloud drifting across the lake. If she went outside right now, would she see that same cloud? Could that strange awareness Jack had harnessed see itself? She pictured the abominable infinity that was created when two mirrors faced one another and felt a little queasy.

"So," Jack said, pulling off those strange mad-scientist-looking gloves, "now that you see that I can run your quarry to ground, if given some time, how about my price? Do we have a deal?"

Renai took a deep breath and held it. This might be her only chance for finding Ramses. She'd be surprised if the spirits she'd collected and changed into a deck of cards on Canal Street did anything but flee if she tried to invoke them, and the usually dependable Sal had basically vanished. Once the chaos of the Hallows started at midnight . . .

She started to slide her hands into her jacket pocket, remembered that she had a coin of Fortune to pay him with right then and there, and put her fists on her hips instead. "What are you gonna do with it?" She expected that anything he said would be a lie, had already decided that he wanted to rebuild his missing soul piece by piece. But the lie he chose could be informative too.

"Does it matter?" he asked. "It's the only payment I'll accept to find your little lost lamb. This isn't a negotiation. You say yes, or you say no."

If she hadn't deliberately placed herself out of reach, she might have hit him. She made herself stare into his unnerving, colorless eyes with all the disdain her mother would have given him. Then she gave him her best you-just-fucked-up smile. "Fine by me. I'll just show myself out." She took a half step toward the door. "You want me to let the next one in to hear your little 'you say yes, or you say no' offer?"

Jack's brow crinkled, unsure of himself for the first time. "What next one?"

"The next one in that long, long line of psychopomps waiting outside. You know, since we're all so eager to get you what you want." She threw her arms up in mock revelation. "Oh! That's right. I'm the only psychopomp here, and I'm the only one coming." She clasped her hands together at her waist and cocked her shoulders. And waited. Patient as the grave.

He broke so quick, it was almost disappointing. He sighed and wilted like that breath was all he had filling up his skin. "I'm limited to seeing what *was* and what *is*," he said. "With some raw destiny to work with, to incorporate into my design, I'll be able to see what *will be*." He frowned and shrugged. "And that's all I'll say."

Renai thought of how easily and callously Jack had dug up every petty little secret Ramses possessed, and tried to imagine what a man like that would do with the ability to see the future. It was not a pleasant thought. Still, Jack's computers—his demons, she reminded herself—hadn't been able to tell Jack what Opal had seen: that Ramses was more than human. She took some comfort in knowing that this soulless whatever-he-was wasn't truly omniscient. Nor, without a soul, did she have any way of ensuring that he held up his end of the bargain.

And that gave her an idea.

"First you find Ramses for me," she said, "and then you'll get your coin."

Jack laughed without kindness. "Sure," he said, "no problem. You want my wallet, too? How about the Rolls downstairs? I've got the keys around here somewh—"

"You think we carry bags of Fortune around with us?" Renai grabbed the corners of her jacket and held them out at arm's length, revealing her shirt, her waist. "You want me to turn my pockets out, too?" She felt her face flush with the lie, with the bluff, but she hoped Jack would attribute that to frustration, if he noticed it at all. "You know what I am. You think about why I might be looking for somebody? The *only* reason somebody like me come calling?" The arrogant smirk slipped from Jack's face, but Renai kept talking, wanting to drive the point home so he wouldn't question it. "Did it occur to you that in order for me to break you off a piece of soul, I gotta find one to collect first?"

"Okay, okay," Jack said, raising his hands in surrender. "You make a fair point." He steepled his fingers and pressed them against his lips. Without pupils or iris, it was impossible to tell if he was looking at her, waiting for a response, or if he was staring off at nothing, lost in thought. The silence drew out, became obvious that he considered weighing his options more valuable than her time.

Renai managed to keep her reaction to just a lifted eyebrow, but inside she seethed. You had to be some kind of prick to just stop talking to a person in the middle of a business negotiation. Though she'd long since used up her patience with Jack, for some reason his rudeness didn't trigger the righteous storm inside her. Maybe she'd used up her whole day's mojo on those fugitive spirits. Maybe frustrated indignation just wasn't the right kind of anger. Maybe the tempest knew, like she did, that the satisfaction of double-crossing him would be worth the wait.

Or maybe, she thought, *his creepy-eyed Big Brother ass scares the storm as much as he scares me.* If the spirit heard her, it gave no answer.

Jack's lips compressed, and for a second Renai thought she'd spoken out loud, but then he nodded to himself and cleared his throat, and she realized that he'd just come to his decision. "If I were to agree to this," he said, "I would need to secure some collateral from you."

Renai licked her lips to keep from cursing. "Like what?"

"Your name—your *true* name—and a drop of blood."

Any petty satisfaction she felt at the possibility of tricking Jack went spilling out of her. Renai was no practitioner of magic, but she knew enough about spells and workings to know that Jack's request was both perfectly reasonable and absolutely destroyed any hope she'd had of double-crossing him. She couldn't turn away from Jack's ability to follow Ramses, nor could she just pay him with the coin in her pocket, not now that she'd made such a show of not having one. She'd backed herself into a corner by trying to be tricky. *Tell the truth and shame the devil,* she heard her grandmother say.

"Fine," Renai said. "You got a pen?"

Jack opened a drawer in his desk and took out a small wooden box. It opened and unfolded more than once, like an intricate puzzle. When he finished, it lay flat on his desk and revealed its contents: a small sheaf of paper, a squat, dark bottle, and the elegant gossamer swoop of a single white feather. The sight of that feather filled Renai with a dread she couldn't name or shake, nothing to do with its function as a pen, but something older, something half-remembered. She watched as Jack plucked the stopper out of the inkwell with a hollow little *plunk,* as he dipped the quill's nib into the ink with smooth, delicate gestures, waiting for her aversion to the feather to pass. When it didn't, when Jack held the quill out to her, she pushed it down and reached for the pen anyway. She had no time for weakness, especially not her own.

RENAISSANCE DANTOR RAINES, she wrote in the blocky, spare handwriting that no penmanship teacher in all her years of Catholic school had ever been able to twist into cursive. She pricked her thumb with the sharp nib of the quill—her stomach writhing with nausea when she did so, not from the pain or the blood, but from that damned white feather—and mashed a bloody print onto the paper next to her name. Jack tore the strip of her name off and curled it into a little tube, which he slid into a glass vial. Renai had the sudden impulse to check the scrap of paper that Seth had given her to see if it, too, bore a brown smear of dried blood. She'd have noticed that, wouldn't she?

Jack closed up his writing case with a series of little wooden clacks and slid it back into its drawer. He pulled his mad-scientist gloves back on and reached once more for the map of the city. This time, though, once he'd pulled it free from the monitors, he squeezed it and folded it and twisted it until it was small enough to fit in just one of his hands, too small for Renai to see. He held it close and molded it, manipulating it over and over with the bending and creasing gestures of someone folding origami. Once he was satisfied, he stood and held one hand out to Renai.

Cupped in the palm of Jack's gloved hand was a hole in reality the size of a peach pit.

"Go on," he said, "take it. It's what you came for, after all."

Unsure of what she might find, but more willing to endure pain than to show this man any uncertainty, Renai reached into Jack's offering hand and, with two fingers, picked up the product of his work. It felt like a small glass bead, smooth but irregularly shaped, cool to the touch and without any real weight. When she held it up to get a good look at it, the light didn't refract through it the way it ought to; instead, images swam around inside it.

"Like this," Jack said, pantomiming a gesture like someone peering through a jeweler's loupe. "Look *through* it, not *at* it."

She copied him and saw Ramses St. Cyr once more. He sat in Opal Brennan's classroom, head bowed to his work, taking notes from her lecture. Everything moved in double or triple time, like a movie on fast-forward. Renai couldn't help but smile. Eventually this would lead her right to him. She started to thank Jack, asshole though he'd been, but he'd already turned back to his computers, their business obviously concluded.

The seeing stone found its home in Renai's jacket pocket—the one without a coin of Fortune in it—and she found her way to the exit. The doors opened for her without the electric buzz, but the locks clunked tight as soon as each one swung shut behind her. As she made her way down the stairs and through the strange server room, Renai tried not to think about the power that this Jack Elderflower possessed, nor the fact that she had no idea who, or what, he truly was.

She did know, however, with that strange resonance that plagued her more and more since Ramses' disappearance, what waited for Elderflower should his unnaturally extended life come to an end. The Sixth Gate, presided over by a skull-faced god who called himself Barren, was where the soul met the Scales of Judgment. If she had managed to lead Miguel Flores through all the other Gates, down into the vast depths of the Underworld, it was at this Gate that the coin of his Fortune would be weighed and measured. Where the life he'd lived would be compared to the destiny that had been measured out for him at the moment of his creation. Where his Essence would either be allowed to pass through to meet the Thrones, or cast into the nothingness of oblivion, personified by a beast known as the Devourer. Without a coin of Fortune to place on the scales, Elderflower had no hope for any destination other than the Devourer's belly.

You'll never meet anything more dangerous, Renai heard her father saying, *than a person without hope.*

Thinking about the Sixth Gate and the Devourer, and her fleeting memories of her own time there, brought to mind the man she'd—erroneously, as it turned out—thought was waiting for her when she'd first entered Elderflower's weird-ass wizard's tower. The man who was partly responsible for her being a psychopomp instead of just another dead girl. The man with a knack for finding lost things. The man she and Sal probably should have turned to as soon as Ramses St. Cyr went missing from his own death. Except he wasn't just a man anymore, now that she thought about it. Hadn't *ever* been just a man. These days, Jude Dubuisson was a *god*—the Fortune God of New Orleans, in fact.

And his fine ass owed her a favor.

CHAPTER THIRTEEN

OF THE MILLIONS of moments you experience each day, only a handful are truly impactful. Glancing at the bulletin board at a coffee shop instead of your cell phone. Smiling at the stranger in the bar who will one day be your spouse. The flat tire on your way to a job interview. The pill you forget to take. We call this destiny, or fate, or luck, and its influence is incorporated into the unique pattern of each person's life the moment they come into existence. But the book of your life is written in pencil, not ink. You might be visited by Budai, an exuberant monk in robes too small for his girth, who will share the good luck he carries in a cloth sack thrown across a shoulder, or by Mammon, the demonic figure whose gift of wealth is actually a curse. You might burn incense, the scent that pleases Dedun, Nubian god of wealth, or you might bake miso and attract the attention of a binbōgami, a dirty old man with only one sandal, carrying his fan and his broken toy and a cloud of misfortune. You might pause amid the alder trees and receive the favor of Leib-Olmai, or you might seek the blessing of Legba and discover instead that Kalfou has closed all the doors that were once opened to you. Lakshmi and her elder sister Jyestha, one who offers aid and the other who brings calamity. Ganesh, elephant-headed remover of—and creator of—obstacles. Fortuna, with her ship's rudder, her horn of plenty, her wheel of fate.

Our lives are both predestined and uncertain. Fate and Fortune: two sides of the same coin.

⧗

Finding Jude Dubuisson proved harder than Renai thought it would. After filling Cordelia in on Jack's method of finding Ramses and what he wanted in return—which earned a snort of derision from the little bird—Renai had told the psychopomp that she needed a few hours to herself. Cordelia hadn't liked it, but when Renai couched it in terms of "call it a test," she'd agreed to meet back up with Renai at midnight at the First Gate, freeing her to seek out the fortune god on her own. Renai couldn't be sure if she wanted this solitude because she wanted Jude's attention all to herself, or if she just simply didn't entirely trust Cordelia—she didn't—but now that she'd wasted three hours driving around to all the places she hazily remembered as Jude's stomping grounds and failing to find him, she was glad Cordelia wasn't here to witness her frustration.

She knew that as New Orleans' resident god of fortune, Jude must still live in the city, but that didn't mean you could find him on Google. The last time she'd spoken to Jude—she had a brief, colorful flash of memory of talking with him on the parade route the Mardi Gras after she'd come back from the dead—it had been Sal who tracked him down. The dog-shape her mentor wore had a nose that couldn't be fooled, not even by gods, which made his inability to find Ramses all the more disturbing. Her current struggle to find Jude just showed her how much she'd relied on Sal's nose. How much she'd allowed herself to become someone's sidekick. In her search, she'd been to the now-vacant apartment in the Warehouse District that Jude had once called home, the office in Canal Place, just at the edge of the Quarter, and had walked past the tarot card readers and caricature artists in Jackson Square where he'd once had a table offering to find lost things for tourists.

Now she rode Kyrie away from the Quarter, aimless. They were on Canal again, headed in the direction of the cluster of cemeteries, the city of the dead, that lay at its foot. She wondered if one of the other six Gates was at Lake Lawn, or St. Patrick's, or Odd Fellow's Rest.

All this time as a psychopomp and she'd only ever been to the First Gate.

Part of her was looking forward to midnight. Once the clock ticked over and it was officially Halloween, the Gates couldn't stay locked. Not even the Thrones could keep the living and the dead apart during the Hallows. She'd be able to find Sal and he'd be able to find Ramses, and that would be the end of it. Simple. Clean.

If that was true, though, why had Sal been so insistent that they find the boy before that? Why did she feel so driven to solve this on her own? Why did the thought of the Hallows starting also fill her with a dread she couldn't explain?

If only she'd been able to find Jude. Twilight had come and gone, taking her hope of finding the fortune god with it. Kyrie changed lanes, sensing Renai's capitulation right as it happened. She might as well head to her meeting with Cordelia at the First Gate and wait for midnight. Without Salvatore to guide her, she'd need the devil's own luck to find Jude. That thought, coupled with what she knew of Jude's nature, gave her an idea. One last desperate shot before she gave up and admitted to Cordelia and the Thrones that she'd failed their test.

Kyrie seemed to appreciate her change in intent, because the bike dropped down into a lower gear and swung back the way they'd come—narrowly avoiding one of the red streetcars ambling down the tracks—and then went roaring down Canal, heading toward the river. They wove through the blaring, growling symphony of traffic and around the muttering, humming crowds, darting through red lights like they were hunting or hunted, the wide-open space of Canal getting brighter and brighter amid the towers of glass and neon, the hotels and the bars and the theaters—the Joy and the Saenger—lighting up the cloudy, moonless night.

When they reached their destination, Kyrie was so eager that she hopped the short curb onto the wide sidewalk and drove straight for the stairs. Renai twisted the handlebars and pulled Kyrie into a tight spin that made her back tire screech against the pavement, kicking up a brief plume of pink smoke, intense enough that a handful of tourists actually noticed her for a moment, gawping at her until her aura kicked back in and they lost interest.

Renai patted the hot chassis of her bike. "Easy, girl," she said. "We don't know for sure he's in there." The more she thought about it, though, the more right it felt.

The building before her was huge, almost a city block in girth and at least three stories tall, more palace than tower. A line of palm trees—not native to the city but transplanted any place that rich people wanted tourists to associate with the license of the tropics—stood in front of a wide flight of stairs. Columns rose between the stairs and the face of the building, every inch granted to glass door after glass door. *The devil's house got plenty of doors,* she heard her grandmother say, *but ain't none of 'em let you out the way you come in.*

The cornice was lit up to display the sculptures that had been placed there in some pseudo-Greco-Roman style—at least, Renai assumed they were fake, since they were illuminated by garish purple neon lights. A woman in robes to the left, a couple of struggling figures on the right—though they were so twisted around each other it was hard to say who was restraining whom—and in the center: a huge male face, open-mouthed and wide-nosed, with some sinuous something either spilling from his lips or being drawn within. It was eerie in the daylight and full-on ominous in the dark, thanks to the shadows created by the spotlights, but Renai had a feeling most of the people who entered this place didn't bother to look up.

Renai swung her leg off of Kyrie, whose engine still rumbled for a few moments even after Renai left the bike's side and started up the stairs, the motorcycle's enthusiasm infectious and getting her pulse throbbing. Though Renai had seen this place many times, she'd died before she'd been old enough to get inside.

Harrah's was the largest casino in the state and the only one in the city that sat on land. If the people who worshiped luck and wealth had a church, this was it. The temple where they prayed their desperate prayers and sacrificed their fortunes one turn of the cards at a time.

The perfect home for a Trickster.

The cacophony of the place hit Renai full in the face the moment she stepped through the glass doors: the electronic dinging and whirling and whistling and bleating of hundreds of slot machines, all at once. A deep, compelling voice offering "new and better ways to play" from the TV screens that were everywhere—anywhere—she looked. Late '90s pop music, like the place was one giant elevator. And over it all, people shouting. Shouting drink orders over the gibberish of the slots, shouting into cell phones over the shouting of drink orders, just shouting in joy or despair as the wealth poured in or the luck ran out.

It took Renai over a minute of stunned immobility before she became numb to the noise, before she could hear her own thoughts again. Her first coherent one was: *I've made a big mistake.* The Jude she knew wouldn't be a part of all this naked greed, all this empty flash and gaudy excess. Not because he was above filling his pockets with the wealth of the gullible—he'd do it with a smile—but because his tricks were more subtle, his cons more slick. Of course, he was a god now. He might not be the Jude she'd known.

Renai—confronted with the immensity and the chaos of the place—reached into her pocket for her phone so she could check the time, sure that if she wasn't careful, the few hours between here and midnight would slip through her fingers and she'd end up missing the time she was supposed to meet up with Cordelia. She realized just then that she didn't trust the psychopomp not to cross through the First Gate without her.

Her phone showed a text had come in from a blocked contact. Her first thought was that it came from Opal, the only person who had her number, but the message was too strange even for an oracle. *Take the elevator to your right,* it read. *Top floor.* She looked in that direction and, sure enough, an elevator took up the space between the men's room and the ATM. She hadn't noticed it before, maybe because of the OUT OF ORDER sign taped to it.

Or maybe it just hadn't even been there the last time she'd looked.

Despite the sign, the elevator dinged as soon as she pushed the button, and the doors slid open, splitting the sign right down the middle. Renai stepped inside, greeted by mirrored walls bisected by a bronze railing, thick maroon carpet, and a quartet of gilt statues shaped like large toads huddled in each corner. No, not statues but *ashtrays*, one with someone's still-lit stub of a cigar left on its lip. They came up to her waist and were all profoundly ugly and strangely out of place, since smoking was illegal in casinos now. The doors shut behind her just as she realized there were no buttons anywhere on the mirrored walls.

Renai spun around, tension swirling in her chest that had nothing to do with the tempest sleeping deep inside her. No, this was a mixture of fluttery panic and frustration with herself for walking right into what felt like a trap. She'd gotten arrogant, spoiled by the powers of the storm and the ghost word. *Too big for them britches,* her father would have said. After a moment, all the restless energy inside of her spilled out as a sharp, cynical laugh. "Trickster gonna trick," she said to her own reflection.

Someone else in the empty room cleared their throat.

Having grown comfortable with just this kind of weirdness since her resurrection, Renai turned her attention to the ashtrays: fat, golden-skinned toads with bulging eyes of some faceted red stone, clawed feet that gripped the piles of coins that held up their bulk, and their wide mouths weighed down in stern, possibly even angry, expressions. The only difference she could see was that one of them bit down on a foul-smelling stogie, whereas the other three had coins pressed between their lips: round and engraved with four Chinese characters surrounding the square punched out of the center.

"Hello?" she said in the direction of the one that was smoking.

The toad statue let out a stream of syllables in a language Renai didn't know, but was pretty sure from the tone that he wasn't pleased with her. One clawed foot came up and swiped the cigar out of his mouth, freeing him to mutter at her some more. When she didn't answer, his faceted eyes squinted at her and returned the cigar to his mouth. When the statue spoke again, in English accented with what sounded like Chinese to Renai's ears, his words were in the slow, carefully enunciated cadence of someone speaking to a child. A not-too-bright child. "Do. You. Have. Coin."

Renai's hand crept into her jacket pocket and clutched the coin of Fortune she'd collected from the corpse in the morgue. She'd refused to give it up to Jack Elderflower, but here she might not have a choice. It was this or try to escape from a mirrored, magical prison cell on her own. She fidgeted with the coin in her pocket, turning it over and over as if it would tell her what to do, as if she could stall long enough for a statue to betray its thinking. The toad stayed perfectly still, thin tendrils of smoke rising from its nostrils, ash flaking onto the carpet. Renai pulled the coin out of her pocket and — following the example of the other statues — reached out to put it between the cigar-smoking toad's lips.

The toad yanked his head away, cursing loud and long in his native tongue. "Do I look like a child?" he asked.

"No," she said, trying not to smile, unsure whether his grouchy outburst was a teasing exaggeration or actual foul-natured distemper.

"Then why feed me like one?" He tapped ash onto the floor and then held that same hand out, two claws clutching the cigar and his palm up, expectant. Since Renai saw no other options and her time was short, she gave him the coin, which he snatched away, bit to test it, and then — grunting in seeming surprise at its genuineness — swallowed it. The wall behind him faded away, revealing only darkness beyond. He moved out of her path, somehow shifting both his weight and the mass of coins beneath him. She saw now that it had always just been the two of them, that the other statues had only ever been reflections or illusions. "Top floor," he said, waving her through as though she had any reason to trust the darkness he presented her with. When she started to protest, he made a growling noise deep in the back of his throat. "You paid for entry, not for questions. Go now."

With little choice, Renai stepped through the doorway into a space that felt hugely open, despite her inability to see. The light from the elevator vanished, leaving her in a dark silence that her adjusting eyes and ears strained to pierce. She was trying to decide whether she should use the ghost word's strange vision or her cell phone camera to see just what she'd gotten herself into when a door about ten feet in front of her creaked open, spilling light into the huge, unfinished room she stood in—bare concrete floors and wood framing and exposed wiring—a doorway that seemed to be standing in a frame by itself.

Leaning against that frame, smiling his Trickster's smile, was Jude Dubuisson.

CHAPTER FOURTEEN

THE MAN LEANING across the threshold of that impossible door looked every inch a New Orleans god of fortune, long and lean-muscled, with a smile as dangerous as a knife and eyes the crisp green of freshly printed money.

He wore a solid dark turtleneck under a bright blue vest covered in golden stars and silver crescent moons, impressionistic whorls and splotches of color, like a Van Gogh painting. With a clean-shaven jaw and his hair cropped close to his head, he was that difficult-to-place kind of light-skinned: maybe a black man fair enough to pass for white, maybe Latino, maybe Indigenous. Renai knew that Jude himself didn't know, having never met his father.

His hands were half-tucked into tight piebald jeans — a patchwork of reds and yellows and blues rough stitched together like a jester's costume, like a quilt turned inside out — that should have been ridiculous, but somehow he pulled them off. *Might have something to do with how low he wearing 'em,* Renai thought, trying to keep her eyes off the "V" in his hips, realizing as she did that she was biting her lip, that Jude's grin widened like he'd read her mind.

Mortal or divine, dead or alive, this man could always get her feeling some kinda way as soon as she laid eyes on him.

And what was worse: he knew it, too.

"Renaissance Raines," he said, in a deep honey-filled voice that made her insides squirm in a pleasant, distracting, infuriating way, "as I live and breathe." A look of feigned concern washed over his face. "I do still live and breathe, right? You ain't here on business?"

Renai felt her lips betray her by twisting into a grin. "Jude I used to know never tried to separate business and pleasure," she said, walking closer to him, trying to summon some sashay into her stride. Jude moved, rising to his full height and shifting his weight so that his body blocked the half-open doorway. He reached behind him, pulling the door almost closed, but ensuring the lock didn't catch. It was too casual a move not to be deliberate. "You hiding someone from me?" she asked. "Afraid I might get jealous?"

She'd meant it to be a joke, a flirtatious way of getting him to open up, but something in her tone or her choice of words made Jude frown, a flash of annoyance or disappointment that was gone as quickly as it appeared. "I think we both know that nobody can hide from you and your people, Renai. Not even me."

Renai wanted to take her words back, wanted to rewind to the teasing back-and-forth that she'd somehow ruined, but that moment was gone, and she didn't have time to try and get it back. Midnight was coming, one way or the other. "Couple of days ago I'd have agreed with you," she said, "but it turns out we're wrong. That's why I'm here. Believe it or not, we've lost—"

Jude held up a hand to stop her, shaking his head. "Sorry to say, but I can't help you." Renai couldn't say anything, not because he'd done something to her—though she knew he had the magic to silence her if he wanted—but because the sudden flush of frustration robbed her of the ability to speak. Her eyebrow's arch said everything she needed to say anyway. He did actually look genuinely apologetic, but that only irritated her even more.

Jude held up his hands, as if he could ward off her anger, and then turned it into a rueful shrug. "Are you really that surprised?" he asked, a hint of laughter in his voice. "Things are different now, Renai. We don't play for the same team anymore."

Renai spoke through clenched teeth, heard her mother's voice coming from her own lips. "You best stop talking out the wrong side of your mouth at me, Jude. I am not the one."

"Not the one what? Not the one who serves the Thrones?"

"What does that have to do with—"

"I'm *Trickster*, Renai. They're *Death*. They send you to evoke the appointed end at the appointed time, right? Well, I'm the lucky break that avoids you." He pointed one finger at her in a slow, dismissive gesture and said, "Fate," then turned that same finger toward his own face and said, "Twist." He frowned and tilted his head in a what-can-you-do gesture. "I'm afraid it's just that simple."

Renai reached down deep for the power within her but found nothing there. Much as she'd love to hurl a little wind and flood at Jude's annoying, smug face, he wasn't wrong. And both she and the storm knew it. "If you weren't gonna help, why did you even bother letting me up in here?"

"Didn't know it was you. Just knew you could afford the buy-in. Which reminds me, your money's no good here." He dug in the pocket of his stars-and-moons vest and pulled out a coin, which he flicked into the air, sending it ringing and spinning straight at her.

Even before she closed her fingers around it, the psychopomp inside her knew it was a coin of Fortune, recognized it as the same one she'd given the toad in the elevator. She tucked it back into her jacket.

Before she could say anything else, before she could even *think* of anything else, Jude was talking again. She'd forgotten that he loved the sound of his own voice as much as she did. "The thing is," he said, "even if I could help you, I really can't. You've been wrong about this misplaced soul of yours from the beginning."

Renai narrowed her eyes at him. "You wanna collect yourself and try again? You just said a whole lotta nothing."

Jude chuckled, low and deep and hungry. "Just because you *heard* nothing doesn't mean I *said* nothing. Why did you come to me?"

Renai took her time to consider her answer. There were a number of reasons. The fact that she knew him, that he owed her a favor, because she needed help she could trust. But he'd emphasized the *me* in that sentence. Why had she thought *he specifically* could help her? That was simple. "Because you can find lost things," she said.

Understanding eased into her like a lock clicking open. "So if you can't find him, it means he isn't lost at all. It means he's right where he wants to be."

Jude tapped a finger to his temple and then pointed it at her. "That'a girl," he said.

What started as a disgusted, dismissive growl from Renai turned into a full-fledged shout, a wordless cry of frustration. She couldn't help it, it just slipped out of her. All that time and energy worrying about some child lost so bad not even death could find him, and that clowning motherfucker was *running* from her? Oh, no. Oh, *hell* no.

She took some small amount of satisfaction from the worried glance Jude threw over his shoulder at his red door, like her outburst might have disturbed whoever—or whatever—he had waiting on him in here. When he turned back to her, though, he was smiling once more. "I do have a consolation prize for you," he said. Without waiting for a response, he beckoned her closer. Just a few steps took her near enough to breathe in his scent: crushed almonds and roasted coffee and dark, dark rum. He reached into the leather satchel at his waist—his bag of tricks, she remembered—that she hadn't seen up until now, that she was pretty sure hadn't been there until just this moment, and a thrill of something ran through her; danger maybe, but not quite fear. All she really knew about his satchel was that it held some potent magics, that he could pull just about anything out of there.

When he pulled his hand free, her first thought was that he held nothing at all in his fist. In the darkness of the room, and the blackness of what he held, the object practically vanished. But then he tilted it just so, and the light danced across its surface like the shine on a piece of glass, and she saw that he held a knife. He spun it in his open palm and held it by the blade, so that the handle was presented to her. She took it without stopping to think whether it was a good idea.

It looked at first to be made of smoked black glass, but as she studied it, she thought it was some polished stone, maybe even obsidian. The blade curved up from her bottom knuckle in a wide arc and then tapered to a sharp point, curved like a talon or a thorn. The grip wasn't what she expected, a knotted cord wound tightly around a core of wood or stone, and the blade itself seemed more accidental than fashioned, its jagged, serrated edge more like something broken than something shaped. It was a wicked, dangerous thing, suitable only for rending, for destruction.

It felt absolutely *right* in her hand.

"See?" Jude said, startling her. "I'm still your boy if you've actually lost something."

"And here I thought you couldn't help me," she said. She found it difficult to pull her eyes away from the knife, like the blade's gleam would show her something other than her own reflection if she stared hard enough. It felt both familiar and unknown, like it belonged to those memories of hers that had been wiped away.

Jude pursed his lips and waved her off, playful, like they were pals, like he hadn't just told her they were fundamentally opposed to one another. "Well, I do owe you one. After you helped me in the Underworld the way you did, I couldn't let you out of here with your pockets turned out."

Renai tried to keep her ignorance from showing on her face, but Jude seemed to read it there anyway, frowning at whatever he saw. "You don't remember that, do you?" He glanced behind him again, like someone late obsessively checking their watch. She wondered how close to midnight they were. "I'll have to tell you about it sometime," he said, backing slowly toward his impossible door, "you were a real badass that day."

She followed him, matching his slow, inching pace, but not letting him get away, either. "Why wait? You got something better to do?"

"Not better, just urgent."

He showed her his back, almost at the door now. "But I've lost my memories," she said, a kind of breathless desperation making her words come out plaintive, needy. She hated the sound of it, but it made Jude pause, his hand pressed to the door but not pushing it open yet, so she kept going. "Wouldn't those help me more than some knife?"

"Depends on the knife," he said over his shoulder. "Besides, the memories are like the kid. They're not lost. They just don't belong to you no more."

And then he turned, just enough for one last look, to shoot her a brief fuck-you grin, and then the red door swung open at his touch. In the brief glimpse through the doorway that Renai managed to steal, she saw a small room dominated by a poker table filled with horrors: a brown-skinned, shirtless man with protruding eyes, a smear of paint on his forehead in the same shade of dark blue as the crown of feathers he wore, and a beast's cruel fangs curling down over his lower lip; a scrawny, dirty child with bright red skin and an elongated, dangling tongue that seemed somehow obscene; a woman of Native ancestry — judging by her light brown skin and thick black hair — who had two slender arms waving above her head in a slow, hypnotic dance and two more resting on the table; Seth, with his awkward, ugly face and his filthy red hands; and a person-shaped mound of cockroaches, writhing and skittering and repulsive.

Then the door slammed shut, and she was once again alone in the big, empty dark.

"To hell with *this*," Renai muttered. Though she could barely see, she reached for where she thought the knob would be and, after a couple of missed attempts, managed to find it with her free hand. She twisted it and threw her shoulder against the door, expecting it to be locked—

—and went sprawling into the bright cacophony of the main casino floor.

She nearly lost the knife in her confusion. A glance back showed her the trick: the door she'd burst through led into a janitor's supply closet, mops and bleach and rolls of black garbage bags. She let out a harsh bark of a laugh. "Guess that's what you get for fucking 'round with those Tricksters," she said, mimicking Sal's sardonic drawl. She was surprised at how much she missed the psychopomp, even though it had only been a few days since she'd seen him. She hoped he wore his dog-shape when midnight came around, so she could throw her arms around his big stupid neck. And then she'd skin him for abandoning her like he had. She already had the perfect knife for it.

The blade seemed even more sinister in the fluorescent lights, tar-black and sharp as flint. Prehistoric. Primordial. For the first time in a long time, Renai felt the itch of eyes on her and looked up. Gamblers at slot machines, waitresses carrying cocktails on little silver trays, security guards in maroon jackets with walkie-talkies in their hands, all of them kept glancing her way and then doing double takes, *seeing* her before shaking their heads and turning away. Even her aura of disinterest couldn't fully hide her if she waved around a black glass hell-knife, it seemed. Nor, she realized, could she drive a motorcycle while holding the damned thing.

Would it have killed that fool to dig a sheath out of that bag of his, too? she thought. She scavenged some thick cardboard and duct tape out of the janitor's closet, rigging up a case for the blade that let her tuck it into the back of her jeans without cutting herself. It wouldn't last long, but it was the best she had for now. Maybe Sal would know what to do with it.

She hurried out of the casino to where Kyrie waited, already running, to carry her to St. Louis No. 1, to midnight and the First Gate and the start of the Hallows. Renai felt as eager as the bike, her hunger and her anticipation of getting some answers leaving her light-headed. As they wove through the traffic of Canal—the crowd tame compared to what it would be tomorrow night—Renai's thoughts turned to something Jude had said, about her helping him in the Underworld.

She was struck by one of those strange memory-visions: this time of the Seventh Gate, the Final Gate, the one that waited between the twin empty Thrones who ruled over the entirety of the Underworld. She could see it clearly, almost as if she'd stood there herself more recently than the five years since she'd died, the image more intense, more *real* than any mere dream or recollection.

She saw herself there, dwarfed by the massive rough-hewn empty chairs of the Thrones, her hair long and twisted into dreads, still wearing the lacy white Confirmation dress that she'd been buried in, Sal in his dog-shape at her side. Miguel stepped forward, stripped of Name and Shadow, the coin of his Fortune already off to wherever they went once their appointed psychopomp delivered them to the scales, prepared to face the decision of the Thrones. The Final Gate opened, a soothing, warm light that suffused Miguel and set him alight, made him luminous, like dust motes dancing in a sunbeam. She smiled, both the Renai on the bike lost in her own thoughts and the other Renai in the other world, because this was what she'd thought her purpose would be when she'd agreed to be a psychopomp, to guide souls to this moment, their just reward.

It was especially satisfying when that afterlife was a happy one.

Then she remembered that no one would get to the afterlife they deserved if the Gates stayed locked, and that tenuous grasp on happiness was snatched away from her. Anxiety and questions about Ramses' disappearance quickly took its place. On the one hand, whether he lived or died wouldn't matter in the grand scheme of things. She didn't like considering a human life from that angle, but the truth wasn't always pretty. Black boys his age died from bullets all the time in this city. If Ramses hadn't avoided his fate, if he'd met that bullet two nights ago like he was supposed to, it would have been just another tragedy. He might have gotten half a minute on the evening news before they pivoted to forecasting the weather and next week's Saints game.

On the other hand, she now knew that Ramses wasn't just human, that he hadn't slipped free of his appointed end by accident. That he had *run* from his death, from her, which ought to be impossible. He'd done something that threatened to upend one of the fundamental principles of existence: that when it was your time to go, you *went*. So while his life or death shouldn't matter in one world, it ought to be hugely fucking important in the other. And yet, aside from a dirty-handed god who came asking for help on his behalf from a psychopomp trainee, no one on the other side seemed to give a shit.

The question was: Why the hell *didn't* they?

⧗

By the time Renai pulled Kyrie up onto the neutral ground across from St. Louis No. 1, she thought she had an answer.

Oussou's spot next to the cemetery's entrance was still empty. Cordelia waited for her on the statue where Renai had first seen her, an innocuous little bird perched on a bronze shoulder. "I was starting to think you wouldn't show up," Cordelia said, before Renai had even gotten off the bike. Suspicion and ire replaced her usual jocular, facetious tone of voice. "Did you find anything useful?"

Renai felt the sudden, inexplicable desire to keep the black blade to herself. As she eased off of Kyrie's seat, she tucked the knife's handle underneath her jacket. "Nope," she said. "No luck at all." Strange, how quickly she'd gone from more or less trusting the little 'pomp to keeping secrets from her. She'd be glad when she had Sal back, when she had a partner she could rely on at her side. Still, she was glad that she'd had Cordelia to bounce ideas off of in her mentor's absence. "I've been thinking, though. We looked high and low for Ramses, right?"

"Right." Cordelia fluttered from the statue's shoulder to Renai's. "When the Thrones ask, we can say we did our due diligence."

"No, that's not what I mean." Renai waited for the light to change and then crossed the street, imagining she could feel the moments between now and midnight ticking away. "I'm saying if we couldn't find him, maybe it's because he doesn't *want* to be found, you know? That he's running from us." Renai stopped in front of the wrought-iron gate, peering through to the other side. Still nothing but plaster tombs and palm trees. Not yet time.

Cordelia hopped off of Renai's shoulder and flapped up to a NO PARKING sign, putting her just over Renai's head. "He wouldn't be the first to flee the embrace of the grave," she said. "What of it?"

"The best place to hide is where the person chasing you would never expect. So if death is hunting you . . ."

Cordelia's beak gaped open. "You hide in the land of the dead. That's actually quite brilliant." Renai pantomimed dropping a microphone. Before she could say anything else, the alarm she'd set that morning went off. Midnight.

At first, nothing of note happened. Renai pulled out her phone and silenced the abrasive braying. She tugged on the gate and found it both locked and still merely wrought iron. She turned and looked up at Cordelia. "Are we supposed to knock or something?" The truth—the one that Renai had been avoiding thinking about until now—was that she didn't really know what happened during the Hallows, even though she'd lived through five of them as a psychopomp. Those three days were another hazy gap in her memories. Not lost, if Jude could be believed, but not *hers,* either.

And then, suddenly, the Gates opened.

All of them, all at once.

When Oussou opened the First Gate, she'd only ever seen a glimpse of the other side, fog and wandering shades and a world that was both New Orleans and somewhere else. When the Hallows began, those two worlds weren't separate any longer, if they'd ever truly been two worlds to begin with. The dead were all around her, silent and sad and blinking at their surroundings like they could see them for the first time. Renai turned in a slow circle, taking it all in. How could she have forgotten this?

Behind her, the iron gate creaked open on rusting hinges. She spun, just in time to see Salvatore's dog-shape twisted and frightening—fur bristling, saliva glistening on his muzzle, teeth bared in a snarl, a beastly growl deep in his chest—before he leapt at her with a howl of fury. Time seemed to slow. He rose through the air, neck muscles straining, fangs coming straight for her throat, and then he sailed past her even as she flinched away. But he hadn't lunged for her at all.

It was Cordelia he sought.

His jaws chomped down at the little bird with an audible snap. But as horrific, as confusing as that was, Renai only had eyes for the girl who stepped through the cemetery gate after him.

She had long dreads that were bound up in a loose bundle away from her face, her dark brown skin in stark, alluring contrast with the dazzling white dress she wore, a thing of lace and satin, like she'd just come from a wedding, or a prom, or her Confirmation. Red sneakers peeked out from her hem.

Renai knew her, knew every quirk of her lips, the exact shade of her eyes, knew where she'd gotten that tiny scar dimpling one eyebrow.

Renai knew everything about the girl in front of her and nothing at all, because the girl in the white dress was Renaissance Raines.

PART TWO

THE NEXT WORLD

CHAPTER FIFTEEN

SOMETIMES THEY ARE benign spirits. Heralds and watchmen. A first-comer that the Norse called a vardøger and the Finns called an etiäinen: the scent of your perfume or the sound of your voice announcing your presence to others before you've actually arrived. Other times they are more ominous, spectral doubles that appear only as ill omens, as harbingers. Lincoln saw his as a death-pale reflection in a mirror, but you might meet your fetch or your wraith or your haint in a nightmare, or a vision, or on the internet. Sometimes they are sinister beings meant to replace you. When the Scottish trow replaced you in the cradle, you were called a changeling; when your loved one notices your replacement today, they say she is suffering from a Capgras delusion. Replicants and clones, illusions and shadows and doppelgängers. They have your hair and your eyes, your scars and your smile, the same embarrassing laugh and the same morning breath. They are no mere twin or reflection. They are you, and they are not you. They are a perfect copy of all your imperfections. Their wonder and their horror and their power lies in their impossibility. Their conflicts. Their contradictions.

⧖

One of those contradictions was a young woman named Renaissance Raines, and she sat in a coffee shop in Mid-City—or more accurately, in the part of the Underworld that looked like New Orleans—waiting for death.

She nestled deep in a plush leather armchair, her legs tucked beneath her and her attention fixed on her phone, scrolling through Twitter and trying to ignore the gawking, relentless stares of the shades all around her.

Even though it was late October—just over a week until the Hallows began—she wore a dark blue Captain America tank top, khaki shorts, and flip-flops, desperate for the first true cold front of fall to arrive and tease the temperature out of the nineties. She'd coiled her dreads high and tight on top of her head to try and keep cool.

As she flicked one finger across the phone's screen, her other hand toyed idly with the St. Christopher medal that hung on a silver chain around her neck. In one sense, she had the coffee shop all to herself: no one sipped a latte while tapping away at a laptop keyboard, no one pulled shots of espresso from a hissing, clanking machine, no one had a banal conversation just a few decibels too loud. She was the only living soul in the place.

In reality, there was nowhere in the Underworld that she was ever truly alone.

All around her, the vaguest impressions of people flickered in and out sight, as intermittent and inscrutable as a spiderweb dancing in the breeze. These shades—the restless dead who had crossed over into the Underworld but failed, for any number of reasons, to continue on to the Far Lands—were drawn to her, watching her every move, following her wherever she went. In her five years in the Underworld since her resurrection, she hadn't been able to puzzle out a reason for their attraction to her. As far as she could tell, she was as unreal to them as they were to her; she was just the flame to their moths.

The shades were one of many of the details of her post-resurrection life that she'd had to force herself to accept, like her disjointed, scrambled puzzle pieces of a memory, her duties as a psychopomp, or the strange dreamlike flashes she'd get of an *other Renai*—one who'd managed to cling to a place in the world of the living.

Despite being crowded with wisps of forgotten dead—or maybe because of that fact—the small sitting area of the coffee shop was almost silent. The only sound, save for her own breath and the occasional *click* or *ping* from her phone, was some weird indie-pop/Lord-of-the-Rings-soundtrack/angelic-choirs-chanting music filtering through from the living side of things. She'd been listening to it long enough that she'd almost started to like it. Since it came from the other side, though, it sounded distant, muted, like she was underwater or the speakers were in a passing car, instead of on top of the used-books-and-board-games shelf right next to her. She could drown it out with music from her phone, of course, but after five years of being the Underworld's only flesh-and-blood girl, she'd grown fond of any intrusion from the world of the living into the silence of this place.

That had been one of her first and hardest lessons when she'd awoken to this new life in the land of the dead, that while the dead could communicate with each other—eerie whispers that were closer to telepathy than creating sound—the ability to speak belonged solely to the living. At first, she'd thought it was just that the dead, who no longer had bodies, didn't have the vocal cords necessary to create sound. But her mentor, a psychopomp named Salvatore, taught her that what the dead truly lacked was the ability to influence those around them, a capacity that he called their Voice. Sounds were just ripples in the air. Someone's Voice could take the form of spoken words, or sign language, or written text, or art, or music; anything that could impact others. Voice, simply put, was magic. And only the living possessed it.

Which was why—along with the three cups of coffee she'd drunk in the last hour—she nearly pissed herself when a deep honey-filled voice behind her said, "Is this seat taken?"

Renai managed, barely, to control her bladder and her voice, though a little croak of surprise snuck out of her throat.

The speaker didn't wait for a reply, just threw himself into the chair across from her with a grateful sigh and propped his feet up on the small table between them, his Jordans worn and dirty, as if he'd walked every impossible mile between this world and the other. He wore a long-sleeved purple dress shirt with the sleeves rolled up and tight black jeans. Although the experiences of death and resurrection and the pressures of living in the Underworld had been hell on her memories, Renai recognized the man across from her immediately: Jude Dubuisson, Trickster and fortune god, fine specimen of the male form, and the reason she was sort-of-but-not-really alive instead of moving on to the afterlife she'd earned.

"You got a lot of nerve dropping in on me like this," she said, her voice raspy from disuse, "after the shit you pulled."

The smug, satisfied expression slid away from his face in dismay. It was almost worth the frustration of seeing him, sudden and unwelcome, after all these years. Jude straightened in his chair, his hands held up in defense, his eyes stretching wide. "Whoa, whoa," he said. "I thought we were friends."

"Friends? *Friends?*" The words came out louder and far more shrill than she intended, and she was standing over him before she realized she'd risen to her feet. The shades surrounding them backed away in a group, not so much moving as being pushed by the force of her voice. "When someone gives up her chance at an afterlife so that your triflin' ass can return to the world of the living, would a *friend* just up and vanish? For *five goddamn years?* Because that don't sound like a friend to me. That sounds like some fuck-boi Trickster bullshit to my ears."

Jude's head dropped, staring down at his hands. For a moment, Renai saw herself standing in front of the Thrones once more, those empty chairs that represented all the power of Death, trading her eternity to save Jude from annihilation. It was one of the few memories from her death and resurrection that wasn't hazy and incomplete. She'd done it willingly, happily even. The next thing she remembered clearly was Sal telling her that he'd train her as a psychopomp, but that she couldn't ever go back to the world of the living. That her place now was among the dead.

Blinking away the memory, Renai looked down at Jude and saw his shoulders shaking. She felt, at first, a deep swell of pity, but she pushed it away. She'd need a damn sight more than some crocodile tears before she even considered forgiving him. Which was when she realized that the sounds coming from him weren't moans of remorse or swift sobbing breaths, as she'd expected.

He was *laughing* at her.

Renai checked the nearby tables for something she could hit him with. "Are you for real?" she said, so furious that she moved past anger and into genuine confusion. Jude had been shady and way too pretty for his own good, but she hadn't known him to be cruel. Then again, she hadn't known him to be the kind of person who would abandon a friend, either. Maybe godhood had changed him. "Just who the fuck do you think you are?"

"Who, indeed," he said, in a voice that wasn't as deep, that had a hint of an accent that Renai couldn't place. A voice, in other words, that didn't belong to Jude Dubuisson. Nor, when he looked up, did his face. This man had darker skin, though not by much, thicker eyebrows, and a hooked nose. Still far too pretty to be trusted, though. And that smile, when he turned it toward her, that smile was just as dangerous as Jude's.

And as thrilling.

"I have to admit," he said, "I always knew Dubuisson was a bit of a bastard, but I never knew he had full-on betrayal in him. That's a real surprise."

"Yeah, well, Trickster gonna trick." She pursed her lips at him. "Who're you?"

"I am He Who Keeps the Flocks. Ram-Bearer. Slayer of Argos. Thrice-Great." Renai pressed her fists to her hips and raised an eyebrow at him. Some of his charm wilted away. "Comrade of the Feast? Bearer of the Golden Wand?"

Renai kissed her teeth. "You're about to be He Who Catches These Hands if you don't cut the bullshit. What's your name?" She really hoped he didn't call her bluff. She didn't need a name to know that she spoke to a god. Didn't need to know *which* god to know that she was in way over her head.

He waved a hand at her, as if shooing away her demands as he would a fly. "Names and titles are, obviously, of no use to you. You may call me Mason. And I owe you an apology. I wore the shape of one I thought to be your friend because I'm desperate for your help." He frowned. "Shame, though."

Renai relaxed her hands but kept them on her hips. She hadn't missed the fact that owing her an apology wasn't nearly the same thing as being sorry. "How's that?"

That dangerous, seductive grin returned. "It was quite a pleasing shape to wear."

Renai barked out a laugh in spite of herself. She started to tell Mason that his own shape was plenty pleasing, but the last thing she needed was to start flirting with another damn Trickster.

"Why would you ever need *my* help?" she said, instead. She flopped back into her chair, throwing one leg up over the arm. She fought the urge to smile when she noticed Mason's eyes take in the long stretch of her bare toned leg. Tricksters were all the same. "Seems to me a man who can wear somebody else's face just so he can ask a favor might be better served by doing the thing himself."

Mason sighed and reached into the chest pocket of his dress shirt, pulling out a smartphone. "Certainly have to explain myself less," he muttered, low enough that he could pretend like he hadn't meant her to hear it, loud enough that she knew he had.

She didn't recognize the logo on his phone, expecting a bitten apple or a single word or a multicolored letter, but Mason's device had a symbol embossed in gold: a circle with a downward pointing cross and a swoop, like horns, above. She thought, at first, that it was the Love Symbol from when Prince had just been "The Artist," but no, that wasn't it, though she only got a brief a glance at it as Mason swiped quickly on his screen and then slid the phone back into his pocket.

Just then her own phone made a soft *ding*. "I've just sent you the name of someone who will soon come under your jurisdiction," Mason said. He held up a hand to stall her protest before she had a chance to voice it. "All I need is some information. He's . . . acquired something very important to me. I'd like to know where he's keeping it. If you insinuate yourself as his guide, he should be more than willing to share." His grin grew feral, hungry. "After all, it's not as though he can bring it here with him."

"What's in it for me?" The words were out of her mouth before she could stop them. She didn't know why she'd jumped right to quid pro quo. Maybe it was because Mason had worn the face of a man who had betrayed her, maybe she was getting tired of just doing whatever Salvatore told her to. Once asked the question, though, she was glad she'd chosen that one out of all the others whirling through her mind. She'd been waiting years for an opportunity like this.

If the question surprised Mason, he gave no sign. "What is it you want?" he asked, his voice dropping to a conspiratorial purr.

Once, she'd have found that question difficult to answer. She'd gone to college because that's what you were supposed to do, but had died before she'd had to declare a major. She'd gotten a job at a voodoo shop run by her eccentric Aunt Celeste, not out of any real desire to convert, but to piss off her Catholic parents. Her father had once told her that she had the soul of a thunderstorm, a powerhouse of passion and energy that was willing to drift wherever the wind took her. He'd meant for it to galvanize her, to goad her into taking control of her life. Young Renai had simply shrugged and agreed with him. After five years of lonely monotony though, five years guiding the souls of the recently departed through the Underworld—those that made it all the way through, anyway—without any hope of reprieve or advancement, Renai had gained a sense of purpose. She finally knew what she wanted.

"I want to die," she said.

Though he hid it well—a hand raised to his mouth that he turned into a scratch of his cheek, a lick of his lips instead of an answer—her statement surprised Mason. Whatever he'd expected her to say, he hadn't planned on this. *Rendered a god speechless*, she thought. *Achievement unlocked.*

When he recovered his composure—which happened in the time it took Renai to blink—Mason had painted his Trickster's grin back on. "That should be simple enough to arrange," he said. "Though I'm not sure why you would ever need *my* help." He repeated her own statement back to her, emphasizing the same words she had, implying, as she had, that Renai might be better off handling the task herself.

"Easy now. I'm not having a *Hamlet* moment here. I know exactly what dreams may come. That's the problem. Every life gets one trip through the Gates, one chance at eternity. Mine has come and gone. Traded my ever-after away on some trick who didn't deserve it. The Thrones brought me back, but you know as well as I do that they don't ever let go of someone for good. Maybe it's tomorrow, maybe it's fifty years from now, but I'll die one day. If I'm not heading for the Far Lands, where do I go when my time comes? The Devourer? *Trickster, please.*"

Mason chuckled. "So if I can secure your passage to one of the Far Lands without the oversight of the Thrones—"

"Not 'one of' them," Renai said, making the air quotes with her fingers even though she hated when people did that. "I get to pick. That's the deal."

Closing his eyes, Mason reached up and rubbed at the bridge of his nose, the gesture of someone whose glasses had grown tedious, even though he wore none. "I suppose," he said, without opening his eyes, "that you've already chosen your destination?"

"The Fortunate Isles."

The corners of Mason's lips curled down in a small frown, and he clicked his tongue in a thoughtful, staccato rhythm. "I see you've done your homework," he said.

When the ancient Greeks died, they were either tortured in the pits of Tartarus, languished in the boring, tepid Meadows of Asphodel, or—if they had lived an exemplary life—rewarded with the comfort and bliss found in the land of Elysium. A true hero, presented with the paradise of Elysium, might choose to return to the world of the living. Only after three lives and three deaths, earning a place in Elysium all three times, was one worthy of the Fortunate Isles.

It was the heaven even people in Heaven wished they could get into.

"Does that mean you can't do it?" Renai asked, trying to keep too much sass out of her voice.

"It's not beyond my reach," Mason said, choosing his words with care.

"Then we have a deal." Renai glanced down at her phone, saw that Mason's text had come through. "I'll bring you whatever this soon-to-be-dead guy managed to steal from you—"

"No!" Mason hurled himself to his feet, his voice like a thunderclap. He towered over her as if he'd doubled in size. The light in the room dimmed, or seemed to, because he held a golden sword in his fist that burned like it was made of the noonday sun. "You will not touch it, you will not seek it. Swear!"

Renai found it hard to speak, her heart pounding so hard that her pulse squeezed her throat with every beat. "I swear," she managed to wheeze out. "I'll just find where he hid it, that's all."

Mason's smile was terrible to behold. There was joy there, but it was the fierce joy of a predator about to pounce. "Then, yes, we have a deal, Renaissance Raines. Remember the name, and send word when he's told you what I want to know." And then he was gone, leaving behind a faint whiff of incense, the glowing red afterimage of his sword burned into her retinas—which didn't merely fade away, reinventing itself as a throbbing ache behind her eyes—and a message. A name.

It took Renai more than a few minutes to recover from Mason's outburst, first to calm her racing heart, and then to let her vision return to normal. It took a while longer—turning their conversation over and over in her mind—for her to come to the conclusion that she'd probably done exactly what the smiling god had wanted her to do. Trickster gonna trick, after all. Only then did she open the message and read the name Mason had given her.

"Ramses St. Cyr," she said. "I don't know what you stole, but I hope it was worth dying over."

Renai let the door slam shut behind her when she left the coffee shop — phone and flip-flops tucked away into the messenger bag slung over her shoulder — unconcerned that she might lock herself out of her favorite place to steal Wi-Fi and stale muffins, since she'd learned long ago that nothing ever stayed locked in the Underworld.

Not that anyone but her on this side of things even *used* doors. The shades drifted through walls like they — or the walls — were made of smoke, and none of the other psychopomps seemed to much like being inside for some reason. Probably because most of them wore animal shapes, even on this side where they weren't bound by the rules of the living world. The gods, the few of them that she'd met in the last five years anyway, seemed to do whatever they damn well pleased, popping in and out of existence like the doors and the walls and the laws of physics were all equally trivial.

Outside, the Underworld was a city reclaimed by wilderness. The coffee shop stood at the edge of a clearing, its purple-tiled roof unusual in both color and material, its bike rack filled with bicycles that never moved, its nearest neighbor, a two-story home with a full porch on its second story just barely visible through the Underworld fog. A silver-painted fire hydrant jutted up out of the ground amid a handful of cypress knees, half a foot of black pipe visible from where the earth had settled. Directly opposite the front door, where the two lanes and neutral ground of Bienville ought to run, a stand of cypress grew thick-waisted and tall, a curtain of Spanish moss dangling down to the swampy, wet ground below.

Renai had never been able to decide whether the buildings of the human-built New Orleans had been superimposed on the natural world so that the dead would have a frame of reference on this side of things, or if the spirits of the trees — towering cypress and thin, rigid pine and broad, domineering oaks, mostly — had crossed over to this world when they'd been torn down in the other to make way for concrete and steel, for asphalt and streetcar tracks and drainage canals, digging their ghostly roots into the land of the dead. Whatever the reason, there were no roads in the Underworld, no cars and no planes, which meant an eerie silence hung in the pristine air, unbroken by the incessant, tidal roar of engines and tires on concrete she'd known all her life. When she'd asked Sal about it, he'd acted like she couldn't handle the truth, which is what she figured he did when he didn't know the answer.

Thinking of the gruff psychopomp, Renai glanced at her watch — a relic from her childhood, a cheap elastic band and a tiny digital display embedded in the molded-plastic trash can of a green cartoon monster who said "Get lost!" when you squeezed a button on the side—and saw that the conversation with Mason had taken longer than she'd thought, long enough that she didn't have time to walk and wade through the long span of Underworld swamp that separated her from the First Gate where she was supposed to meet her mentor.

Smiling, Renai dug her toes into the cool, dew-kissed grass and let her wings unfurl—those impossible gossamer spans of magic and light that she'd possessed since her resurrection—letting them unspool from the strange nowhere space where they lived when she wasn't using them. Wide and diaphanous, they caught the slight breeze and tried to tug her into the sky as soon as she released them. They weren't the feathered and dove-white angel's wings her fourth-grade religion teacher had taught her to expect upon her death—these were shaped and colored like those of a monarch butterfly: a deep sunset orange with thick black lines streaking across them like veins and flecked with spots of white at the edges—but Renai thought these suited her more. She'd never had the temperament of an angel before she died, and she certainly had no interest in being one after her resurrection.

She was pretty sure it had been an angel who'd killed her, after all.

Lifting into the air took less effort than holding on to the earth, so flight, she'd found, was as simple as letting go. In truth, her gentle swaying ascent was more floating than flying, the tumble and flutter and glide of a butterfly instead of the powerful swoop of a superhero that she'd envisioned when she'd first discovered her wings. Nor could she manage to climb much higher than the treetops, her bare feet skimming across the leaves like something out of a kung fu movie. She'd tried to fly higher once but found that the sweet-scented easy breeze that bore her up quickly became a punishing gale that threatened to tear her from the sky if she dared to challenge it. The experience had reminded her of a story from when her sophomore English class had studied Greek myths. A quick Wikipedia search had found the winged boy's name: Icarus. The dense fog of the Underworld might diffuse the sun's warmth across the whole span of the heavens, but Renai knew the point of his story had nothing to do with beeswax and heat, so she kept her flights to the winds that wanted her there. She wasn't about to go out like some white boy who couldn't respect boundaries.

Once she rose above the canopy, most of New Orleans sprawled out beneath her in a patchwork green-and-gray carpet of foliage and mist. The office buildings in the CBD, the eggshell-white curve of the Superdome, and the big hotels in the Quarter all stretched up higher than the monotony, of course, as did Touro hospital Uptown and a handful of buildings behind her in Metairie, but the majority of the city was so flat and close to the earth that the fog shrouded it all.

Renai usually didn't fly this high, finding it unnerving at how quickly she lost her sense of direction without all the familiar landmarks and the comforting pattern of city streets, but she didn't have time for comfort. Fortunately for her, all she had to do was head toward the Quarter—south as the psychopomp flew, but "Toward the River" in a New Orleanian's cardinal directions—and wait for Sal. The First Gate would announce itself when it opened.

It took less than five minutes for her to get across the city, even moving at her slow, delicate pace, her home much smaller from above than she'd ever realized with her feet on the ground. When she reached St. Louis No. 1—estimating her position based on the Hotel Monteleone sign on her left and the Dome on her right—she hovered there, wishing Google Maps worked in the afterlife. This side was as devoid of cell towers as it was roads, though, so she'd never been able to get a signal, even though she checked whenever she unlocked her phone.

It was strange. Wi-Fi and sound sometimes seeped through from the other side, and her charger worked in any electric socket she tried, but phones simply refused to make a connection. It felt deliberate, like something the Thrones had done to keep the living and the dead separate. Maybe the Thrones had some reason for allowing the internet in the Underworld, but Renai thought maybe they just didn't know it existed. That thought was far from comforting.

But she knew firsthand that even Death made mistakes.

The First Gate opened behind her, a trumpet blast of noise that made her whirl around just as a spear of light pierced the fog and stabbed up seemingly forever. Her guess had been close, just a city block or so away.

She flew toward the open Gate, descending as she glided closer. The inscrutable heavens of the Underworld pulled away to reveal a stark night sky speckled with a handful of stars, the glow of light pollution and the hot stink of car exhaust and the muted roar of the Quarter all spilling through.

Renai breathed it all in, basking in the heat and the life of the place. Of home. It didn't do anything to help her headache, still throbbing since Mason's deity tantrum in the coffee shop, but she reveled in the sensation all the same.

Once, when she'd been high above the cemetery like this when the Gate opened, she'd tried to cross back through to the world of the living, only to find that the image of the other side was just that, an image, intangible as a sunbeam shining through a dusty room. She'd managed to hide her tears from Sal that day, but only just. She'd hoped, for a while, that Sal and the Thrones would let her be a true psychopomp—the kind who crossed over and guided the dead through their whole journey—once she proved herself, but after five years, she'd let that hope die. Now her only hope was that she could find her way to the other side of the Final Gate and into the Far Lands.

All too soon the Gate swung closed, leaving the Underworld silent once more. Renai slid down through the fog and into the plaster and brick tombs of the cemetery. Her descent was slow and gradual, even though part of her wanted to drop from the sky and land with one fist pounding the earth like a superhero. She could fly, damn it, why shouldn't she enjoy it? *Because,* she told herself, in her older sister's have-I-taught-you-nothing voice, *if you twist your knee or break an ankle, there ain't no doctor on this side who can fix it. But if you feel like carrying a limp for all eternity just so you can play Iron Man, you do you.*

So, badass winged psychopomp she might be, but she eased out of the air like an old man wincing his way down the stairs. She hopped and skipped to a stop once she reached the ground, her wings flexing and trying to carry her back up. She folded them away, which felt more like an act of will than a physical movement. Her wings didn't just lie flat on her back when she didn't need them, they vanished entirely, which was equally weird and convenient. On the one hand, she didn't have to worry about tearing one of her gossamer-thin wings every time she sat down or got dressed. On the other, her wings literally came from nothing and returned to it, even though they were unmistakably a part of her when she stretched them out. Kind of like people. Here and then gone.

It was this thought—the from-nothing-and-returning-there aspect of both her wings and the human spirit—that followed her on her brief walk to the cemetery's entrance. There she found Salvatore, wearing his raven-shape, perched on the shoulder of a dead Latino man whose wide eyes seemed to be trying to take in the whole Underworld all at once. As most of the dead did when they first arrived, he tried to speak with lungs and vocal cords and a tongue that he no longer possessed, and so said nothing at all.

"Renai," Sal said, "this is—" He stopped midsentence, his feathers ruffling.

"What?" Renai asked.

"Renaissance, where the fuck are your *shoes?*"

Renai laughed. "Seriously? What, you afraid I'm gonna catch cold? You got a lot of fashion tips for a 'pomp who goes around naked in *both* his shapes. Boy, bye." Sal started to answer, but Renai put her hand right up to his beak, a gesture both playful and confident. "Not now, Sal. We got work to do." She turned her hand over so that her palm faced up. "His coin?"

Making the gap-beaked gape at her that was his raven-shape's version of a smile, Sal pulled the coin from beneath his wing and dropped it into her hand. As soon as it touched her skin, the whole life of the man whose Fortune it represented flooded through her. Miguel Flores filled her heart and mind, his loves and his family, the joys and sorrows of the child, the boy, and the young man, his struggles and triumphs and fondest memories, his weaknesses and failures and crimes. She saw him at his birth and at his death. She knew him, as his father would have said, from asshole to appetite. Because of this connection to him, Renai felt the words that the dead man kept trying to say.

Lady of the Elegant Skull, he called her, except the words he wanted to use were in Spanish. She didn't speak the language, but that didn't matter here. Since the dead didn't speak, only shared meaning and intent, their communication transcended language. The name he gave her carried with it a flicker of an image: a skeleton wearing a brightly colored dress, tight in the shoulders and bodice but flaring wide at the hips and cascading to the ground in a wave of embroidery, flowers, and lace, like something out of *Gone with the Wind,* her eyeless skull grinning from beneath a wide-brimmed, fringed hat. Renai recognized the figure from pictures of Day of the Dead celebrations.

The dead, she knew, saw what they wanted—Sal would say what they *needed*—to see on this side of things, and that sometimes included her. That knowledge had unnerved her at first, the thought that in the eyes of her dead she might be an icon, a goddess, a beloved ancestor. She'd found it hard to connect to the souls she was meant to guide, and that made it easier for them to stumble off their path. To become a shade: irrevocably lost, forgotten, identity wiped away until they were as featureless as the mist they'd wander through forever. They were erased so entirely that even Renai couldn't remember them once they were gone.

Though Renai couldn't remember even the number of the dead she'd lost, she knew it was too many, so now she leaned into their narrative, played whatever role they created for her. Whatever it took to keep them on the path. She dipped into a curtsy, ridiculous in her bare feet and khaki shorts, but in the dress Miguel saw La Catrina wearing, it would fit perfectly. "Come, Miguel," she said as she rose to her full height, "we have a long way to go." The fog swirling along the ground at the dead man's feet parted, revealing a single paving stone jutting out of the grass. Miguel took a tentative step forward, resting one foot upon the stone, and the fog parted further, as though his footfall had thrown up a brief gust of wind. The stones continued deeper into the cemetery, a full stride apart and worn smooth by innumerable footsteps from previous travelers.

With a flutter of dark wings, Sal leapt from Miguel's shoulder and flew to Renai's, his claws clutching at her bare skin, sharp, but taking care not to scratch. "How come you never curtsy for me," he muttered into her ear. She shook her shoulder to shush him, though she grinned just the same. She worried, for a moment, that it would spoil the solemn mood of the beginning of Miguel's journey, and then she remembered that to him, her fleshless skull was always grinning.

Renai turned and walked down the path of paving stones, which led all the way to the far edge of the cemetery and then through a hole in the wall that she knew didn't exist in the living world. A glance back told her that Miguel was following, struggling against a wind that Renai couldn't feel, that didn't disturb the fog on either side of the dead man's stone path. A wind that existed for Miguel alone. She hoped he had the strength to endure it, to endure all the trials ahead of him.

She hadn't lied to him; he had a long way to go before he could rest.

The way through the Gates was never the same, and yet it was the same every time. In guiding her other dead, Renai had seen endless staircases and impossibly long hallways, narrow bridges and perilous mountain paths. Once, when guiding a child who'd died far too young, she'd walked down a road made of yellow bricks.

She knew her own part well, the Gatekeepers Miguel would face, the parts of himself he would sacrifice along the way, but each person saw the journey from their own perspective, translated the trials and challenges of the Underworld into their own unique dialect. She knew that the most difficult part for her would be facing forward, restraining the urge to constantly check that Miguel hadn't strayed from the path.

In the Underworld, she'd learned, you never looked back.

CHAPTER SIXTEEN

OVER A SPAN of a few hours that felt like they lasted for days, or over a few days that were squeezed down into a matter of hours — time was squishy on this side of things — Renai and Sal led Miguel through the Gates and into the depths of the Underworld. Each of the Gates stood at the center of a different New Orleans cemetery, and each one opened into a deeper level.

Ascending was simple. All Renai had to do was release her hold on the earth and she would rise, easily, almost involuntarily, as though she was naturally buoyant here, as though she belonged on the level of the First Gate, right on the threshold of the living world. The only way she'd ever managed to descend was through the Gates.

The journey through the Gates, a unique series of trials and choices and tests for each of the souls that Renai led, had taken on the casual familiarity of routine for her over the years. Some of the dead stayed behind in the Underworld, forever tending the garden that Nibo offered at the Second Gate or attending Babaco's eternal revels at the Fifth. Others were unable to meet the demands of the other Gatekeepers — like Plumaj, who took their Name at the Third Gate, or Bridgette, who took their Shadow at the Fourth — and were lost. Some managed the entire descent, only to be weighed upon Barren's scales at the Sixth Gate and found wanting. As much as it wounded her to lose one of her dead, though, they weren't, ultimately, her responsibility.

Their Fortunes were.

Whether a soul ended up a lost shade or a denizen of the Underworld or, like Miguel Flores, made it all the way to the bottom of the Underworld and through the Final Gate to the Far Lands, Renai's duties were the same. Each day she met Sal at the First Gate, took possession of a coin of Fortune, and carried it all the way to the Thrones at the very bottom of things. There, she handed the coin to Papa Legba, the voodoo loa of the Crossroads, the being who opened the Final Gate to the Far Lands. What Legba did with the Fortunes, Sal had told her, was way above her pay grade. His too.

Once she'd delivered the coin, Renai would—with a wave and a "smell ya later" to Sal—let her wings unfurl and carry her out of the cold, silent darkness of the Thrones' domain. As she rose through the different levels of the Underworld, the world around her changed. One minute she flew blindly through an impenetrable night, the next in the depths of a thundercloud, the next through thick, cool fog eerily illuminated by moonlight and streetlamps. When she reached the top level of the Underworld—as close to the world of the living as she could get and where she chose to spend most of her time— Renai would stretch her wings and glide toward the one place she wanted to be, the place she'd never be able to go to again.

Home.

Renai slipped down through the fog and the tree canopy, swooping past the campus of Tulane University and the row of Greek housing and into the residential neighborhood that lay beyond. This area hadn't changed much in all the time she'd known it; even after the storm it had just gotten taller, with most folks rebuilding their homes and raising them up five feet in case another once-in-a-lifetime flood happened the following year. The houses in this part of Uptown were a more diverse bunch than you'd find in an older neighborhood. There, street after street was filled with identical shotgun doubles. Most of these were bigger single-family, two-story homes, the first floor converted from what had been just a dusty crawl space before the storm.

Even amid the mist and the trees and the strangeness of the Underworld, Renai could walk down these cracked and broken sidewalks with her eyes closed. She didn't need a map to know that Plum Street Sno-Balls was that way, that the Nix branch of the library was over there, and that Palmer Park, where she had stolen her first kiss from a neighborhood boy named Trent, was off in that direction. It was all so familiar that when she reached the house, she had to stop herself from checking the mailbox. There were no cars in the driveway, of course, but there was her father's herb garden lining the front where there used to be a porch, and there was her mother's lemon tree peeking up over the back fence.

Turns out you can *go home again,* she thought. *So long as you don't mind haunting it.*

A long set of stairs climbed from the sidewalk to the old front porch, now a screened-in balcony on the second floor. The front door, she knew, would be unlocked, as all doors were in the Underworld. Her childhood home would be full of everything she remembered: an antique curio cabinet that both her folks hated but couldn't get rid of because it had belonged to Renai's great-grandmother, a dining room table full of opened bills and grocery store receipts and clean laundry that had been folded but not put away, a mantel crowded with family pictures and junior high trophies and a souvenir coffee mug full of pens, above all of which hung a picture of Jesus, his heart visible in the center of his chest, glowing and crowned and encircled with thorns like barbed wire.

They hadn't kept her room "just the way she'd left it" as some kind of shrine to her like they did in the movies — her grandmother now slept in her old bed, even — but they hadn't tried to erase her from their daily lives, either. Pictures of Renai were everywhere, and bits and pieces of her life had survived her, a throw pillow once on her bed now on the family sofa, a school art project taped to her wall was now framed and hung in the kitchen. Every day without fail, her mother wore a cheap bracelet that she'd found in Renai's nightstand.

Renai knew all this because she could still catch glimpses of her family in the obsidian mirror that she could pull out of the same nowhere place where her wings lived, so long as her family was in the house on the living side of the veil and she managed to get the angle on the mirror just right. She'd watched them in the five years since her death — *spied* on them, honestly — her younger brother overcoming a learning disability in school, her parents moving her grandmother in when it became obvious she couldn't stay on her own anymore, her sister and her partner struggling to conceive. She'd read their lips and laughed when they did, even though she couldn't hear the joke. Wept sometimes, too, though they kept laughing.

Much as she could use the small measure of comfort that looking in on their lives granted her, Renai didn't make her way up the stairs. Partly because she didn't have the energy to struggle with the mirror, and partly because—even though they were literal worlds away—she knew better than to track the mud from her filthy feet onto her momma's fresh cleaned floors. Instead, she went around the side of the house, to the small apartment that her father had built in the former crawl space when they'd raised the house, hoping to rent it out to college kids to help pay off the ongoing Katrina repairs that the insurance company had screwed them out of. Since the ceiling down here barely cleared six feet, he'd had trouble attracting tenants for long enough to be worth the hassle. So now the family used it as storage space, and Renai took advantage of the old furniture and working bathroom to make herself a place to live in the land of the dead.

After a long, hot shower, Renai felt like a human being again, or as close as a dead-and-resurrected girl like her could get, anyway. She put on a pair of pajama pants and a moth-eaten Tulane T-shirt that had once belonged to her older sister. Her whole wardrobe had come out of a box of stuff that was supposed to go to Goodwill and ended up down here. After a quick meal of a peanut-butter-and-honey sandwich—she made a mental note to scavenge some more non-perishables from the hurricane supplies in the pantry —she lay down on the inflatable mattress that served as her bed and scrolled through her phone, hoping she could distract herself from the events of the day long enough to quiet her mind and fall asleep.

When memes and celebrity gossip brought her no satisfaction, she propped her phone up on a pillow and started the next episode of *Treme*. In life, she'd been more into horror movies and dark fantasies, having been in the grip of a minor goth phase in the part of her teens when she developed those sorts of tastes, but since her resurrection, she'd found herself desperate for any depictions of modern-day life, especially of New Orleans.

Hellraiser lost a lot of its menace when you had actually seen a doorway into Hell.

After only a few minutes, Renai gave up on the show, too, and shut her phone off, rolling onto her back and staring up at the ceiling. Her mind kept chewing on the events of the day. Some souls were easier than others, and Miguel had been a hard one, but she'd gotten him down to the Thrones and the Final Gate. After that, she no longer felt the weight of responsibility, neither her self-imposed obligation to her dead nor the Thrones-induced burden of the coin of Fortune. She hoped that Miguel was satisfied with the Far

Land the Thrones had sent him to, but those decisions weren't hers to make. She was a guide, not a judge.

So he wasn't what kept her thoughts churning. It was all her extracurriculars: Mason and Ramses and her memories and Sal.

In the five years she'd been a psychopomp, she'd had little contact with the gods — aside from the Gatekeepers, of course — so Mason coming to see her felt portentous in a way that twisted everything else that had happened to her since.

She hadn't said anything to Sal about meeting a god, nor was she entirely sure why she'd kept it a secret. She'd checked for the name Ramses St. Cyr in the giant eerie book where Plumaj kept the names of the dead, but she'd only managed to steal a quick peek without Sal noticing. Her mentor had seemed anxious and cagey, too, especially when she'd brought up the Hallows. *I know how it weighs on you when the Hallows are comin' up,* he'd said, and he hadn't given her a chance to ask him what that meant. He knew that her memories were as full of holes as a pair of cheap stockings, but did he know that she remembered nothing at all about the Hallows? That those three days were blank spaces in every year since her resurrection? Did he know why?

Could it be a coincidence that Mason, whoever he really was, had chosen a time when the Underworld's order was thrown into chaos to ask a psychopomp for help?

Above her, the passage of someone — some family member she'd only see in her mirror's reflection ever again — made the ceiling groan and creak. She wondered if they ever heard her moving around, if they knew they were haunted, or just thought they had another family of possums living down here. She didn't even know for sure who the footsteps belonged to, and she missed them so much that it ached. She'd given up on ever seeing the living world again and, in the same way, had given up on remembering what happened to her during the Hallows. She'd tried notebooks and Polaroids and digital recorders, none of which had survived until November 3rd, when she'd wake in the grip of what felt like an epic hangover and no memory of the previous three days.

Renai groaned and sat up, pressing the heels of her hands against her eyes like she could squeeze the thoughts out. Her chances for sleep were diminishing rapidly. She reached out and turned on the small flat-screen she'd . . . acquired . . . her first year in the Underworld, when she'd found her brother's old Nintendo buried at the bottom of the Goodwill box. She didn't know if the television on the living side of things had disappeared from the house on Greek row that she'd taken it from, or if only echoes of things were carried over from one side to another. Frankly, she didn't care. She was dead and bored, and they were frat boys. Fuck 'em. After a couple of weeks, she'd gone back and taken their PlayStation, too.

In the flickering light of the TV, Renai saw a couple of shades watching her from the corner of the room. They didn't bother her too much here for some reason, but she never managed to escape their presence for good. She wouldn't mind them following her everywhere if they could hold a conversation. Just listening would be nice, if they would respond to her in any way that was more than repulsion or attraction. She'd tried, but talking to a shade was like talking to a rock. Worse, because rocks didn't bring their friends to help them creepy-stare-at-you for hours. She was so starved for human contact that she'd be cool with the shades hanging around if all they did was pick up a controller and play video games with her once in a while.

Her game finished loading, and she swirled the camera around her character, reminding herself where she was and what she'd been doing. She'd last saved out in the Capital Wasteland, about to descend into a cave that she'd finally gotten to a high-enough level to take on. Her character, who she'd named Bey, looked as close to her own appearance as she'd been able to get in the hours she'd spent tweaking it, except this version of her wore bulky power armor and carried a laser rifle. The hair was wrong, though; they always had such shitty options for a black woman's hair.

She had a flash, almost like a memory, of herself in the living world, wearing a badass leather jacket and her hair in a short natural puff. It occurred to her that she'd designed Bey to look just like this other Renai. She shook that thought away like all the others, though, and in just a few moments, she'd lost herself in this other world, Mason and Ramses and Sal and even the Hallows all forgotten. She couldn't solve any of that, not tonight anyway. Not by worrying about it.

But she could damn sure kill a few ghouls.

⚱

Almost a week went by, and every day was practically indistinguishable from the rest. Renai woke and wasted time scrolling through social media or playing video games or attending to her body's physical needs until she was scheduled to meet Sal at the First Gate, where he would hand over a coin of

Fortune. She'd guide that day's dead through the Gates, always checking Plumaj's book for the name Mason had given her and not finding it, nor getting a moment alone with the angel to ask if they'd remembered where they'd heard the name before.

She'd sign up for another random soul and then continue on, more and more convinced each day that Mason had tricked her somehow. She'd lead her soul through the rest of the Gates, showing them their true self with her mirror, cleansing them of their Shadow with the magic inside her, and leaving them at Barren's streetcar. She lost one soul to the fog, another to Babaco's never-ending party, and carried a third—a crib death who had spent only a few weeks in the living world—the whole way down to the Thrones and the Final Gate. Renai found it hard to hand the small bundle of Essence to one of the other dead there, even though she'd known all along that she wouldn't be able to cross the Gate herself, had known that she couldn't carry the soul on to Paradise, the Far Land that the infant had earned in her short joy-filled life.

Each day Renai intended to ask Sal what he knew about the Hallows and Mason and her place in everything going on, and each day she found herself too exhausted or emotionally frayed or just plain scared to actually ask. Each night she'd find herself back here, either so worn out that sleep dragged her under without giving her a chance to reflect or so tightly wound with anxiety that she couldn't trust any of the conclusions that came to her. Each day blended so seamlessly with the one before it that she'd practically forgotten about Mason and his deal and the thief he'd asked her to find until four days before the Hallows began when, leading an elderly dead man through the Third Gate, she saw in the giant book of the dead that the next soul she'd been assigned to lead through the Underworld was none other than Ramses St. Cyr.

⌛

Even though Renai spent most of that night building Ramses up in her mind as some culture hero who laughed in the face of the gods, Death, and anyone else he damn well pleased, when Sal didn't show up at the First Gate like he was supposed to, it still took her by surprise.

She just stood there, stunned, struck by that disconnected feeling that came from closing your eyes for a few minutes in the afternoon and waking up in the dark of night hours later. She fidgeted with the dangling shirttails of one of her father's old blue dress shirts—coffee-stained and sleeves rolled up and still smelling of his aftershave—that she'd tied in a knot at her waist.

Renai dug the toe of her low-top canvas sneakers in the dirt. She checked her watch to be sure she had the time right. She called Sal's name, first like he was just in the other room, then shouting like he was lost.

A quiver of what-felt-like-memory from that other version of Renai told her that on the living side of things, she was used to waiting on Sal. But the Sal she knew was always on time. She gave him five minutes, then ten. After that she gave the Gate—on this side of things: a huge pair of brass and ivory doors that were, impossibly, too big for the frame that held them—a half-hearted shove, not surprised to find that they didn't budge.

"Well, what the hell am I supposed to do now?" she muttered to herself.

Sal's voice came from one of the trees above her. "How about you start by explaining yourself?" he asked.

She looked up but couldn't spot him among the foliage. Her heart began to flutter, a nervous, guilty feeling. The psychopomp sounded pissed, suspicious even. Something had gone wrong with Ramses' collection, that much was obvious. The question was, how bad? Had Sal known about her deal with Mason and guided the dead boy himself, just to keep Renai away from Ramses? Or was it something worse?

It occurred to her, then, that she really had no idea what Salvatore was capable of doing, what he might know. She'd always thought of him as a friend, but she couldn't trust that he had her back on this one. The stakes were just too high; bigger than life or death. Salvation or damnation. *This is what I get for fucking around with gods,* she thought, and then, in her grandmother's voice: *You ever got to choose between a truth and a lie, tell the truth and shame the devil.*

So that's just what she did. She told Sal all about meeting a god in a coffee shop, and the deal she'd made. Tried to explain how desperately she wanted out of the monotony and the loneliness of the Underworld, even if it meant crossing through the Final Gate and into the Far Lands. Admitted that she'd been waiting for Ramses' death to show up in Plumaj's book, that she'd been deceiving Sal for days, even if her lie was one of omission.

As she spoke, she found a vine climbing the exposed brick of a crumbling, unmaintained tomb, and stared at one of its leaves as it trembled in the soft breeze of the Underworld, fixing her gaze on it in order to keep herself from searching the trees for Sal.

The words spilled out of her in a kind of meditative trance. She didn't know for sure that Sal was alone, or even if he was still there. For all she knew, the only ones hearing her story might be the small group of shades that had gathered among the tombs as she spoke. Once she began, though, it was less about Sal hearing and more about getting the whole thing out. It felt strangely familiar, unburdening herself of something unpleasant and secret to an unseen listener, like a trip to the confessional from her youth.

When she finished, Sal said nothing for a few seconds that felt like hours. When he spoke, he no longer sounded angry—only tired. "There just ain't no side of this ain't fucked from hell to breakfast, is there?" he asked, though it seemed rhetorical. Then she heard wing beats and claws scrambling on granite, and she turned to find him perched on a nearby tomb.

"How long have you been—"

Sal squawked out an angry caw, whipping his head around to glare at her with one black eye. "Nope. We are not at the Renai-gets-to-ask-questions part of this yet. The fuck were you thinking, making a bargain with a god like Seth?"

Renai's own anger, rising in her own defense, slipped away in sudden confusion. "Hold up. Who said anything about a Seth? The god who came to see me called himself Mason."

"Ugly sumbitch? Goofy ears and red hands?"

"Yeah, no. My dude was too pretty and he knew it. And his hands were as brown as the rest of him."

"And I bet you dollars to dick-punches he wasn't no bricklayer, no matter what he called himself. He give you anything? This nose a'mine might know him. These fuckin' deities leave their stink all over anything they touch."

"No," she said, "he texted me Ramses' name."

"Figures," Sal muttered. "Why would they make it easy for us?"

"But whoever he is, I think he's a Trickster like Jude." She started to tell Sal how Mason had worn the face of Jude Dubuisson at first, but didn't get far before Sal spit out a sentence that was just the word "fuck" in all its grammatical flexibility. "Yeah," Renai said. "That's what I thought, too."

"Tricksters! Why's it always gotta be Tricksters? Like my thrice-be-damned Hallows ain't complicated enough with—" He bit down on whatever he was about to say, his feathers ruffling in frustration. "So we got some coffee shop god after this missing dead kid, too. Wonderful. This Mason tell you what he wanted?"

Renai shrugged. "Just the location where Ramses is keeping whatever he stole from him."

Sal blinked, and then, despite the fact that he didn't have any, whistled between his teeth. "Well," he said, "I hate to crap in your cornflakes, but there's a teensy bit of a problem with that particular exchange." Renai shrugged at him, spreading her hands in a spit-it-out-already gesture. "Your boy Ramses did us a runner. He wasn't there when I went to get him."

"Like, he died somewhere else, or—"

"He. Wasn't. There." Renai raised an eyebrow at him, and Sal dipped his beak in apology. "Sorry. Just been a shit day that's like to get shittier." He explained, then, how he'd gone to collect Ramses at the moment of his death, like any other, only to find that the boy wasn't anywhere to be found. And that his escape, however he'd managed it, had left a wound behind, a stinking, shrieking place of *wrongness* that said that finding him wasn't so much a matter of "if" as it was "how soon."

When he finished, Renai couldn't think of anything to say. She wanted to make a joke, but all that was running through her mind was a lame "disturbance in the Force" joke that she didn't think would do the trick. Thankfully, Sal broke the silence for her. "So this death-dodging so-and-so caught a Trickster with his pants down and robbed him blind, huh?"

Renai flushed. She had a feeling she and Sal didn't have the same idea of what Mason would look like without pants on. "Seems that way," she said. "That give you any ideas on how to find Ramses?"

"Not a one. But it means I'm starting to like this little bastard in spite of myself."

Renai grinned. "So now what?"

"Now is what I came here to do in the first place. Gotta check with all the 'pomps who made deliveries today, and hope that this fuck-up is of the misfiled-paperwork kind and not the breaking-a-fundamental-rule-of-reality kind." He rose to his full height and turned, in little shuffling steps, until his beak faced more or less north, "Toward the Lake," as a New Orleanian would say. Toward Holt Cemetery and the Second Gate, Renai knew. He glanced back. "You coming?"

"But what if it is?" she asked, unfurling her own wings.

"What if it's what?"

"The rule-breaking kind of problem."

Sal sighed. "Let's cross that apocalypse when we get to it."

CHAPTER SEVENTEEN

JANUS'S TWO FACES keep watch in both directions at once. Qin and Yuchi ward off both evil spirits and mundane threats. A bull, a dragon, an eagle, and a giant all stand guard, together protecting the whole of Iceland.

They are depicted in stone throughout the world: the mace-wielding warriors called dvarapala; the fierce, nurturing lions called shí shī; the grotesque monsters called gargoyles.

Likewise stand vigil the ravens in the Tower of London; the decommissioned fighter jet at the entrance of a military base; the angel with the flaming sword outside the Garden of Eden.

They stand always at the gates: Protectors. Watchers. Guardians.

⧗

Renai followed Sal in a short flight across the city. The journey that usually meant hours of walking along whatever path the Underworld had dictated for the dead she was leading took only minutes on the wing. They mostly skimmed across the treetops, with few landmarks breaking the monotony: a church steeple here, the stretch of Bayou St. John there. She glanced down through the gap in the trees at the water that ran too viscous, too dark to actually be water. Sometimes the Underworld made the dead brave a narrow bridge over a bayou filled with blood or tar or molten iron in order to get to the Second Gate. Sometimes they were only given stepping-stones. Sometimes they had to swim. Renai couldn't tell what kind of crossing waited for the dead in the brief glimpse she caught of it, but she was glad for her wings all the same.

Just on the other side of the bayou, they slid in a slow glide down to the ground, Sal barely waiting for Renai's feet to settle on the earth before he scrambled to a perch on her shoulder. She didn't need the directions he grunted at her—she knew the way to the Second Gate as well as he did—but she'd long ago grown used to Sal's gruff demeanor.

After a few minutes of walking through trees and fog, past shotgun doubles—most of them homes, but many of them converted into law firms and boutiques and bookstores and coffee shops—and a supermarket, past the bright red bulk of a Museum line streetcar half-sunk into the mire, past a handful of wandering solitary shades, Renai cleared her throat. "I've been thinking," she said.

"Thought I smelled somethin' burnin'," Sal muttered, but it was a knee-jerk response, devoid of both bite and mirth. Renai ignored it.

"Since we're here, we ought to ask Nibo if he's seen Ramses," she said.

"And that wouldn't be an obnoxious waste of time because . . ."

"Because Nibo is the loa in charge of the unburied, unremembered dead?"

Sal was quiet for a few steps, and then chuckled. "Not bad, Raines," he said. "Not bad." When the gray concrete and black iron gates of Holt Cemetery rose up out of the gloom, Sal tapped her shoulder with his clawed foot. ".Since it was your idea," he said, "why don't you do the talking?"

Holt Cemetery had originally been a potter's field—a burial ground for those who could afford nothing better—and it was one of the few cemeteries in New Orleans where the dead were laid to rest in the earth. In the world of the living, it was sad and gray: a few struggling patches of brown grass, a sprawl of crowded plots with leaning or broken headstones—sometimes no stone at all, just a wooden cross with a hand-lettered name—all tucked behind the fence of a community college's baseball field. In the land of the dead, Holt Cemetery flourished: every plot covered with vibrant flower beds growing over and into one another, a striking, vibrant riot of color, like a garden planted by Jackson Pollock. At its center a gigantic oak towered over the whole seven acres, and at the base of that oak stood the Gatekeeper, Nibo.

Like Oussou and Masaka—who Renai knew by reputation but had never met, since the twins always opened the First Gate from the living side of things —Nibo was a loa of the Ghede family. His long, lean frame was wrapped in a tailor-cut three-piece suit, dark pants and a cream-colored waistcoat. His light blue jacket was covered with a pattern that belonged on an old white lady's sofa: blooms of long, thin petals in pastel shades of red, orange, and yellow with pale green vines snaking all over. Set in contrast with his dark brown skin and in the confident way he wore it, Nibo made every inch of that jacket work.

He leaned against the giant oak like everyone who saw him owed him money. As they drew closer, Renai watched him pull a pistachio from his coat pocket, crack it open, and pop the green nut in his mouth, letting the two halves of the shell drop to the ground. He did it with the mechanical, unconscious motion of someone cracking their knuckles, over and over. When Renai and Sal got close enough that he recognized them, Nibo's typically dour expression brightened. His smile revealed teeth flecked with diamonds.

"Look at these muh'fuckas rightchea!" he shouted, his high, nasal voice shattering the silence of the graveyard. Once they crossed over to him, he spoke in a quieter voice. "I say, what you done brought your old friend Nibo, today?"

"You a poet now, Nibs?" Renai said, a smile teasing at the corners of her lips.

Nibo peered at her for a moment, until her meaning caught up to him. "Girl, you play too much. But f'true? Ain't the rhyme that makes a poet, it's in the soul." He rested his fingertips lightly on the lapel of his jacket. "And you know poor Nibo has always had a sensitive soul."

"Sensitive is one word for it," Sal muttered.

"Oh, hush, you," Nibo snapped, not unkindly. "Them Thrones shoulda gave you an old hound dog shape to wear, the way you go moping 'round with that sour puss." He craned his neck to peer past Renai's shoulder at the empty path behind them. "Well, now, y'all done lost your dead already?"

"Something like that," Renai said. "We were wondering if you'd seen him."

Nibo reached into his vest pocket and pulled out a pair of gold-framed spectacles on a thin chain, the rings on his fingers winking with diamonds and amethysts. Holding the glasses up to his eyes, he took a step closer to Renai, studying her. Nibo's impeccably shined shoes crunched on the pile of pistachio shells littering the ground at his feet. "Have I seent your lost dead, mmm? Guess that means he ain't one a'them shades flittin' about. You think he a'one of my little flowers?"

"The thought had crossed my mind," Renai said.

He dropped the glasses so that they hung, dangling, from his vest, and slipped his arm, as casual as if he'd done it a hundred times, around the crook of her elbow. He gave her a gentle tug, more playful than actually insistent, and clicked his tongue at her. "Well, come on and have a look, then. Let's see if we cain't find this lost lamb a'yours."

Nibo waved an arm at his garden cemetery and the fog parted, revealing a sparse crowd of the dead. They were working amid the flower beds, pulling weeds and pruning vines and watering the soil, but they didn't appear to be toiling. Here and there, two or three were gathered, chatting in those eerie, whispery non-voices the dead possessed. One man appeared to be napping. "We got Buddy Bolden here, bless his heart. Genius with that cornet, but he come to us penniless and crazy as a shithouse rat. We got Robert Charles, too, him and a few others of them that died in the riot he was at the center of. Some of them boys from the UpStairs Lounge fire, too. Most of my flowers you wouldn't know, though. That's 'cause I tend to them that got no one else to care, them that died unremembered, unburied."

Renai had to turn away, swallowing past the sudden lump in her throat. She knew that Nibo's garden was a comfort, a best-case scenario for many of the dead, but no matter how many times she'd seen his "flowers," as he called them, it struck her to the core every time.

"So what you say, gorgeous?" Nibo asked. "You see anybody you recognize?"

Renai reached up and nudged Sal with a knuckle. "You awake up there?" she asked.

"We never actually saw him," the psychopomp said. "All we have is a name. Ramses St. Cyr."

Nibo said nothing, just gave a curt nod, and the fog rolled back in. He crossed over to the oak, his footsteps crunching on discarded pistachio shells once more. From the pocket that wasn't filled with nuts, he took out a black iron key shaped with the whorls and sharp edges of his veve, which he slid into a hole in the oak, turning it with a loud click. The base of the giant tree split and cracked into the shape of two doors. The Second Gate.

His meaning was clear, and disappointment sank to the bottom of Renai's belly like a stone. *Did you really think it would be that easy?* she thought. She mumbled her gratitude to the loa and stepped toward the Gate, but he stopped her with a gentle hand on her forearm.

"I ain't said no 'cause I won't," he said, his voice gentle and kind, "but 'cause I cain't." He held a glass bottle now instead of a key, filled with a mostly clear liquid that had particles of something leafy floating in it, like loose-leaf tea that hadn't been brewed. She hadn't seen him reach into his jacket for it or pick it up from the ground, because he hadn't. One minute it hadn't been there, and then it was. A nice little reminder that as friendly and as compassionate as Nibo was, he and all the other Gatekeepers were still loa. Still gods.

Renai took a breath before she asked her next question, doing her best to scrub the frustration from her voice. "And why can't you?" she asked.

"If this boy a'yours had made it to my garden, I'd know him, clear as sunshine. But if he's lost 'neath the waters? I gots ta be on the other side of things where my Voice has real power in order to call him up." He raised the bottle toward Renai and then to Sal in a gesture equal parts "sorry" and "to your health," before putting it to his lips and taking a few swallows. As the liquor swirled around, Renai could see the bundles of herbs and the split-open pepper pods that made up Nibo's special recipe. The loa swore it could heal any wound, if you could stand its fire. Sal swore it would strip the paint off a Buick.

Nibo pulled away from the bottle with a grateful sigh, smacking his lips. "That'll make you say shit and goddamn," he said, letting out a loud *woop*. "That'll make you say mothafucka!"

Sal squawked out a laugh and launched through the Second Gate, vanishing through the oak tree into the fog of the Underworld at its center. Before Renai could follow, Nibo spoke again. "Couple three days," he said. "Once them Hallows start. Then I'll be able to slip over to the other side and look for this boy a'yours. Deal?"

"Deal," Renai said, grateful for the way Nibo had turned things around and made it seem like she was doing him a favor. She wouldn't call Nibo a friend, exactly, but he was kind to her when he didn't have to be. And yet, as she stepped through the Second Gate and down into a lower level of the Underworld, she couldn't help thinking that if they hadn't found Ramses by the time the Hallows started, it would already be too late.

Moving through the Second Gate had left them standing in Holt Cemetery once more, but a level deeper in the Underworld. The changes from one level to the next were small at first. Trivial, even. Renai would almost say irrelevant, except that no one, not even the dead, failed to notice that something was different.

The most obvious change on this side of the Gate was that what obscured their surroundings here wasn't fog, but a thick, relentless rain. In the living world, she knew, the rain would be hissing against hot pavement and rushing toward catch basins, but here in the forest of the Underworld, the ground underfoot turned into a squelching muck almost instantly.

The other change was more subtle, a feeling more than an observation. Everything here felt less real than it did on the other side of the Gate: flatter and dingier and more vague, like the special effects from a movie ten years old. And things only got more and more abstract the deeper you went, she knew.

"Least it's warm out," Sal said to Renai over the hushed white-noise sound of the rainfall. "Especially since we're only a couple of days away from the Hallows. Come next month, I'll be freezing my nuts off."

Renai let out a sarcastic huff. "Do birds even have—"

"The dog-shape's got balls to spare, thank you very much. And ten nipples that hate the cold, too."

Renai smiled and started to answer, but that was right when the first arrow came whizzing out of the sky and plunged into the soft earth, its shaft still quivering, humming like a plucked guitar string.

Then came another, and another. Sal cursed and took to the air, realizing just as Renai did that they'd gotten caught up in a trial of some soul—led by some other psychopomp—and though he didn't need to say it, he yelled for her to run. Sal was small enough to hurtle through the hail of arrows in the air, but Renai's huge, diaphanous wings would get chewed up if she unfurled them, so she tucked them tight against her back and ran.

Renai couldn't say how long it took for them to escape—she lost herself in the motion, the slapping of her feet against wet earth, the tense and flex and swing of it, her concentration locked on ensuring her footing and breathing deep and trying not to flinch when an arrow sliced the air close enough that she could feel it slash by. She didn't stop when she felt a punch of pain in her left shoulder, only glanced at it long enough to see that her skin there was unbroken. Whether the arrows were blunt-tipped or if she was impervious to them, she didn't know, but either way she ran on with a wild grin on her face.

One of the things she'd learned on waking up in this strange new life of hers was that a storm lived inside of her. It rose when she was excited, when she was horny, when Sal said something really, really clever. She'd learned to channel its power, to use it in her work, but sometimes—like when she hauled ass through deadly rain, for instance—Renai's thoughts were empty of everything but the fierce joy of the howling of the wind and the pounding rain. So she ran, and at some point the arrows quit falling and the rain slacked off and she reached the low iron fence that surrounded the raised tombs of Lafayette No. 2, but she didn't remember any of it happening. It was only when she stopped at the entrance of the cemetery—a gate but *not* a Gate— that Renai managed to push the spirit back down to where it lived inside of her, so she could see and think clearly once more.

That's when she realized that she'd run so fast and so far that she'd left Sal behind.

Renai waited for a while at the cemetery's entrance, catching her breath, squeezing the rainwater out of her dreads as best she could, expecting Sal's raven-shape to come winging out of the downpour any second. She chewed at her lip and checked her watch every minute or so for ten minutes, and still he didn't come. *Okay, girl,* she thought, in her mother's voice, *you might be pretty as a rose and strong as an oak, but God ain't gave you roots. You got to get moving.*

She knew what she ought to do. As a psychopomp, she'd gotten used to leaving people behind. She could hear Sal in her head: *'Pomps only move in one direction, Raines. Forward.* Her main responsibility was always to the coin of Fortune she carried. No matter what happened, she had to deliver it to the end of the line.

That need crawled inside her, a physical thing, like a rumbling hunger and nagging, nervous tension and that maddening have-to-sneeze-but-can't-itch all rolled into one. A contract scrimshawed onto her bones at the moment of her rebirth. She had no idea what would happen to her if she couldn't find Ramses, couldn't find his coin. Would the need fade? Would it consume her? Continuing to look for Ramses meant turning her back, but it's what Salvatore would tell her to do. It's what she'd been taught to do her whole life when she didn't know what choice to make.

You did the work.

Besides, Sal could handle himself. He might wear the shape of a scavenging bird or a tired old dog, but what lived within that skin was a spirit of Death. No one lived forever, but Renai was pretty sure it would take more than an arrow—or even a whole sky full of them—to do real lasting damage to her mentor.

She'd been wrong before, though. She rubbed at the still-tender bruise on her shoulder, where the arrow had hit her. She knew for a fact that they could hurt. Maybe Sal wasn't as tough as she'd thought. Maybe he'd been wounded and was even now waiting for her to come back and rescue him. And what if the arrows really had killed him?

What happened to psychopomps when they died?

Renai had to grit her teeth to keep her wings from unfurling. For every day of the last five years, Sal had been by her side: guiding, teaching, consoling. For the first time, he needed her. She didn't care that flying into that hail of arrows might mean sacrificing her wings, didn't care that she had a deal with Mason and an obligation to the Thrones.

The only thing that stopped her from going back to look for her mentor were the words he'd told her over and over again. Only one direction. Forward. Renai closed her eyes and slipped her wings away into whatever nowhere place they went when they weren't unfurled, allowed herself just a single moment of weakness—one last glance behind her to see if Sal had found his way through the hail of arrows—and then she put it all behind her and followed the path of raised, smooth paving stones to the center of Lafayette No. 2, where the Third Gate awaited.

⧖

Lafayette No. 2 looked like a combination of the cemeteries that housed the first two Gates: it shared the customary aboveground tombs made of brick and mortar and plaster with St. Louis No. 1, but it also had a number of concrete slabs about half a foot tall that marked belowground burials, like in Holt. Unlike the other two cemeteries, though, on this side of things the Third Gate's location didn't teem with flowers or grass in all of the areas surrounding the graves.

In the Underworld, it was filled with bookshelves.

It always felt like something out of a dream for Renai—even more so than the rest of the Underworld—to walk out of a forest and into an archive, without leaving behind the trees. There were no walls save the fog that hung everywhere, no ceiling save the canopy of oak leaves high overhead. All the bookshelves were built exactly the same, over ten feet tall and just a few feet wide, with six shelves and a ladder with dangerously thin rungs built in. The books they held were also all identical, thick and tall and bound in brown leather, with gold lettering on the spine indicating a year and a span of letters, like encyclopedias or dictionaries.

She'd always wondered how the books never got rained on, how the moisture from the fog never spoiled them, but Sal had never had an answer for her. Renai tried not to think about Sal and kept walking down the center aisle of the cemetery. The pristine condition of this archive had just become another one of those things about the Underworld that she'd had to accept. She'd never had to wonder what was recorded in all those books, though, because the Gatekeeper of the Third Gate was the one who'd written them all.

As Renai approached the center of the cemetery, her view of the Gatekeeper was partly blocked by a huge lectern, a tall, broad bookstand made of wrought iron and gold. The edge of an open book peeked up above the carving of an eagle, its wings spread and talons outstretched, that adorned the top of the lectern, its wings forming the platform where the huge books that lined the shelves in this place could lay open and flat.

The base was iron and made up of the busts of twelve men, all but one of them facing out, one turned inward. The Greek letters A and Ω were stamped on the lectern's broad column in ivory and gold. Depending on the faith or heritage of her dead, the letters might be א and ת in Hebrew, or a phrase in Arabic script that Renai hadn't yet been able to find on the internet. When the letters changed, the iconography on the lectern changed as well. Off to the side of the lectern, a microphone—a slitted chrome bulb the size of Renai's fist—stood on its own stand, a single thick wire trailing off into the trees. Once Renai was close enough to hear the soft persistent *scritch-scritch-scritch* of a pen nib on paper, she could smell the licorice-sweet scent of fennel, coming from the angel writing in the book.

They called themselves Plumaj and answered to the title Ghede like any other Gatekeeper loa. While Renai had learned in her time in the Underworld that the gods had a habit of wandering from one pantheon to another, she'd always wondered if the other loa were also angels, or if Plumaj was somehow special. It had always seemed impolite to ask.

Plumaj had pale beige-tinged white skin, like the flesh of an under-ripe pear, and the soft, brown wings of a barn owl. Like the only other angel Renai had ever met, Plumaj had stark white, pupil-less eyes, and—also like that other angel—dressed like they'd run through a thrift store and grabbed whatever their hands touched. Plumaj wore a faded red flannel button-down shirt with frayed cuffs and the buttons undone over a Ninja Turtles T-shirt, an inflated yellow life vest from a commercial airplane, and bright purple pants with GEAUX written in cracked gold lettering down one leg and TIGERS down the other, a price tag still stuck to the waistband. The angel was short and wide, with thick thighs stretching the legs of the sweatpants and multiple chins folding up when they bent their head to their book.

The angel leaned their head out from behind the book and smiled, a warm, genuine gesture that should have made Renai feel welcome. Instead, her scalp felt tight and her mouth went dry. She had to tell herself to stay calm, to breathe. Plumaj had never given Renai a reason not to trust them. In fact, they'd been kinder to her than anyone else on this side of things, up to and including Salvatore. If any of the other Gatekeepers had treated her the way that Plumaj had, she'd probably be tight enough with them to have a special handshake with them by now. But Renai couldn't get past those cold, empty eyes.

The same eyes as the angel who had killed her.

"Renaissance Raines," Plumaj said, in the soft, pleasant voice of an elementary school teacher. "I was starting to wonder if you'd grace us with your presence today." Most people who said shit like that were trying to make you feel bad for being late. Coming from Plumaj, it sounded like they'd actually been thinking about her.

"Caught a little drama," Renai said, waving her hand behind her to show the absence of the dead man she ought to have with her, and of Sal. "So the only presence you're getting graced with today is mine."

Plumaj clicked their tongue and frowned. "No one laments the loss of one of the flock quite like a shepherd."

For a brief second, Renai got a chill, thinking that Plumaj knew that Ramses had gone missing, that this wasn't the calamity Sal had worried it was. But then it occurred to her that the angel just thought that, like so many others, Ramses had wandered off the path and become a shade.

"I do not envy you your task," the angel continued. "Is there any aid I might provide?"

Not unless you want to fly on upstairs and ask your boss if he can spare a minute, Renai thought. She didn't say it, though, because despite their pleasant, accommodating nature, Plumaj didn't have much of a sense of humor. They wouldn't be offended by the joke, exactly, but they'd either take it literally or think Renai was mocking them. Either one wouldn't go well.

"Yeah, maybe," she said instead, trying to keep her voice casual. "What can you tell me about Ramses St. Cyr?"

The angel's brow furrowed in thought, and they tapped their lips with the tip of their pen, a quill made from one of their own feathers. "There is a certain familiar ring to it," they said. "Of course, I've always been partial to saints." They leaned a wink in Renai's direction, a gesture made eerie by the angel's pupil-less eyes. Renai's laugh sounded forced even to her own ears. Plumaj made a come-closer wave toward Renai with the feather in their hand. "Shall we have a look?"

From where she was standing, Renai could see the open pages of the book, but the text all looked the same to her, as if Plumaj had simply written the same letter—a ligature of A and Ω—over and over again. Humming a tune that Renai recognized from years of Christmas Eve masses as "Gloria in Excelsis Deo," the angel used a ribbon to mark their place, and another to open the book a few dozen pages further along, coming to a list written in English: a column each for names, times, and locations, and a space for a brief description of a manner of death.

Each day of her life since her resurrection, Renai had chosen a name from this book or one just like it, the name of a person living in New Orleans whose time in the living world was coming to an end. And every following day, Sal would guide that soul through the First Gate and give her their coin of Fortune. Yesterday, since she'd been watching for it ever since her deal with Mason, she'd chosen Ramses' name from this very list.

Today, his name was gone.

If the dead made it this far, they would write their Name in the book, a scrap of their Essence left behind so that their memory could live on in the living world without them. Once they'd given up their Name, the dead became less distinct, blurring at the edges like an image projected by a lens just slightly out of focus. Not ghostly, like the shades, but definitely less like a breathing person and more like the memory of one.

Renai had done the same thing once herself, though she didn't remember it, didn't like to think about it. Had resurrection returned her Name to her, or had it remained here in one of Plumaj's books? Could that explain why her memories were all jumbled up? Why she had a storm living inside of her? And was that why Ramses' name had disappeared as well?

She'd gotten so caught up in her thoughts that it took Renai a moment to realize that Plumaj had stopped humming, had turned back to one of the other pages in their book, the strange, indecipherable records of each person's deeds and misdeeds in their time in the living world.

Plumaj stared down at the page in front of them, their lips pursed. After a moment, the angel shook their head. "I apologize," they said. "I seem to have spoken in error. That soul is not among my records."

Plumaj's face twisted in frustration, mirroring Renai's own feelings. It seemed strange that the angel couldn't remember the name of the boy Renai had chosen just yesterday, but then, he was one name out of all of those who died in this city, day after day. Maybe it wasn't so surprising.

"And yet," Plumaj said, "that name seems so familiar. I can't recall—"

Renai cut the angel off. "Can't you just look up the last thing you wrote about him?" she asked.

Plumaj frowned again. "It does not work that way, I fear. Though it is my charge to transcribe every event and choice and triumph of the lives that pass through this Gate, I am not granted the vision to see that life until it is their appointed time." They set their pen down and folded their hands, their usually expressive face suddenly unreadable. "And why, Renaissance Raines, have you come to me asking after this person? Who is Ramses St. Cyr to you?"

Renai lifted one shoulder in a halfhearted shrug. "Just somebody I promised to help find," Renai said. Somehow, she didn't think Sal would want her talking about a soul going missing; he'd seemed far too eager to keep it quiet until they knew exactly what they were dealing with. The fact that Ramses had somehow been wiped out of Plumaj's ledger told her that whatever this was, it was bad.

Plumaj nodded. "'Of all tools used in the shadow of the moon,'" they said, quietly, as if they didn't care whether Renai heard them or not, "'men are most apt to get out of order.'"

"That's deep," Renai said. "Is that from Psalms?" Like most cradle Catholics, Renai couldn't recite the Bible chapter and verse like other Christians seemed able to.

"That ain't scripture," Sal said, "it's fuckin' *Moby Dick*." Renai spun around and there he was, his shaggy fur and mournful eyes and his lop-sided doggie grin. She lunged at him, throwing her arms around his neck and squeezing him tight. "Aww-right, aww-right," he said after a moment, pulling away from her, "easy on the fur, Raines."

"What the hell happened to you?" Renai asked, letting Sal get far enough away that she could look at him, but not taking her hands off him. "You stop off somewhere for a couple of daiquiris?"

"Later," he said. "We still got miles to go before we sleep."

"You don't sleep," she said, not caring how much sass was in her voice, grateful that Sal was okay and pissed that he'd vanished on her all at once.

But if Sal heard her, he ignored it. "You mind letting us through?" he said, speaking to Plumaj over Renai's shoulder. "We got an appointment downstairs."

Plumaj, who had gone back to writing in their giant book as soon as Renai's back was turned, nodded absently and plucked an iron key from the pocket of their flannel shirt. They pressed it into their book, into the crease where the leaves were bound together. A turn of the wrist, a click, and then the book and the lectern and the sky and the earth all split in two as the Third Gate swung open wide.

Sal went through first just like before, without a word of thanks, without looking back to see if Renai was following. *Taking that "psychopomps only move forward" advice a little too literal,* she thought. She didn't know if he'd heard what Plumaj told her, didn't have any idea where he was leading her. She'd never seen him so driven, so distracted. *Who is Ramses St. Cyr to you,* Plumaj had asked her.

But the real questions is, she thought, as she followed the psychopomp through the Gate, *who is Ramses to you, Salvatore? Who is he to you?*

CHAPTER EIGHTEEN

ALMOST AS SOON as they crossed through the Third Gate, Sal started telling Renai why he'd fallen so far behind her. According to the psychopomp, an arrow had hit him right in the wing bone, which sent him tumbling out of the sky. "I tried to tough it out," he said, "you know, walk it off, but when it still hurt like a bastard after a few minutes of hopping along like a fuckin' windup toy, I gave the damn thing up for broken and slipped on the dog-skin. So I hate to say it, but we're grounded until the other shape heals up."

"I don't mind walking," Renai said. "I'm just glad you're okay."

For a few minutes, they walked in silence through a New Orleans that felt increasingly like a dream. Even though the rain had stopped and the fog had lifted, Renai still couldn't see much beyond the trees surrounding them. Night had fallen and, without a moon or stars or streetlights, the world had turned into an inky-black void. They didn't have far to walk through this darkness, thankfully, even though Saint Roch's was—in the living world— miles away from Lafayette Cemetery. The deeper one went into the Under- world, the closer things got. It was as if each Gate was a funnel, squeezing the city into a more compact version of itself. So a journey that would have nor- mally taken hours on foot only lasted about twenty minutes.

Something about Sal's explanation nagged at Renai, felt off. She tried to picture it as he'd described it. She'd seen Sal change skins before, one form vomiting up the other, even though the dog was an order of magnitude larger than the raven. It was both revolting and fascinating. She had no idea how the process worked, though, didn't know if he had an infinite number of the two shapes inside of him like an eternally renewing set of Russian nesting dolls, or if he swapped out his shapes from the same nowhere place where her wings and her mirror came from.

What she did know is that when he swapped shapes, it happened pretty much instantly. Which made her wonder if he was telling her the whole story. *Girl,* she thought, *you're letting the lower levels get to you.*

Down this deep, there were shades everywhere, blending in so perfectly with the gloomy night around them that it seemed like the air itself shifted and moved and *watched.* It made her skin crawl and got her—as her grandmother would have said—skittish as a five-tailed cat in a room full of rocking chairs. Nor did it help that the lingering presence of some soul's trial had their surroundings filled with rustling noises in the trees and an occasional growl from some large restless predator. It had to be that. Had to be. Because if she couldn't trust Sal, who *could* she trust?

But no matter what she told herself, she couldn't just let any dog, sleeping or otherwise, lie.

"Figuring out you had a broken wing took all that time?" she asked, trying to keep any suspicion out of her voice, not even looking at him, trying to make it sound like she was just trying to fill the silence.

"Huh?"

"You were gone a minute. Did you try to hop the whole way across the Underworld?"

"Oh." Sal flicked his ears in a dog's version of a shrug. "Naw. I ran into Link, one of the 'pomps we're looking for? Obviously, she didn't know nothing 'bout Ramses, or I'd have told you." He cocked his doggie grin up at her. "Why, were you worried?" He thumped against her leg, playful.

Renai snorted. "Boy, please. The thought of handling my business without you weighing me down had me like"—she took a few steps in an exaggerated strut, shuffling her feet so her toes turned toward each other, kicking a leg behind her every other step like she was showing off her footwork at a second line, those uniquely New Orleanian walking parades of revelers and brass bands that followed social clubs and funerals and weddings.

She stopped for an instant, her whole body gone still, her hand held up to her mouth as if she'd shocked even herself with her skills, and then fell out laughing. She didn't know if it was relief that Sal had an explanation for his absence, or just the joy of moving, but she felt better. Or at least, as good as one could feel this deep in the Underworld.

When she glanced down at Sal to see if she'd impressed him, the 'pomp only grunted at her to keep moving. She reached down and scratched the old grump between his ears anyway. "So how did you of all people know that Plumaj was quoting *Moby Dick*?"

"You instigating that I don't know how to read?"

Renai smirked at his word choice, somehow both wrong and poetically accurate at the same time. "You're just forever quoting old movies is all. Never heard you mention any books."

Sal chuckled. "Yeah, I'm just bustin' your balls. Ain't a shape I wear can turn pages worth a damn. Only *Moby Dick* I know's got Gregory Peck in it. Well, that and the one with Thor. I only knew Plumaj was quotin' the book 'cause they *always* quote that book. Fuckin' love it. Rumor is they used to be a Muse and that one was their Mona Lisa."

Sal's comment about Plumaj's rumored Muse-hood turned Renai's mind toward Muses and gods, psychopomps and mortal souls, and so she spent the rest of the walk to the Marigny — where Saint Roch's Cemetery and the Fourth Gate waited — lost in thought.

Before she'd died, she'd thought she understood how the world worked. Raised Catholic but fallen away in her teens, she'd placed her trust, her faith, in technology. After all, praying for help on a history paper hadn't done anything for her, but Google and Wikipedia had worked miracles.

So by the time she was filling out college applications, she'd settled into a quiet atheism, certain that the world she lived in was the only one that existed. Not having any beliefs of her own had made it easy to ask her Aunt Celeste for a job when Renai and her father had argued about her plans after high school.

She'd known Celeste's genuine faith in the loa and voodoo rites would upset her father, the kind of man who was at Mass every Sunday, who confessed his sins once a month, a man who still toyed with the idea of becoming a deacon. To her, though, Celeste's calling on Papa Legba to open the way for the other loa had seemed just as futile as her father's prayers for the intercession of angels and saints.

And then, to her great surprise, death had carried Renai into a world where not only was *she* wrong, but *both* her father and Celeste were right. Where the gods of every faith existed, where the afterlife that every religion promised could be reached if you could manage the crossing, where a young woman who'd believed death was just an off switch could become the guide that led souls to their just rewards.

Most people would have found a way to accept the truth of this revelation after five years. For Renai, it was the kind of epiphany that gave birth to more questions. If Plumaj could be a Muse and an angel and a loa all at once, did that mean everyone's roles were equally fluid?

She'd been there when a demigod became fully divine. Could a human attain that kind of immortality? What about psychopomps? Most of them that Renai had met were mere spirits, without anything resembling autonomy or personality. Was that what she had to look forward to, a slow slide into a kind of single-minded senility? Or did she have the potential to evolve? She'd bargained with Mason, told him she'd trade this Ramses St. Cyr for escape, but maybe she should have asked for more.

She hadn't found satisfactory answers to these questions in her five years as a psychopomp, so she wasn't surprised when she still hadn't come to any conclusions by the time the entrance to Saint Roch's Cemetery rose out of the gloom. Two brick buildings—squared off and crenellated like a couple of guard towers at the drawbridge of a fortress—stood on either side of the elaborate iron gate that bore the cemetery's name, flanked by a pair of statues: two women, one with her palms pressed together in prayer, the other with her hands clasped together in penitence or grief. The gates were closed and didn't open when Renai pushed on them. After a brief lurch of panic, Renai peeked through the iron bars and saw why.

The long avenue of the cemetery led straight back to a tall chapel designed to look like a miniature cathedral and, in front of that, an altar. In the living world, a statue of three women praying at the feet of a crucified Christ occupied this space, but in the Underworld, it was just a table of bare marble. A short row of stairs led from the altar to a dais that held a black iron cauldron, from which flames crackled and leapt.

The Gatekeeper—Maman Bridgette, a white woman with shockingly red hair done up in a bunch of elaborate braids—was there with an elderly dead woman and her guide, a fat little brown bird with a hooked beak that Renai didn't know. Renai asked Sal if the other psychopomp was one of the ones they were looking for, but he answered her with a negative grunt.

Inside the cemetery, Bridgette took the dead woman by the elbow and guided her to the top of the stairs and into position, her back to Renai and Sal, facing the flames roaring in the cauldron. The shadow she cast stretched out long and flickering behind her, darkening the altar where her whippoor-will psychopomp waited.

Beside her, Sal curled up on the ground, his head laying on his paws. For some reason that Renai had never gotten him to admit, he always tried to avoid this part of the dead's journey. It wasn't fear, exactly, that she saw in him. Something closer to sadness. Like watching Brigette at her work made Salvatore think about something he'd rather forget.

Renai turned back toward the Gatekeeper just in time to see her reach into empty air and pull out a large ornately decorated mirror. Holding it in both hands, Brigette angled it so that the dead woman could look into its depths.

Seeing the Gatekeeper using her mirror made Renai's hands itch to reach for her own, which lived in the same nowhere place that her wings went to when she folded them away. Hers looked nothing like Brigette's; hers was made of obsidian—smooth and cold and polished until it gleamed—an oval of black glass about a foot long and half a foot wide with a handle of bone wrapped in rough ancient twine.

Once, there had been two handles, but the opposite end of the mirror ended in a jagged crack, where the other handle and a sliver of the mirror had broken loose. She'd tried only once to grip the mirror on its cracked side, and the damned thing had sliced her palm open, its edge so sharp that she hadn't felt the pain until after she'd seen the blood. Like the wings, she couldn't re-member the first time she'd used the mirror, didn't know if Sal had taught her to use it or if she'd just known her role instinctively. Nor did she know why hers was different, or why she had one at all, since Bridgette always used hers on the dead who made it to the Fourth Gate. All she knew for sure was that when she needed it, the mirror was there.

Bridgette tilted and adjusted the reflective surface until she had it just right, until the dead woman facing this trial could, for the first time in her whole existence, truly see herself. Renai knew the moment that it happened, because the shadow she cast on the altar behind her took on definition and di-mension, became a copy of the dead woman in every detail.

Every person alive, Renai had learned, had an image of the person they wanted to be, a single quality prized above all others. Courage or conviction or success, devotion or ambition, understanding or intelligence or wisdom. Though we'd like to think we possessed all of these, we knew deep down that perfection was unattainable. And so we chose one quality to strive after, one virtue on which to place all our hopes. Compassion sacrificed in the pursuit of success. Devotion to an ideal drowning out the capacity for understanding. Ambition allowed to die so that wisdom might flourish. It was not a conscious decision but a yearning of the soul, and as such happened without our awareness, even though it defined the trajectory of our lives and determined our consequences in the world to come.

Humans were beings defined by conflict, however. There were always two sides to a coin. It wasn't as simple as good and evil. Choosing one virtue meant that its vice followed after. Within every courageous person, there lurked a coward. The truly compassionate were nonetheless capable of intense cruelty. The most intelligent person you'd ever met proved, once in a while, to be an idiot. They followed us always, these opposites, these traitors to the most fundamental aspect of our lives, hounding every step, mimicking every move, watching every moment.

They were our Shadows.

Sometimes—in drunken revelry, in fits of passion or rage, in the madness of youth or the infirmities of age, in dreams, whenever we are weak, in short—these Shadows drove our choices. They spoke with our tongues and acted with our hands. They ruined what we built, they hurt what we sought to heal, they hoarded what we would share, took when we would give. Weakness was human; times of failure were inevitable. No one could outrun their own Shadow. But if you weren't careful, the Shadow assumed the role of the virtue. Isolated moments of weakness were replaced by occasional shows of strength. The compassionate child grew into a callous adult. The hardworking youth fell into sloth. The intelligent student, convinced of their own superiority, became a rigid, foolish teacher.

When the dead looked into Bridgette's mirror, they didn't merely look upon a reflection. The flames in her cauldron revealed both the virtuous self they were meant to attain and the Shadow self that had haunted them their entire life; the glass indicated which of the two they'd most often chosen to be. Above all else, the dead woman facing the trial of the Fourth Gate had been an honest woman. She'd broken laws—and promises, occasionally, which was more important in this place—but mostly she'd told the truth, even when it was inconvenient. She'd been a faithful lover, a steadfast friend, a straightforward employee. The lying, deceitful, untrustworthy Shadow at her back had been denied far more often than it had slipped into her shoes and twisted her tongue.

Which made it easy for Bridgette, drawing an ancient iron dagger from the sheath on her belt, to cut the Shadow from the dead woman in swift, decisive motions, like an experienced hunter skinning a kill. As Bridgette separated the Shadow self from the dead woman's Essence, the dark shape shared less and less of her characteristics, first her facial features and clothing melted away, then her posture and even the semblance of hair, until only a vaguely human shape lay on the altar. As Bridgette worked, it coalesced into something like cloth, thick and billowing and fluid. It took only a few moments for Bridgette to slice the dead woman and her Shadow completely free from one another, gathering the dark material in her hands and stuffing it into a large cloth sack hanging from her belt. There was no blood, since the dead no longer had any, but that didn't mean the process didn't hurt. In the mirror's surface, the dead woman was forced to examine every moment of weakness splayed out before her: every lie, every time she'd withheld the truth. Renai imagined that wounded her deeper than any blade ever could.

Whenever one of her own dead reached this moment in their journey through the Gates, Renai would have to fight down the tempest that lived inside her, that fierce, whirling power that responded to her joy with a zeal that bordered on euphoria. She didn't understand what this power was, but she knew it was a contradiction as potent as the soul's Shadow. It was a destructive force, but it was a cleansing, purifying kind of energy. The kind of destruction that paved the way for new growth, for reinvention. The kind of death that preceded resurrection.

Renai could feel it moving within her, waking in response to the dead woman's change, her sloughing off of her Shadow like a snake shedding its skin. The storm wanted to help, wanted to facilitate that change. Wanted to scour away every last shred of the deceit from the dead woman the way a driving rain washed everything clean.

Because she was expecting it—because she'd braced herself for the storm's surge—Renai was able to push that whirling wind back down to where it slept within her. Because in truth, the dead woman *wasn't* truly free of the things she'd done.

Renai could hear her father's voice reciting the part of Mass where parishioners would ask forgiveness from both God and their fellow faithful for having sinned: *in my thoughts and in my words, in what I have done, and in what I have failed to do.*

Once they'd truly seen themselves, the dead had to endure it all, the big mistakes they'd regretted their whole life, and the little failures that they'd mercifully forgotten. Bridgette's mirror was a test, not an absolution. The Gatekeeper might cut away the Shadow self that had been drawn to those acts, but the dead had been the one to commit them. They would still bear their weight when they faced the Scales of Judgment. When they faced the Thrones.

By the time she finished quieting the tempest—restraining its power, even though she'd been prepared for it, felt like it got harder and harder each time—Bridgette had unlocked the Fourth Gate, which opened in the center of the altar, and let the dead woman and her whippoorwill guide pass through. Once she closed the Underworld Gate, the iron gate of the cemetery unlocked and swung open on creaking hinges. Renai went through first, with Sal sullenly shuffling close behind.

"Girlfriend, you look a mess!" Bridgette said as they approached, her voice thick with the burr of an Irish brogue. She wore a wide-skirted dress with a tight bodice that showed an intimidating amount of cleavage, an elaborately sewn garment full of pearls and lace, all in black, like a wedding dress designed for a funeral. "Has this mongrel the Thrones saddled you with got you digging graves with your own hands, then?"

Renai hadn't fully realized it until the loa said it, but her run through the rain and the mud had left her filthy. Now that she thought about it, every part of her felt grimy, like dried sweat and dirt encased her in a second skin. Nothing she could do about it now, though. "You know how he does," she said, shaking her head in an exaggerated rolling of her eyes. "He says we're making graves, but he's just hunting for bones."

"That so?" Her green eyes glittered and shined, literally glowing in the darkness like a couple of distant stars. "Well, if it's a bone he's wantin', I'm sure my faithless husband will be willin' to provide." Bridgette was married to Baron Samedi, a skull-faced god who went by the name Barren. He was the chief loa of the dead, and though they were both famously promiscuous, they loved one another fiercely.

"Don't mind me," Sal said. "You ladies just go ahead and talk about me like I ain't fuckin' standing here."

"Right you are," Bridgette said, snapping her fingers with both hands like she was clapping at a poetry slam. "My dear old mam always said that men were creatures of the earth, the best of them dumb as a stone and hard as a rock."

Sal barked out a laugh in spite of himself. "How is it every time we meet, you end up talkin' about my prick?"

"Och, sensitive subject is it? Have the Thrones finally gone and gotten you fixed, then?"

Renai cut in before Sal could respond, knowing they could go on like this for a while. "Speaking of the Thrones," she said, tilting her head in the direction of the Gate, "we've got an appointment—"

The loa showed Renai her palms, nodding. "Say no more, dear, say no more." She reached into her impressive cleavage and took out an iron key. "Death ain't exactly one to be kept waitin'."

CHAPTER NINETEEN

THIS **DEEP IN** the Underworld, the trees had given up on any pretense of reality and were as flat and as uniform as the stage scenery in a high school play. *Lights, camera, action!* Renai thought, still a little giddy from the exertion of restraining the spirit within her. A few minutes' walk brought the two of them to a huge house at the foot of Elysian Fields that didn't exist in the living world, an old plantation-style mansion. The growling, frenetic horns of a brass band called from within, and a crowd in fancy evening dress spilled out onto the lawn, flirting and mingling and laughing. At least, they were as loud as they could be, band and crowd both, given that they played and spoke in the desperate whispers of the dead.

At the entrance to the property, a small white fence separating the revelers from the rest of the Underworld, a loa named Babaco waited. Babaco was an older black man, wearing a practical brown suit with a matching fedora tilted just so, who leaned on a cane and smiled wide as they approached.

Everything about the Fifth Gate should have been comforting: a fancy party where the black folks were doing the eating and drinking, instead of the ones serving the drinks or carrying the trays, and a grandfatherly figure, clean-shaven and warm-eyed and kind. The sight of this place filled her with dread. She'd been here before—on her own journey through the Underworld, as part of Jude Dubuisson's schemes—but her memories of that time were brief and jumbled and awful.

And the worst of them happened at this never-ending party of the dead.

At her side, Sal cleared his throat. "How 'bout I handle this one," he said. "I know you ain't exactly Babaco's biggest fan." Renai just nodded, thankful that they didn't have any dead with them who would be forced to listen to Babaco's line of bullshit.

It didn't matter how many times she heard it, the offer made by the Gatekeeper of the Fifth Gate pissed her off every time. This was the last chance before the end, he'd tell them. Before the Thrones. Before the scales. Babaco offered the dead an extension. A deferral from judgment. What he didn't mention—unless the dead could manage to ask, anyway—was that this choice would last forever. That if they chose to stay here at the party in the depths of the Underworld, their coin of Fortune would continue on without them, and they'd be trapped here for all eternity.

According to Sal, it wasn't such a bad deal. The music was good and the food was rich and the wine was free—what more could anyone ask for? Every once in a while, Renai would remind him that he'd asked for more back when *he'd* made this trip. He didn't like that answer very much.

She knew, logically, that she couldn't have chosen to stay here. She had too vivid a memory of standing before the Thrones, awaiting her own judgment. No, her unease had something to do with all of Jude's trickery surrounding her resurrection. She had flashes of an angel's wings and a big heavy revolver like something out of a cowboy movie. Red doors and gods laughing and the dead fleeing and a great wave of fear.

She'd lived and died once already in these scraps of memory, and whatever had happened to her inside that mansion had still scared her worse than dying again. So she was more relieved than she could say when Babaco unlocked the Fifth Gate and let them through.

Before they reached the location of the Sixth Gate—the streetcar stop at the foot of Canal Street—Renai managed to climb up out of her feelings.

Here, three cemeteries spread out in a fan. Cypress Grove was to her left, a largely Protestant graveyard where they'd built the Katrina Memorial. Its entrance of tall white pillars and a pair of pyramid-sloped roofs looked to her like the gate into an ancient city. Odd Fellow's Rest was to her right, a small cemetery hidden by high brick-and-plaster walls, its name carved, in bas-relief, into its granite entryway. Greenwood Cemetery was right in front of her, huge and lavish, a true city of the dead complete with its own landmarks, like the massive, grassy mound topped with an imposing bronze elk of the Lodge's tomb or the Firemen's Monument, rising like the spire of a Gothic church, the statue of a man wearing a fireman's helmet taking the place of a church bell.

In the living world, according to Sal, this intersection had been closed off for months due to construction extending the tracks across City Park Avenue. Soon, he said, the streetcar stop would be a well-lit brick structure on the neutral ground that ran beside Greenwood. Here in the Underworld, though, the streetcar stop at the foot of Canal remained as Renai remembered it: an uncomfortable bench that only seated about half as many people as the streetcar could, sagging beneath a rickety Plexiglas overhang, its single wall covered in scratch-etched graffiti, its roof offering as little protection from the rain as from the sun.

Sometimes there were other dead here with their guides, two or a handful or even a crowd. Sometimes, like now, Renai and Sal were alone. Sometimes her dead used this time to question her, if they'd managed to figure out the dead's version of talking, anyway. They'd ask about members of their family, or what would happen to them next, or whether they'd lived a good life. Sometimes they'd even ask questions she was able to answer.

She and Sal sat there in silence. Sal yawned, his tongue lolling out the side of his muzzle, and seeing it provoked a similar yawn from Renai. In that sliver of time between when her gaping jaws squeezed her eyes shut and when she opened them, the streetcar appeared.

It didn't come rumbling and squealing to a stop, didn't announce itself with the signature jangling bell, didn't move down the tracks at all. It was just there all at once, an Underworld streetcar that only partly resembled its counterparts in the living world: a glossy black carriage with a row of small square windows running along each side, a set of thin folding doors at all four corners, and a single headlight at the front and back that somehow managed to pierce the gloom of the deep Underworld.

The general shape and function of it matched the streetcars in the living world, but here dark silk hung in drapes along the side instead of advertisements, and the interior was lit by lanterns filled with eerie blue flames instead of simple electric bulbs. The streetcars on the other side were either green or red, depending on the line they serviced, but here the black surface of the streetcar had a shimmery iridescence, like an oil slick, like the sheen on a raven's wings. The carriage's abrupt appearance was startling, but in an almost childish way, like jumping out from behind a corner and shouting, "Boo!" The eerie streetcar was the Sixth Gate, and unlike any of the others, could carry them pretty much anywhere in the Underworld that they wanted to go.

Assuming they could convince the driver to take them there, anyway.

"Why's my dude always gotta be so *extra?*" Renai said, more to herself than expecting Sal would hear her.

Sal chuckled. "You're one to talk."

The folding doors creaked open, and Baron Samedi, the Gatekeeper of the Sixth Gate, leaned out. His entire head was a fleshless skull painted with vibrant, stylized images of flowers and stars, like a Día de Muertos sugar skull.

Without lips, his teeth—clamped tight around a thick, hand-rolled cigar—stretched into a constant leer. He came correct though, in a three-piece suit, charcoal gray and pinstriped, with an eggshell dress shirt and gloves to match, a tie the dark purple of a glass of merlot, and a pair of fresh polished black-and-white oxfords.

Just the sight of him made Renai feel dirtier and more busted than she already felt. The loa in the streetcar's doorway went by many names: Baron Cimetière, Bawon Lakwa, Saint Saturday, Mr. Same Day, Baron Criminel. Renai had hazy memories of him from her time spent with a fortune god named Jude, so she called him what Jude had called him: Barren.

Even though he had nothing but deep wells of emptiness inside his eye sockets, Renai could feel Barren's gaze look her up and down. "When I asked the good god Bondye to send me a woman who liked to get filthy," he said, his voice raspy and dry, "this ain't really what I had in mind."

Renai had no response. Her ears filled with a persistent whine, like she'd been standing too close to the speakers at a concert, and it drove anything resembling coherent thought away. She couldn't swallow and her chest felt tight, and she only realized her hands were clenched into fists when her forearms started to ache.

Barren affected her like this, sometimes, though the reason why eluded her, lost in that haze of memories from her death and resurrection. It was worse than Plumaj, worse than Babaco, maybe because she at least had an idea of why those two Gatekeepers unsettled her. Barren, charming and flirtatious as the rest of the Ghede though he might be, just plain scared the hell out of her.

Sal knew what Barren did to her, and—bless him—stepped forward so she wouldn't have to answer. "Yeah," he said, "and when I asked the Thrones for a shape that would let me chase tail for all eternity, they made me a damn dog. You gonna let us on, or what?"

"Salvatore, you old so-and-so," Barren said, cigar smoke rising up from the slits in his face where a nose ought to be, "you know I'll take you anywhere's you like. Just so long as you pay the fare." It was a familiar exchange, not rehearsed exactly, but—like many of a psychopomp's interactions with any of the Gatekeepers—as much ritual as it was conversation. An act performed for the benefit of the dead, even when the audience wasn't present. With the others Renai could play her part, but far too often Barren's presence robbed her of any speech at all, much less playful banter.

For the dead, paying Barren's "fare" meant giving up their coin of Fortune. Once he had it, he'd drive his streetcar all the way down Canal to the Mississippi and onto a ferry that would carry them halfway across the river, only to sink down, down, down to the silty, dark riverbed. There, at the very bottom of the Underworld, they'd find the Thrones themselves: the pair of huge empty chairs from which Death reigned. Barren—sometimes the skull-faced voodoo loa, sometimes an Egyptian death god with a jackal's head, sometimes a winged, haloed man in white robes and bronze armor—would weigh the dead's heart, their Fortune, on his scales. If they passed that final test, the dead would walk between the Thrones, through the Final Gate, and into whatever afterlife they'd earned. Where the coins of Fortune went after that, Sal had often told her, was above her pay grade.

In the Underworld, commerce between psychopomps and gods and spirits and anything else that found its way down here wasn't nearly as regulated and relied more on a constantly shifting economy of barter and favors and oaths. Sal and Barren bickered back and forth for a moment about the cost of Sal's ride, and then the skull-faced god stepped aside, beckoning them in with a wide, sweeping bow.

For some reason that Renai had never had the stones to ask about, Barren had never once asked her to pay.

Renai followed Sal up the stairs into the streetcar, the floor trembling from the engine's rumble. Just as she dropped into one of the lacquered wooden seats, the whole thing lurched forward once, shuddering, and then leapt into motion.

"Almost there," Sal said, his ears twitching back as he glanced up at her. "You doin' okay?"

"Yeah," Renai lied. "It's just been a long couple of days."

"Yeah. Must be hard on you with the Hallows on the way." His ears flattened against his skull, what would have been a guilty shit-did-I-just-say-that-out-loud frown on a human face. He kept talking, though, didn't give her a chance to call him on it. "Tell you what," he said. "I'll buy you a drink. First round's on me."

And that's when Renai realized just where Sal was leading her.

There were places in the Underworld where the dead couldn't go, markets and hotels and theaters and libraries that were nothing like their counterparts in the world of the living. The Sylvain, an opera house that had been on this side of things since the French Opera House burned down in the living world in 1919. The Docks, a restaurant stitched together from the West End places that got washed into Lake Pontchartrain by Katrina's storm surge. The Oubliette, a prison that held the demons and the wild spirits and the corrupt souls that the Far Lands wouldn't take.

The Last Stop, where psychopomps drank away their sorrows.

On the living side of things, it was called Carrollton Station, an Uptown neighborhood bar across the street from an electric grid transformer yard and the once-abandoned streetcar repair station that gave the bar its name. In the Underworld, the only sign of the streetcars were the straight lines cutting across the field outside the bar, the only places where the tall grass didn't grow. In place of the constantly humming power lines and transformer towers in the living world, here a giant bonfire roared and crackled, always consuming but never dying down. Renai only needed one look at it to decide that she didn't want to know what was burning there.

As they walked up to the pale green building of The Last Stop and beneath its sheet metal awning, its security gate and corner door both left hanging wide open, Renai tried to shake whatever panic the sight of Barren inspired in her. They'd left the skull-faced loa behind when they'd exited his streetcar, but Renai swore she could still feel his eyes on her. Waiting. Weighing. She gave her body a full shake, like a bug had gone skittering across her skin, and turned her attention to what was in front of her.

She'd only been inside Carrollton Station a handful of times when she was alive, but she found the same green and white tile on the floor, the same combination of wood paneling and dark green paint on the walls, the same row of lights outlining the steps that led to the stage in back that she remembered.

The main difference between the two bars was that The Last Stop was full of death.

Psychopomps were everywhere, of course: a solid white dog drinking beer out of a pint glass at the walnut brown bar; a calico-feathered owl flipping through the channels by pecking at the television remote; a crow at one of the small tables, its wings waving back and forth as it told a story to a pair of hooded, shadowy figures with corpse-pale hands.

They weren't the only occupants of The Last Stop. A camazotz—a Mayan Underworld demon that looked like a horn-nosed bat stretched out to human proportions—hustled back and forth behind the bar serving drinks, his wide veiny ears twitching, the skull-and-crossbones tattooed on one of his leathery wings showing every time he stretched up for a bottle of liquor on the shelves above him. On the stage in the back, a thick white woman in a long, slinky green dress, her eyes red-rimmed like she'd been weeping, helped a trio of skeletal, black-cloaked musicians set up their instruments—a banshee accompanied by specters.

At a small table in the corner, half-hidden by the darkness of a burnt-out lightbulb, a white woman with high, pointed ears, a vulture's curved beak taking up the lower half of her face, and hair made of snakes played a game using both chess and checkers pieces against a brown-skinned, shirtless man with protruding eyes, a smear of paint on his forehead in the same shade of dark blue as the crown of feathers he wore, and a beast's cruel fangs curling down over his lower lip. He wore a belted loincloth that only covered his privates, while his opponent wore a tunic-style dress clasped at the shoulder with an ornate gold pin, which draped across her body in such a way that it revealed one of her small, flat breasts.

Sal saw Renai watching the gamers and grabbed her hand in his teeth, not hard enough to break the skin, just nipping at her to get her attention. She yanked her hand away, startled, scratching her palm in the process.

"Jesus," she said, "what?"

"Eyes front," he said. "We're here for a couple of 'pomps, remember? Not them." And then, lowering his voice so that she could barely hear him over the murmuring crowd, muttered, "You done fucked around with enough gods for one Hallows, you ask me."

"At least tell me who those two are."

Sal sighed, scanning the occupants of the bar as he answered. "The one with the feathers is Tlaloc. He's an ancient water deity. Brings the rains that bring the crops that bring the life, y'know? And the one with the snakes is Too-Chew-a? Too-too-chew? I don't fuckin' know. Somethin' like that. She's an old-school death god. Real fond of games."

"What's a life-bringing rain god doing in the Underworld?"

"Same thing a god does anywhere else," Sal said. "Whatever the fuck he wants." He grinned up at her, his tongue dangling over his lower jaw.

Renai raised an eyebrow at him. "Seriously, though."

"The serious answer is that the gods got two sides to 'em just like people," he said. "He might be all rain and life and happy times right now, but flip that coin? Hurricanes. Rage. Death. Trust me. He belongs down here as much as the rest of us."

Motherfucker got some kinda nerve showing up here, Renai thought, *god or no.* She knew all too well how easily a storm god could be a death god, like everyone else in this city, but she'd never really seen the other side of that coin. The bitter twist to her inner monologue made the spirit within her swirl and surge, wanting, as it always did, to help wash away her pain. Sal didn't seem to notice the discomfort that she was sure was showing on her face, so she pushed that all away. Instead, she considered the gods she knew best, the Gatekeepers. Considered what they represented. What they were gods of, Barren in particular. Which side of their coins did she know?

Sal made a happy, triumphant sound in the back of his throat, interrupting her thoughts. "Jackpot," he said. "Howl's right over there. Let me do the talking. She's a sharp one, and I ain't talkin' 'bout her claws."

The psychopomp named Howl wore the shape of a chubby gray cat with sleek, thick fur and short, stubby ears. She sat on the bar, her tail wrapped daintily around her paws, lapping wine out of a nearly empty glass. Howl glanced up as Renai and Sal approached, and some combination of the posture of her ears and the curl of her mouth gave off the impression of a sly, knowing smirk. Renai couldn't tell if the brief gesture had revealed some quality of Howl's personality, or if it was just the way cats looked at everyone.

"Salvatore," Howl said in a voice made of velvet, drawing out the syllables as if she were stretching out a kink in her spine as she spoke. "To what do I owe this dubious pleasure?"

Just those few words told Renai that Howl possessed more charm and personality than all the other 'pomps Renai had ever met combined. Usually, the spirits who guided the dead through the Underworld moved through the Gates like automatons, answering questions in distracted, one-word responses, like they were half-asleep or all-the-way-stoned. Like the souls of the dead didn't matter to them one way or the other. When she'd asked Sal about it, he'd told her that most psychopomps were deeper in the Underworld than the two of them, that the act of collecting a soul and guiding it through the Gates was more of a recurring dream for them than a conscious, deliberate act. Howl was the first 'pomp Renai had met who, like Sal, seemed to have a mind of her own.

"We got a couple of questions for you," Sal said, "if you can spare a minute."

Howl inspected and then licked at the space between two of her toes, revealing her claws in the process. "Mmmm, I don't know. Might be difficult to say much, seeing as I'm so parched." With her other paw pressed against her throat, she made a delicate little cough. Sal laughed and raised a paw of his own in the direction of the bat-thing behind the bar, who swept over and refilled the cat's wineglass without slowing. Howl returned to her bath, without so much as glancing at the demon fulfilling her request. After a moment, she paused, flicked a pair of golden eyes at Renai, and then started to clean her tail. "Ask your questions," she said. "But please, darling, don't be boring."

"Who did you lead through the Gates today?" Sal asked.

Howl froze mid-swipe. She stood and stretched, a long, exaggerated movement full of disrespect. Renai half expected her to knock the wineglass over next. Instead, she turned her back to them both and started to slink away, her tail high and twitching.

"Thought you said she was sharp," Renai said to Sal, loud enough for the cat to hear them. "You must have been thinking of some other—"

"I asked for one thing," Howl said, her head and shoulders turned back around toward Renai. "Just one. And yet this lout asks me a question that is a matter of public record. The definition of banal. Perhaps you think you're up to the challenge?"

"How about a soul who managed to evade his own death?" Renai asked. "Does that tickle your fancy?"

Again that sly feline smile crept across Howl's posture. "Oh, *yes*," she said, "that's much more like it." Her tail dropped down and started swishing back and forth, like she'd seen a particularly fat and delicious bird within pouncing distance. "I presume the boy in question is the one you were meant to collect?"

Renai exchanged a glance with Sal, not exactly asking for permission, but close to it. She read agreement in the shift of his eyebrows. "His name is Ramses—"

"St. Cyr," Howl said, some emotion flickering across her face that was too fast for Renai to read. "I know."

"How do you know that?" Sal asked, the words hissing out of him.

Howl waved Sal's tone away, splaying her toes and extending her claws in a slow, playful gesture. "Because I peeked, you silly thing, how else?" She leaned down and lapped briefly at the wine in her glass. "One can learn so many interesting little tidbits from Plumaj's book."

"And here I thought curiosity *killed* the cat," Renai said.

"Do me a fuckin' favor," Sal muttered, and Renai had to bite her lip to keep from laughing. If Howl had heard them, she was pretending not to, hadn't even stopped talking.

". . . and that's when Plumaj caught me looking," she said. "They tried to close the book, but it was already too late. I saw it all." Her eyelids pulled back, her pupils expanding until her eyes were almost entirely black. "Oh," she said. "I understand now. You didn't read Ramses' entry." She bent down and lapped noisily at the wine in her glass. When she spoke again, it was in a singsongy gloat. *"I know something you don't know,"* she sang.

Sal growled deep in his chest, but Renai had a feeling that Howl would respond to aggression by hissing and vanishing, and they needed to know what she did. Needed to know what the Gatekeeper had hidden from them. Renai kissed her teeth. "Quit being a cliché and tell us what you want," Renai said. Sal shot her a questioning look, but Howl just sat up straighter on the bar, the tip of her tail swinging back and forth contentedly.

"Simple. I want to come with you," she said, purring.

"Come with us where?" Renai asked, at the same time that Sal blurted out, "The fuck you will."

"The three of us are going to have to go all the way to the top with this one," Howl said, speaking first to Renai and then down to Sal, "which, for the likes of us, means going all the way to the bottom."

"The Thrones?" Renai asked.

Howl glanced back at her and flicked her ears in a cat's version of shaking her head no, the gesture so slight that Renai almost missed it. *"The very bottom,"* she said.

Beside her, Sal barked out a bitter laugh. "Fuck you, kitty," he said. "Maybe you got nine lives, but I ain't got but the one, and I ain't throwin' it away fuckin' around with no Fortune Tellers."

"Oh, but you *will*," Howl said, smiling her wicked cat's grin, "because what I learned from Plumaj's book is this: this wasn't the first time Ramses St. Cyr was supposed to die."

CHAPTER TWENTY

ONE SPINS THE thread. One takes its measure. One cuts it clean. And they do it all sharing a single eye between them. They are sisters identical and united, they are a single face seen in three mirrors, they are three photographs of a woman taken throughout her life. They are all of these at once. When the path before you is wide and clear and easy, bless the names of Clotho, Lachesis, and Atropos; of Urðr, Verðandi, and Skuld. When the burdens on your back are more than you can bear, send your curses to Saraswati, Lakshmi, and Parvati; to Badb, Macha, and Nemain. Seek them — should you be so desperate or foolish or brave — in the cave beneath the World Tree or on the field of battle or just behind the throne. When they carry vengeance in their talons, we call them Erinyes. When they hold back the end of all things within the stars, we call them Auroras. When they speak the truth to Macbeth, we call them the Weird. The Morrígna and the Moirai, the Norns and the Charites, the Tridevi. The highest of gods and the smallest of spirits must bow to their will. One spins, one measures, one cuts.

The power to create, and to preserve, and to destroy.

"I don't understand," Renai said, following Sal and Howl out of The Last Stop. "How could Ramses have avoided his own death more than once? How could he *have* more than one death?" She was, of course, intimately familiar with reincarnation, both in her own experience and in many of the dead she guided through the Gates: Buddhists and adherents of Wicca, Hindus and Voodousants, she'd led them all down through the Gates, knowing that their turn at the scales would likely return them to the world of the living instead of sending them through into the Far Lands.

Renai didn't think Howl meant that Ramses was part of a cycle of death and rebirth—and judging by his reaction, neither did Sal. Howl seemed to be implying that, not only had Ramses somehow managed to sidestep the moment he'd been destined to die—which shouldn't be possible—he'd done it more than once.

"Ain't nothin' to understand," Sal said, snapping the words over his shoulder at her. "This 'pomp don't know what she's saying." When Howl chuckled in response, he said, "She don't," again, but quieter, like he wasn't entirely sure.

"No?" Howl asked. "Then why are we walking in the same direction?" That direction was vaguely toward the Quarter, unless Renai had gotten more turned around than she thought in all the trips back and forth across the Underworld that she and Sal had made.

"So's I can show your smug ass just how wrong you are."

Oh no, Renai thought, *Mommy and Daddy are fighting.* She had to stifle a laugh, knowing that her confused nerves would spit it out as a giggle, a panicked one she'd find it hard to stop. Choking back her humor turned it into a cough.

"You okay?" Sal asked.

"I will be soon as you tell me where we're going. Who we're going to see."

He didn't turn around, but Renai saw Sal's sides expand and swell as he pulled in a deep breath and held it, then shrank as he sighed. "You know how you're always askin' me what happens to the coin of a person's Fortune after their Essence moves on?" Renai hummed an affirmative. "Well, you're about to see for yourself."

As they walked, Renai could feel their descent in her belly, like a shift of inertia in a moving elevator, even though the New Orleans on this side of things was as flat as it was in the living world. The psychopomps were leading her down through the levels of the Underworld without needing to pass through the Gates themselves, a trick that she'd never been able to pull off. She could ascend just fine on her own, but if she wanted to go deeper, she always had to go the long way.

"What are you getting out of this?" Renai asked Howl, more to distract herself from the unsettling sensation of the ground falling away beneath her feet and the abrupt changes in her surroundings—now fog, now smoke, now deep, dark night.

"I've never met the Sisters," she said. "I hate being bored, and doing this is the least boring thing I can imagine."

"If you want to see them so bad," Renai asked "why do you need us? Are they hard to find?"

Sal laughed. "What she needs is an excuse! You don't go interrupting the Weird Ones at their work, no, ma'am. Not unless you got a good goddamn reason."

"They are . . . important," Howl said, a hushed awe in her voice. "Powerful."

"*Scary* is what she means," Sal said. "They're powerful fuckin' scary."

A minute or so of walking had carried them all the way to the Quarter, to Jackson Square, or at least, the poor facsimile of it that existed this deep in the Underworld, the black iron lampposts made of plywood, the cathedral itself nothing but a half-sized facade duct-taped to some rickety scaffolding. And then, strangely, impossibly, between one step and the next, they delved even deeper, *beneath* the Underworld somehow, a thought that made Renai a little queasy, even as the grass beneath her feet and the buildings around her, fake as they'd been, became nothing but ash and shadows. Sal and Howl had led her to a place where only the three of them existed, a nothing place, a nowhere.

So why did she hear ringing bells?

Renai turned in a slow circle, and there it was, a low brick building with three entrances, a brown-shingled roof with a pair of windows slanting out, and smoke coming from the slender chimney in the center of the building. Since its architecture was unique among buildings in the Quarter, most of which had the second-floor balconies favored by the Spanish who'd built it, she recognized it at once as Lafitte's, an old bar, one of the oldest structures in the city, one of the few that had survived both of the great fires that had destroyed almost the entire original Quarter between them.

This *had* to be where Sal and Howl were leading her, since it was the only thing she could see in this nowhere place, the only thing that existed aside from her two companions, the soft, orange glow coming from inside the only source of light that she could see.

Lafitte's hadn't always been a bar, she knew. In its earliest days, it had housed a blacksmith's shop. And that's when she realized that the rhythmic *TING-ting-ting* she heard wasn't a ringing bell, but the sound of a black-smith's hammer pounding on metal.

Focusing her attention on the occupant of Lafitte's filled Renai with a sudden, intense dread. Not that she could see more than soft firelight from where she stood, or even had an inkling of who might be inside—but just *wondering* seemed to be enough to pin her in place. Only a few feet separated her from the entrance right in front of her and literally nothing stood in her way, and yet Renai found it impossible to move closer. In fact, the only comforting thought was one of escape, her back muscles twitching with the wings' eagerness to unfurl and carry her away from this place.

It wasn't malevolence she sensed, wasn't fear that poured into her, but something more primal. A presence of immense and overwhelming will was aware of her, and some part of her mind—the oldest part—knew it was better not to be seen. Howl and Sal had tried to warn her, but nothing could have prepared her for this. She couldn't move, couldn't speak. Tears threatened to leak from her eyes. Even when standing in front of the Thrones, Renai hadn't felt this small.

Which meant whatever dwelt in this small cottage at the empty bottom of the Underworld was more powerful than Death.

And after a time—if time even existed in this place—this impossible regard ebbed away from her. She found herself able to think, to breathe without effort. Her wings still wanted to flee, but she shrugged them back down. She hadn't come this far just to run away now.

"*Christ on a cracker,* this was a bad idea," Sal said. But he followed anyway, so close to her that they brushed against each other every time they moved.

Renai kept her eyes fixed on the entrance and focused on putting one foot in front of the other. That—and not pissing herself—took all of her focus, so she didn't know if Howl was following them inside, or if she'd fled, or if she'd simply ceased to exist when faced with the power before them. In this place, any of those possibilities seemed equally plausible.

Each step was easier than the last, as if Renai had passed through some gauntlet. Each motion toward to the entrance made the tidal, irrepressible potency of the being inside recede just a bit more. By the time Renai slipped inside, her surroundings felt almost normal.

Within, she found a low ceiling held up by simple brick columns, racks of metalworking tools meticulously aligned and hung on the walls, an uneven floor of dirt or dust or ash, and a forge—an anvil of some glittering black metal and brass bellows churning and churning without cease and a circular, arched hearth made of ancient gray stone, its bricks fitted seamlessly without mortar—dominating the center of the room.

Though heat crackled against Renai's face and roared in her ears, she saw no flames in the hearth, no source of light other than the white woman pounding her massive hammer against the anvil.

The woman had long dark-with-sweat hair pulled back in a ponytail and wore a leather apron over a pair of basketball shorts and a black sports bra. A shadow obscured half of her face, but the rest of her burned bright, an incandescent glow emanating from her. Everything about the blacksmith exuded power, from the bulging musculature of her arms and shoulders, to the fluid sway of her thick hips and legs, to the sharp, focused barks of exertion that squeezed past her lips each time she heaved the hammer—a maul that the blacksmith wielded one-handed, its worn head as big as an engine block—in a smooth, precise arc, to the way Renai felt the impact in her bones when the hammer came hurtling down to meet the anvil.

Even though that terrible pressure had left her, Renai couldn't bring herself to speak, to interrupt the woman's stride, her process. Even the thought felt wrong, like stopping Serena Williams mid-serve to ask for an autograph. The blacksmith, whoever and whatever she was, just took far too much joy in her work, her teeth bared in a smile focused and joyous and fierce all at once.

Instead, Renai took a closer look at her labors.

In the hand that wasn't busy with the hammer, the blacksmith held a pair of tongs, which she used to grip a coin of Fortune, heated to a white-hot sheen. The coin withstood blow after crushing blow without bending or changing at all, without even throwing any sparks.

Renai thought it strange that something so malleable in her own hands could be so rigid under such an onslaught from the blacksmith's. The rhythm of the hammer's strikes was seductive, hypnotic, and Renai felt her vision relax, like she was just at the edge of sleep. Instead of seeing coin and anvil, hammer and hearth, she looked through the forge and saw something . . . more.

The glittery black metal of the anvil spread and stretched until it filled her vision—like the night sky, like a sprawl of diamonds on black velvet, like a glimpse of heavens she'd only seen in pictures, having lived her entire life in the shroud of New Orleans's light pollution: the sprawling, flowing liquor of the Milky Way. At its center, instead of a fireless forge, Renai saw the massive absence at the center of the galaxy, a furnace that burned hotter than thousands of suns which shed not a single photon of light. A nothing whose rage not even destiny could deny.

And then, with a clang as sudden and as discordant as the Big Bang, Renai returned to herself as the coin of Fortune shattered.

The blacksmith turned to the three psychopomps who had crept into her forge while she worked, her chest heaving in time with her bellows, and grinned at them with the gleeful abandon of youth. What Renai had taken for a shadow across the young woman's face, she could see now was a headscarf pulled so low that it covered one of the blacksmith's eyes. The other, gray and piercing and knowing, didn't match the rest of her. From head to toe the blacksmith was young, barely out of adolescence, but that eye was *ancient*. That eye had literally seen it all before.

"Renaissance Dantor Raines," the woman said, in a voice that was almost disappointingly normal. Renai had half expected her ears to bleed when the blacksmith spoke. Thankfully, though, her tone said she was both happy to see Renai and unsurprised at her presence. That ancient eye moved slightly. "She Who Howls With Lament. He Who Liberates From Peril." She winked, and even though she only had a single eye, the wry twist of her mouth and the crinkle of her cheek made her gesture clear. "Be right with you."

The blacksmith turned back to her anvil and scooped up the still-glowing shards of Fortune from the coin she'd destroyed—all but one tiny sliver that got left behind—sweeping them right into her cupped palm. She dumped them into an unpainted ceramic bowl filled with other broken bits of Fortune, and then reached down for her hammer, only when she picked up the same instrument, it was now a long iron pole. She set the bowl into her forge, which—changing as abruptly and as silently as the hammer—was now a kiln, and waited for the Fortune to melt into a single orange-golden mass.

The goddess—for what else could she be—stirred the puddle of molten Fortune with the pole, gathering a glowing, viscous lump of it, raised the pole to her lips, and blew. The shimmering, coppery knob of Fortune bulged and grew into a wide bulb. When she was satisfied, the glassblower—for that was what she'd become—shifted her grip on the pipe and snatched a tool off the wall with the other hand, a wicked-looking pair of forceps. Easing down onto a stool with the pipe across her thighs, she spun the bulb with one hand while she shaped and pinched it with the forceps. After a moment, it went into the kiln again to heat back up, while she selected another tool, a flat stone paddle. It went on like this for a while, shaping and heating and shaping again.

When Renai pulled her attention away from the glassblower's work to study the artisan herself, Renai found that the goddess had aged decades between one moment and the next. Her skin had tightened, her muscles shrinking and hardening like a gnarled old tree. Hair turned a steely-gray, corners of the lips and eye pinched with laugh and frown lines, knuckles swollen into knobs and her posture slightly stooped. Her single eye, if anything, now appeared even more ancient.

Her movements were no less confident, her presence no less commanding. Her joy at her work no less a thing of beauty. She twirled and stretched and clipped and smoothed the pliant lump of Fortune with a surety that came from experience and skill, unlike the blacksmith, who had relied purely on strength. With a simple tool, like a chisel as small as an ink pen, she pressed a handful of characters into the surface of the Fortune. It looked to Renai like cuneiform writing on clay tablets at first. It was only when the glassblower finished—mashing the Fortune flat and smoothing its rounded edges into the shape of a coin—that Renai recognized the glyphs.

It was the same as the indecipherable writing that she'd seen in Plumaj's book.

Because she was looking for it this time, Renai saw when the elderly goddess changed—a sudden, seamless transition between one blink and the next—into a middle-aged version of herself, cheeks plump and brown hair just slightly touched with salt, breasts heavy and belly gravid with pregnancy. She groaned to her feet, one hand holding the handle of a precision tool that had been a long and hollow iron pipe a moment before, the other knuckling the small of her back.

Shuffling over to her anvil—which was now a workbench holding sheaf after sheaf of blueprints—the architect peered through the now-transparent piece of Fortune as though it were a magnifying glass, studying the topmost of the drawings, which seemed to be either a constellation or a schematic for an intricate clock or the building plans for a massive cathedral, measuring with a pair of calipers and muttering to herself. She stopped, and smiled, and

—pulling a stub of pencil from behind her ear—made a single deft mark on the paper.

With a soft *plink*, a newly minted coin of Fortune fell to the tabletop. And the goddess who'd created it tossed the coin into a nearby chest full of them, a pirate's treasure of destinies.

The artisan stretched to her full height, turned her attention to the psychopomps once more, and smiled. "Now," she said, wiping her soot-stained, spark-burned hands on the hem of her leather apron as if it were a washrag, "what can I do for you three?"

For a long, terrible moment, no one spoke, and Renai panicked, thinking it would be up to her to break the silence, certain only that she had no idea what to say. And then Salvatore—bless him—hunkered low to the floor, like he was bowing or kneeling, and began, in a stilted, formal voice that was almost a moan, "Many thanks for your attention, oh most Kindly Ones—"

"Please," she said, holding up a calloused, powerful hand, "call me Grace."

It was so genuine and so equally absurd that Renai coughed up a laugh. Thankfully no one, especially not the seemingly omniscient being that she'd just laughed at, called her on it. And that gave her the courage to speak. "We're here because one of the deaths I was supposed to collect has disappeared, even though that shouldn't be possible. We were hoping you might have some guidance for us."

Grace frowned, and the simple fact of having disappointed this being made Renai want to cover herself with the ash of this place and never speak again. Grace reached into an apron pocket and pulled out a pack of American Spirits and, just when Renai imagined she would have to watch a pregnant uber-deity smoke a cigarette, blinked into the youthful version of herself. It was only slightly less unsettling when she leaned over to her hearth and casually used the energy radiating from a supermassive black hole to light it.

"So, let me get this straight," she said, blowing out a long plume of smoke. "You've lost one soul among the literal billions that I've forged just this *century*, and you stopped by so I could tell you where you left it?"

Next to Renai, Howl made a little gasp of dismay and started stammering an apology, just as Sal started cursing, but Grace couldn't keep up the pretense for long. Her frown cracked into a wide, affable grin. "Awww, I'm just screwing with you guys," she said. Her smile faded when no one else seemed amused, but only a little. "Sorry," she said, "I couldn't resist. Don't get many unscheduled visitors down here, you know?" She took another drag and pointed with the fingers holding the cigarette. "Tell you what, you've got my undivided attention until I finish my smoke break. I presume you've already seen the angel about this wayward lamb of yours?"

"We, uh—" Renai began, freezing when she realized what she was about to say. Sal rescued her from having to accuse the Gatekeeper.

"This particular soul is a real tricky little bastard," he said. "This wasn't the first check they managed to skip out on payin'."

"Ah," Grace said, "you got one of *those*." She plucked a loose bit of a tobacco from the tip of her tongue and flicked it away. She was silent for a moment, pensive. "That makes things a good bit harder for you, I'm afraid. If this was just your garden-variety twist of fate, I could point you right to 'em. But I can't really tell you where somebody's supposed to be if they've gone and wandered off the path I put 'em on. Frankly, this soul of yours could be anywhere."

"How is that even possible?" Renai asked, proud that she'd managed to speak to this being without her voice betraying her.

Grace tilted her head and pursed her lips, a how-do-I-even-begin-to-answer-that gesture. "There's a reason I shape Fortune into a coin. Doesn't matter if you're a mortal or a spirit, a god or whatever else, you spend your Fortune, little by little, until the only bill you can afford to pay is the final one. And just like any other commodity, it can be stolen." She shrugged. "Or you can spend it all at once on something big, the moment of your death included."

Howl hissed and Sal said, "Fuck me," like Grace had just told him he had a tumor.

"What?" Renai asked, looking down at the psychopomps that had brought her here. "What does that mean?"

"It means Ramses St. Cyr has made a deal," Howl said, her tail lashing back and forth.

"The sell-your-soul-to-the-Devil kind," Sal said.

"Sure," Grace said. "Any ol' devil will do."

Watching the artisan flick away ash from the tip of her cigarette, Renai had to restrain herself from asking for one herself. She breathed in deep, the scent comforting. Mundane. Grace must have seen the question on her face, though, because she shook one free of the pack and held it out to Renai. When she took it, though, Grace didn't offer her a light. *I'm definitely not going anywhere near that forge,* Renai thought.

There were so many questions to ask that it felt impossible to choose, much less figure out how to put one into words. Did Grace know who Ramses had sold his Fortune to? Or what he'd gotten in return? If Ramses no longer had a coin for Renai to deliver, did she even need to bother searching for him? Or should she be looking for his coin, instead?

All of these options, and what slipped past her lips was: "If immortality is that easy, why doesn't everybody do it?"

Grace turned her full attention to Renai, that knowing, inescapable gaze. "You know that answer better than anybody," the goddess said. "You died before you were supposed to, which left you with an excess of Fortune. You spent that on someone else's behalf, so now your needle has well and truly hopped out of its groove. Every breath you take isn't a part of the destiny I mapped out when I forged your coin." Her smile, when it came, was sad. "So why doesn't everybody do it? How's it working out for *you?*"

Renai opened her mouth and closed it. The most powerful being she'd ever met had just told her that she no longer had a destiny. That her existence no longer had an expiration date. That knowledge ought to be liberating. Empowering. But all it did was explain why she always felt so empty.

Grace stubbed out the last remaining embers of her cigarette on the anvil and flicked the filter into the abyss of the hearth. "Wish I could give you three some more of my time," she said, "but my wheel is always kinda turning, if you know what I mean."

She slammed closed the lid of her chest full of Fortune coins and hoisted it, effortlessly, onto one shoulder. A blink, and the middle-aged, pregnant version of Grace carried the weight, rapping a knuckle on the side of the wooden box. "There's a whole bunch of creation deities waiting for these babies."

Because Grace seemed to be waiting for it, Renai forced a polite chuckle, which Howl echoed. If the expression on the pregnant deity's face was any indication, it hadn't been convincing.

"And people say Fate doesn't have a sense of humor," Sal muttered.

Renai winced, but Grace only smirked at the psychopomp's insolent tone. "Do they now?" she asked. "That's funny. After all, I'm always the one who gets the last laugh."

And then she was gone, taking all the light in the world with her. Neither Sal nor Howl stuck around long in the vast, empty darkness Grace left behind; Renai felt their passage out of the bottom of the Underworld like they kicked up a breeze as they passed by. But Renai waited, some detail or unresolved question nagging at her, despite her wings trembling in their desire to carry her out of there.

After a few moments her eyes adjusted to the darkness, and she realized that Grace must have left something behind, some source of illumination that allowed her to see. She thought, at first, that the slight glow must be leaking through the seams of the kiln, light spilling out of the melted-down Fortune left simmering there, but then her pupils dilated a bit more and she saw that it came from the thin sliver of the shattered coin that Grace had broken on the anvil. Renai had crossed over to the shard and reached out for it before it occurred to her that this whole setup might be a trap.

As her fingertips touched the slender needle-sharp sliver of Fortune, a shock ran through her. A single thump of a pulse; an instant of sudden, intense pain; a long, drawn-out exhale; a last flicker of thought before sleep. The psychopomp within her recognized the sensations for what they were: a single moment. A crucial one. A final one. A death no longer connected to a lifetime's course, no longer tied to any destiny.

Renai picked up the sliver of Fortune, careful—oh so careful—not to prick her finger with the point. She whispered a little prayer of gratitude to Grace and, after a moment's consideration, pressed the sliver of Fortune into the cigarette, rolling it between her fingertips so that it drilled deep into the tightly packed tobacco leaf, sharp end first. When the Fortune was completely embedded in the cigarette, she tucked it behind her ear, equal parts hiding place and safety precaution.

Unnerved by the now-absolute darkness, Renai unfurled her butterfly wings and let them carry her out of this place, trying to decide whose destiny-less life Grace intended for Renai to end. Because if Grace was right about Ramses—if he'd sidestepped his death by giving up the entirety of his Fortune—one poke of this needle and Ramses' next moment would be his last.

But then, since Renai also lacked a destiny, it could also do the same thing for her.

CHAPTER TWENTY-ONE

WHEN RENAI ROSE to the next higher level of the Underworld, the one she'd always thought was the bottom of everything, she found Salvatore waiting for her, pacing and alone. He whirled to face her as soon as her feet touched the damp earth. "Where have you been?" he asked, his tone somewhere between incredibly relieved and pissed-as-hell.

Renai's first impulse was to take his concern for her well-being as sweet, if unnecessary, but when she hesitated for a moment, trying to think of how to explain her impulse to remain behind, he ruined it by saying, "The truth shouldn't be that hard to come up with." Growled it, really. And suddenly his worried big brother act was just him being a presumptuous asshole.

"First," she said, hearing her mother in her voice, "I don't appreciate that tone. I'm a grown-ass woman. Only man who gets to speak to me like that is my father, and you don't look like Charles Raines to me, my dude. Second, I would really like to know where your habitually tardy self gets the damn *nerve* to come at me over a few minutes of —"

Sal made a noise that was half-laugh and half-trying-not-to-choke. "A few minutes? You kept me here waggin' my own fuckin' tail for over an hour!"

"No —" Renai began, drawing the word out, but she broke off when the truth occurred to her, when she saw her realization echoed in Sal's eyes. She glanced down at her watch, at the top of the screen where a single LCD dot marked the day of the week. It was days further along than it ought to be. "No," she said again, though this time in quiet disbelief.

Sal's ears swiveled around, like he was trying to pinpoint the location of a strange noise, and then he squinted up at the moonless, starless night sky. "Sheeeee-it," he said, when whatever he saw there confirmed his suspicions. "I guess time really does fly when you're having fun." He glanced over at her, his eyebrows drooping. "Sorry. For, you know, jumping your shit."

Renai felt haughty threaten to twist her face and tightened her lips into a thin line instead. "Yeah, well, thanks for saying so. I'd have been pretty pissed too, I guess." She was proud of herself for not mentioning that Sal had done this very thing to her more than once. "Guess that's why Howl bounced, huh?"

Sal chuckled, but sounded more nervous than amused. "No, she took off when she figured out where Grace sent us."

"Which is?"

"Come and see for yourself," he said, nodding for her to follow him into the flat, poorly painted trees. Renai followed, even though she wanted nothing more than a long shower and an even longer sleep. She'd been awake for so long that she was starting to get that fuzzy, disconnected feeling that came midway through an all-nighter, her eyeballs tight and dry in their sockets, her body and especially her head increasingly susceptible to gravity. But they only had a matter of hours before the Hallows began. She'd just have to tough it out.

Following Sal through the cardboard cutout forest of the deep Underworld, Renai tried to piece together everything they'd learned about Ramses, but it all felt too slippery, like she only had part of the story. At least she was too tired to be nervous about the fact that she never remembered the three-day span of the Hallows. Right now, a three-day nap sounded like a gift. Then the Underworld version of Orleans Parish Prison came into view, and Renai reconsidered her earlier thought; now she wanted nothing more than a reason to stay out of that place.

Built like a fort and carved from a single block of black ice, the prison smoked and steamed in the relatively warm air, but never seemed to diminish in size. It rose high above the tops of the false trees, its solidity among artifice making it even more imposing. Not that it needed help. Every surface of the prison was sharp or hard or both, as though its architect had only used thorns and broken glass in its construction. Worst of all, the prison's entrance stood open, a wide, gaping maw that wasn't so much a sign of welcome as it was a statement of authority. Whoever ran this place had so much confidence in their security that they didn't even bother locking their door.

"Welcome to the Oubliette," Sal muttered. "Talk about 'abandon all hope,' huh?"

"I thought Hell was one of the Far Lands," Renai said, unable to make herself speak any louder than a harsh whisper.

"It is," Sal said, matching her low volume. "This is just a piece of it. A little slice of eternal damnation right here in the Underworld."

"Like an embassy?" She was only talking to keep her mind busy, she knew, trying to distract herself from how swiftly they were drawing closer to the prison, almost to the entrance now.

"More like a tumor."

Renai glanced down at the psychopomp. He seemed off, distant. His movements were hesitant, almost timid. Not in pain, exactly, more like he anticipated—dreaded, even—some agony yet to come.

"Why are we here?" Renai whispered. When the psychopomp didn't answer, she repeated herself, and this time she didn't lower her voice. "Salvatore. Why are we here?"

Her answer came from the direction of the prison when a rough, deep voice she recognized and wished she didn't said: "I was wonderin' the same damn thing my ownself."

The young black man who had spoken leaned against the wall just beside the open door, his hands tucked into his pockets and one bare foot crossed over the ankle of the other, as if the frost and the razored edges didn't bother him. They probably felt like home. He wore a three-piece suit of dark red fabric tailor-cut to his broad shoulders and his narrow waist, without a tie and with his dress shirt unbuttoned halfway down his chest. A pair of horns jutted up from his forehead, as sharp and cruel as the prison itself. His otherwise handsome face was marred by the tears of tar that bled from his eyes.

Whenever a voodoo priest began a ceremony, the first loa they called on was Papa Legba, the ancient, benevolent god of the crossroads between the world of the living and the world of the spirits. Nibo and Plumaj and all the others had charge over a single Gate, but Legba—the opener of the ways—controlled them all. The loa that waited for them here, his insolent smirk as unsettling as the black tears that streaked down his face, was the Petwo side of Legba—the Shadow of his soul if he were mortal. He was pride and rage and lust. He closed the paths that Legba opened, locked them so tight only Legba or the Hallows could reopen them. He called himself Cross.

Renai had forgotten just about all the details concerning the circumstances of her resurrection. She knew that Jude Dubuisson had tricked her into giving up her afterlife for him. She suspected that an angel had been the one to kill her. And even with those memories firm in her mind, it was Cross's face who visited her nightmares.

"Speak of the devil," Sal said. "You're just the loa we were looking for."

"The fuck you were," Cross said, lurching away from the wall and swaggering toward them. "Don't talk no caca-shit at me, boy." He waved one long-nailed finger at Sal, like he was chastising a puppy who had piddled the carpet. "I ain't your podna, me."

"Sal, what's he talking about?"

Cross curled his whole face into an elaborate, overwrought sneer. "'Sal,'" he repeated, in a whiny, mimicking voice, "'what he talking about?'" He spit on the ground. "Like you ain't got no part of this escape."

Shit, shit, shit, Renai thought. *The deal with Mason. Cross knows.* Her heart started hammering in her chest, and before she could stop them, her wings unfurled. They swept her into the air, reaching up for the next level of the Underworld and—

Nothing. She hovered a few feet off the ground, but she could ascend no higher. Her first panicked thought was that the Oubliette had hold of her somehow, but then she heard the loa's harsh, humorless laughter and, remembering his role in the Underworld, realized what had happened: Cross had locked the Gates.

All of them.

Renai forced herself back to the ground and folded her wings away. Her mind raced, but she could see no way out. Maybe that explained why Sal just sat there, ears flat against his skull, tail tucked between his legs. Cross reached down and clutched at himself, adjusting his crotch before stuffing his hands back into his pockets.

"Go ahead," Cross said, "say you don't fuckin' know nothin' again. 'Cause tryin' to fly away ain't made you look guilty at all, no."

"We really don't," Renai said. "We're tracking down a lost soul."

"Peculiar-ass place to be doin' that," Cross said.

"You know as well as I do that lost souls end up here all the time," Sal said. "It ain't just the ones who deserve it in there."

"Ain't no one in there." Cross reached into his coat pocket and pulled out a short stub of a cigar, which he lit by rubbing its tip against the pad of his thumb. The smoke it emitted was acrid and foul, like burning tires. "Seein' as every devil, black spirit, damned soul, and toppled god that's supposed to be on ice in there done absconded in the fuckin' night."

"*What?*" Sal asked, so surprised that he didn't even curse.

"Right before the Hallows," Renai said, more to herself than actually expecting a response. "They'll be able to go wherever they want."

Cross made a grunt of affirmation, grinning past the cigar clamped between his teeth. He tucked it into the corner of his mouth so he could speak. "Them we ain't already caught by then, anyways."

"That's why you locked the Gates," Sal said. "To make it harder for them to escape."

Cross tipped an imaginary hat in the psychopomp's direction. "For all the good it's gonna do us. Them Gates is gonna be 'bout as useful as a half-inch dick come midnight. Which I guess was the plan, huh?"

Which was when Renai realized what Cross had meant by her being a part of the escape. Judging by the high-pitched whine coming from Sal, he'd figured it out, too. "You think *we* did this," she said.

"Ain't no 'think' about it. I know it for a fact. This place has got y'all's stink all over it. Only thing—"

"That's from the other side!" Sal shouted. "Check with Plumaj! We collected a death from—"

Cross waved a hand at Sal and muttered a word that sounded familiar to Renai, which was strange, since it was in a language she didn't even recognize. Whatever the word was, it made the air vibrate like a thunderclap without sound and snapped Sal's mouth closed mid-word. "*Only thing,*" Cross repeated, "I can't figure is why you come back. You leave something behind? Or y'all just that caca-shit-for-brains stupid?"

Renai truly didn't know what to say. Not only was she being accused of something she hadn't done—couldn't have done if she'd wanted to—she felt like she was missing some crucial detail. Cross said he'd smelled them both here at the prison, while Sal claimed that the scent he was picking up was from the living side of things, when he'd gone to collect Miguel Flores from Orleans Parish Prison. But that was impossible, wasn't it? Unless her memory lapses were far greater than she thought. Or Cross was lying to get them to confess. Or she and Sal were getting framed somehow. Beside her, Sal was grunting against the gag of his sealed jaws, but Renai couldn't tell if the word he wanted to say was "run" or "wait" or "no" or "yes." Probably something else entirely.

So, certain that she couldn't lie well enough to fool Cross, and knowing that he wouldn't believe the truth of their innocence no matter how many times she proclaimed it, Renai opened her mouth and said what she'd been wanting to say since Sal first came through the First Gate without a soul to deliver, spoke the words that had been crowding her tongue throughout their search through the depths of the Underworld.

"I want to talk to the Thrones," she said.

Cross's mouth stretched open so wide that he dropped his cigar, laughed so hard that he had to bend down and clutch his knees. Renai would have thought the loa was faking it, if not for the strained, high-pitched giggling tearing out of his throat. No one would make that embarrassing a sound if they could help it. It would have been the perfect opportunity to make a break for it, except they had nowhere to go.

When Cross recovered—still grinning and shaking his head—he sighed. "Thrones ain't lookin' to help you, no. What you think, you gon' lawyer up?" He waved his hand at her, like shooing away a fly. "Fuck outta here with that noise. You got your head up in them TV shows too much, girl." The way he said the word "girl" let Renai exactly what Cross thought of women. "This here is my place. My rules. You 'bout to tell me everything you know, everything you done. Your little dog, too. And when I'm finished, ain't even your own shadows gon' recognize you."

Shadows, Renai thought, and with it came an idea, a desperate grasp at a fleeting hope. She didn't know if it would work, since Cross had closed the Gates. But she had to try. Cross came toward her, not hurrying, knowing he didn't need to. Hands loose at his sides, a humorless grin plastered on his face. Nothing threatening—except everything about him was a threat. She tried to see the world from his perspective, tried to imagine what it must be like to be closed off from everyone and everything. To be bound—not only by his role as a god—but as only a reflection of another. To be perpetually an antagonist, to be seen, first and always, as a devil.

No wonder his eyes never stopped weeping.

When she found that tiny seed of compassion, she reached down deep and woke up the tempest within her. The power burst through her skin like the slap of scalding hot water, the winds lashing out and the rain pelting down, hammering Cross full in the chest and driving him back. His laughter howled like the tempest she'd hurled at him. He leaned into it, slanted almost sideways, and crept forward, his bare toes digging into the muddy Underworld earth, his coat flapping behind him. The tempest whirled around her, with Renai at its calm, still center. She felt Sal, fur sopping wet and shivering, huddle against the back of her legs. She gritted her teeth and pushed harder, trying to scour the flesh from Cross's bones. He kept creeping forward.

"Ain't no storm can hold me back, girl!" he shouted. "Can't nobody stop me but me!"

"That's what I'm counting on," Renai said, and pulled her mirror from the nowhere place where it resided. She held it up with both hands, where Cross couldn't help but look into its surface where his other half waited. Behind him, Cross's shadow twisted and bent, the horns flattening and spreading into a hat's brim, an arm stretching down to become a third leg. An old man, leaning on a cane.

Papa Legba.

Renai felt her magic take hold, her destructive capacity as a death spirit as wild and terrible as a hurricane. She gripped Cross with this power, as tightly as she could, and *tore*. She couldn't pull him free from his Shadow; they were too linked, too complete a circuit to be separated, but she could break Cross's hold on this place. She strained, bearing down on Cross with all her strength, not pulling back even when she tasted blood, and then, with a scream of rage that cut off midway through, the young, horned man melted into darkness and an elderly black man in a lavender suit stood in his place, nearly toppled by the tempest the instant he appeared.

Renai didn't restrain the storm's power so much as she simply exhausted her strength, the wind and the rain vanishing in an abrupt silence, like a singer's voice giving out mid-note. She wavered on her feet, nearly dropping to her knees, but her wings unfurled and fluttered, keeping her upright.

"My oh my oh my," Legba said, shaking the rainwater from his trilby hat and grinning his gap-toothed smile at her. Everything about him was different than Cross, even his voice. When Legba spoke, his tone was soft and kind and tinged with a Caribbean accent. "Strange weather we're having, don't you think?"

Much as she wanted to beg the loa for his help, Renai needed some time to regain her strength. She dropped to the ground with her back against one of the fake trees, hands trembling and head spinning and skin slick with sweat. Sal wandered off to just at the edge of earshot, shaking himself dry and cursing and muttering, though Renai couldn't make out what he was saying. Legba seemed content to wait for them, smoking from a clay pipe he'd stuffed with some sweet-smelling dried leaf.

Renai kept telling herself that she didn't have time to rest, and then kept struggling—and failing—to rise. She'd been on the track team in high school and remembered once going all weak and jittery like this during an especially hot summer practice. Her coach had taken one look at her and sent her into the locker room with a trainer, saying she was right on the verge of heatstroke. The trainer had told her she was lucky that she was a girl, that the football players got told to tough it out. Renai hadn't been able decide if that was more infuriating to be thought weaker because of her sex, or more sad on behalf of the boys.

The next day, she'd clocked the fastest mile she'd ever run.

Eventually—second after precious second until midnight slipping away—her skin cooled and her heart stopped fluttering in her chest and she managed to haul herself, shakily, to her feet. Sal came trotting over. There were things she needed to know, questions about the Underworld and the holes in her memory and the circumstances of her resurrection, but before either she or Sal could speak, Legba pointed in their direction with the stem of his pipe and said, "The both of you got someplace else to be, no?"

Sal sighed. "The Thrones, right? How pissed are they, on a scale of one to wiping-us-from-existence?"

Renai felt a spike of guilt tinged with a flicker of hope. Part of her had known, from the moment that Sal came through the First Gate alone, that they didn't have the jurisdiction or the knowledge or the power to handle Ramses' disappearance on their own. That they were, to quote her father, "trying to stuff ten pounds of shit into a five-pound bag." But Mason's offer had made her greedy, which had made her stupid. She'd been so focused on finding Ramses, so desperate to trade what he'd stolen for a one-way ticket into the Far Lands, that she'd done everything but plug up her ears and yell "I can't hear you" to her own conscience. She had no idea why Sal had gone along with it. But now they were caught. Now the authorities could handle everything. Now Death could sort it all out.

But then Legba went and ruined everything.

"Not Les Morts," he said, shaking his head. "This call come from the Marketplace."

"That means the living world," Sal said to her, speaking to her without turning his head.

"If there was ever a time for you to not mansplain at me out the side of your mouth . . ." Renai said, letting the rest of her threat go unspoken.

Legba's lips quirked, and he put his pipe back into his mouth to keep from smiling. After a few puffs, he took it out again and said, "I can't reopen the Gates until after the Hallows begin, not without risking another struggle with my dark side, but this I can grant. No need to thank me."

He gestured at them with his cane, which clattered like a ceremonial rattle, and suddenly they were bathed in a harsh, hot glare. Renai tried to find the source of it, but it was like looking directly into a spotlight. Her eyes watered, and her heart started pounding, though in anticipation of what, she couldn't say. Sal squeezed as close to her as he could.

From somewhere far, far away, Renai heard the sound of a trumpet being played. It was just at the edge of hearing, but she swore that if she could just hear it a little better, she'd be able to recognize the musician. Maybe even the song.

And then, with an abrupt explosion of momentum like a ride in an amusement park, Renai was yanked all the way to the top of the Underworld.

And then out of it entirely.

CHAPTER TWENTY-TWO

A YANTRA WOVEN, THREAD by thread, image by image, into a fine carpet. Chalk on a gravestone sketching out a shaky veve that won't last through the next rain. A temenos built of marble that survives for centuries longer than the forgotten deity who made it sacred. A mandala sculpted out of colorful sand, poured with the grace of deep meditation. A Solomonic circle, drawn according to a precise formula. Ancient as the kivas of the Anasazi, modern as the copper mesh of a Faraday cage. Arcane symbols and geometries, ritual and craft and symmetry. Sacred spaces, messages, prayers, boundaries, traps. The universe made small, the soul writ large. Circles within circles, all with one purpose: to let the magic in and keep the darkness out.

⧖

Renai knew she wasn't in the Underworld anymore before she even opened her eyes. After the sterile, still silence of the other side, the living world roared and reeked and rioted all around her. She smelled the baking cake scent of lit candles, the bleach bite of cleaning products, the old pennies taste of metal polish, and the greasy, rich aroma of fried chicken. She heard the bluster of traffic, engines and horns and sirens, the rumble of an old AC unit, and the constant hum of electrical appliances. The plaintive croon of a brass instrument had stopped the moment she arrived.

She found herself kneeling on a hard, cold floor, her skin itchy and too tight, like her anxiety had become literal, her flesh crawling. Her eyes she'd kept squeezed shut, a headache pounding between her temples, genuinely afraid to see who, or what, had the power to pull her—and only her, Sal got ripped away from her before she left the Underworld—past the boundary of the First Gate so easily.

"You sure it's her?" A voice she almost recognized, deep and raspy and thick with an old-school New Orleans accent.

"Last time I trusted something from the Underworld, I ended up with a tattoo on my tit and a nasty case of the clap," a second voice said, higher-pitched, but harder-edged than the first one.

"That a no?"

"That's a no." A throat cleared. "Hey. Creepy little death spirit. Your name Renaissance Raines?"

When Renai opened her eyes, the world was a wash of primary colors, blues and reds and yellows, the blurred haze of thermal imaging. Streaks of crimson and deep pools of indigo filled the room; not heat, but magic. Wards and talismans and—surrounding her—the twisting geometries of a sum-moning circle. Two human-shaped figures stood side by side within their own smaller circle burning like fireworks. Then the colors slipped out of her vision. Slowly, like the afterimage of a blinding camera flash fading away, and she could see normally again.

She'd been summoned by a petite white woman with short auburn hair and a tall, lanky black man with round spectacles and a trumpet hanging loose in his hand. The woman wore jeans torn at the knee and a T-shirt with a symbol that Renai was pretty sure came from *Star Wars,* and the man had on tan slacks, a white dress shirt that hung baggy on his lean frame, and a brown vest. She had rounded cheeks and smooth skin; might've been any-where from her late twenties to her early thirties, maybe even older if she was a four-times-a-week-yoga-health freak. He had the complexion of a man aged by years of long nights spent in bars, but Renai's assumption might have been biased by the instrument in his hand.

The two seemed familiar somehow, but if Renai knew them, the memory of it had been wiped out by her resurrection. When she finally recognized the musician, it was from her memories from before her death: an album cover from her father's vinyl collection. "You're Leon Carter," she said.

The woman snapped her fingers three times in quick succession at Renai, a gesture both irritating and effective. "Try again, Sparkles," she said. "We didn't ask for *his* name. We asked for *yours.*"

"Sparkles?" Renai looked down at herself and saw that she wore the floofy, lace-covered white dress and the red sneakers she'd been buried in. She tugged at it and felt the pull on her wings at her back. She flexed them, finding them smaller and more rigid than their counterparts in the Underworld, certainly nothing that would carry her weight. Reaching back, she ran a hand along the fragile, paper-thin tip of one wing, coming back with fingertips covered in glitter.

Whether it was shock from being pulled across the First Gate, or some effect of the summoning these two had worked, or just simple exhaustion, Renai's thoughts felt sluggish and thick. She wanted to ask why she should trust either of them, why she would confirm information as intimate and magically potent as her name for a couple of kidnapping strangers who obviously had both the knowledge and power to use it against her, and where they'd learned her name in the first place. What came out instead was "My name?"

"Yes," Leon said, patient and coaxing. "Tell us who you are."

"Oh, suck my dick with this pussy-footing shit," the woman said. She made a twisting, grasping motion with one hand, and the chalk circle around Renai flared phosphorescent-bright.

A sensation like the sudden need to vomit gripped Renai, and words came ripping out of her mouth, "My name is Renaissance Dantor Raines! I'm a psychopomp and I'm searching for Ramses St. Cyr and I've forgotten so much of the last five years that it scares me!"

"Regal, that's enough," Leon said. He grabbed the woman's wrist and shook the gesture out of her hand. The compulsion to speak ebbed out of Renai. She'd managed to hold back Sal's name, and her deal with Mason, and her desire for a one-way trip to the Far Lands, but only just. If Leon hadn't stopped Regal — assuming something so fake-sounding was actually her name, but then again her own parents had called her Renaissance, so who was she to judge — she'd have told these two everything she wanted to keep secret, down to who she thought about when she touched herself on long, lonely nights and the time she'd cheated on an English exam in high school.

The thought that this woman had that much control over her made her want to throw up for real.

She locked eyes with Regal and saw a person who just straight-up did not give a fuck about her. Renai had seen that expression before. Sometimes because she was a woman, sometimes because of the color of her skin. Her youth, her piercings—back before resurrection had sealed the punctures in her lip, eyebrow, nose, and ears—her neighborhood, her idiolect, the education that taught her words like "idiolect," all of it meant that people thought they knew her just by looking at her. Renai felt her spine straighten, her thoughts clearing like she'd been nodding off and had jolted awake. She smiled at Regal, but really it was just showing her teeth.

Sooner she was done with this bitch right here, the better.

"What do you want from me?" Renai phrased it as a question, but her tone made it a command. Regal smiled too, a mirror of Renai's own. Good. They understood each other. That meant the woman finally saw her at least —instead of whatever image she'd looked down on.

That, she could work with.

Before Regal could say anything, Leon—who must have read the room based on the placating tone in his voice—said, "The dead are restless. Spirits can't cross over, bodies up and walkin' 'round. Couple, three days now, far as we can tell. Can't none of us on this side figure out why, and if y'all sent us messages, we ain't got 'em."

Since Cross locked the Gates, Renai thought. *Of course. 'Pomps are trapped in the Underworld, the dead are stuck here. Maybe that's why we couldn't find Ramses. Maybe he's been here all along.*

"And?" Renai crossed her arms and cocked her hip. "None of that explains why you brought me here." *Or how you knew my name*, she thought.

"We can't unfuck your shit until we know exactly how bad you taint sniffers fucked it," Regal said. "Is that a satisfactorily succinct explanation?"

Renai kissed her teeth. "Girlfriend," she said, "you keeping runnin' that mouth and you'll find out what I think is satisfactory. You really think Death needs your help? A couple of souls in need of a guide to the hereafter?" She gave them a dismissive backhanded wave. "Child, please."

Regal smirked and raised her hand, fingers already twisting into the crooked gesture that had forced Renai's earlier word vomit. Renai stepped to the edge of the circle, her breath misting its surface like she breathed on a mirror. "Go ahead with that truth juju on me, too," she said. "I can't *wait* to tell you just what I think of your ratchet ass."

"Oh, I like you," Regal said, dropping her hand and shooting a grin in Leon's direction. "Guess that makes *you* good cop, Voice."

Leon frowned at Regal, an I-told-you-so gesture that Renai didn't have the context to fully understand. "Me and her," he said to Renai, tipping his head in Regal's direction, "we can't stay clear of this. Ain't even Death got a say in that. I'm the Voice of this here city, and Regal Constant is her Magician. When New Orleans got a problem, we aim to be the solution."

Renai wished it could be that simple, that she could just accept their help. They were certainly offering more than anyone on her side of things. But Sal had told her from the very beginning that there were rules about cooperation with the living. That the Gates kept things separate for a reason. The living weren't their enemies, exactly. More like their competition. If Sal were here, he'd refuse to help them, in language that would give Regal a run for her money. But he wasn't. They'd summoned *her*, not him. And she wasn't so sure she should take Sal's every word as gospel anymore. He'd been acting strange for days and keeping secrets for far longer.

Besides, Legba had opened the way for her to come here. He had to have known who was on the other end.

Hell with it, Renai thought. *Especially since they can just squeeze whatever information they want out of me.* Renai sighed and nodded to herself, like she had come to a decision instead of merely accepting the inevitable. "The Gates to the Underworld are locked," she said, "so nobody gets in and nobody gets out. Legba letting me come here was a special case."

"Why?" Regal asked. She'd taken out a little black notebook, scribbling in it like some kind of cop.

Renai shrugged. "Maybe 'cause you two are so powerful and important?"

Regal started to say something, but Leon put his hand on her shoulder and stopped her. "Why did Papa Legba lock your doors, she mean to say. We do somethin' wrong? You know a way we can make it right?"

Right then, when Leon's first impulse was to blame some flaw in himself, to seek reconciliation instead of triumph, that was when Renai decided to trust Leon, to tell him everything she knew and accept his help. It would only be much later that she'd realize she'd done so because he reminded her of her father.

"It wasn't Legba that closed the Gates, it was his other side, Cross." When she heard his name, Regal literally snarled, curling her lips and growling like a cornered cat, but said nothing. Renai chuckled. "That's him, all right. And as bad as you got it now, it's about to get worse."

Regal snorted. "Worse than a constipated soul chute and streets full of zombies?"

"Ain't zombies," Leon said, snapping at Regal like she'd dropped the n-bomb. "No spirit, no mind. Just a corpse that ain't got the sense to know it oughta be in the ground. Name 'a that is ghoul, not zombie."

Regal muttered an apology, and Renai broke the uncomfortable silence that followed. "Anyway, yeah. Worse. 'Cause Cross locked the Gates to keep the dark and nasties from slipping through into your side. But once the Hallows start, that won't matter."

"That this Ramses St. Cyr you lookin' for?" Leon asked, just as Regal said, "What the actual fuck is a Hallows?" It took Renai a second to separate the questions enough to answer them.

She looked to Leon first. "No, Ramses is just a lost soul I'm looking for. Not connected at all." But as soon as she said it, she doubted herself. A mortal who made a deal with a devil slips out of his appointed death — for a second time, no less — right when all the devils in the Underworld get busted out of jail? That was a massive coincidence. Regal held up her hands and widened her eyes in a I'm-still-waiting-here gesture that shook Renai out of her thoughts. "And the Hallows are when the world of the dead and the world of the living are aligned." She couldn't stop herself from letting a little bit of petty slip out. "Here I thought you knew everything."

Regal frowned, shrugged. "I had more of a . . . hands-on education, let's call it."

Renai held up one hand, palm up, facing the other woman. "Let's say this is the world of the living, okay?" Regal nodded. Renai held up her other hand. "This is the world of the dead. The Underworld."

"With you so far."

Renai touched the tips of her index fingers together. "When you're alive, if you believe in the afterlife at all, you think it's like this. You cross over from one world to another." She pressed her palms together. "But in reality, it's more like this. It's all the same world, just two sides of the same coin. The dead and the living are always side by side, we just can't see each other." She entwined her fingers together, so that her two hands made one big fist. "During the Hallows, it's like this. For three days, we can see each other, interact with each other, if we really want to."

Regal snapped her fingers. "The three days from Halloween to All Souls' Day."

"Exactly. So starting at midnight, it won't matter whether the Gates are open or closed. They won't really exist at all."

"Lettin' your dark and nasty come struttin' into our house," Leon said.

"Like I said, it's about to get worse."

"So what do we do?"

"What we can," Renai said. "I'll meet you at the entrance to St. Louis No. 1 at midnight. You help me find my lost soul, and I'll bring as many 'pomps as I can to solve your ghoul problem."

"And the dark and nasty?" Regal asked. "If it's over here when the Hallows end, won't Cross keep the Gates locked?"

"We'll have three days to figure that out," Renai said. She checked her watch, just an hour until midnight and the Hallows began. "But for now, you gotta send me back. Don't know what might happen if I'm still on this side in a summoning circle when midnight hits, but I'm in no hurry to find out, feel me?"

Regal started making passes through the air with her hands, tugging at the threads of magic that held the summoning circle together. "What I can't believe is that this shit happens every year and my fuck-knuckle ass didn't notice. Shouldn't the dead, like, way outnumber the living?"

Renai grinned. "Yeah, well. There's this world, the Underworld, *and* the Far Lands. To really explain things, I'd need three hands." She left out the part where she honestly had no idea what the Hallows were like because those three days were a constant blank space in her memories every year.

Leon chuckled, while Regal started speaking in a harsh, sibilant tongue. Renai could feel the working breaking down around her, the implacable gravity of the Underworld pulling her home. "He said you was funny," Leon said.

"Who did?"

"Jude Dubuisson. Said if we ever needed to talk to somebody on the other side to call you up." He smiled at her. "Ain't you wondered how we knew your name?"

Regal finished her magic with a sharply barked word and a clap of her hands that cracked the air like thunder. All the candles went out at once and the bottom fell out of the world and Renai went hurtling back across the barrier and into the Underworld.

She cursed Jude's name the whole way down.

⧖

When Renai came back to herself, she was once more in the Underworld, in the same one-car garage that Regal and Leon had summoned her to, still wearing the frilly white dress and red sneakers she'd worn on the other side.

Outside, she found the dew-slick grass and thick forest and idyllic atmosphere of the highest level of the Underworld. Exhaustion dragged at her. She'd been awake so long that she'd gone past tired into feeling like she had the flu, bones achy and head tight. The Voice and the Magician were lucky she hadn't curled up inside their circle and taken a nap.

She started to leave the garage, but saw that her shoe was untied and so bent down to tie it. Why had Regal's magic dressed her in the clothes she'd been buried in, anyway? Was that just how Jude remembered her, and that impacted the spell? Or was it significant in some way that she was missing? She wondered if these were the dress shirt and jean skirt she'd been wearing before transformed into something new, or if she'd left those clothes behind the way she'd left Sal. A giggly, sleep-deprived thought occurred to her, and she pictured herself shooting up from the depths of the Underworld bareassed as the day she was born.

Amusement turned to panic, and her hand went to the side of her head so fast she smacked herself. She let out a breath when she found the cigarette still tucked behind her ear, relieved that she hadn't lost the sliver of Fortune that held a moment of death. If she lost that, the whole trip beneath the Underworld would be for nothing. Her mother's St. Christopher medal still hung around her neck, too. A flush of shame went through her when it occurred to her that her first concern had been over possibly losing the sliver of Fortune.

Outside, she wandered for a while until she found a landmark she recognized, the teal and white awnings of Commander's Palace, its sign spelling out the name of the restaurant in individual bulbs, its corner tower appearing out of the fog like a lighthouse, a cemetery across the street. She checked her watch. Only half an hour until midnight, and this far Uptown, she'd never make it to her meeting with Regal and Leon if she didn't use her wings. Hopefully Sal would remember telling her that if they ever got split up to meet back at the First Gate.

Renai clenched her jaw, hesitant to let her wings unfurl. Trust had become a precious commodity lately. She knew Mason had some kind of backstab planned. He was a Trickster, that's how they thought. They saw the world in schemes and traps. Like Jude. The fact that Leon trusted him, ironically, made him *less* trustworthy. Which sucked, because she liked the musician, felt comfortable around him in a way she hadn't in a long time. Not since her resurrection.

Which brought her to Sal and the Thrones and the Gatekeepers. They were keeping things from her. It was a fact she simply had to face. They all knew more about her missing memories and Ramses' disappearance than they were telling her. The only question was whether it was some misguided keep-you-out-of-it-to-keep-you-safe sort of lie, or something more nefarious. Regal? Well, at least Renai could trust her to speak her mind.

And that brought Renai to the real source of her anxiety. She couldn't trust her own mind. Her missing memories, her lack of control, the strange, powerful tempest that lived within her. She didn't know who she was anymore, didn't know if she'd recognize herself if she looked in her mirror. Would she be able to forgive her own mistakes as easily as she washed away those of the dead she escorted through the Gates?

She had no answers to any of this, only doubts. No faith that she was doing the right thing, only desperation. And worse, no time for any of this. The Hallows were coming whether she was prepared for them—whether she'd remember them—or not.

And with that oddly comforting lack of options, Renai let her wings slip free. They billowed up behind her, far larger than they'd been on the other side, grabbing at the air like sails and carrying her up into the mist. She leaned into them, doubt swept away for just a moment by the sheer exhilaration of flight, and they carried her in the direction she wanted to go.

It took most of her remaining time to reach St. Louis No. 1, skimming along just high enough to move quickly and just low enough that she didn't lose herself in the fog. She circled once and saw Salvatore—still wearing his dog's shape—pacing back and forth by the cemetery's wrought-iron gate. She descended as quickly as she dared, but Sal didn't wait for her feet to hit the ground before the questions started.

"The fuck happened? Renaissance? You okay? Why did you change your clothes? Where have you been?"

In spite of her worries and her doubts and her fears of what was about to happen, his concern made her smile. She tucked her wings away, dropped to one knee, and hugged him, scratching her hands through his fur and squeezing him tight.

She had a plan, she wanted to tell him. If Ramses really had sold his soul to a devil, they could find both by finding the boy. The sliver of Fortune would end his life — which should have ended days, maybe *years,* ago — the devil could be named and caught, and everything could go back to normal. Simple. Clean.

Before she could answer any of the questions he'd fired at her, though, her watch beeped, and all across the Underworld, bells began to toll the hour.

Midnight.

⧗

When the Hallows began, when all the Gates opened and the world of the living mingled with the world of the dead, Renai was grateful for her brief jaunt to the other side. The sounds and the scents and the heat that swept over her might have overwhelmed her, otherwise. She stood, gathered the dangling strands of her dreads into a loose bundle, and started toward the physical front gate of the cemetery.

"Renaissance, wait—" Sal began, but Renai cut him off.

"I'll tell you everything, I promise," she told him, "but first there's some people we have to meet."

She gave him a little follow-me wave over her shoulder, a gesture she realized too late could be taken the wrong way, like she was telling him to heel. She winced, but if Sal minded, he didn't say anything, just trotted to catch up to her so that they reached the gate at the same time. Through the wrought-iron bars, Renai saw a little brown bird with a spiky crest perched on a NO PARKING sign, and a young black woman whose back was to her, hair cut short and natural and pulled into a tight bun, wearing a worn leather jacket and jeans and black combat boots that Renai coveted as soon as she saw them.

"*Discord,*" Sal said, a growl in his throat making him sound more savage than she'd ever heard before. She glanced down at him and saw that his fur was bristling, his head hunkered low and ears pulled flat, his lips peeled back in a quivering snarl. He shouldered the gate open, a long, slow creak, and then time seemed to slow as things started happening very fast.

Sal raced across the sidewalk, quicker than Renai had ever seen him move. The woman in the leather jacket turned, just as the psychopomp in the dog-skin leaped, a dog-catching-a-Frisbee glide that would have been funny if the object of his attention wasn't an innocent little bird that disappeared into his jaws when he snapped them closed.

And then the woman turned all the way around and Renai saw her own face.

CHAPTER TWENTY-THREE

RENAI'S VISION DOUBLED, and in a nauseating swirl that her mind could just barely handle, she saw both of herselves seeing each other, both disbelieving and confused and inexplicably full of rage.

Doppelganger, she thought.

Demon, she thought.

One thought belonged to a woman who had spent five years in the Underworld, and one thought belonged to a woman who had spent five years living in a world that couldn't see her, and both thoughts were hers, and both thoughts belonged to the other that wore her face. She crept closer to herself step by inevitable step, pulled closer by curiosity and revulsion and an implacable gravity. She saw herself—dreads and white dress and red sneakers and surrounded by shades—and she saw herself—boots and leather jacket and Sal behind her, jaws gnashing and head thrashing back and forth, and she couldn't remember which one was her and which one was *her.*

She reached out—and she reached out—and fingertips touched and palms touched and she pulled herself into herself. Scalding heat raced across her skin, so intense it felt cold; pain so sudden and powerful and deep that it felt like a frisson of pleasure, like the ache of desire. For one agonizing, blissful moment, she was no one at all. And then a strain, a pop, like a joint snapping back into place, and—for the first time in a year—a whole and complete Renaissance Raines opened her eyes.

Just in time to see the broken, bloodied lump of brown feathers being savaged by Salvatore's teeth shudder and flicker and become a tall white woman —with a long, elegant neck that stretched down to lean muscled shoulders, hair black as night accented by a slender white streak running from scalp to tip, her body sheathed in a black and gold gown that dragged the pavement and hugged her hips and left her strong, toned arms bare—an abrupt transformation that stretched the dog's jaws so wide that he released her with a yelp and backed away.

"We meet at last," said the being who had pretended to be psychopomp pretending to be a bird.

Cordelia, Renai thought, and then, *Discord.*

With a howl, Sal leapt at her again, but Cordelia reached out—a motion that was both casual and confident—and grabbed him by the throat. She pulled back a fist and punched him over and over again, her arm moving so fast that it blurred, before finally, mercifully, hurling him back to the pavement. Renai heard something crack, and he flopped onto his side, gasping for breath.

Renai was moving before she thought about it, dropping to her knees and cradling Sal's head in her arms, his tongue lolling out. Tears swirled in her eyes, fear and anger and confusion welling up and spilling out. She reached for the storm but couldn't grasp it, felt it whirling within her but just out of reach.

The ghost word, she thought, and *my wings,* and thinking two different things at the same time made a tearing sensation rip through her head, a pain so sharp that flecks of light danced in her vision.

Cordelia laughed, a musical, beautiful, cruel sound. "What am I to do with you, little psychopomp?" she said, more to herself than to Renai. "Like you, I'm of two minds." She smirked behind a hand daintily pressed to her mouth, a gesture that was condescendingly forced, a cat toying with her food. "Forgive my little aside, I simply couldn't resist. And yet, the question remains. What is to be done?" She came closer, a graceful sweep that was more glide than walk. She crouched down, wrinkling her perfect nose at Salvatore. "I hadn't counted on this tiresome stray spoiling my surprise quite so soon. I'd hoped you'd find the boy for me before I had to reveal myself." Sal struggled in Renai's arms, his claws scratching at the concrete, a growl in his throat. Renai didn't know if he was trying to flee or bite, but she could tell he didn't have the strength for either.

The goddess—she was certainly no mere psychopomp—looked up at Renai, and their eyes met. Cordelia's were deep pools of night: vast and dark and terrible. But not as terrible as her smile. "I could simply destroy you now, of course. Spare you the conflict that's already tearing you apart." She tilted her head back and forth, as though she were considering her options, a scale tipping one way and the other. "But then, I'd have to find that troublesome child on my own. Do I have time for that? No, I do not. I barely have the patience for this conversation."

Sal made a coughing, gasping noise that Renai—even with the pain lancing through her skull and the fear pounding through her veins—recognized as laughter. "Me. Fucking. Either," he said, each word a wheeze. He'd definitely have to change skins after this. Cordelia had beaten the hell out of him.

Cordelia flicked her eyes in Sal's direction, literally looking down her nose at him, an expression Renai had never understood until this moment. When the goddess turned her attention back to Renai, her whole face was lit with brutal glee. "I do so love it when a solution to a problem presents itself so neatly, don't you?" When Renai opened her mouth to answer, Cordelia shushed her with a finger held to her own lips. "I don't actually care what you have to say. I just want you to watch and *remember*."

With that same finger, Cordelia reached down and touched Salvatore between his eyes. The psychopomp stiffened, whether from pain or in anticipation of it, Renai couldn't tell. "Like you," Cordelia said, "I am a being of dissolution. Of endings. Of destruction." She squinted at something only she could see, her eyes roving around, seeking. "Ah, here we are," she said, her pretty mouth twisting into a sneer. "A perfect ending for a disgusting mongrel like you."

"No," Renai whispered, as if, somehow, she knew what was coming. From far away, almost as if she were imagining it, she heard screeching tires, saw a blur of motion in her peripheral vision, and then heard a thud and a truncated yelp of animal pain, sickening and final. A death snatched from the nowhere of possibility and forced into the here and now. In her arms, Sal collapsed in on himself, bones crunching and organs squelching and his face broken. She watched the light go out of his eyes.

"*No,*" she whispered again.

Cordelia bounced to her feet, buoyant and satisfied, swiping her hands against each other in a pantomime of a job well done. "That's settled," she said. "Now you've the proper motivation—"

Renai didn't know what the goddess intended to say next, because her vision went white and a profound silence filled her ears. Even though she couldn't hear herself, she knew she was screaming, in rage, in pain, in grief. The two halves of her each tried to act, each straining for the storm inside, for the destructive magic that lived in one's capacity for hate and the other's for empathy. The power that exploded from one version of herself when faced with injustice, that spilled from the other to break the bonds between the dead and their Shadows. Because she felt both hate for Cordelia and empathy for Salvatore, both sides of her reached for the same power, and she fought herself, wrestling for control of mind and body and magic, hammering at the crack in the foundation of her being.

As the sweet release of darkness rose up to claim her, Renai's final thought was to wonder who would guide her through the Gates, now that Sal was gone.

PART THREE

THE FAR LANDS

CHAPTER TWENTY-FOUR

SOMETIMES THE TWO are opposites, one good and bright, the other dark and malevolent. Ahriman and Ahura Mazda, locked in eternal combat. The twins Chernobog and Belobog, one with hair like pitch, his brother with eyes like the noonday sun. Glooscap and Malsumis, formed from the dust left over after the creation of man, one tasked with creating a perfect world, the other bent on building a land of misery. Avuncular St. Nicholas, who brings good children gifts and delight; demonic Krampus, who steals bad children away to be tormented. Sometimes one is found on the other side of the coin, not in opposition but in balance. The savage Enkidu comes from the wilderness to humble and tame the urbane, city-building Gilgamesh. The fierce Erzulie Dantor protects the children borne by her other aspect, the seductive Erzulie Freda. The self-centered Mait' Carrefour, who closes the ways that the benevolent Papa Legba opens for us all. Sometimes the one is a part of the whole that has slipped away: the Norse fylgja, the Egyptian Ka, the psyche's id.

Nothing is ever only itself. Everything is a part of something greater. Every light casts a shadow.

Renai woke up, relieved to find that it had all been just a terrible dream. Morning sunlight filtered in through a nearby window, and she let herself sink back beneath the covers, trying to remember what day it was. The bustle of her family moving about the house as everyone started their day—murmured conversations and a shower running and something sizzling in a pan and the scent of coffee—were as warm and comforting as the blanket she curled beneath.

And then a pan slammed against the stove and Regal Constant yelled something that sounded like "cock-nosed fuck-weasel," and Renai came all the way awake to the missing-the-last-stair realization that it was all real, every horrible second of it.

She closed her eyes and willed herself to fall back asleep, but gave it up after only a few heartbeats. She rolled over onto her back, pinning one of her wings uncomfortably beneath her. Groaning in frustration, she sat up, to find that someone had undressed her before putting her to bed. Her cheeks flushed.

That's when she noticed the scars.

Renai yanked the covers back and hopped out of the bed—a wide four-poster affair that had the baby-powder-and-peppermint-muscle-cream scent of an old lady's sheets—to get a better look at herself. Thankfully, whoever had put her to bed had left her panties on, so at least all her business hadn't been put out into the street. But they'd taken other liberties. Thick, livid red lines stretched down the center of each leg, crisscrossed over her belly, looped and swirled across her chest and around her shoulders, and then ran down her arms to her wrists. Each wrist had been circled multiple times, ending in what looked like an elaborate knot.

Tentatively, she ran a fingertip along one of the lines on her stomach and found that it didn't hurt. Nor was it exactly a scar. Instead of rigid flesh darker than the rest of her skin, the raised line on her belly was scarlet red and was rough and pliant to her touch. It felt, impossibly, like spun cloth that had adhered to her skin. It was as bright as the ink of a fresh tattoo and itched like one, too.

Same color as the stains on Seth's hands, she thought. It was a single person's thought, without conflict or confusion—a person who had met both Seth in a bar in the world of the living and Mason in a coffee shop in the world of the dead, who had collected Miguel Flores's soul in Orleans Parish Prison and then guided him through the Gates to Barren's streetcar. Renai remembered it all and more, things neither self had been able to recall: her time with Jude and her resurrection and those missing days during the Hallows. For a moment the room spun, and Renai had to hold on to one of the posts to stay upright.

Then she pushed it all down and focused on what was in front of her.

The Hallows had started, so both spirits and ghouls were running the streets. Seth and Cross and Mason and Cordelia all had some kind of scheme going—either working together or against each other—to turn the confusion to their advantage, and the Thrones didn't seem to give even half a fuck. And at the center of it all: the absent, elusive, infuriating Ramses St. Cyr. Her own shit would have to wait.

But first, she needed to find her damn clothes.

She was in a small bedroom with hardwood floors that creaked whenever she moved, with walls empty of pictures—likely all lost during the storm—and covered in peach paint; a queen-sized bed ate up most of the floor space. An alarm clock on a nightstand told her that it was late in the morning, closer to noon than dawn. A vanity hutch stood against the wall directly opposite the closed door, its mirror covered with a dusty black sheet. On the table beneath the mirror, neatly folded, she saw an assortment of the clothes she'd been wearing the night before.

She saw the boots first, remembered both wearing them and coveting them, and her vision swam for a second. *Don't wallow in it,* she thought, *just move.* So she shimmied into the frilly white dress—a maneuver complicated by the cumbersome butterfly wings growing out of her back—and stuffed her feet into the combat boots, glad that whatever power had decided on her wardrobe had given her something to cover her boobs, at least, but pissed that they hadn't left her any socks.

"Beggars and choosers, Renaissance," she muttered to herself as she yanked her laces tight, "beggars and choosers."

She scooped up the jacket, knowing that there was no way she'd be able to endure its sturdy weight crushing her wings against her back, and checked the pockets. Empty. Of course. The messenger bag holding her tablet, her jeans and her phone, the coin of Fortune and the black glass knife and the deck of Shadow cards and the seeing stone and the cigarette holding the sliver of death, all gone.

She reached into the nowhere place where she kept her mirror, and, after a moment of waving her arm around in awkward jerks, like a white person shaking a handkerchief at their first second line, she managed to get a hand on it and drag it into reality. *Least I still have this,* she thought, patting the mirror's surface.

Her moment of triumph was short-lived, however, when she thought of all she'd lost to get here, wherever *here* was. What was the damn point of any of this? She clenched her teeth and fought down a scream. All that time and effort, and all she had to show for it was a cheap watch, a pair of wings too small and weak to carry her, a broken mirror, and a jacket whose magic she couldn't use, since she couldn't even wear it.

She ran a finger along the line of red that ran across her shoulder, and a terrible possibility occurred to her. She didn't consider herself a vain person, but the thought that these marks might also crisscross her face made her shudder. She looked into her broken mirror and found, to her relief, that her face remained as she remembered it. Her hair, though, had changed, her dreads still as long and tightly twisted as they'd been in the Underworld, but now they shimmered when she moved, iridescent as a raven's wing. She grinned, imagining what Sal would say when he saw it, and then she remembered, and grief took the wind out of her like a fist to the gut. She sank back down onto the bed, and let it loose, tears streaming and sobs racking her body, no amount of willpower able to force away the memory of holding him when he died.

Renai had known loss before—a grandmother to age, an uncle to a heart attack, a classmate to drunk driving—but this hurt worse, because she knew for a fact that Sal was just *gone*. No afterlife, no journey through the Gates, no chance at the Far Lands. Just a spirit. Just a part of the machine.

Expendable.

After a while, she managed to draw in a shaky breath and hold it, to sit up and wipe the tears from her puffy eyes and send the mirror back to the nowhere place where she'd found it. It felt like she'd been weeping for a long time, but when she checked the clock, only a few minutes had passed. *Time flies when you're havin' fun,* she heard in Salvatore's voice, and a gasp of a laugh burst out of her, a sigh that she sucked back in so that it didn't become more crying. *Okay, Sal,* she thought, *let's do this.*

The door opened onto a dining room, a table just big enough for four, an ugly rug on the floor, a half-wall that formed a bar looking into the kitchen the next room over. Regal and Leon sat across from each other, plates of food in front of them, both silent and now looking at her.

"Morning," Leon said, at the same time that Regal said, "Glad to see you're still in one piece." Leon swiveled around in his chair and, though his back was to Renai, she knew he was giving Regal some serious stank-eye. Before Renai could say anything herself, though, she smelled eggs and coffee and biscuits, and her stomach yowled like an angry cat, and then everyone was laughing and whatever tension had filled the room slipped away.

Renai was filled, suddenly, with a sensation she couldn't explain; she just knew that it felt deeply and profoundly good to be around people again. People who saw her for more than an instant, people who were alive with more than a shade's lurking, silent presence.

She moved toward the kitchen, but Leon motioned her to sit at the table and went into the kitchen himself. The next few moments were filled with a kind of blissful domesticity, Leon asking what she wanted to eat, Regal telling her her hair was "seriously badass," and Renai just soaking it all in, knowing it wouldn't last.

And then the food was in front of her—scrambled eggs and biscuits made from scratch and grits so full of cheese that they were orange—and she was shoveling it away, barely pausing to breathe, much less hold a conversation. When she'd just about cleaned her plate, a third voice spoke from the far side of the room, one that Renai recognized right away.

"If I had any suspicions about who you is, the way you eat like my good-for-nothin' sister surely done eased my mind." Renai spun around, and looked into the smiling, tear-streaked face of Celeste Dorcet: the voodoo priestess who had taught her everything she knew about the loa—her mother's sister, and the last human being who had seen Renai before she was murdered.

They were hugging before Renai realized either of them had moved.

⧖

Celeste had aged since the last time Renai had seen her, round cheeks eroded to an ascetic hollowness, gray hairs peeking out from beneath the headscarf wound around her head. More than the five years that had passed weighed on the woman. She stood in the kitchen doorway, a cup of coffee in her unadorned, nail-bitten hands.

The Celeste that Renai had known had gone to the same nail salon every Thursday, had covered her fingers and wrists with rings and bracelets. She'd always said that a mamba's hands were her ambassadors to the world. Well, to be completely accurate what she'd said was *Don't nobody want healing from a pair of busted-up paws look like they too poor to take care of they ownself*, but it was practically the same thing. Renai knew from one glance at Celeste's hands just how much had changed.

Celeste Dorcet, the Voodoo Queen of New Orleans, a mamba who could trace her lineage in both teaching and blood to Marie Laveau, had turned her back on her faith.

That hadn't made her any less sharp, though. "I see you throwin' them eyes my way, so you might as well ask," Celeste said.

Renai couldn't think of a polite way to word it, so she just said it. "What happened to you?"

Celeste's lips tightened to a thin line. "What you think happened? You *died*, child."

The memory swept through Renai unbidden. That night in the voodoo shop in the Quarter, the same day that she'd met Jude Dubuisson for the first time. The scent of cinnamon, a movement at the corner of her vision, and then —

Renai put her hands underneath the table, so no one would see them shaking.

Next thing she knew, she was being led through the Underworld. Not by Salvatore, but by one of the psychopomps who were little better than shades themselves, an unspeaking, unsmiling woman in robes made of light. Renai knew more, knew she'd gotten caught up Jude's wake in the Underworld, that she'd stood before the Thrones and earned her passage to the Far Lands, that she'd traded it away to give Jude a second chance, a resurrection that had saved the city's soul and cost her greatly.

Now that she could remember all of it, she had conflicting feelings about the Trickster who had turned her life upside down. On the one hand, she'd made her own choices. He hadn't tricked her, like the part of her that had lived in the Underworld believed. On the other, if he hadn't come into Celeste's shop, she'd have lived the life she was meant to have, which took away some of the shine the part of her that had lived in this world had seen in him.

"I thought I was strong," Celeste said, shaking Renai out of her thoughts.

"I thought after the loa took my husband so young, that I could bow my head to their wisdom, no matter what load they put on my back." Her jaw trembled, and she tilted her head back, narrowing her eyes like someone fighting back tears. "But when I had to scrub your blood from off my floor, I cursed them with every breath. From the littlest loa ain't even got a name to the Great Bondye himself, I cursed them all. That's what happened to me."

"Jesus," Leon muttered.

Celeste let a half smile slip past her guard. "Cursed him once or twice, too," she said.

"And that's why you closed up the voodoo shop?" Regal asked, for once reading the room and softening her voice. "Me and Jude always wondered where you went. You know, after."

Celeste made a noise halfway between a laugh and a grunt of disgust. "Naw," she said, "that was on account of the got-damn tourists."

"The what?"

The onetime voodoo Queen of New Orleans let out a little groan as she eased into the empty chair left at the table. "Tourists. You know" — she slipped into an impression of a stereotypical white person, her words clipped and overly enunciated and spoken through her nose. "Gosh, look-ee here, Becky, a, uhhh, a magic voodoo candle!" She raised an eyebrow, her face twisting into exactly the same expression of haughty weariness that Renai's mother would have worn.

When she spoke again, her voice was her own. "One of them tour guides read about our Renaissance here in the paper, and before you know it, every time I look out my window there's a crowd of them, swarming like termites. Sweaty, hung-over, wearin' Mardi Gras beads all year long. And up in front, some no-account takin' money from these fools saying the police called it a robbery gone wrong. Then he suggests, just *suggests*, mind, that maybe this young woman lost her life in some ritual. That's because I can't sue his pasty ass if it's" — she paused and her voice shifted to her white-person impression again, her nose lifting into the air with snooty superiority — "merely speculation."

She chuckled, and it wasn't a kind sound. "I told him speculatin' was enough to get a pox conjured up for his pecker, but he kept on leadin' them tourists to me just the same." Celeste snorted. "And here I am just got quit of all them fools askin' where Katrina happened." She took a swallow of her coffee, grimaced, and glared down at her mug like it was the coffee's fault. "I wasn't stickin' 'round for more of that, no indeed. I locked my doors and ain't been back."

Renai let out a long, slow breath and wiped her palms on the hem of her dress, her breakfast making a solid, painful knot in her stomach. She'd been around more than enough death to know that it always had consequences, that her leaving this world would have left a wound. Maybe not as literal as the one left by Ramses, but an absence nonetheless. She'd been able to catch glimpses of her family from the Underworld, knew that her sister was struggling to conceive, that her brother was kind of a fuck-up, but that was all. If Celeste was any indication, Renai's life wasn't the only one that the fallen angel had impacted.

Regal scooted forward in her chair. "But what about—" she began, only for Leon to cut her off.

"Regal, no," he said, shaking his head and grinning in spite of himself.

"She can't lay that kinda sweet seductive shit out there and not finish me off, Carter," Regal said, smacking her hand on the table hard enough to make the silverware jingle. "I'm not about to stumble around all brain be-fuck-eld because I got my mind chewing on a case of narrative blue balls."

Celeste closed her eyes and rubbed her temples. "What nonsense is this foul-mouthed sorceress talking?"

"Did you pox that pecker or not?"

Renai burst out laughing, a tension coming out of her that she hadn't fully acknowledged, her giggling turning frantic, unrestrained. The others chuckled and grinned, but Renai laughed until tears came out of her, until her belly hurt, until she didn't know whether she was laughing at Regal's words or the embarrassing sounds she was making or the fact that she couldn't stop. It took a minute or two for her to calm down, to suck in a few ragged, snickering breaths.

"You okay?" Leon asked, quiet. Renai had no idea how to answer that, so she just nodded.

"The answer is no," Celeste said her voice entirely serious, "that was just somethin' I said. I don't do conjure work, 'less it comes bargin' in my door in the dead of night wearin' my niece's face." She shot a pointed glance in Renai's direction. "But even if I did, I never had a hand in no gris-gris like that. That's callin' on the loa's Petwo side. That's that bokor shit."

Regal nudged Leon with her elbow. "Why do I feel like I just got insulted?" she asked, without taking her eyes away from Celeste.

"'Cause you *did*," he said. "Your kind of power is unseemly, Magician."

"Shiny." She winked at Celeste, and then turned and pointed a finger at Renai. "That's as good a fuckin' segue as I think you're gonna get, Sparkles. So how about it."

All the eyes in the room turned toward her. "How about what?"

"How 'bout you tell us what happened to you," Celeste said. It wasn't a question.

"Well, first I died," she said, "but you already knew that part." Renai felt her way through the story as she told it, relieved to be able to remember the sequence of events in their entirety, but shaky on both the details and how many of them she could share with the living. "I met Jude in the Underworld, and we made a deal with the . . . with Death. I got resurrected and he caught a ride in my head." Celeste, who already wore an expression of stern disapproval at Jude's name, frowned in full-on displeasure at this comment. Renai plowed on ahead. "We tracked down his, well, his corpse, I guess. And he pulled himself back together. Body and soul and magic."

"Thrilled as I am to hear that Jude motherfucking Dubuisson came out smellin' like magnolias, we asked about *you*, child." Celeste did not, in fact, sound thrilled.

"The thing that killed me was a fallen angel. Jude pulled a trick, told the angel that he had this revolver that was able to kill a god. But it actually was cursed, so the angel tried to use it and got trapped instead. That was the trick: only an innocent hand could use the gun, but once you turn to violence, you're no longer innocent. The revolver pulls the evil out of you, but the fallen angel was pretty much all evil by that point so—" She made a sucking noise and closed her hand into a fist. "Like I said, trapped. And then, you know, the bad guy gets caught and the good guys win, right? But I was stuck. Dead too long to just creep back into my old life, and I didn't want to face —" She bit her lip, couldn't meet anyone's eyes. "Look, there's shit about the other side I can't say, y'know? I just can't."

Leon reached across the table and covered her hand with his own. "Say as much as you can," he said. "Ain't nobody at this table don't understand at least some of what you been through."

"I couldn't come back," Renai said, squeezing Leon's hand in thanks and then pulling away, "and I couldn't move on. They found a place for me in the Underworld as a psychopomp." She looked at Celeste. "That's a—"

"I had plenty of schoolin', me," Celeste said. "When you got somethin' to teach me, I promise I'll let you know."

Regal widened her eyes and mouthed "oh snap," but Renai pretended she didn't see it, that she hadn't heard the clapback in Celeste's voice. She cleared her throat. "Right. So things were fine for the first few months. I collected souls on this side of things, guided them on the other. But the longer it went on, the worse I felt. Part of me struggled with the Underworld side of things. Having to help people leave the worst of what they'd done in this life behind them? That was hard. And part of me struggled with what I have to do here. Sure, it's their time and all, but when you get right down to it, I'm the one that does it. For all the souls I've carried, I'm Death." She shrugged. "I tried my best, at least I think I did, but I just couldn't do it. Being a psychopomp was too hard. I was falling apart."

"Fault ain't entirely your'n, child," Celeste said. "The loa gave you an impossible task. Spirits are simple. Don't matter if they loa or gods, spirits or angels or demons, they only ever really one thing. Healing. Motherhood. Hunger. Death. Why you think Papa Legba got him a whole other person just to close the doors that he opens?"

Renai nodded, and it felt like some flower was blooming inside of her. None of the other psychopomps had tried to do both parts of the job like she had. There were the Gatekeepers, like Nibo and Bridgette, who helped the dead cast off the aspects of life that they'd clung to. And then there were the ones like Sal, who seemed only concerned with ending a life and carrying the coin of Fortune down to where it would end up in Grace's hands. Maybe the Thrones had expected her to choose one or the other. Or maybe they hadn't considered that she'd even try to do both. She hadn't thought of her struggle as a psychopomp in just that way before, and it made what she was about to say next make a whole lot of sense.

"Then came my first Hallows as a psychopomp. Those three days are always hell for 'pomps. It's like all the shades wandering in the Underworld get a hard reboot. Instead of one dead to guide through the Gates, you get dozens at a time. Every one of them wants to see their families, most of them plotting to stay on this side of things when the Gates go back up." Celeste opened her mouth to say something but thought better of it. Renai had a feeling anything she'd have asked would have come from her aunt, not from the mamba, so she was relieved that Celeste left it unsaid. The last thing she wanted to talk about was why she hadn't contacted her own family in the five years since her resurrection.

"So I'm running myself ragged, still having to collect the dead, but also trying to keep all the shades on the other side of things when All Souls' Day comes. Then at midnight, the world of the living and the world of the dead splits in two. And so did I." Regal made the sign of the cross, and Leon pulled a face like he'd just bitten his tongue. Only Celeste seemed unsurprised. "I'm not sure how to explain it. Honestly? I get to feelin' some kinda way just thinking about it." That woozy, light-headed sensation made her vision swim every time she tried to hold two separate thoughts or memories in one brain, but she thought she might be getting the hang of it. "But for the past five years, except for the three days of the Hallows, I've been living two lives. One on this side, and one on the other. My memories were cut in half, my emotions, everything." *And a storm spirit moved into the empty spaces inside me,* she thought, *stretched across the seam between the living world and the Underworld like some shadowy rubber band.* She realized that she was picking at a stitch in the tablecloth and clasped her hands together.

"But you yourself again come the Hallows, yeah?" Leon asked.

"No," Renai said, a little sharper than she meant to be, "during the Hallows it's worse. I'm two people crammed in one body, one mind trying to think in two directions at the same time. It's agony. Three days of crippling torture." *That's why Sal always gets jumpy around the Hallows,* she thought. *Always got jumpy. He knew what he was about to have to watch me endure.* She waved both hands at herself, in a gesture meant to indicate her whole state of being. "This is the first time I've been myself in years. I don't know how—"

"Things is different for you this time on account of this," Celeste said, dropping a small bundle of rough cloth onto the table. When no one else made a move for it, she turned her eyes toward the ceiling in exasperation and unwrapped it herself. Inside, a human figure made of sticks and twine—an effigy bound together with a single strand of thick red yarn, a twisted lock of hair pinned to the place where the figure's head should be—and a gris-gris pouch of supple brown leather, its mouth wound closed with a coil of barbed wire. The sight of the effigy made Renai's head swim for a moment, and then her vision locked together with eerie clarity, like a pair of binoculars going from blurred inconsistency to sudden, perfect alignment. *Yarn,* she thought, *that's what those lines all over me are. Not tattoos or brands. They're stitches.*

"Fuck me with a lightsaber," Renai muttered, "I thought voodoo dolls were just in movies."

"This ain't got nothin' to do with the loa," Celeste snapped, "this here is hoodoo. Conjure work. My people learned it from your'n, not the other way 'round."

"Bokor shit," Leon said, nearly a whisper, his voice distant and sad.

Celeste fixed her eyes on Renai and seemed not to have heard Leon at all. "You understand what I done for you, child?"

Renai nodded, forcing herself to meet the voodoo woman's eyes. "I do," she said. "And I'll make it count, I swear." What people didn't understand about voodoo as a religion was that it was nothing like the movies. Deep down, it was a faith based on respect: for one's ancestors, for one's community, for this world and the next and one's place in it. You asked the spirits for help, but you abided by their answer. If you made a charm to ward off a curse or mixed a salve to heal some hurt, it was because the loa had directed you to, were using your hands to help them shape this world. Hoodoo, like all magic, was the opposite. It was a refusal to accept the will of higher powers. It was arrogance made manifest in the world.

For someone who had devoted her life to the religion of voodoo, working some hoodoo without the blessing of the loa — even for healing — was a grave sin.

Something about the leather pouch tugged at Renai's attention. If it was anything like the talismans that Celeste had made back when Renai was alive, it could contain dried herbs and sticks gathered from ceremonial fires, stones with a loa's veve scratched on them, pictures of loved ones or saints, maybe even bones or teeth. Though some could be turned to evil purposes, in Celeste's hands they were always protective charms, imbued with a tiny fraction of a loa's power. Unlike the effigy, Renai wouldn't have found it strange that Celeste would have made one, except that she claimed to have given up her faith entirely. "I get what the doll is for," she said, "but why did you gather me up a gris-gris?"

"You had that on you when we found you," Regal said.

Which meant that it could be anything, a ward against harm or a curse that would bring it, a charm to bring luck or a fake with no power at all. Renai reached out for the gris-gris, unable to stop herself, even though she knew it might be a trap left by Cordelia. When she picked it up, its contents clicked and clacked as the small hard objects within fell against each other. The psychopomp inside of her felt the faint whispers of an Essence: a gruff, often vulgar, sense of humor, a love of old movies, an affinity for art, a cynical outlook and a bitter temper and a tendency toward screwing up words with more than two syllables. She knew that if she unwound the wire and opened the gris-gris, she'd find a handful of sharp teeth and small bones, a couple of broken raven's feathers, and a piece of spray-painted concrete. Knew that the inside of the leather that made up the bag was covered with soft brown fur.

Neither Cordelia nor Celeste had made this gris-gris. *She* had. And it held the fragile remnants of Salvatore's Essence.

Hope leapt within her. She held the leather bag out to Celeste. "Can we—"

But the former Voodoo Queen was already shaking her head. "You listen close, child," she said. She tapped her finger on the table next to the effigy, as if reluctant to touch it. "Won't nothing in this world make me stain my hands with this filth more than once. I might not shake the asson no more, but that don't mean I'm about to stoop so low as some backdoor hoodoo woman. I did this on account of you bein' family, to ease your pain these last days. I'll make sure your people are at the cemetery come All Souls' Day. You say your goodbyes. You let them know that you rest easy in your grave. And then you let go of this world." She tried to say more, but her voice broke, and she had to swallow hard before she could continue. "Renaissance, I love you like you was my own, but I best never see your face again, you hear? I do, and I swear by Damballah on high and all the Ghede in Guinee, I'll cut you down my ownself."

She stood, leaning heavily on the table, her movements slow and cautious as a much older woman's. She breathed in deep through her nose and straightened to her full height, posture impeccable as she walked away, though it obviously cost her to do so.

Celeste paused halfway out the room, spoke without looking back. "I'm gonna lie down for a spell. Y'all lock the door behind you when you go."

The three of them endured an awkward silence for only a handful of breaths, and then Leon stood, collected their breakfast plates, and moved into the kitchen. Renai watched as he rolled his sleeves up at the sink and got to work, his hands busy, not having to speak to anyone, actually accomplishing something productive. She wished she'd have thought of that. Anything to avoid what she knew was coming next. At least she managed to ask the question first, so that she passed the responsibility of answering it on to Regal.

"So," she said, "where do we go from here?"

CHAPTER TWENTY-FIVE

CENTRALIA, WHERE A coal seam has been burning underground for over fifty years. Kolmanskop, where the diamond boom went bust. Shi Cheng, where a hydroelectric station dammed up Qiandao Lake. Plagues and landslides, economic collapses and rising tides. Cahokia and Chernobyl and Roanoke and Thonis-Heracleion and — perhaps one day — New Orleans. Humans build and the world changes and humans leave, their homes and their schools and their temples all standing empty, like the husk of a cicada left clinging to a tree.

We call these places ghost towns. The dwelling places of the djinn. Haunted. Because we know that whether it is a house or a body or an entire town, we always leave a part of ourselves behind.

Regal leaned back in her chair, the old wood creaking ominously. She propped one sneaker up on the edge of the table, stretched her other leg out on top of the tablecloth. "I seem to remember somebody talking a big game about taking care of the ghouls dropping all their corpse-bits up in my streets. How's about we start there?"

"But Cordelia is still trying to find Ramses," Renai said, more to herself than making an argument.

"Who?"

"Ramses is that dead boy she tryin' to find," Leon said, raising his voice so he could be heard from in the kitchen. Renai had no idea how he'd heard them talking over the sounds of the running water and the dishes clanking in the sink, but somehow he had.

"Not *him*," Regal said, waving a hand at Leon without looking at him. She narrowed her eyes at Renai. "The other one. Cordelia. What haven't you told us?"

Renai sighed. *Tell the truth and shame the devil,* she thought. "When you summoned me from the Underworld, I told you everything I knew. But that was only half of it." It took another cup of coffee and a handful of Regal's swears to get through it, but Renai told them everything. Or at least, everything she thought would be important.

She started with Ramses' disappearance, explaining to them how she and Sal had shown up at moment of his death only to find the wound his absence had left in the world. Then she told them about Cordelia—who Sal had named Discord right before she killed him—and how she'd pretended to be a psychopomp to gain Renai's trust and follow along with her while she'd searched the living side of New Orleans for Ramses. The more she thought about it, the more Renai realized that Cordelia had never really said she was anything but herself. She'd let Renai jump to conclusions all on her own.

Their biggest accomplishment together had been convincing a magic-using hacker to help them track Ramses down. Renai couldn't help but wonder if Cordelia had been less interested in finding Ramses and more interested in making sure *Renai* didn't. But then why kill Sal? Why not kill her, too? Nothing Cordelia had said or done really made any sense yet, so Renai moved on and told them about her journey with Sal through the Underworld in search of Ramses—though she kept the details hazy, since she might very well have to answer for every drop of tea she spilled—how they'd discovered that Ramses had been destined to die once before, that he'd sold part of his soul for immortality. At that, Leon had been the one to season the conversation with some impressive vulgarity.

And then she told them about the start of the Hallows and Cordelia's betrayal.

She left out the parts about Seth's offer and Mason's deal and her less-than-helpful conversation with Jude, partly because she didn't know how much longer they could sit around here talking before Celeste threw them out, and partly because she didn't think these meddling gods were anybody's business but her own.

But mostly because the last time Renai had trusted someone, they'd murdered her best friend.

"So there it is," Renai said, swallowing the last of her cold, bitter coffee. "I'm still not exactly sure what this kid and Cordelia have to do with each other, but I know damn sure I'm gonna find him before she does." She squeezed her hands into fists so tight that her knuckles cracked. "I just wish I wouldn't have lost everything I had on me when I . . . reassembled. I had a seeing stone that would have led me right to him." She turned to Regal. "Hey, you think Jude—"

Regal spit out a bitter little laugh and let her feet drop to the floor with a thump. "I'm afraid the Fortune Choad of New Orleans has other duties," she said, making a loose fist and shaking it back and forth.

Leon, who'd come back into the dining room during Renai's story but hadn't sat back down, leaned his forearms on the back of one of Celeste's chairs. "Jude got a game going. Say the best way he can help us is to keep these cats occupied."

Renai had an image flash through her mind: a peek into the fortune god's card room, the assembled horrors she'd seen gathered around his table. "What kind of game?"

Regal shrugged. "Bunch of storm deities and gods of destruction to hear him tell it. Apparently some lame-ass card game is the only thing stopping a bunch of sentient hurricanes from hitting the Quarter like coked-up frat boys. Like anybody'd notice." That last was muttered to herself as she leaned down to reach underneath the table to retrieve something. "But we don't need that immortal prick anyway," she said, dropping a child's *Princess and the Frog* backpack onto the table. "You didn't really lose any of your shit. We sorta stole it."

Renai unzipped the backpack and dumped out the contents on the table. It was all there: her knife—still in its half-ass cardboard sheath—the seeing stone she'd gotten from Jack Elderflower, the Fortune coin, and the cigarette —now in an empty medicine bottle with the label peeled off—and the lost spirits she'd transformed into a pack of playing cards, all of it. Everything she'd spent half the morning thinking she'd lost.

Renai turned her best glare in Regal's direction. The spirit rose up in response to her anger, different than it had ever felt before. Easier to control than the part of her from this world remembered, far more destructive than the Underworld side of her could believe. The temperature in the room dropped a few degrees. The hiss of rain hitting hot concrete whispered in Renai's ears, the crisp stink of burnt ozone filled her nostrils. A spark leapt and popped across her fingertips.

That was new.

"You'd best have an explanation," Renai said, and Leon widened his eyes at the threat in her voice. If Regal felt any fear at Renai's display of power, though, she didn't show it. Instead, she leaned closer, a slow, satisfied grin curling across her lips.

"I *knew* I liked you," Regal said. "As for why I took all your toys away, take a look at yourself. Maybe it was a dick move, but I don't think I made the wrong call. When we found you in front of the cemetery, you were like *Hunter S. Thompson* fucked-up. Muttering nonsense, holding that gris-gris bag in one hand, and calling down lightning with the other. Until the sleep charm I threw at you actually worked, I wasn't sure you were even human. I had no idea who was going to come out of that room when you woke up: the girl who needed our help, or death in a pretty dress." She shrugged. "So yeah, I went through your pockets. Sue me."

Renai took a deep breath and pushed the power back down into her belly, pleased at how obediently it responded. There was none of the fight she'd expected, none of the weakness that came from wrestling with the storm. The ease with which she called the magic to heel took some of the edge off her anger, made it easier to slow her pulse. "I guess that makes a certain kinda sense," she said forcing an apology into her voice that she didn't really feel.

"So we cool?"

Oh good, Renai thought, *now she's trying to speak the language.* She kissed her teeth. If Regal wanted a stereotype, she'd give her one. "Yeah, fam," she said, "we cool. You just gotta reco'nize and respect, y'eard?"

Regal nodded, not seeming to pick up on the mocking 'hood tilt to Renai's words. *Bet she tells people she's "woke," too.*

To give her hands something to do, Renai scooped up the child's bag and started filling it back up, the coin of Fortune and the pack of cards going in first, then the gris-gris bag of Sal's Essence, and the stick-and-yarn conjure figure — re-covering the effigy that was holding her two halves together with its cloth wrapping — knowing that she'd have to be very, very careful with it.

"Does any of what you just said mean y'all can keep from killin' one another for five minutes?" Leon asked, his voice full of fatherly disapproval. "'Cause a brother could use a smoke." He didn't wait for either woman to answer before he stomped past Renai, muttering to himself on his way out the door.

"Speaking of," Renai asked, picking up the pill bottle with the cigarette in it, "whose idea was this?"

"Celeste did that. She touched that thing and yanked her hand back like it burned her. Said it was death to touch it. I was like, 'no shit, surgeon general, it's a fuckin' cigarette.' But I get the feeling she meant something else?"

Renai hummed in agreement but didn't elaborate. She picked up the knife and pulled off the cardboard covering its blade. The jagged, curved edge of it had a wicked gleam, even in the dining room's dim light. As soon as her palm closed on the handle, she recognized it for what it was: the broken-off piece of her Underworld mirror. She remembered holding it that first time the Hallows ended and she broke in half, the mirror cracking right along with her. She thought about reaching for the other larger piece and trying to press the edges back together, but she knew what would happen if she pulled something from thin air in front of the Magician, and she'd spent enough of her morning answering questions.

She covered the broken glass blade with the pieces of cardboard and — acting like she was putting the knife into the backpack, but really just hiding her hand and the blade from Regal's view — reached into that nowhere place that held the mirror and slid the knife inside. A little frisson shook through her when it vanished, the taped-together strips of cardboard remaining behind.

Regal drummed her fingers on the tabletop and fidgeted, her toes on the floor and her heels driving up and down, like her body was trying to run away from whatever her brain was fighting with. Renai picked up the stone she got from Jack and bounced it on her palm, expecting a dozen questions from the other woman before she could look through it, but Regal's attention was fixed on the front door, where Leon had gone. *Something is up with those two,* Renai thought.

Trying not to get her hopes up, telling herself that the stone might show her Ramses asleep in his own bed or still in class or somewhere else unhelp-ful, having not caught up to his current time yet—or worse, nothing at all—Renai closed one eye and held the stone up to the other.

Through the hole in the stone, Renai saw Ramses in bright daylight walk-ing along an empty stretch of road. Judging by the sweat soaking through his uniform shirt, he'd been walking for a while. She searched the image for any kind of landmarks: buildings, street signs, anything, but there was nothing. Just palm trees growing in a wide neutral ground that separated four lanes of empty road in two, and overgrown foliage on either shoulder. The absence of identifying signs was itself a bit of a clue—she knew he wasn't anywhere in the city proper, at least—but he could be on any long stretch of road going nowhere on the edges of the city, maybe in New Orleans East—the suburb of the city that had suffered the most and struggled the longest in the after-math of the storm—or even out somewhere on the West Bank for all Renai could tell.

She opened her other eye and saw that Regal had taken out her phone and was scrolling through it but kept glancing up to the door. Renai smirked. "So you sweet on Sweetwater Carter, huh?"

Regal's wince was covered up so quickly that Renai could have convinced herself that she imagined it, except for the red flush creeping over the other woman's cheeks. Renai couldn't tell if it was embarrassment or anger or in-fatuation. Probably some combination of all three. To spare her a little dig-nity, Renai closed her eye again, turned her attention back to Ramses and his empty road.

After a moment, Regal spoke. "Wouldn't matter anyway," she said. "That man is puckered up tighter than a priest on Ash Wednesday. I know he's got history with Legba, and that he's a pretty famous musician here in the city even though nobody anywhere else has heard of him, but that's all informa-tion I got thirdhand. Voice of this whole shameless painted whore of a city, and I can't get him to say five words to me ain't about our limp-dick *duties*."

Renai fought a smile. She hardly knew this woman, wasn't sure she even really liked her, but it was strangely comforting to know that even with all the weird shit they dealt with, with all the power they possessed, relationships were always awkward. "Might have something to do with him being High John de Conquer," Renai said, more to herself than anything. Even though she couldn't see the other woman, she felt Regal's nervous jittering go sud-denly still.

"His real name isn't Leon?"

Renai looked away from the stone entirely, to see if Regal was joking, but from the expression on her face, it was clear she had no idea what Renai meant. "I guess it's more of a title, really. The original High John was like King Arthur for the Africans abducted during slavery. You know, that whole part about him coming back one day when his people need him most? That was one of the first things I learned on the other side. The loa have been waiting for years for Leon to claim his crown, to really *become* High John. I imagine it weighs heavy on him, you know?"

"I ever tell you I used to have King Arthur's knife? Whisper the right charm and it made you practically invisible. It was sweet as fuck." She drew out the last word into a long drawl, punctuated by a little sideways shift in her chair.

The abrupt shift in subject didn't really fool Renai, but she didn't press it either. The other woman's love life—or lack of it—was her own concern.

Renai held the seeing stone back up to her eye and found that Ramses had turned off the main road and was now slipping through a hole in a chain-link fence. On the other side of the fence, amid a dense tangle of undergrowth, a massive sign rose on two dark blue columns. The top and sides had once been a bright red, but over a decade of neglect had faded it to a light pink. The main image had been similarly bleached by the sun:

SI_ ____GS

was all that remained, and even that had faded almost to obscurity. The only portion of the sign that hadn't been impacted by time was the small marquee board beneath the main logo, which read:

CLOSED FO_R STORM

Renai wrapped the stone in her fist and hissed out a quiet "Yes!" to herself.

"Good news?" Regal asked.

"That depends. Did you two drive us here?"

Regal barked out a laugh as she bounced to her feet.

"What's so funny?"

"You can't get Leon Carter to give a single straight answer to a question about himself, not for love nor pussy." She stretched, straining her arms toward the ceiling until her spine popped, and she let out a satisfied groan. "But try, Sparkles, just *try* to shut him up about his fucking car."

The car in question was a light green Rolls, gleaming like he'd just finished polishing it. Leon leaned on the hood, smoking a cigarette and reading a copy of the local paper *The Advocate*—folded in half so he could hold it in one hand—that he must have taken off Celeste's front lawn. He wore black pinstripe pants, a matching vest, and a charcoal-gray dress shirt. Behind him was a two-lane road and the grassy rise of the levee, and a train clanking and rumbling by. A cool breeze blew in from over the levee, carrying with it the subtle brackish scent of Lake Pontchartrain.

When Leon saw them come out of Celeste's house, he cocked one knee and scrubbed out his cigarette on the sole of his glossy wingtip shoe, tucking the butt into a vest pocket. "Where we headed?" he asked, holding open the back door for Renai and the passenger door for Regal.

Renai had a moment, just one, where she considered lying to them. The people around her lately seemed to end up either traitors or victims, and she didn't want that to be true of either of these two, especially not Leon. She could get them to take her back to Kyrie and—assuming the bike had waited for her—ditch them and go after Ramses on her own.

But Celeste's effigy would surely only hold her together for another couple of days. Sal was gone. She was out of time and out of options. Whether she wanted it or not, she needed their help.

Regal slid into her seat, and then both she and Leon looked at Renai. Waiting. Expectant. So Renai said the only thing she could:

"We're going to Jazzland."

CHAPTER TWENTY-SIX

FROM THE BEGINNING, Jazzland was a series of mistakes waiting to happen, an amusement park complete with roller coasters and
a Ferris wheel out on the far edge of New Orleans East, on land that
most people in the city thought was Federal Wildlife–protected swamp. In
its inception, it doubled down on every cliché of a tourist's idea of the city
even when they didn't make any sense, combining Cajun terminology with
vaguely French Quarter–inspired architecture and hyperbolic historical ref-
erences in a bland, tasteless stew, like gumbo served in a Cleveland airport.
When it was bought out by Six Flags — who added vapid cartoon characters
to everything in a veneer of Americanization and based their publicity cam-
paign around a thin, tuxedoed, frenetically dancing white actor in a creepy
old man mask — everyone in the city still called it Jazzland.

To everyone's amazement, when the storm hit, the Ferris wheel and the
huge coasters stayed standing. Unfortunately, they were standing in seven
feet of filthy, salt-dense water for over a month. The gates were closed and
hadn't opened since.

Not to the public, anyway. Teenagers left their spray-paint tags on everything in sight, and drug deals went down, went bad. A couple of movies used
the park for filming, particularly the parking lot that was the size of an air-

port runway, and the police started patrolling the area, trying to keep out the gangs and the thrill seekers and the urban decay bloggers.

Teenage kids in school uniforms could still slip in unseen, apparently. Maybe Ramses' ability to evade the patrol had something to do with whatever inhuman nature Opal had recognized in him. Or maybe security had just gotten lax.

Either way, while Leon's and Regal's attention was focused on the road in front of them, Renai pulled her black glass knife out of its nowhere place just long enough to cut two slits in the back of the jacket the Thrones had given her—the blade slicing through leather and fabric without effort, without even a whisper—big enough for her to push her wings through as she shrugged it on.

She transferred most of the contents of the child's backpack to her pockets—the playing cards and the cigarette and the coin of Fortune—but left the pouch of Sal's Essence and the stick figure effigy in the bag, which she left locked in the backseat of Leon's car. It was way too hot outside for a jacket that heavy, and she didn't know if its magic would even work anymore, given the way her wings and her mirror had changed thanks to the Hallows, but there was no way she would go into the ruins of Jazzland without the jacket. Nor would she risk those things most precious to her—the gris-gris pouch of Sal's Essence and the effigy that was holding her together—by bringing them inside.

After all, things even hungrier than junkies, more territorial than gangs, and way more dangerous than the police made their homes in ruins.

That thought got her pulse jumping when Leon pulled the Rolls over onto the gravel-strewn shoulder, the realization that they might encounter something in there that she couldn't reason with or intimidate with her connection to the Thrones. Something that she might have to destroy. It scared her, of course, but even more than fear, she felt anticipation. She'd been confused and broken for far too long—and now the tempest inside of her was ready to break some shit of its own.

The three of them got out of the car, and Leon walked around the back to pop open the trunk. He reached inside and pulled out a half-sized baseball bat, like something a toddler would use, and a thick black duffel bag. He handed both to Regal, who slung the bag's strap over one shoulder and gave the bat a couple of loose-wristed whirls.

Renai saw that arcane symbols and runes had been carved deep into the wood of the bat. Before she could ask about it, Leon reached back into the trunk and took out a battered instrument case and the jacket that matched the rest of his suit. When he spun it around to slide his arms into the sleeves, the coat billowed up enough for Renai to see that symbols had been sewn into the lining, similar to the ones on Regal's bat. The two of them—this Magician and Voice duo—moved like they'd done this a hundred times before, handing things to one another without needing to ask, without getting in each other's way. *Like an old married couple,* Renai thought, not bothering to hide her smile.

Regal glanced over at her and did a double take. "Holy Sex Pistols, Sparkles!" she yelled, and Renai felt her face flush. If she was sure the ghost word would work, she'd have used it right then to disappear. "Check her out, Sweets. She looks like a punk rock faerie princess!"

The heat in Renai's face shifted to a different emotion. "Don't play," she said. "If you think I'm about to stand here and get laughed at—"

Regal smiled. "No, seriously, I mean it. That jacket is the *tits*. What's it do?"

"It's a jacket. Keeps the rain off and the cold out."

Regal's smile faded. "Now who's laughing at who? I can practically taste the magic coming off of that thing."

Leon slammed the trunk shut and picked up his case. He cleared his throat and said, "I strike either one 'a you as a man who aims to idle here in the sun and sweat through this suit?"

Man had a point. End of October it might be, but the first cold front of fall was a week away at least. With no clouds in the sky and humidity so high they might as well be swimming, Renai could already feel the heat draining her. For a moment, she considered the merits of watching Ramses' journey into Jazzland through the seeing stone while they waited in the car with the AC on full blast. She was going to feel pretty foolish if all he did was creep in, take a selfie to prove he'd been there, and then hurry out again.

But no, she knew what she'd seen through the stone. She hadn't seen a group of boys egging each other on to commit some mischief. Nor had she seen a pair of young lovers sneaking into a place where they were assured privacy. Ramses had been alone, and he'd been focused, and he hadn't looked back. Whatever brought him here, Ramses had come to Jazzland with a purpose.

Renai pointed across the street, at the concrete barriers blocking what used to be the entrance to the theme park, the chain-link fence and the massive overgrowth of brambles and weeds, the sign that, via the seeing stone, she'd seen Ramses walk past without glancing up. "There," she said, "that's the way he went in."

⧗

Walking down the service road that led to the huge empty parking lot felt like something out of a post-apocalyptic novel, the inexorable weight of nature breaking the asphalt into jagged chunks, a long, slow trudge down a span that —in a more civilized time—would have taken mere moments in air-conditioned comfort. Renai wondered why the soft breeze tickling through the treetops did nothing to ease the oppressive heat, only to realize that what she heard was actually the constant rush of traffic on the nearby interstate. Occasionally, a bird let out a harsh, grating call off in the distance, but otherwise they traveled in silence.

Renai checked Ramses' progress a couple of times as they walked, the sped-up nature of the stone's observation meaning that he was already in the ruins of the park when she saw him—once throwing rocks at the remnants of windowpanes, once pissing into the weeds behind a twisted metal shape whose original function she couldn't even guess at—and each time she peeked through the stone, his day swooped closer to evening.

She couldn't be entirely sure which day of Ramses' life she was spying on —she might have missed the moment when he escaped his death, for all she knew—but given the fact that he was still wearing his school uniform, she had a feeling this day was his last. She tried to walk with one eye on her surroundings and one eye on Ramses, but every time she went more than three steps with the stone pressed up to her face, she stumbled on a loose stone or a well-anchored tangle of vines. So she and Leon and Regal crept along in the present while Ramses leaped toward his future. A creeping anxiety settled in to the back of her head, the certainty that when the vital clue revealed itself in the stone, she wouldn't be watching to see it.

When they reached the three guard shacks that had once barred or granted entry into the parking lot, Renai paused and looked through the stone again. She saw Ramses staring down at his phone, and then he held it up, its camera facing back at him. Renai felt a brief stab of panic, instinct screaming at her to flinch away before he caught her even though she knew logically that whatever demon animated the stone would be invisible to Ramses, and also that what she was seeing had already happened. Sure enough, even though it felt like he aimed the phone right at her, all she saw on his screen was him, pulling a goofy face at the doodle of a unicorn someone had spray-painted onto a wall.

Renai slid the stone back into her jacket pocket. The sight of Ramses taking selfies made her wonder where her own devices had gone, a thought quickly swept away by the realization that Ramses definitely wouldn't have posted that picture to any site that his mom had access to, which meant that aside from all the other shit he was into, Mr. St. Cyr was good at hiding his tracks online, too. She wondered if Jack Elderflower had been as thorough as he'd claimed. She'd ask, but with her phone lost to whatever abyss it had vanished into, she'd have to see him in person again to find out for sure, which was an option that was even less appealing than wandering around an abandoned theme park.

"Which way?" Leon asked. Way down the parking lot was the main entrance, with a boarded-up ticket counter and multiple turnstiles beneath a massive awning, while just off to their left a gap in the trees showed a paved strip just wide enough for a single car, the remnants of a fence long since collapsed and dragged away. Renai nodded toward the smaller, closer entrance, trying to project a certainty that she didn't possess.

She was starting to worry that the sense of purpose she'd seen in Ramses had just been wishful thinking. As for taking the smaller entrance, that was just an educated guess. She hadn't actually seen Ramses enter the park, but it stood to reason that the main gates would have some kind of barricades set up, and besides, when she was a teenager, she'd have relished the chance to use an entrance that wasn't meant for her.

The moment they passed the threshold, leaving behind an abandoned stretch of parking lot and entering the ruins of the amusement park, a prickling, creeping sense of dread ran across Renai's skin. That ominous lizard-brain feeling that you were being watched. The random birdcalls, the buzz of insects in the trees, all of it fell silent, eerily still. Debris marked a few places where nature and time and gravity had torn some structure down, a maintenance shed, maybe, or a decorative facade. Most of the sturdier buildings were more or less intact, though they were filthy and graffiti-covered and dilapidated. The rides towered over everything, skeletal and huge, like the bones of some metal leviathan that had died long ago. A faint stench hung in the air, stagnant water and rot, stale cigarettes and mold and rust. The stink of decay, of entropy.

Regal visibly shuddered. "You guys feel that? Like there's eyes everywhere?"

Renai nodded, and Leon said, "Like somebody done walked over my grave."

"Scopaesthesia," Renai said, and then grinned sheepishly when the other two exchanged a look. "What, I like knowing big words." What she didn't say was that it wasn't coincidence that she knew the term, that she'd searched for it often enough to remember it, that the sensation was one she was intimately familiar with.

That the atmosphere in Jazzland reminded her of the deep, unpleasant parts of the Underworld.

They walked along the empty path of what, based on the signs, must have been a delivery access road until it came to an end at an intersection with the wider, more worn concrete of the walkway open to park guests. To their left, what looked like a target painted on the concrete—a blue circle ringed by white ringed by red—where the exposed piping of what had once been a fountain jutted up from the ground, and beyond it a miniature clock tower standing in front of a collapsed facade of some mansion. To their right, a couple of columns whose writing had long since worn away, a boxy, aluminum warehouse, and the looping, metallic spire of scaffolding that had once been one of the smaller roller coasters. "I think I know where we are," Renai said, pointing at the warehouse. "They used to have haunted houses in there."

"This whole damn place a haunted house," Leon said, locking eyes with her. "Sooner we out of here the better." Renai caught his meaning and dug in her jacket pocket for the seeing stone.

When she put it up to her eye, she saw Ramses sitting on the raised tracks of a roller coaster—not the huge wooden one that was visible from the interstate, but one of the smaller steel constructions that was still higher up than most of the surrounding pine trees—watching the sun set. The sight of him that high up, on a structure that had been deemed unsafe a decade ago, made Renai's stomach clench. Even though she might very well have to end his life once she found him, she dreaded finding his broken body in this desolate place. And then she realized that it wasn't the orange burn of sunset that had grabbed his attention, but a golden glow coming from inside the park. *This is it,* Renai thought, *whatever he stole from Mason, he found it here.*

"At some point," Regal said, intruding on Renai's concentration as she watched Ramses make his way down the tracks, "you're gonna have to tell me how you magicked up an honest-to-goddess seer stone. Just out of professional curiosity, you understand. Last guy I saw tried some shit like that, his whole face melted off like a fuckin' Nazi at the end of *Raiders of the Lost Ark.*"

"I didn't do it," Renai said, only half paying attention to the other woman, "you'll have to ask Jack."

"Wait," Regal said, grabbing Renai's wrist and pulling the stone away from her eye. "Jack *who?*" Leon sucked in a breath like something had pained him.

Renai tried to pull her arm away, but the other woman's hold was too strong. "He said his name was Elderflower, but I don't think that's the name his momma gave him, y'know?" She tugged again, thinking Regal had just gotten overzealous, but no, she wouldn't let go. Renai felt Leon move behind her. The storm rose up, unbidden but welcome. "You want to take your hands off me," Renai said.

"You never said you were working with that shit-breathed bastard," Regal said.

"You never asked." She saw Regal's other hand, the one holding the bat, tighten its grip. "But just so you know: I'm not."

Regal's cynicism came out in an ugly, snorting laugh. "Sure. You expect us to believe a pap smear like Elderflower just gave you a talisman with this kinda juice"—she forced Renai's arm up, and gave the hand holding the stone a little shake—"out of the goodness of a heart that he doesn't fucking have?"

"Believe whatever you want," Renai said, "you obviously made up your mind already." It was getting hard to hold back the tempest, that crackling energy that had shown itself for the first time in Celeste's dining room. Mostly because part of her *wanted* to hit Regal with it. Wanted to put her down hard. With the spirit's strength filling her, Renai managed to yank her arm free of Regal's grasp and took a long step back. She half expected Leon to grab her, but he shifted out of her way, moving to stand between her and Regal.

"Okay," he said, "how 'bout we quit this foolishness? This ain't the time, and it damn sure ain't the place."

Renai clenched her molars together and tried to summon a sense of calm. Leon was right. Regal had filled herself with as much of her own magic as Renai had. She could practically taste it in the air. And if *she* sensed it, then so could whatever lost, broken things that called these ruins home. A breeze kicked up years of dust off the concrete around them, swirling and cold, blowing strong enough to make the nearby Ferris wheel creak and groan. Renai reached out for the wind, to pull it back inside of her. It was only when it slipped away from her that she realized that the wind hadn't come from her at all.

And that it carried with it the faint sound of children laughing.

Based on their sudden disinterest in Renai, the others heard it, too. "Well, shit-balls," Regal said, turning in a slow circle and scanning the debris for threats, then she glanced at Leon. "Guess this is the part where you say you told us so?" Leon spit between his teeth, dropping to one knee to unclasp his instrument case and pull out his trumpet. Regal started spinning her bat, like she was limbering up her wrist, faster and faster, a shadowy presence uncoiling from the wood grain, the weapon letting out a harrowing buzz. Renai didn't know exactly what magic Regal was calling up, but it felt nasty. Renai swallowed, her control over the storm's power leaching away from her in the face of her fear. She considered trying the ghost word but decided to save that as a last resort. Instead, she reached into her nowhere place for the glass knife.

Renai felt the threat coming before she saw it. She was a psychopomp, after all. Spirits were her job. "Over there," she said, pointing at the shape coming down the wide sidewalk, half-hidden by the gloom cast by the warehouse Renai had recognized.

She thought at first that it was just a large person — either exhausted or injured or drunk — staggering toward them. But the perspective was all wrong. As were the number of limbs. And then it stepped into the light and she saw it for the marionette cobbled together from the ruins that it was.

The walking ruin had steel girders for legs and lengths of coaster tracks and plumbing for arms — one still had a sink attached — of which there were at least four, if not more. Renai couldn't tell exactly how many, because the body of the lurching puppet was most of an attraction that had once held riders in chairs as it whirled around and around, which it still managed to do, tilting and spinning as it staggered closer. Its face was one of the cartoon characters that the park had licensed, a scowling-mad cowboy with a bushy, flame-red mustache; its voice a chorus of screaming children, a cacophony of shrieks and squeals that might have been exhilaration and might have been terror.

She couldn't see the individual spirits that animated it, but she could feel them, a whine in the ears like an old computer monitor, a vibration to the air like a hive of bees. "Play," the ruin howled, its bumper-car foot pounding the ground so hard that Renai felt it shake beneath her feet. "Play!"

"Nope," Regal said, "just no, nope, and no fucking thank you." She aimed her bat at the walking ruin and muttered some other word, a word that tickled unpleasantly in Renai's mind, a word of magic. She'd heard that word before, but she couldn't—or didn't want to—remember when. A shadow surged along the length of the bat—the tatters of Essence that the sorceress had used to animate and fuel her magic, Renai realized—and a spurt of molten fire dribbled out of the bat's tip, squirting out less than a foot away, and oozing into a burning puddle on the concrete. Regal steadied her feet, gripped her weapon with both hands, and shouted the word so loud that her voice cracked.

Liquid flame burst from Regal's cudgel like a firehose, a fountain that arced across the hundred feet or so that separated them from the ruin, striking it first in its whirligig chest, and then tracing a clinging, scorching line down to one of its legs. The ruin kept moving forward, one step, then another, but Regal's stream burned white hot, so intense that it melted through the steel and sent the thing toppling to the ground.

Regal hissed out another word that made the fire cease and punched the air with a triumphant shout. "How you like that?" she yelled toward Renai, and then she turned back to the ruin, sliding the bat into a hand held at her waist like she was sheathing a sword. "It was a pleasure to burn, motherfucker!"

The whirligig spun, its multiple arms scraping against concrete and gouging up chunks of earth until it righted itself, its spindly arms now crablike, insectile legs, its cartoon face now dangling from its belly, its two legs—one of them half the length of the other—pounding together like a battering arm.

Renai and Leon and Regal exchanged a few glances, and they all saw the same conclusion in each other's eyes. They did the only sensible thing they could: they ran. The ruin followed, its skittering legs and swinging arms and shrieking voices, but its bulk made it slow. "You can't kill it," Renai said, once they rounded a corner and put a little distance between them and the ruin, "it's not real."

"There!" Leon shouted, pointing to a squat cinder-block building that seemed more sturdy than the ones surrounding it. Renai ran toward it, her youth and her runner's stamina letting her pull ahead of the other two easily. The entrance wasn't a door but an alcove that bent around a sharp corner into a dark, windowless room. She was already inside before she realized that Leon had steered them toward what had once been the public bathrooms.

Regal and Leon came running in behind her, crowding into the corner together instead of going all the way into the darkness inside. They stood for a minute, catching their breath, needing the oxygen but trying not to suck in too much of the hot, thick air. The smell wasn't as bad as Renai expected, just more of the same funk of decay and dust and rot, only more concentrated in the enclosed stagnant space. In fact, what little she could see of their sanctuary in the darkness—tile floor and faux-marble sinks and a row of toilet stalls in the back—seemed improbably clean. Outside, the ruin crashed into something with a metal-on-metal screech.

Regal peeked around the corner, and when she ducked her head back inside, her expression wasn't hopeful. "So tell me, Sparkles," she said, digging through her duffel bag, "how exactly is the world's shittiest Transformer out there 'not real'?"

"It's not only one thing, is what I meant. Not something you can kill, or even hurt. It's like . . ." Renai waved her hand, as if she could scoop up the words she was struggling to find. "You know those birds? The ones that make a big flock and swoop around and fill up whole trees?"

"Starlings," Leon said, "and the word ain't 'flock.' When they in a group, they called a murmuration." Regal pulled away from her search to look at him, her head turning slow and deliberate, her brow creased with incredulity. Leon grinned at her, a quick flash and it was gone. "What? I like big words, too."

"Sure," Renai said, "it's like starlings. Only instead of birds, you got a tree full of spirits. Or shades, or devils, or whatever you wanna call them. All the little wisps of magic and soul that don't have anywhere else to go? They like abandoned places. Ruins. This whole theme park is like their tree and their swirling, murmur-whatever all balled up together. That thing out there is just a puppet. You could burn chunks off that ruin all day long, and the spirits would just gather up the pieces and start over."

"So we burn down the tree," Regal said. There was no humor in her voice, no question, either. Just will.

"Bad idea," Renai said. "Be like fire ants in a flood. You know, how they—"

"They cling to each other in a ball and float to dry land, I get it," Regal said. "Christ on a crutch, between the two of you it's like watching the goddamn Discovery channel. I should make a recording for when I can't fall asleep." Outside, the ruin shrieked like a dozen schoolchildren hurtling through the air, cackled like a hundred wheels hurtling down a pair of tracks. Regal let out a disgusted huff. "Can't you do something? Seems to me spirit problems fall under the psychopomp's jurisdiction."

Renai thought about what she'd done to the fugitive spirits, the destructive wind that had ripped them apart and forced them to take new forms. She tried to picture doing that same thing here, but all she saw was failure. The dead she'd turned into playing cards had been haunting spirits, true, but they'd also been afraid of her role as a psychopomp and softened by centuries of ennui. They'd been waiting for change. The spirits animating the ruin outside, on the other hand, were ravenous, desperate beings made of fire and shadow and dust. Whatever they'd been once, they'd already changed, already chosen this new identity, or had it chosen for them. They were too violent, too feral, too *many* for Renai to try to control.

She never got a chance to say any of this, though, because Leon—carrying only his trumpet and an expression of grim determination—walked past her and out into the sunlight. He was already playing when she and Regal caught up to him, his cheeks ballooning out so elastically that it would have been funny if not for the giant mass of metal and machinery and trash lumbering toward them.

At first he played only a single note, bright and loud and clear, but the piercing scream of his trumpet soon shifted into a throaty, brassy growl, a gently cascading melody of drawn-out melancholy sounds. There was magic in the song he played, not merely in his skill or his artistry—though he demonstrated an abundance of both—but a literal, potent charm that radiated through the air and resonated through the earth from where he stood. Unlike Regal's sorcery, this magic came from deep within him, drew on the fire of his own soul to fuel it.

The ruin slowed and then stopped, or at least it stopped coming closer, but it swayed where it stood, like a tall, tall tree rocked back and forth by the wind. The eerie, laughing shrieking chorus of its voice fell silent. Leon played his soothing, muffled tune, and the world listened and went still. He leaned into it with his whole body, straining for every note, to produce a sound that hung in the air, delicate and achingly sweet.

The psychopomp part of Renai could feel the shadowy, haunting spirits that animated the mound of trash and metal being lulled into calm, their rage soothed by Leon's music. And then, piece by piece, the ruin slumped to the ground. First the great trunk of it, the whirligig with its gaudy gilt frame and its dozens and dozens of burnt-out or shattered lightbulbs, and then the appendages—which had only ever been connected by force of will anyway—came undone and succumbed to gravity. He played until Renai felt the last of the spirits dissipate into a kind of sleep, and she put a hand on his arm and said he'd done enough.

When his last note faded away, Renai felt like something pure—glimpsed only for a moment—had flown away.

And then Regal bunched up a fist and punched him in the bicep. He grunted in pain, and she flinched at him like she was going to do it again. "The hell got into you, woman?" he asked, moving away from her and back toward the bathroom, rubbing his arm.

Renai followed and Regal chased him, shaking her fist at him. "You did, you shit-heap, plague-dicked, stupid son of a—" Leon whirled around, making a sound in the back of his throat, the one you made when a child reached for something you'd just told them not to touch, and pointing one long, slender finger right at Regal. She stopped mid-word, grimaced, and then turned that baring of teeth into an insincere smile. "Son of a very nice lady," she finished. "Where do you get off risking yourself like that?"

Leon continued walking back to where he'd left his instrument case, his long strides carrying him quickly around back into the darkness of the former bathroom. "You reminded me that these spirits were sleepin' when we got here," Leon said. "Y'all the ones woke 'em up with all that yellin' and callin' up magic." He shrugged. "Figured least we could do was leave 'em how we found 'em."

"Leaving is a very good idea," Renai said, hurrying to interrupt whatever Regal was about to say next. "Let's just get what we came here for and go, okay?" Regal grunted her approval, snatching up her duffel bag like it had offended her. Renai dug the seeing stone out of her pocket and held it up to her eye, only to look straight through the hole without any image appearing: no Ramses, no glimpse of the past, not even a shroud of darkness. Just the other side of the stone.

"What you see?" Leon asked.

"Nothing. Nothing at all." She handed the stone to Leon, who looked through it and handed it to Regal.

"I don't understand," Regal said.

"Neither do I. Maybe whatever demon Jack put in there got put to sleep when Leon played his song. Maybe whatever power helping Ramses elude his moment of death was stronger than the magic in this stone. Maybe Ramses died here in this theme park, and we missed it." She chuckled, even though she didn't find any of this very funny, but it was either laugh or start crying. "I really, really just don't have any idea what I'm doing. All I know is I'm probably not ever going to find Ramses, so I might as well give up and enjoy my last couple of days before I tear myself apart again."

For a moment, everything was quiet. And then, from the darkness at the back of the bathroom, came the sound of a weight being dragged along the floor. It was a brief sound, maybe a roach or a rat, but it made the hairs on the back of Renai's hair stand up. When it came again, louder, the black glass knife was in her hand before she thought to reach for it. Leon and Regal moved to either side of her, but that was something she felt more than saw. Every sense strained toward that impenetrable absence of light, where some new threat shifted and slouched its way forward.

"Wamtheeth?" a soft, creaky voice said, lisping the word. "You want Wamtheeth?" Renai hadn't sensed it back there at all, which meant it wasn't human, wasn't alive. And then the shuffling, timid creature reached the edge of the light, just enough for Renai to see that it had a human shape, though it only had the height and scrawny shoulders of an adolescent. For a moment, they looked at it and it watched them. And then a sudden, heartbreaking possibility occurred to Renai.

She reached out to the skinny creature in the darkness and said, *"Ramses?"*

CHAPTER TWENTY-SEVEN

THERE ARE WAYS to see that which the spirits would keep hidden. Sip of the tea brewed of the ayahuasca vine, or the wine of Dionysus, or the water from Mimir's well, or Indra's soma. Chew the peyote button, the dried psilocybin mushroom, the petals of the lotus flower, the bark of the iboga tree. Lick the bufotoxin from the back of a frightened toad, or the paper that has been soaked with lysergic acid diethylamide. Breathe in the smoke of the cannabis leaf, the tobacco leaf, the volcanic fumes of the oracle at Delphi.

Dosage determines whether they are medicine or poison; culture determines whether they are sacred or profane. Whether they reveal a deeper truth or inspire a dreamlike madness, however, is entirely a matter of perspective.

⧗

The shape in the darkness made a wet, rasping chuckle. "Īe. Aka knowth Wamtheeth, but Aka no Wamtheeth. What you want for him?"

It took Renai a half second to comprehend what the voice was saying, to understand that it — Aka, it called itself Aka — wasn't Ramses, made a joke about it, and then asked why they were searching for him. She'd thought at first that Aka had offered to buy him. Leon held his arm out across her waist, like a dad reaching out for his kid when he slammed on the brakes. Misguided patriarchal bullshit aside, Renai didn't understand why he and Regal still seemed afraid of Aka. There was something infantile in the voice, a childlike quality that went beyond just the lisp and the simplicity of language. Renai adjusted her own diction to match it.

"Ramses stole something," she said. "Something important from someone dangerous. We want to get it back before something bad happens." Not entirely true, of course, but close enough to the truth that she didn't feel bad about saying it.

"Hai," Aka said, "Yeth. Aka knowth. Aka thaw."

"You saw him take it?" Only Leon's arm stretched out in front of her kept Renai from stepping forward. If Aka saw what Ramses took, maybe they could find out where he'd gone, if he'd managed to get out of the park at all.

"You understand that Parseltongue shit?" Regal asked. Her abrasive tone made Aka retreat a step back into the darkness.

Renai spun around to confront her. "What?"

Regal aimed her bat into the gloom where Aka had vanished. "You know what that thing is saying?" She leaned around Renai to look Leon in the face. "It's not just me, right? You hear somebody gargling a throat full of spooge, too?" When Renai turned to him, Leon shrugged and nodded.

"Ain't the words I'd have used," he said, "but yeah, it don't make a lick of sense to me, neither. And I don't like the way it don't come into the light."

Renai breathed out through her nose and moved Leon's hand out of her way. To come this close, to have finally found someone who could point them in Ramses' direction, only to have it slip through their fingers? She couldn't just walk away. "Aka," she said, "my friends can't understand you. And it makes us nervous when we can't see you. Can you come into the light, please?"

"Nathty mouth dropth down her thick firtht."

"Regal, put the bat away."

"Is that what it said? You know, I think I'm starting to pick up on the language. Here, translate this." And then she hocked up a wad of phlegm and spat it on the tile floor at her feet. "How was that? Did I get the pronunciation right?"

Suddenly, the tempest was back, quick as the flush of anger that raced across Renai's skin. She and the presence living inside her might not have a lot in common, but neither one of them liked bullies. A spark arced back and forth between Renai's palms, snapping the air with a loud crack with every leap. In the camera's flashes of brightness that flared through the bathroom, Renai caught a few fleeting glimpses of the demon named Aka, before it went shrieking into one of the stalls.

Aka had bright red skin and long grease-slick black hair. She—Renai, to her own embarrassment, had looked—was naked and filthy and so emaciated that Renai had seen the slats of her ribs, the knobs of bone at her hips. Her fingers were twice as long as they ought to be, curling and multi-jointed as spider legs, and her feet each tapered to a point, one squat toe with one wicked-looking nail. Mostly, though, it was Aka's tongue that Renai noticed—thick and muscular as a tentacle, hanging down all the way to Aka's navel, slavering and questing—because it was the tongue that Renai recognized from the first time she'd seen Aka.

Sitting at the table in Jude Dubuisson's card game full of destruction gods.

⧗

It took a number of apologies and more than a little pleading—and Regal being forced to leave the bathroom entirely—before Aka crept out of her hiding place. While she made her way back to where Leon and Renai stood, wary as a feral cat, nails clicking with every step on the tile, Renai tried to think of what best to ask this creature, whether the status of the card game was more immediately significant than whatever information she might have about Ramses.

"Okay," Renai said, once Aka had settled into a crouch a few feet away from them, "nasty mouth is outside. It's just us. Can you tell us what you saw Ramses steal?"

"Prith firtht," Aka said, stretching one hand out flat and then stamping it with the thumb of her other hand. "Aka no thay unlethh rai den girl gifth Aka rei." She seemed intensely serious for a moment, but then she broke off into her raspy, choking laughter. "Aka wordth make muthick."

Leon leaned over to Renai without taking his eyes off of Aka. "What's it sayin'?" he asked, his arms folded across his chest, his trumpet held at the ready. He'd told Renai—when she tried to get him to wait outside with Regal—that while he trusted that Renai trusted Aka, that didn't mean *he* trusted her, which was the kind of nonsense bullshit only a man could say and actually mean it.

"She," Renai said, tilting her head as she said the word to emphasize it, "she said that if I want to hear what she knows, I gotta pay for it. At least, I think that's what she said." Renai glanced back at Aka and saw her licking Regal's spit and snot from the tile floor. Delicately, as if she were savoring it. Renai choked back a gag, suddenly understanding why this bathroom was as clean as it was.

"You *think?* I thought you understood . . . her."

"I do. Mostly. But I don't really know what she wants."

"Thtone," Aka said, saying it slow and enunciating as best she could with her massive tongue blocking her mouth. She stretched out one index finger, and then pressed her thumb and index fingertips to it to form a triangle, which she held up to her eye. "Theeing thtone," she said, one beady eye glaring through the gap of her own fingers.

"Oh," Renai said, "okay." Part of her recoiled from the idea, since less than an hour ago it had been her best chance of finding Ramses. But it didn't show her anything now, much less Ramses. Before she could get caught up in some internal debate about it, Renai pulled the seeing stone out of her jacket pocket and dropped it into Aka's slick red palm.

Leon sucked in a breath between his teeth. "You sure 'bout that?" he asked.

"Sure," Renai said. "Damn thing's broke, anyway." The demon sniffed it, smiled up at Renai, and snapped it in two like a dry twig.

Leon grunted out a chuckle. "Damn sure broke, now."

Smoke rose from the broken edges of the stone, oily and thick and sluggish. The psychopomp in Renai reached out for the smoke, the same part of her that ached at the sight of the shades in the Underworld. Whatever demon or spirit Jack Elderflower had trapped in the stone, Aka had just set it free. Before Renai could ask what she intended to do with it, though, Aka's tongue lashed forward, coiling around the spirit and scooping it up and dragging it to her lips. There was something grotesque in the sight, her tongue bulging and quivering as if it moved of its own volition.

Leon coughed into his hand in an attempt to disguise the low moan of disgust in the back of his throat. "What is she?" he asked, having the decency, at least, to whisper it. Renai hoped Aka couldn't hear them over the slurping noises she was making, and then felt her own belly squirm with nausea.

"I think she's a destruction goddess, more or less. The whole world is in balance, right? Everything dies, everything gets eaten. Well, what happens when a spirit gets too weak to continue its task? Or when scraps of memory and emotion get left behind when a soul crosses over? Or when a god dies? That's where Aka comes in. She's a scavenger for the spirit world; a bottom feeder, like crabs or catfish."

"Yeah? Well, I like my catfish fried and my crabs boiled, me. Not suckin' up dead spirits like the marrow out a bone."

"Just be glad she didn't offer to share," Renai said, and grinned when Leon coughed again, hacking like he nearly lost it. To Aka, she said, "I gave you what you wanted. Now tell us what you saw Ramses take."

The red-skinned demon beckoned her closer. She reached out and let the two halves of the seeing stone spill into Renai's hand, closing her fingers with her own. "What I thaw," Aka said, "ith ethier to thow." Before Renai really even understood what Aka said, much less had a chance to ask what it meant, Aka's tongue stabbed forward and slithered into Renai's mouth, cold and wriggling and foul.

Renai gagged, unable to stop herself from imagining that impossibly long appendage snaking down all the way inside her, but Aka's tongue withdrew as quickly as it had intruded, leaving nothing behind but a burning taste, like bile, and a pungent, mildewy slime that Renai spat and retched onto the floor, on her hands and knees with no memory of falling. She felt more than saw Leon lunge for Aka, but the demon went skipping into the darkness and vanished.

Leon handed her a water bottle from Regal's duffel bag, and she rinsed and spat, rinsed and spat, gagging still, until the water was gone and Leon half helped, half dragged her to her feet. He led her out into the light, Regal asking what happened and him trying to explain and everything going fuzzy and indistinct, music playing somewhere, just a single piano note plinking over and over again, and it smelled like popcorn with liquid butter and it smelled like rotten, stagnant water and it smelled like fresh-cut grass. Leon looked funny with that crown on his head, just like Regal looked sad with all that blood on her hands. Renai flicked her wings and they were made of rainbows, and Regal was shaking her and yelling in her face, and she was flying and she was flying and she was gone.

The next thing she knew, it was night and dark, and she was walking through the ruins of Jazzland with Ramses St. Cyr. They were heading toward a golden glow, so radiant bright that Renai could see the rays of light coming off of it, like a sun on the horizon in a child's drawing. She'd flown here on the cascading wings of a rainbow—did that mean this was a leprechaun's pot of gold? She laughed, but Ramses didn't think it was funny. Or he hadn't heard her. Or she hadn't said it out loud.

She reached out to him, she had to stop him, she had to tell him not to do what he was about to do, she had to find out who he'd sold his soul to, but then, no, she didn't reach out at all. Nothing happened, she just thought she should reach out and then decided not to. Something was wrong. She stopped, except, no, she didn't do that either. She laughed again. Obviously, she was going to walk with Ramses until he did what he did so she might as well pay attention.

When they reached the source of the golden light, it was too bright to look at, so she looked down at her feet. Birds lay there, wings sprawled and still, and a cat, and two dogs, and a fox. They weren't dead, she realized after a moment, their chests still rose and fell, rose and fell. They were asleep. A few steps closer, and there was one of the private security guards who patrolled the park after hours. He snored, a surprisingly delicate sound from a man so large.

But if whatever spell dominated this place could strike down a man that size, surely a boy of Ramses' small stature would have succumbed. And sure enough, he swayed on his feet, lids drowsy and heavy, a slow smile creeping across his face. Was this it? Had he been dreaming his life away in this place the entire time she was searching for him? His head bobbed once, twice, and Renai wished he'd just sit down—if he fell to the concrete he might hurt himself—and then his chin dropped to his chest and he was asleep on his feet.

And then Ramses St. Cyr lifted his head and opened eyes made of fire.

He grinned, quick and confident and far too cynical for a boy Ramses' age. "Not bad," he said to himself, reaching across a shoulder and patting himself on the back. "Not bad at all." And then he wasn't Ramses at all, but a whirlwind of fire that wore a boy named Ramses like a comfortable pair of jeans. He reached out to the glow at the center of a ring of sleeping creatures and when he touched it, the glow faded enough for Renai to see it for what it was: a golden rod, about a yard long, capped with an orb and a pair of outspread white wings, with the carving of two serpents twined around the haft. Renai had seen it before, but she couldn't remember where. Knew it belonged to someone she should know, but she couldn't remember who. The being of fire inside Ramses St. Cyr looked down at this object of divine power, shrugged, and tucked it into the back of his school-uniform khaki pants.

He knelt down at the place where he'd found the rod and reached down into the hole it had left behind. His tongue crept out and wiggled at the corner of his mouth as his hand sought and searched, reaching deeper and deeper until his arm was down in the hole up to his armpit, and then his face shifted into a triumphant expression and he pulled out a cloth-wrapped bundle. The thing that wasn't Ramses unwrapped it, humming to himself, stepping over the still-sleeping forms of the guard and the dogs and the birds. The cloth came free, and Renai saw that he held death in his hands.

She'd held it once, too, the gun, the cursed revolver that had trapped a fallen angel. She screamed and she made no sound. She ran and she went nowhere. She spread her butterfly wings, her fragile shards of rainbow, and fled, rising into a sky that held no stars, that was no escape. That gun, like all guns, was evil, an engine of only destruction, but unlike any other gun, it could kill literally anything, humans or spirits . . . or gods.

And now it was in the hands of a devil.

When Renai was herself again, she was sitting on an uncomfortable sofa whose springs were digging into her thighs, in a living room she didn't recognize. She didn't feel like she'd been asleep, more like a switch had been thrown in her mind: a moment ago she'd been wandering through roman-candy-scented rain clouds toward a stage where Donald Glover, in his Childish Gambino persona, wore furry pants and white paint streaks and sang a song he'd written just for her, and now she was here, in a loft apartment she'd never seen before, exposed brick walls and high ceilings and the flat-screen television mounted on the wall playing *It's a Wonderful Life* with the sound turned off.

Her mouth felt full of cotton, and her limbs were as sore as if she'd finished a hard run and hadn't bothered to stretch after. Her hair and her skin and her clothes were damp, from sweat, she thought at first, but then she heard the *pock-pock-pock* of rain drizzling outside. She knew she ought to feel some kind of way about all this, confused or angry or afraid, but instead a kind of languor sat in her chest and took the edge off of everything. So she sat there, calm, and waited for something to happen.

After a moment, one of the doors—which led into a bedroom from what

Renai could see—opened and Regal came through, wearing a long blue coat with brass buttons, her arms filled with plastic masks. Her hair had been slicked back and forced into a tight ponytail, and she had a fake goatee pasted onto her face. The soles of her knee-high boots thumped on the hardwood floor.

"Why are you wearing a disguise?" Renai asked. Her words weren't slurred as she'd expected, instead, her throat felt raw, like she'd just left the Dome after a Saints game.

"Glad to have you back," Regal said, dumping her armload of masks onto the counter. "And it's not a disguise, it's a costume. It might be a re-reboot of *Night of the Living Dead* out there, but it's still Halloween. You dress like the consequences of Tinker Bell and Joey Ramone's busted condom, so you're good, but if you think I'm going out there in street clothes like some god-damn plebe, you're as confused as a cat with two assholes, my friend. I'm the Magician of New Orleans. I got a rep to maintain."

Renai wasn't fully collected yet, still recovering from whatever poison or drug had been on Aka's tongue, but the more Regal talked, the more came back to her. The Hallows. The ghoul problem. The need to find Ramses. "Where's Leon?" she asked. "And who are you supposed to be?"

"Leon's on the phone, trying to reach Jude," Regal said.

Oh, good, Renai thought. But why was it good? Why did that thought bring her relief? Renai knew something about Jude, something that she had to tell Leon and Regal. Something about Aka. But she couldn't grasp it. She knew something about Ramses, but she couldn't grasp that either.

"You really don't recognize my outfit?" Regal cocked her head to the side. "Are you still tripping balls, or just bustin' mine? I thought I did a pretty good job." She struck a pose, one hand on her hip, the other pointing straight into the air. "How 'bout now?"

Renai shrugged. "Pirate? Vampire? Pirate vampire?" Except that didn't make sense. There were no vampires in New Orleans anymore. Not since Jude had kicked them out, the same night that he—

And then she remembered everything.

She lunged to her feet, the pad of paper and pen that she hadn't realized was in her lap falling to the floor. "I know what happened," she said. "I know what Ramses stole."

"Yeah," Regal said, "you told us. 'Bout eighty times now. You check out your drawings yet?" Renai reached down and scooped up the pad, saw that she'd scrawled a half-dozen drawings of the serpent-twined staff that she'd seen Ramses take, and that she'd written the words IN THAT SLEEP OF DEATH over and over and over again. "It's called a caduceus," Regal said. "The staff of Hermes. You gave us sleep, snakes, and staff, and Google did the rest. I know it's a bad situation all around, gods are pissed, the dead are walking, yadda, yadda, yadda, but I gotta admit, I'd have taken that motherfucker, too. Sleep on command? Wake the dead? Hell, yes."

"It wasn't Ramses, though—"

"He's possessed. Yeah, we got that part, too. And the gun. You want a cup of coffee or something, Sparkles? Because we kinda need to hit the ground running here, you know?"

"And Aka? You know she was at the card game with the other destruction gods?"

Regal nodded. "Yep. That's why Leon's trying to get in touch with El Juderino. To see if Aka slipped out early, or if the game is still keeping the others ocupado." The other door rattled and opened, and Leon came in, carrying with him the funk of a recently smoked cigarette. "Here he is now," she said. "What's the word, Sweets?"

"No answer," Leon said, tossing Regal a phone. "Called his phone and the casino number, from both my phone and yours. Best I can figure, he's still dealin' them cards." He gave Renai a curt nod. "Glad to see you shook whatever that demon stung you with. She won't get a second chance, you got my word on that."

"Great," Regal said, shifting from foot to foot with impatience. "Wonderful. And now that she's functional again, will you *please* come pick one of these so we can get this shit-show on the road."

Leon crossed the small room in a couple of long strides. When he reached the counter, he sifted through the collection of masks—some just cheap plastic dominos, others more elaborate ones that covered half the face or more—with a dubious twist to his features. "Remind me again why I need to make a fool of myself like this?"

Regal threw her head back and let out an exaggerated groan. "Because where we're going, you'll need to be in costume to blend in. Especially you, with your picture on the cover of every one of your inexplicably popular albums."

"Hey, now," Leon said, just as Renai asked, "Where are we going?"

The half smile he always seemed to have in response to Regal's antics slid off of Leon's face. "You didn't tell her?"

"I figured it would be better if we discussed it on the way."

"Tell her what?" Renai asked, though her tone made it more of a demand. She felt the storm spinning within her, driving away the last dregs of confusion and calm. Leon scooped up one of the masks at random, a half-face pink rabbit mask with big floppy ears. He gestured toward Renai in a well-go-on-then wave.

"Me and Leon got to talking," Regal said, "while you were, you know, giving all the glory to the hypnotoad. You wouldn't shut up about Ramses being possessed, and how without the stone you couldn't find him and—" Leon cleared his throat and tapped his wrist, even though he wasn't actually wearing a watch. "Okay, right. So we figured, it's real goddamn convenient that the stone quit working right when we got close, right when a possessed theme park and a destruction spirit were waiting to ambush you. And we asked ourselves, who had the ability to watch you and orchestrate that whole thing? Who sure seems to know a lot about spirits and possession?"

"Jack fucking Elderflower," Renai said. It all made a painful kind of sense. Cordelia had brought her to him. He'd worked so hard to convince her that his stone was the only way to find Ramses.

He and Cordelia had been playing her from the start.

Regal shot her the finger guns. "The very same. So we went to pay that immortal turd-stain a visit." She reached into one of the wide pockets of her coat and pulled out a plain white envelope. "But this is all we found." She held it out to Renai, tilting it to make sure she saw the name written on the front: RENAISSANCE RAINES. Inside, Renai found a digital recorder.

When she pushed the PLAY button, she heard hollering and laughter and slamming lockers and the strangely muted shout of someone speaking from a PA speaker, and she knew what was coming next before the woman started speaking. "Spooky Girl and Miss Feathers," Opal Brennan said. "So bad news first . . ." Renai let the rest of the message play, but she didn't need to. Renai had heard it all the first time around, when the oracle left it on her voicemail. She'd lost it when she lost her phone, but that wouldn't stop someone like Jack, now would it? The question was, why had he left this message for them? Was it a clue? A threat? "Last time anybody heard from our boy," Opal continued, "he was supposed to meet up with some friends to ride the

Ghost Train." And then, even though Renai knew there was more to the message, the recording ended with a click that sounded all too final. Which meant that Jack had wanted those to be the last words she heard. Wanted to emphasize them.

"This is some kind of sick joke," Renai said. "He's got her, you know that, right? That soulless bastard grabbed up an innocent woman off the street just so we would come running into his trap." The spirit—already awakened by the way Regal and Leon had talked about her like she wasn't in the room—kept whirling within her, rising in response to her rage, begging to be set free. Renai ached to let it loose. To cut a path across the whole damn city if she had to.

"We had a similar notion," Leon said.

"And you came back here to *change into costumes?* Are you—"

"We came back for this," Regal said, reaching out and snatching something off Renai's forehead, pulling it off with the skin-tearing yank of a Band-Aid.

"The fuck?" Renai's hand went involuntarily to her skin, checking her fingers for blood. Regal slipped the thing into Renai's hand, a curl of thin paper that was sticky on one side, like a pore cleanser or a nicotine patch. There was a thin paste on it that smelled like berries.

"I used to party like a rock star," Regal said, giving Renai a rueful grin. "After the third time I had to sleep in my car all night because my shitty friend never stayed sober when it was her turn to be the designated driver, I whipped these up. Makes your piss burn like lit gasoline for a couple of days, but that's the price you pay for making out with strangers in bathroom stalls. I wasn't sure what weird-ass roofie you swallowed when Aka slipped you the tongue, but I figured this would straighten you out. And it did, so we're good to go." She looked at Leon, who nodded, and then back to Renai. "Right? Right."

"But we know it's a trap. We're really just gonna stroll right in like he owes us money?"

"Of course not," Regal said, handing Renai a domino mask designed to look like a butterfly's outstretched wings. "That's why we're wearing disguises."

CHAPTER TWENTY-EIGHT

I WAS DARK when they left Regal's apartment, the air heavy with the moisture of a recent rain, the clouds still grumbling overhead and threatening more. They piled into Leon's Rolls and set off, the tension potent and unspoken. Aside from Leon constantly glancing up at his rearview mirror to check on her, and Regal's half-hummed, half-sung rendition of that girl-kissing song from that white-as-hell pop singer—changing the lyrics to replace "I" with "Sparkles" with no regard for meter—the ride was pretty quiet.

Renai spent most of it staring out the window at the gathering crowds, trying—and *failing*—to spot any ghouls, which was strange; given the number of people she knew died in the city each day, there ought to be plenty of animated corpses shuffling around in the streets. Regal and Leon had thought it was enough of a problem to summon her from the Underworld, even. So where were the undead?

If Regal or Leon noticed the absence of the ghouls, neither mentioned it. They both seemed content to leave Renai to her thoughts on the short drive across town, which—once she gave up wondering where the restless dead had wandered off to—she appreciated, because she felt like she was on the cusp of understanding the greater picture behind Ramses' disappearance.

He'd obviously made a deal with some devil to save his life, a deal that allowed his body to be possessed by whatever Underworld spirit he'd traded his Fortune to. Whether that deal and that possession was part of Cordelia's plan, or merely a convenient reality she'd taken advantage of, it was pretty clear that she was orchestrating some plot that involved Ramses, and either the caduceus, the cursed revolver, or both.

Renai had to hand it to Cordelia. The timing was perfect. A missing kid here, a spiritual prison break there, all of it building up to the Hallows, when the whole system designed to keep the living and the dead separate from one another was split wide open. It was like robbing a bank during Mardi Gras, when all the cops were on the parade route. The only thing she couldn't wrap her mind around was the one that would lock it all in place. The end goal. The why. Cordelia was obviously some kind of goddess. She could come and go to the Underworld whenever she pleased. Why would she *need* all this confusion in this world and the other? What move was she hiding?

She tried to see it from every angle, trying to remember what she and Sal had been doing in the Underworld at the same time the other half of her had been in this world with Cordelia. When it occurred to her that her dual nature was why Cross had accused her and Sal of being at the prison when the demons were released—because they'd been at OPP in the living world collecting Miguel Flores from his moment of death—her vision caught a little slant in that now-familiar sensation of trying to hold two separate memories in the same brain at the same time, but with the addition of a sharp pain at her wrist. She slapped her own skin, absently, thinking it was merely a mosquito, but when she looked, it was far worse.

The yarn bound to her flesh by Celeste's effigy magic was beginning to fray.

Renai tried to tell herself that she'd known that the magic tying her two halves together was only ever a temporary solution, that it made sense for something that was only supposed to last for three days to start wearing out after one. But she couldn't deny that needle-prick of pain. She'd caused this. By remembering as both Underworld Renai and Living World Renai at the same time, she'd put a strain on the magic that it couldn't handle. Which meant that if she pushed herself too hard, this strange compromise with herself that Celeste had forced on her could rip apart a lot sooner than the end of the Hallows.

To distract herself, she tapped Regal—who was on her third or fourth

rendition of her "Sparkles Kissed a Girl," each one more filthy than the last
—on the shoulder. She sang one more line, something about "bathroom
floor flavor ChapStick," and turned around, leaning one arm across Leon's
bench seat.

"What's up?" she asked.

"What have you got against Jack Elderflower?"

Regal made a face like she'd been the one who'd had to endure Aka's
tongue. "A restraining order would be nice," she said.

Renai lifted an eyebrow and twisted her mouth. "For real? You got
jokes? Now?"

Leon jerked the wheel, cursing, trying to avoid a pothole too late, and the
Rolls bottomed out with an alarming thump. No screech of metal, though,
so they should be okay, Renai thought. He slowed to a crawl, nonetheless.
Regal, who had been thrown to the side, turned back to Renai, saw that her
expression hadn't changed, and frowned. "Okay fine. The truth about Elderflower. Well, first thing's first, you might know him by another name.
Jacques St. Germain?" She paused, as if that should mean something. Renai felt a salty response rising to her lips, but then the name did tickle at her
memory, some half-remembered detail overheard from one of those tours in
the Quarter that had driven Celeste from her shop. Only they had called him
the Comte de St. Germain.

And they'd said he was a vampire.

"Wait," she said, "that can't be right. He's—"

"Not a vampire, no," Regal said. "There are no vampires in New Orleans, not anymore. They get that wrong in those tours. What they get right,
though, is that he's been in the city since the early 1900s, and he was apparently over a hundred years old when he got here. He claims to be a count,
but that's probably bullshit, just like all of his other names. The only thing
I know for sure that's true about him is that he's an alchemist, among other
things. You know, lead into gold, commanding spirits, attaining immortality.
That whole deal. As for why I hate him? Well, the short version is, he and
my father, they—"

Don't say "had beef." Please don't say "had beef."

"—they had beef. And I sort of inherited it. Elderfucker got his dick all
bent out of shape when I tried to resolve things some years back, and I reacted poorly." She got an almost-wistful expression on her face. "I may have
actually cursed his dick to hang crooked? I forget."

"Seriously?" Leon said, surprising Renai, who hadn't even known he was paying attention.

Regal shrugged. "It was right after Katrina. I was in a bad place."

"Ain't nobody in a good place after the storm," he said, "but you the only one out here hexin' a man's private business. You got you an unhealthy fixation, woman." Renai could see his smile in the rearview mirror, but also his hands flexing and gripping the steering wheel like he could throttle some calm out of it. She recognized their banter for what it was and knew there was a reason they called it gallows humor.

And yet, amid all Regal's cussing and irreverence, she'd said something important: Jack Elderflower commanded spirits. Renai remembered now that he'd said that all of his odd computer wizardry was because he sent out demons to do his bidding. Since she'd been raised Catholic, she had a very specific idea of what a demon was, complete with batwings and a pitchfork, but in truth, it was just another name for a spirit. Maybe he'd summoned and trapped a bunch of demons in his server racks in the same way Regal had bound a spirit to fuel her fire-stick. The same way Renai herself had forced a room full of lost souls to take the form of a deck of cards. Elderflower had told Renai he wanted a coin of Fortune, but maybe he'd had his eyes on another source of power.

Maybe Elderflower knew where all those demons who had escaped from the Oubliette had gone.

"So, anyway," Regal said, "words were exchanged, my FEMA trailer got burnt down; things were tense. Then he up and vanished, and I haven't seen his cowardly ass since."

"Aight," Leon said, turning the Rolls off of the bumpy, pitted stretch of Magazine and into the long, sinuous driveway of Audubon Zoo. "Y'all tighten up. We here."

⧖

Renai didn't know how long the Audubon Society had been putting on this "Boo at the Zoo" fundraiser for Children's Hospital, but she was pretty sure it'd been going on since right after the storm, at least. As a kid, her folks hadn't been big on Halloween — half from the manufactured panic about sociopaths putting razor blades in random pieces of candy, and half from the occult implications that they saw in the holiday — so it wasn't until she was old enough to "run the streets" on her own, as her father had put it, that she was able to really explore Halloween for herself. She'd loved coming to Audubon Zoo on Halloween as a teenager, loved it with every ounce of her little goth heart: the crowd all wearing costumes, the goofy haunted house for little kids and the genuinely scary version for older ones, the transgressive thrill of being in a place after dark when it normally closed in the afternoon, all of it.

And that included, of course, the Ghost Train.

Unlike Christmas in the Oaks, a similar attraction that ran in City Park during Christmas, the Ghost Train at the zoo wasn't a true locomotive, just an electric cart strong enough to pull a handful of four-seat cars in a line behind it, so every year the path through the zoo was a little different, a little more elaborate. Since they closed all the animal enclosures for the event, the Ghost Train could really go just about anywhere on the grounds.

Renai had a feeling this year's ride would be far more trick than treat.

After five years of living with her aura of indifference in this world and the shades in the next, dealing with a crowd of living humans was an unsettling, unnerving experience for Renai. She hadn't stopped at the front gate until one of the security guards blocked her path, hadn't even considered that she'd need money until she was asked for it. Luckily, Regal had done some trick with a napkin that convinced the woman in the ticket booth that they'd paid.

Inside, she felt like hundreds of eyes were watching her, like everyone turned to stare at her as she passed by. It wasn't until a young white girl tugged at her mother's sleeve and shouted, "Mommy, that lady's fairy wings are *flapping!*" that Renai realized that her nerves were wound so tight that her wings were trying to carry her away. The mother grabbed her child by the arm and tugged her away, face reddening and refusing to look in Renai's direction, as if her child had somehow offended her, or more likely that Renai would "cause a scene." Like she was dangerous, not because she had a spirit living inside of her or because she was an emissary of Death, but because of the color of her skin. Renai felt that old familiar flush of shame and anger, an indignity that was almost comforting after so long without it.

Girl, she thought, *when you take comfort in some racist-ass Becky giving you the you-know-how-they-are stare, you got yourself some problems.* She shook her head and tried to focus on what was in front of her.

The plan Regal had come up with was for them to split up, Leon in front, Renai behind, and Regal bringing up the rear, the idea being that Jack had no reason to suspect that either of the other two would be there with Renai.

So when Jack approached her, either Regal or Leon would be in a position to grab him. Renai didn't have any better ideas, so she went along with it, pretending like she didn't know that it was an act-like-we-have-a-plan-so-we-don't-freak-out sort of approach.

Overhead, thunder rumbled through the clouds. Renai almost wished it would rain, just so the crowds would disperse. She wondered if the little tempest inside of her could reach up and quicken a true storm out of the clouds above, but with only anxiety pulsing through her veins, the spirit seemed far out of her reach, and had been since Aka had sent her on a spit-induced acid trip. She could still feel it there, coiled down deep, but it seemed to be sleeping. Or waiting.

Focused on maneuvering through a crowd that could actually see her and didn't shy away from her like the shades did, Renai jumped when Regal's voice muttered from just behind her, "That you?"

"What?" She barely stopped herself from turning to look at the other woman.

"The thunder, is that you?"

"No," she said, "not me."

"I sure hope Jude is keeping those rain-dancing pricks busy at that card game."

Renai was quiet for a second, unsure if Regal was being weirdly literal or just unconsciously racist, wondering if it was possible she was doing both at once. "Aren't you supposed to be keeping your distance?" she asked, taking the next steps on her toes and craning her neck so she could see Leon's rabbit-eared mask over the crowd. He'd turned around and was heading back toward them.

"Change of plans," Regal said. When Renai looked at her, she was holding out her cell phone, which had a text from a blocked number. Up ahead, Leon held up his phone, giving it a disgusted shake.

THANKS FOR JOINING US, the message read. ALL ABOARD!

⧗

The line for the Ghost Train was a long, restless serpent of people that wound its way through the metal barricades set up around the carousel: an elaborate, massive wheel beneath a red and white awning, its rim and its center both decorated with paintings of endangered species and oval mirrors, its spokes twisted, gilt-covered poles that held the menagerie of alligators and elephants and rhinos and flamingos alongside the more traditional horses. Every time it started to spin, Renai flinched, unable to stop herself from imagining the huge thing rising up like the animated ruin at Jazzland.

Renai hadn't really considered that there were unexamined benefits to her aura of indifference, but not ever having to wait in line was sure one of them. She felt her time as herself slipping away from her like there was an hourglass just outside of her vision, a timer ticking down. Not to mention all the dirty looks the three of them were getting from parents whenever Regal muttered something vile within earshot of their kids. She was going on and on about how she should have anticipated that Elderflower would have been able to track their phones, how his demons were everywhere that had wires or circuits for them to possess, only she used words that would have had Renai's mother reaching for a bar of soap.

To make it worse, when they finally got into the lines that led to the cars themselves, some white family's kid—obviously way too young for the ride —started screaming when he saw the bloody aprons and grotesque masks the zoo volunteers were wearing. One of them went so far as to lift his mask to show the shrieking child that it was all just a joke, but that only scared him even more.

The young boy's fear wormed into her, into the half of her that had dwelt in the Underworld, into the compassionate side of her that tried to understand, to empathize. The one that used her power to wash away, not to kill. And so she felt the gulf between her and the destructive power she wanted to face Elderflower with widening, felt the strain of it tugging at the bindings of her flesh.

So it was almost a relief when they finally got onto the train—Renai and Regal squeezing into one seat, Leon taking up the other one by himself in that sprawling I-need-all-this-space-for-all-my-junk way that men sat—even though they were, in a sense, just walking into Elderflower's trap. Once the train started moving, pulling away from the crowd into the relative silence of rubber tires on concrete and the oaks stretched wide overhead, Renai felt some of her anxiety ease. One way or another, they were about to get some answers.

The scenery was pretty tame at first, with fake bats hanging from the trees and speakers blasting out ominous laughter, but Renai knew it would get pretty intense before it was over. Mannequins set up to depict scenes of violence, volunteer actors portraying monsters and killers chasing after victims, then rushing toward the train itself. She didn't know if it was because she'd been a victim of violence herself, or if it was because she'd seen the impact that death had on those around them, or if she was just too aware of the real monsters that the world seemed to ignore, but she didn't relish the thought of those images the way she once had.

Maybe she just knew that this time the danger was real.

At least she wasn't alone in that knowledge. As soon as they made a turn off the paved section of walkway and onto a gravel service road that was normally closed to the public—which had been pretty cleverly decorated to look like part of the fencing had been torn down—Leon took his trumpet out of its case, and Regal pulled her flame-throwing bat from one of her coat pockets, a set of knuckle-dusters carved out of bleached-white bone from the other. Regal reached into the nowhere place and took out her glass blade.

"So tell me, Sparkles," Regal said, tapping her bat against her bone knuckles, "do you really not recognize my costume?" The question dragged a nervous laugh of out of Renai, and a chuckle from Leon. "Because it sort of feels like we're about to die gruesome, and to be completely honest, if there's no *Hamilton* in the afterlife, you're gonna have to bring the big guns out to drag me to the other side."

At that moment, Renai was struck by two very different conclusions at the exact same time. The first came from Regal's words, the phrases "big guns" and "other side" colliding in her mind in a way that brought Cordelia's end game, if not its specific target, into clear and almost painful clarity.

The second came as the foliage on one side of the path and the fencing on the other fell away and they entered the truly scary part of the ride, this year's theme immediately apparent and—just as abruptly—the trap that Elderflower had left for them.

What Renai saw when the Ghost Train came around the bend and slowed to a stop was this: a Honda Civic staged to look as if it had veered off the road and crashed into one of the zoo's massive oaks, an actor "pinned" by the car but still struggling and snarling. Other actors in decaying face makeup and torn, bloody clothes shambling toward the Ghost Train with the stuttering, rigor mortis gait of Hollywood zombies. Scattered among them, their empty eyes and vacant expressions aimed unerringly at the car where Renai and Regal and Leon rode, were dozens of ghouls.

A cold, slack-skinned hand clamped over Renai's mouth just as she started to scream.

CHAPTER TWENTY-NINE

THEY ARE SPOKEN of throughout human history, even as far back as *The Epic of Gilgamesh*. The Germanic peoples of the far north call them afturganga, the "after-walkers." In the mountains of Tibet, doors are built with low lintels, in the belief that the Ro-lang, the risen, cannot bend at the waist. In the myths of the Middle East, it was wise to avoid ruins and abandoned places, for there dwelt the ghūl who seized the unwary. In the folklore of Algonquin speakers, they are called wendigo, the forever starving. They are known throughout the modern world as zombies, a name taken from Haitian voodoo. But a zombie is a living person whose soul has been stripped away, while these revenants, these ghouls, are corpses with only the barest shred of life. Monsters and victims both, these walking dead, these failed resurrections share one thing in common: their hunger for human flesh can never be sated.

▧

Elderflower's trap caught them as soon as Renai saw it. Ghouls who had been lurking in the stands of bushes to either side of the gate stepped out of hiding once the train paused, coming up from behind Renai and Regal and Leon, grabbing their mouths and seizing their hands in silent, inhuman coordination, dragging them from the train car with implacable strength just as it started moving again.

Effectively silenced, the three of them had no way to fight back. Renai managed to swipe at one of her assailants with her knife—the blade passing through the meat and bone of the ghoul's shoulder with no resistance—but succeeded only in lopping off a limb that still clung tenaciously to her face. The few people in the cars ahead of them who saw their abduction—plebes, Regal would have called them—thought it was all part of the show, waving goodbye or pointing the struggle out to their friends. Renai saw one asshole filming it all with his phone.

Renai was hoisted into the air by multiple hands, like she was crowd surfing, and she could tell by the swaying and shifting beneath her that the ghouls were carrying her somewhere, but since she could see only darkness above her, she had no way to guess where they were taking her. To Elderflower, she guessed, and if the muffled shouts next to her were any indication, Regal, at least, was heading in the same direction. Cold, rigid fingers pried at the hand holding the black glass knife, trying to pull it from her grasp, so she slid it away into the nowhere place so that the ghouls couldn't take it from her.

Then she clenched her jaw and reached for the living tempest within her, the power that hung just out of reach. She was caught halfway between her two selves, each one fighting, straining for the storm's magic. The half of her that was an ender of lives had a burning hatred for Jack Elderflower and what he'd done—what he was continuing to do—and was willing to scorch the earth for miles around if it meant her lightning would reach him. The half of her that was a giver of mercy was consumed by an aching compassion for the people whose corpses were now carrying her, people who—because their Fortunes were still coiled up inside their bodies while their Essences wandered—would linger forever outside the First Gate for no fault other than dying in the wrong place at the wrong time.

Here was the crux of all her trouble as a psychopomp. How could she stomach the anger she felt for the injustices of the world when she knew it was full of broken, frightened people? How could she love the world she lived in when it filled her with so much hate?

Aching and straining at the bindings that held her together, Renai didn't realize they'd reached their destination until the ghouls tipped her upright and let her slide to the ground. She stayed on her feet, but she was so tightly restrained by their dead hands that they might as well have held her overhead. Thankfully, she was able to move her head, so she could see where the ghouls had brought them.

The ghouls had crowded together onto a raised wooden walkway, the flat, open area broken up at regular intervals by waist-high structures that revealed themselves, after a few moments of peering into the darkness, to be picnic tables. The crowd of ghouls surrounding them were so still and silent that Renai could hear the murmur of insects in the oaks and cypress trees sprawling overhead, the soft swish and drip of water beneath the boards at their feet, and the buzz and mutter of the crowds enjoying the festivities, way too far off to be of any help. Regal was being held to Renai's left, blood streaming from her nose, Leon to Renai's right, his shirt torn and his breath coming in shallow gasps, like it hurt him to breathe.

Lights sparked to life, revealing a squat one-story building with a wooden overhang and a sign featuring a man in a ridiculous chef's hat stirring a pot, the words CYPRESS KNEE CAFE in two different fonts. Renai knew, then, where they were, and huffed out a laugh in spite of herself. Even if they managed to get away from the ghouls holding them, they'd have to use the walkways in and out of this place to get out. Either that, or go over the railing and fuck with the gators roaming the duckweed-filled waters of the Louisiana Swamp Exhibit.

The man who called himself Jack Elderflower sat at one of the tables on the far side of the cafe's dining area. He wore a green T-shirt with NEUTRAL GROUND SIDE written on it in gold letters, jeans so dark a blue that they had to be brand-new, and a pair of flip-flops. He smiled and gave them a casual half-wave, his ass on the table and his feet on the bench, just a casual bro waiting for his peeps to show. Renai half expected him to offer them a beer.

"So glad you all could make it," he said. "These guys are great at following orders, but they are absolute shit at polite dinner conversation." He made a grabbing you-there-come-here gesture that Renai could easily picture him doing at a waiter, and two of the ghouls stepped forward. One handed him Regal's flame-throwing bat; the other held Leon's trumpet. "Oh, and you brought gifts. How thoughtful. I look forward to taking these little trinkets apart and seeing how they work." He tipped a wink in their direction. "Sort of my thing, you know."

Elderflower set the bat down on the table and hopped up, revealing a bound and gagged Opal Brennan lying on the table behind him. She was unconscious, but her chest rose and fell. From what Renai could see, she hadn't been harmed. Elderflower walked toward them slowly, one hand cupping his elbow, the other tapping a finger against his lips, as if he were debating what to do with the three of them. This whole experience, being bound and helpless in the dead of night, reminded Renai of the night five years ago when she'd faced Cross and Criminel in Audubon Park with Jude Dubuisson's Essence rattling around in her mind. There was something important about that night, something she needed to remember.

Smiling at her with a warmth that didn't touch his empty, soulless eyes, Elderflower peeled the amputated ghoul's hand away from Renai's mouth and let it fall with a thump to the wood floor. "You and I have much to discuss," he said.

"I have your coin," Renai said, blurting it out as soon as the thought occurred to her. "It's right here in one of my jacket pockets."

Elderflower's brow furrowed in confusion for a moment. "Ah," he said, his face uncreasing, "the coin of Destiny I asked you to bring me." He wrinkled his nose in an exaggerated gesture of distaste. "Never had much use for one of those, not even my own. You want to know the secret to immortality? The heart of all alchemical study?" He leaned in, so close she learned that Regal was right about his breath smelling like shit. "You step off the wheel of luck and destiny," he whispered in her ear, a forced intimacy that made her shudder.

He leaned back and grinned at her, mistook her revulsion for something else. "I burned out every scrap of Fortune from my soul centuries ago. It's what enables me to demonstrate free will, while the rest of you pull the yoke and obey every tug of the reins. I am what you might be, were you able to cast off the shackles of the gods." He held up a finger, a teacher emphasizing a point to an inattentive student. "What I truly needed was something that would convince you to carry that stone around so I could keep an eye on you."

Though she'd suspected this very thing, the truth still tasted bitter in Renai's mouth. "So you've been working for that skank Cordelia all along."

He reached out and tapped the tip of Renai's nose with his knuckle. "You're starting to get it! But, skank, really? Discordia is a goddess of primordial night, show a little respect."

"If she's so divine," Renai said, "what's she using a scrub like you for?" Despite the fact that it obviously pained him, Leon laughed behind the hand of the ghoul restraining him. Regal muttered something and, knowing Renai wouldn't understand her, winked to show her support.

"As with everything else, Renaissance Raines, you've gotten it wrong. Discordia is not using me, I am using her. You see, everything we told you was the truth. There's a storm coming."

Renai's stomach clenched when he said that. Hurricane season would end in a month, but everyone in the city knew how powerful a late hurricane could be. Some part of her fear must have shown on her face, because Elderflower waved at her, like he was shooing away a gnat.

"No," he said, "no mere temporary collision of wind and flood. The destruction she will awaken is stronger than that little twist of magic you've got living inside of you, more devastating than any hurricane. The kind of storm that will sweep clean the face of the Earth. If I'm going to survive it, and I have every intention of doing so, then I'm going to have to see what's coming. No amount of stolen destiny will accomplish that. For that sort of prescience"—he aimed a thumb at the unconscious woman lying on the table behind him—"you need the eyes of an oracle." Elderflower's tone left absolutely no doubt. He meant it literally. Opal wasn't just the bait to lure Renai here, she was the fee for his service to Cordelia.

That realization tipped the scales in Renai's internal struggle, and as the rage filled her, so did the spirit's power. She let the winds come pouring out of her, their passage a different kind of strain on the strings binding her separate selves together, a pain that was almost pleasurable in its sharp sting. She let the tempest's power build, the wind making the ghouls sway and stagger for balance, and—

Felt the power pour out of her faster than she intended, faster than it had ever gone before. Elderflower bared his teeth in a gesture that was far more snarl than smile. He held up a hand to show her the brass and iron ring that circled his index finger, a signet inscribed with the Seal of Solomon—a hexagram encircled and inscribed with the words of binding that the ancient king had used to command spirits, djinn, and demons—that glowed bright red as it absorbed the storm spirit. Renai tried to grasp hold of it, to stem its rush out of her, but it was too late. The last shreds of the spirit that had lived inside of her since her resurrection went spilling out of her and into Jack Elderflower's ring.

"And, that's checkmate," he said, rubbing his hands together in obnoxious glee. "Though, really, I feel like I've been playing chess while you three have been playing checkers. It was all right there in front of you. There's only one reason we'd need that boy to carry the revolver for us. Only one place we could be sending him. And you never—"

He sighed and fell silent, hands on his hips. "Nothing to add? No threats to make, no mercy to beg for? I have to admit I was hoping for a little more stimulating conversation than this. It's not like I can let these two speak" —he aimed a finger at Regal and the other at Leon—"one of them being the Voice of New Orleans, and the other being a vicious cunt from whose mouth I never want to hear another word." Regal shouted something into the corpse hand of her own ghoul, the words muffled but the meaning clear. That thought triggered Renai's memory of the fight against the loa in Audubon Park, where she'd learned a potent magical word from the mind of Jude Dubuisson, the same word she'd heard Regal shout earlier that day when they'd fought a ruin animated by spirits.

"I don't know much about checkers or chess," Renai said.

Elderflower's face fell, and his eyes lids fluttered in disgust. "No, see, it was a metaphor—"

"Because the game my family always played was Hearts," she said, smiling at him, knowing that this wouldn't work if she didn't *believe* it would work. "And in my house, you never gloated until the last card was played, or else you got hit with the bitch." And then she shouted the word in that strange, unknown language that she and Regal had both learned from a fortune god, the magic word whose power Regal had bound into the wood grain of a miniature baseball bat like it was a magic wand.

The word that meant *burn*.

Liquid fire came spewing out of the end of Regal's baseball bat, arcing across the wooden picnic tables and the wooden floor of the raised walkway and landing at the feet of a handful of ghouls, none of whom possessed the self-awareness to back away from the roaring flames, standing unnaturally still even as they burned. Elderflower spun around and threw out his hand, the one wearing the brass and iron ring. Smoke streamed out from the ring, some of it gray as morning fog, some of it black as oil.

But Renai didn't wait to see how Elderflower intended to stop the fire. She arched her back and twisted her wrist, angling it so that the blade of her black knife—when she reached into the nowhere place and pulled it out—would slice through the forearm of the ghoul holding her arm. A rush of wind and a huge splash and the stagnant funk of swamp rot told her that she was almost out of time, so she thrashed and cut the other hand that held her, and then was falling free and landing on her knees — a jarring pain that made her eyes water — and she slipped the blade back into the nowhere place and dug in the pocket of her jacket —

Only to be dragged back to her feet by one of the ghouls, its dead hand clamped around her neck. She grabbed its wrist, an involuntary response, her body fighting back even though her mind knew it was hopeless. Renai stared into its eyes, cataract milky and unseeing. Her other hand, though, fumbled in her pocket, found the medicine bottle, and — struggling with the safety catch on the top — crushed its thin plastic in her fist, trying not to picture the hand on her neck doing the same thing to her throat. She tore open the cigarette with her thumbnail, sifting through the loose tobacco leaves for a thin sliver of metal.

Another hand clamped over her wrist, this one warm and pulsing with life. Renai turned and looked into Jack Elderflower's empty white eyes. He sneered. A glance over his shoulder showed the steaming, smoldering tables and deck, soaked from where he'd ordered a demon or a Shadow or a djinn — whatever he chose to call that shapeless creature of will and magic he shackled to his command — to douse the flames from Regal's flame-throwing bat with a wave of swamp water. Leon and Regal struggled and fought, but as Renai knew all too well, there was no fighting the dead.

Elderflower forced Renai's hand out of her pocket, twisting her arm so that he could see what was in her fist. For maybe the first time, Renai saw a genuine expression cross his face: surprise. "A cigarette? Seriously? What, were you hoping to give me cancer?"

Renai pulled in a breath to answer him and found, to her pleasure if not her surprise, that she had no difficulty breathing, that the ghoul was holding her by the neck, but not squeezing. She feigned a struggle anyway, wheezing a little and whispering the lyrics to "I Kissed a Girl," so quietly that she knew Elderflower wouldn't be able to hear her clearly. He leaned in, his smile more ghastly than the corpse that held her neck. "Last words," he said as he leaned in, letting go of her arm to lean on the railing behind her. "I've been waiting a long time for this moment."

"You have waited," Renai agreed, all pretense of weakness gone from her voice, "for far too long." And then she jabbed him in the neck with the shard of metal that was the last, final piece of what had once been an entire destiny. The sliver of Fortune that held only the moment of his death. He blinked once, eyes open just long enough for Renai to see that all along, Jack Elderflower's eyes were a very nice shade of blue, and then he slipped to the ground, having finally reached the end of his long, long life.

Regal and Leon both shouted, their voices muffled by the ghouls still holding them fast. They were, as far as she could tell, celebrating their victory, believing what Elderflower had shown them. Thinking that he was in control, and his death meant that they'd won this round. Renai allowed herself a grim smile, but she knew what they didn't—what they *couldn't* know—that their fight was far from finished. She looked away when their struggles against the ghouls' restraint turned frantic, not wanting to see it on their faces when they began to realize what even Elderflower hadn't known:

That these ghouls were animated by a power other than the spirits he'd commanded.

"You can let us go now," Renai said, talking to the ghoul in front of her from force of habit but knowing that all of them would hear and speak with the same voice. "I know you weren't really obeying that asshole."

⧗

The hand gripping Renai's neck relaxed just enough for her to pull free, and even though she knew anything that could possibly feel pain in the ghoul had died days ago, she kicked its leg as hard as she could. It didn't do anything, but it made her feel better. Regal shoved her way free of her own restraint, and then Leon followed, doubling over almost immediately, a hand pressed to his side. Regal helped him up by draping his arm over her shoulder, and though his face twisted in agony, he rose to standing more or less straight up.

It was eerie, standing there amid a crowd of dead bodies. There could be no doubt that there was no life in them, they were too still, too vacant. And more than a few of them were starting to smell. "You want to tell us what the sweet goddamn is going on here?" Regal said, her voice hoarse from all the futile shouting she'd been doing. "I thought chuckle-fuck over there was the one controlling all these zom—" Leon wheezed something angry toward her. "All these walking corpses that are totally something other than zombies."

"So did he," Renai said. "He thought they obeyed him because of this." She knelt down and pulled the iron and brass ring off of Elderflower's limp finger. The moment it was in her hand, she felt the storm surge back into her:

powerful, trembling, and *pissed*. She let it rage, even though it hurt a little, surprised at how much she'd missed its presence.

"See, there's two kinds of ghouls," she said, rising to her feet. "There's the ones who are mistakes. The recently dead animated by some remnant of their former self. When you summoned me and said you had a ghoul problem, I figured that's what we were dealing with. 'Pomps not able to get to the dead in time, and their spirits getting corrupted. If that was the case, then Elderflower's ring would have let him command the spirits animating all these bodies." She shrugged. "But then, being a psychopomp should have given me the authority to strike them down. And I couldn't. Which means these are the other kind of ghoul, the kind animated by a specific, deliberate magic."

Renai threaded her way through the unmoving crowd of dead, shuddering every time her wings brushed up against one of them. She checked on Opal, who was a little damp from where the swamp water had been splashed on her, but otherwise seemed okay. Aside from being kidnapped and unconscious, of course. Then she picked up the flame-throwing bat and Leon's trumpet from where Elderflower had left them and brought them over to her —well, her *friends,* she supposed, though it had been a long time since she'd had any of those other than Sal—and gave them back.

"See," she said, talking to them, but aiming her words at the ghouls around her, at the power animating them, "the mistake I made was thinking that the ghoul I talked to in the morgue was all on his lonesome. A message, not a soldier. But now I see that there's been another player in this game all along. And since we're all T-for-tight with each other, why don't you come out so we can talk face-to-face." She held up the ring. "Or we can do this the other way."

The mouth of every ghoul gaped open all at once, a hissing, whispering laugh echoing in the night air.

"That's a sound I ain't soon to forget," Leon said, wincing when Regal jostled him in reply.

The ghoul closest to Renai, an overweight white man in a nice dark suit and an ugly mismatched tie, sagged to his knees and then tipped over onto his back. All the air came out of his lungs in a gargling, resigned sigh. A shape moved in the back of his throat, wriggling and scritching its way out of his mouth, climbing up the dead man's swollen tongue and over his thick, bloodless lips. At first it was nothing, a dark shape in the corner of your eye, a trick of the light, and then it was a cockroach, long and fat and glossy black. Its quivering antennae flooded Renai with a sense of immediate revulsion.

The roach spread its wings and launched fluttering into the air, swooping first at Renai—which made her flinch back and squeeze out an involuntary grunt, not out of fear so much as desperation not to be touched by it—and then hovering a few feet away. One by one the ghouls around them dropped, let out their own foul gasps, expelled their own bugs. They fell into place alongside the first roach, first a handful, then a cloud, then a swarm. They were coming from everywhere now, squeezing out from under the door to the cafe, flooding up from the loose boards at their feet, descending from the branches overhead. They clung together in a shifting, grotesque mass—first two stumps and a trunk, then stretching out two spindly limbs, then bulging into a bulb on top—until it was obvious that they weren't just an infestation but a facsimile of a person.

The one Renai had first seen sitting at Jude's card table.

All at once, like puzzle pieces locking into place, all the individual insects stopped moving, and—if Renai let her eyes unfocus and see the whole instead of a part—a tall naked woman stood there, her skin the glossy, almost wet black of a roach's wings, so thin that her flesh stretched tight against her bones, her head bare and bald, her stomach an unhealthy concavity that signaled starvation. The illusion was constantly broken, though, a twitching antenna here, a roach shifting out of place there. Renai couldn't help but notice that not all of the ghouls had given up their animating roaches: at least five of them still blocked the exit.

"Speak," the woman-shaped pile of roaches said, her whispery, dissonant voice coming not from her lips, which didn't move, but from the entirety of her body. "You have our attention."

Regal answered first. "So, like, are you a bunch of bugs that thinks you're a person? Or a person who got turned into a bunch of bugs? Because I have laid down some harsh fucking curses in my day, but—"

The mound of roaches turned to face Regal, not moving so much as shifting from one still pose to another. "We are the eaters of the dead," she said. "We are that which devours. We are Cafard."

Renai opened her mouth to respond, but there was such a strange, implicit threat in that statement that she didn't know what to say. A drawn-out, uncomfortable silence followed, in which Renai realized she could no longer hear the noises of the crowd, that the zoo must have closed for the night.

"Cool," Regal said, "cool-cool-cool. But you didn't really answer—"

"Why did Cordelia bring all of you here?" Renai asked, something that Elderflower said nagging at her even now. "What 'storm' is she going to create?"

The shift from Regal to Renai was more abrupt, almost aggressive. If a human being moved like that, Renai would have called it anger. "None brings us here. We are always here. Here is ours. Ours to eat." Before Renai could ask what that meant, Cafard aimed an accusatory finger toward Leon and Regal. "These stole the feast. Ours to eat. Dead, dying, ours. These took. Now we *hunger*. Soon we feast."

Renai tilted her head so she could aim her words at her friends without taking her eyes off of Cafard. "Any idea what she's talking about?"

Leon tried to speak, but only managed to say, "The city," before he cut off with a low moan. Regal patted his shoulder and spoke for him. "Me and Jude and ol' busted here are the heart and soul of New Orleans," she said. "Not bragging, I mean it literally. All that shit-meets-ceiling-fan fuckery you got caught up in a few years back? That's what it was about. Bringing the city back to life after the hurricane almost killed her."

And now Jude's got a card room full of destruction gods and storm deities who want to go for round two, Renai thought. *Or at least, he did.* Her hands curled into fists, the alchemist's iron and brass ring biting into her palm, and another approach occurred to her. "How do you fit into Cordelia's plan?" she asked Cafard. "Because whatever *she's* offering?" She pointed at the pitiful corpse of Jack Elderflower sprawled out on the floor. "*This* is how she repays her promises."

"We make no plans; we make nothing. Strife promises only our feast, and we follow only while we eat."

"But why?" Renai's voice was hoarse even to her ears. "Where does it end? How much do you have to destroy to be satisfied?"

"Is no why. No end. Is us. We are that which devours. Is all."

"And when you've destroyed everything, and all you have left to eat is yourself, what then?" Tears were leaking from Renai's eyes now, and even though she knew that there would be no conversion here, no victory beyond —maybe—survival, she couldn't help but try to understand, the compassionate side of her unable to fully accept the existence of bottomless, conscienceless greed. "If you devour the whole world," she said, hating the pleading tone she heard in her own voice, "what was the fucking *point?*"

Cafard's hissing laughter was her only answer. Renai's anger rose, and in response so did the spirit, its lightning crackling along her fingertips so eagerly that it made the itching threads wound through her skin stretch until they burned. Part of her knew she should pull back that part of its power. That it would solve nothing. She understood that part of the tempest was the wind that carried seeds to new pastures and rain clouds to drought-stricken earth as much as it was the destructive gales that flattened buildings. She knew that floods enriched and replenished soil as often as they washed away homes. She recognized that lightning represented the power of the storm that could do nothing but destroy, knew that this impulse within her was an echo of Cafard's destructive nature. And she didn't care.

She let it slip loose.

The lightning broke free from her as sudden and joyous as an orgasm, a flash of brilliance and scorching heat and thunder that streaked from her palm and struck Cafard dead center, lancing through her and forking out to capture the still-standing ghouls in its embrace. She shrieked—pleasure and pain and regret and release all at once—but deafened by the resulting clap of thunder, she only felt the strain of her shout in her throat. The release was so potent, so intense, that the storm's rage inside of her calmed instantly, sated and coiled deep in her belly, a sudden void that left an oddly pleasant ache.

Renai sank to her knees, her nostrils filled with burnt ozone and a high-pitched whine in her ears, a languor suffusing her limbs. She was content to wait there for her eyes to recover, for the angry red streak across her vision to fade. When it did, she had trouble believing that the devastation in front of her was the work of her own hand. Where Cafard had stood, only a small pile of burnt roach husks remained, most of them simply obliterated by the bolt she'd struck the destruction goddess with. She'd had a similar effect on the ghouls, the fern-frond, fractal pattern of electrical burns stretched across their flesh, Cafard's influence scorched out of each one.

Renai rose to her feet, slow and tentative, expecting that channeling so much energy would have drained her, but finding the opposite to be true. She ached, but it was with the endorphin-filled rush that came after an intense run. Smiling, she turned to Regal and Leon, her friends, the Magician and the Voice of New Orleans, and saw an emotion in their eyes that only the part of her that had lived in this world all these years was accustomed to seeing: fear.

Now we are become Death, Renai thought.

Regal pointed at her, and in that strangely postcoital calm in the wake of her lightning, Renai half expected some curse to follow, some hex that she, in all fairness, probably deserved. But nothing came. Regal gestured with her finger, saying something that was muted by the persistent whine in her ears. When Renai understood what she meant, she looked down, holding her arms out in front of her, and saw that on each wrist one of the strands of yarn binding her soul together had torn apart.

CHAPTER THIRTY

WHEN THEY COULD hear each other again, Renai, Leon, and Regal quickly found that none of them knew exactly what to say. They were surrounded by corpses, Leon could barely stand without help, and Renai was literally falling apart.

Renai could practically feel Regal's mind churning, trying to decide on which aspect of the situation was best suited to her unique style of shit-talk. Or maybe she was just too afraid of the power Renai had unleashed to try to be funny. Renai really had no idea what was going through the other woman's mind; she was a psychopomp, not a psychic. At that thought, she went to check on Opal, worried that the oracle hadn't woken up in all the commotion. From what she could tell, Opal hadn't been harmed, aside from whatever Elderflower had done to her to knock her out like this.

To both Renai's and Regal's surprise, it was Leon who broke the silence. "This here's another fine mess you done got me into," he said, leaning against the edge of the picnic table that Regal had practically carried him to. The corner of his mouth quirked up, a half grin that he fought to hide, as if actually showing a smile would pain him worse than the ribs he'd almost certainly fractured. He looked from Regal to Renai and back again, his amusement slipping away and replaced with disappointment. "Neither of you ever seen

Laurel and Hardy," he said, a statement he was hoping one of them would disprove.

"Oh, I caught the reference," Regal said. "It's just sometimes I forget how crotch-rot old your AARP ass is."

Leon waved her away like her derision was a bad smell. "Only young people think bein' old is an insult. Only all y'all's new shit gets old. Like classic cars and this here horn; I was built to last, me."

"Who's Law-whatever and Hard-D?" Renai asked, not really sure what they were talking about but pretty certain it wasn't a hip-hop duo like it sounded. In truth, she'd only heard about half of what they'd said, too busy examining Opal like she had a damn clue what she was doing. Keeping people alive really wasn't her specialty. She leaned in close to Opal's neck, where she saw what looked like a puncture mark, so small it might have been just an insect bite.

Leon's groan started out mocking and developed into something real, clutching his side and sucking in a breath through his teeth. "Before your time," he said, after a moment. "And speakin' of—time ain't somethin' we got an overabundance of. So maybe we ought to turn our minds to the task at hand."

"Which is what, exactly?" Renai asked, and then, gesturing at Regal with a curl of her fingers, said, "Can you come here a second?"

Leon dipped his head toward the ground, at the bodies that lay sprawled across the floor where Cafard had left them. "Takin' care of these folk here," he said. He was right; they couldn't just leave all these corpses for someone else to clean up. While the average person looked right past the supernatural —which is why the dead had been able to wander around New Orleans for days without inciting panic—there was no longer anything unusual about these bodies, aside from the fact that they were lying in plain sight for some unfortunate, underpaid zoo employee to find the next morning. Renai nodded but didn't have an answer for him. Instead, she pointed out the mark on Opal's neck to Regal.

"Yeah, that's a needle wound all right," Regal said, her face twisting like she'd bitten into something rotten. "Good catch. Of course that fucking scrote-hole would be a woman-drugging piece of shit." She started digging in her duffel bag. "You go help Leon," she said. "I got this."

Renai moved over to Leon, her hands in her jacket pockets. Ironically, problems like this—dead gods, formerly possessed corpses who weren't where the authorities had left them, and bodies that couldn't be identified because they were older than Social Security numbers—were exactly the kinds of problems that a scavenger god like Cafard usually handled, her solution exactly as grotesque as anyone would imagine. By the way Leon studied the splayed-out corpses and tapped his fingers against the buttons of his trumpet, she could tell he was considering some magic song that might be of use.

"Any ideas?" she asked, realizing in that moment that she didn't really have a clue how his magic worked. It wasn't like the powers the Thrones granted a psychopomp, or the potency the loa lent to the herbs and powders of a gris-gris bag. Nor was it anything like the sorcerous abilities that Regal and Elderflower had displayed. Leon's magic wasn't a separate power that lived in him, like Renai's storm; it *was* him in a fundamental way that seemed more like a god than a man.

Maybe that was what it meant to be High John de Conquer.

"I got me a tune that can wake the dead, but I don't know if it'll work on ones such as these." What he left unsaid was that he might not be able to play a single note, since he couldn't take a full breath. Not that it mattered. There was nothing in these bodies to wake up, the tiniest scraps of Voice devoured by Cafard when she possessed them.

Which gave Renai an idea.

She took out the deck of playing cards that had once been the spirits of fugitive dead, thinking she could shift one of them back into its ghostly form. Since she'd only ever used the destructive magic of a psychopomp out of instinct, though, she had no idea how to manage it. She stared at one of the cards as if it could tell her what to do, its matte-black surface as iridescent as a raven's wing, and as reflective as her broken mirror. She tried picturing it as a piece of origami, something that could unfurl like her wings, and she tried thinking of it as a hole, something she could reach into like the nowhere place that held her mirror. All that happened is that her wings quivered like they were trying to stretch as wide as their Underworld counterparts, and her knife kept appearing in her hand.

So, remembering how she'd transformed these spirits in the first place, she asked the spirit inside of her for wind—a weak breeze was all the spirit could manage to call up so soon after unleashing a lightning bolt—and flicked the card into the air, teasing it with her borrowed magic, making it dance. She thought about what she was now, an emissary of Death, and what Cafard had said about being a creature who could only destroy. And so she made her wind a sharp, cutting thing, bearing down on the playing card with what little strength she had, imagining her power destroying the card bit by bit, layer by layer, like the wearing down of mountains into valleys, like the erosion of rock into sand.

The black playing card dissolved into a fine powder, a gray cloud that coalesced into the shape of a person, the bits of them whirling and furious as a swarm of gnats.

Renai couldn't tell if they'd been a man or woman in life, tall or short, fat or thin, black or white or some other ethnicity. In its truest form, the Essence of a person was none of these things, only Fortune had a gender, only the body had a sex and a sexuality and a skin color. Only in this world did these things matter. In death these definitions could be escaped, though most souls carried some of these traits with them, the ones they remembered, the ones they valued, the ones that had impacted them most in life.

In destroying and reshaping this lost scrap of Essence back in the haunted building on Canal, Renai had wiped away everything that the soul had been in life, leaving them with only those intrinsic qualities—kindness or tenacity, frivolity or avarice—that no one, not even Death, could take away. When Renai realized exactly what she'd done, it made her feel a shame so potent that it turned her stomach. *You can't fix it,* she thought, in her grandmother's voice. *You can't go back. So save your hissy fit for somebody who needs it.*

"Why am I here?" the spirit said, in a voice that was a hissing TV-station-tuned-to-white-noise sound that reminded Renai of the Deadline.

Renai pointed to one of the dead bodies, the fat man whom Cafard had first abandoned. "We want you to take over that body," she said, "and ride it back to the morgue where it was stolen from."

"How they gonna know where to go?" Leon asked.

"Once they're inside the body, inside the brain and the eyes, they'll remember everything that the body experienced in life and in death. They'll know."

"Sheee-iiit," Regal said, coming to stand beside her. "That plan is slick as hell, Sparkles. Tied up in a goddamn bow."

"I have a choice?" the spirit asked, as if they had only heard the words Renai had spoken directly to them.

The itching red strings in Renai's flesh started to burn as she strained in two directions at once. Part of her, ashamed at what she'd done, wanted to just release these spirits, fractured and lost though they were. The other part of her knew that she could simply exert her will over this shade and *make* them do whatever she wanted. She wavered for a moment before she remembered that she didn't have the luxury of internal debates, didn't have time for a crisis of conscience. So she compromised with herself. "Yeah, you got a choice," she said, spreading the other black cards into a loose fan. "You can do as I say, or you can go back to being the six of Hearts."

The scrap of Essence—the Shadow—of what had once been a complete identity swirled there for a moment, maybe considering their options, maybe needing time to process Renai's offer-you-can't-refuse, but ultimately they chose the path of least resistance. Like a flock of birds—*a murmuration of starlings,* she heard Leon say—the Shadow bulged and flattened and thickened and thinned, and then curled into a single swirling tendril that descended on the white man in the suit and into his mouth and filled his lungs with a long, rattling, eerie inhale.

The man—no, the *ghoul's*—eyes opened, and he lurched to his feet. Regal leaned in to whisper in Renai's ear. "What's to stop these turd-blossoms from just taking their two-hundred-and-change pounds of flesh on a joy ride and"—she made a whistling sound between her teeth and turned her hand into a plane taking off—"fuckin' right off to Vegas?"

"You'll stop them," Renai said, not bothering to lower her voice, "with this." She held up Elderflower's iron and brass ring, the one with the Seal of Solomon that would let her command spirits. When Regal took it, Renai pulled another card from her hand and fought back a sigh, already weary and knowing she had far more to do before she could rest. "Okay," she said, "who's next?"

⧗

By the time Renai had destroyed and re-formed enough cards to reanimate all the ghouls that Cafard had abandoned, Regal's instant sobriety patch had done its work and brought Opal around to consciousness. Regal had taken her for a walk, partly to help clear her head, and partly so she wouldn't have to watch the gruesome monotony of rinse, possess, repeat that had been Renai's past couple of hours. She had just scooped the remaining dozen or so cards back into a neat square and tucked them back into their cardboard box when Regal and Opal came back to the wooden walkway.

"Missed one," Leon said, nodding at the jeans- and T-shirt-clad corpse of Jack Elderflower. In death he was as disappointing—Renai had hoped his body would crumble away to dust like in a movie, given his extreme age—and as much of a pain in the ass as he had been in life. Like the other bodies, they couldn't just leave him there for the zoo to deal with, but unlike those once-animated corpses, there was nowhere that Elderflower was *supposed* to be. Not to mention the fact that the last thing Renai wanted was one of those renegade spirits getting their incorporeal hands on all the horrible shit rattling around inside the dead alchemist's head.

Besides, she wasn't finished with Jack Elderflower just yet.

"I'll take care of him," Renai said. "You two just get Opal out of here."

"What are you planning, Sparkles?" Regal asked.

For the first time since regaining consciousness, Opal Brennan spoke. "She's gonna do to him what he was gonna do to me," she said. "Dump his ass over the railing for the gators." Regal and Leon both started to speak at the same time, but Opal held up a hand. "Don't try to bullshit me. I'm a psychic, remember? I know why he brought me here. I know what he was planning." She rubbed at her wrists, raw from where she'd been bound. "Do whatever you have to do, but do it quick, please. I've got a wife to get home to."

Nothing left to say, Regal handed her duffel bag to Opal, hooked one of Leon's arms over her shoulder, and the three of them limped away, leaving Renai alone with the sorcerer who called himself Elderflower. Body and soul.

Waiting for a psychopomp.

The rules were the rules, even for miserable, callous bastards like him. It didn't matter how many people he'd hurt, how many lives he'd sacrificed in his pursuit of immortality, didn't matter how many centuries he'd stolen from the Thrones. Even for him, death wasn't the end. So she pulled the hood of her leather jacket up onto her head, tucking her dreads in so she could see, and—before she could second-guess herself—spoke the ghost word. Thankfully even though she was a whole person now, it worked now just as it had before the Hallows: her vision shifting into shades of purple, that strange, buzzing tightness across her skin. Renai knelt beside him, glad to at least be asked to do something she knew how to do right. When her hands slipped inside him, it barely even hurt.

There was no Fortune, of course. He'd burned that away to avoid his death—or he'd traded it away in a deal with a spirit, like Ramses—but she found his Voice and his Essence just like any other dead. His Voice, which took the shape of an apple when she pulled it free of his body, tasted smoky and peppery and vinegary all at once, and filled her with a vitality that was almost frightening. That wasn't surprising, though. She'd expected the alchemist to have amassed a significant amount of power. After all, the bastard could command spirits. It only made sense that he had magic to spare.

Unlike any other collection of a recently deceased, though, Renai didn't leave any scrap of Voice behind. She couldn't take the risk that his Essence — or any of the shades wandering the city during the Hallows — might enter his body and raise it as a ghoul before the gators had their fill. Nor did she want his memory to have any power once he was gone. So, no matter how much it made her feel like Cafard to do it, Renai consumed the whole of his Voice, apple core and all.

What did surprise her was that when she pulled his Essence free, he gathered himself into a fully formed image of his living self, down to a ghostly version of his iron and brass ring, a process that normally took the newly dead the whole journey to the First Gate. "Guess you spent so much of your life commanding those spirits and summoning those demons into your computers that you knew what to expect, huh?" She wasn't gloating, really. Just treating him like the half-aware, half-asleep dead she was used to.

Yes, Elderflower whispered, in that unspeaking thought-talk the dead could manage, *and I know what comes next, too.*

Renai tried to hide her shock at how quickly Elderflower had mastered that little trick, which usually took the dead well into the Underworld to figure out. She was suddenly very glad that she'd eaten the entirety of his Voice. "Yeah," she said, "what's that?" She spoke out loud deliberately this time, even though she could think her words at him like he was doing to her, because she knew her voice — energized by his Voice, no less — would shake his Essence like thunder rattling a window's glass panes.

Without an obol to pay Charon's fee, I will wander the Earth a restless shade. Eventually I will forget myself, and become the very kind of feckless, gibbering demon whose will I subverted to my own ends.

Renai tucked her hands into the pockets of her jacket and nodded, feigning sadness, a heavy acknowledgment that he was right. As if she hadn't been the one to end his life. She very nearly scuffed the toe of her combat boot against the floor but figured that would be overselling it. She knew what was coming next, both from him and *for* him.

Or, Elderflower whispered, *we could make a deal.*

Renai pursed her lips to keep from smiling. "What did you have in mind?"

I've got a vial back at my place. A little something special I keep for emergen-

cies. You put me back into my body, pour the contents of that vial into my mouth, and leave. It'll take an hour or so to do its work. I don't have any magic left, I watched you consume it. I'll slip away and you'll never see me again. I swear it.

As if his disembodied ass has anything binding to swear by, she thought. Out loud she said, "What do I get?"

I'll tell you where you can find Ramses St. Cyr.

"Counter-offer," Renai said. "I bring you through the Gates down to the prison down in one of the deepest parts of the Underworld. That's where the demons you summoned and enslaved will end up after I release them from all your computer equipment. I'm sure y'all will have a lot to talk about."

And Ramses?

Renai shrugged. "Already know where he's going." She knelt to check Elderflower's pockets, found a money clip full of twenties that she took for herself and a number of charms and amulets that she wanted nothing to do with. She put these back where she found them and then slid her hands and wrists under Elderflower's armpits. The alchemist was heavier than she'd expected, but she was determined. He made a satisfying *sploosh* when he hit the duckweed-covered water below.

When she turned back to Elderflower's spirit, he had his arms folded and a haughty look on his face. *I didn't spend centuries avoiding death's embrace just to be dragged there by some pickaninny. I'll take my chances among the living.*

Ah, she thought, there's *that racism I've been waiting for. Makes this next part all the easier.* She reached out, partly with her will and partly with her physical hand, and grabbed Elderflower by the upper arm. He tried to pull away, which just showed that he hadn't figured it out yet.

"I'm sorry," she said, unable to help herself from echoing what he'd said the first time they'd met. "Did you think this was a negotiation?"

And so, his Voice in her veins and his Essence by her side, Renai half led and half dragged Jack Elderflower out of Audubon Zoo and to Leon's car. She was his psychopomp and he was her dead.

That suited her just fine.

⧖

Renai didn't realize she'd gotten her hopes up that her motorcycle would still be waiting on the neutral ground until she got out of Leon's car at the entrance to St. Louis No. 1 and saw that Kyrie wasn't there. Renai just hoped that she was off enjoying the Hallows and not locked in an impound yard somewhere. She'd managed to convince Leon and Regal to leave her there at the cemetery gate after dropping off Opal—who had been less than thrilled to discover, when Renai showed up to the car with Elderflower, that she could now also see the dead—at her home, despite both of them insisting that she still needed their help.

"I appreciate the offer, really," she said, leaning into the passenger side window to keep Regal from getting out, "but you can't go where I'm headed. Besides, this one here's liable to kill himself if he blows his horn with his ribs all busted up like they are, and we need you holding shit down with that ring." She waited for their grudging acceptance before she continued. "Speaking of which, these are for you." She held out the deck of cards holding the last of the fugitive spirits she'd captured. "I figure with that ring, you can command these spirits to take whatever form you want, dogs, birds, whatever. They're nowhere near psychopomps, but if you need them to hunt down some bugs—"

Regal took the deck from her and slid it into the pocket of her costume coat. "Way ahead of you, sister. Those ghouls are fin-fuckin-ito."

Renai shifted over so she could see Leon and pointed to the *Princess and the Frog* backpack sitting on his backseat. "If you don't mind, I'd appreciate it if you brought that bag back here on All Souls' Day for my—" Her voice caught in her throat and she couldn't finish. "For Celeste," she said at last. "It's got, well, it's got some things I'd like her to have."

Some things I want to keep safe, she thought.

"Count on it," Leon said, grinning in an attempt to hide a grimace of pain. "Come rain or shine, I'll be here. You take care now, hear?"

"I will," she said, pulling out of the window and rising to her full height. To herself, she said, "I'll take care of everything." She waited until Leon put the car in drive and started to pull away, before she raised her voice and said, "Hey, Regal?"

"Yeah?"

"Don't throw away your shot!"

The Magician of New Orleans leaned out the passenger side window as Leon Carter drove away, giving Renai the double middle-finger salute. "I *knew* I liked you!" she yelled, and then they were gone, leaving Renai standing at the Gates of the Underworld, wearing the jacket she'd gotten from the Thrones, a coin of Fortune in her pocket, and—aside from the newly dead soul waiting to be led to his just reward—all alone.

In other words, right where she belonged.

Oussou was right where he belonged, too: on the ground next to the First Gate, slumped over onto his side and passed out drunk. At least him being here meant that the Gates were open again. Renai grabbed Elderflower's ghostly hand and stomped over to the loa, nudging him with the toe of her combat boot. When he showed no reaction, she did it again, a little harder. If anything he snored louder.

A couple of white guys passing by shouted drunken encouragement to her, an abrupt and startling intrusion that set her heart pounding until they were on the next block. She'd almost forgotten what it was like to have to put her back to a wall and fake a not-too-distant-but-not-too-inviting smile. She thought about the aura of disinterest that surrounded the half of her that kept to the living side of things, and wondered if it was worth the lack of memories, the sundering of self, to never again feel threatened by something as mundane as a drunken dick.

If that thought made her rougher than usual trying to shake Oussou awake, that was his fault for crawling so deep in his bottle that he couldn't do his job. Was it even that late? She glanced down at her watch, the cheap cartoon thing that had somehow survived the lightning strike that Regal called her "epic-level bug zapper," and saw that it was already well past midnight, which made it officially the Feast of All Saints.

"The hell is wrong with you?" she said, squatting down and dragging Oussou into a seated position. "Did you drink yourself to—" She froze, a spike of panic at that idea, and then she realized that she'd heard him snoring, could feel the rise and fall of his chest beneath her hands. So he wasn't dead. The rum sloshed around in the bottle that he clutched tightly even in sleep, a bottle that was nearly full. Wasn't drunk either, then. Just sleeping. That's when she understood.

Renai eased Oussou back so that he was leaning against the outer wall of the cemetery, careful not to bang his head against the brick. She'd planned on using the coin of Fortune that she'd been carrying with her all this time to bluff her way past the Gatekeeper with Elderflower in tow, past all of the loa if she had to, whatever it took to get down to the bottom level of the Underworld, to finally stand in front of the Thrones and beg them to tell her what to do about Ramses and Cordelia and all the shit that was going down. But Oussou was sleeping the sleep of the dead and nothing she possessed would wake him up. Only one thing she knew of could lay a god low like that.

The caduceus.

She grabbed Elderflower's hand and led his silent Essence through the First Gate — even though the world of the living and the Underworld over-lapped during the Hallows, rules were rules — finally knowing for sure where she'd find Ramses St. Cyr. The one place Cordelia could have been certain Renai wouldn't find him, the place where his path, Renai's path — *everyone's* path — had been leading all along:

The Thrones where Death sat in judgment.

The moment Renai crossed through the First Gate, she learned that while the Hallows allowed the Underworld and the living world to overlap, some things really were different. Her wings, for example, rigid, decorative ap-pendages in the living world, unfolded into the billowing, eager spans of del-icate, living tissue she'd known in the Underworld. She had just enough time to grab Elderflower by his ghostly hand, and then she was in the sky, soaring.

She worried, at first, that being whole and complete would make it more difficult for her wings to carry her, as if the parts of herself that had existed only in the living world had an actual physical weight. She found the oppo-site to be true, though, the wings more responsive, more obedient, and more powerful. She rose higher than she ever had before and — the eerie fog of the Underworld dispersed by the Hallows — saw all of New Orleans spread out beneath her.

There were ghosts everywhere, not just the shades of once-living people walking the streets, but here the shadowy outline of a thriving black neigh-borhood — its main street lined with hundred-year-old oaks — razed to make room for an Interstate overpass, there the diffuse outline of an Opera House, burned and rebuilt and burned again. So much had been destroyed here, sometimes to make way for something better, but more often out of oppres-sion or accident or negligence or greed. The storm rose up in her — the kill-ing kind — ready to meet fire with fire, power with power.

All the tempest wanted was someone to blame.

Renai swept down out of the sky and into the garden of Holt Cemetery, the splendor of Nibo's flowers a ghostly bouquet spread out across the cem-etery. The loa himself was fast asleep, of course, slumped against the base of his tree, the Second Gate left open wide. Renai pulled Elderflower through the Gate, ignoring his whispered questions, and then took to the air once more. She bounced across the city, hurtling through the Gates and deeper into the Underworld, into Plumaj's book, through Bridgette's altar, past Babaco's party, and then through the doorway of Barren's streetcar.

Every sleeping loa she found made her more frantic, every gaping-open Gate urged her to get to the Thrones as quickly as possible. If the caduceus could overpower even Barren—who, among other things, was the highest of the Ghede—then its power might not have any limit. She was torn between two states, hopeful that she was finally on track, that she might find Ramses before the end of the Hallows and her tenuous compromise, and despair that she might already be too late.

After she crossed through the Sixth Gate at the foot of Canal Street, darkness nipping at the heels of sunset, the cemeteries rising up around her, it took all of Renai's self-control to turn away from the Final Gate beneath the river—every instinct inside of her yelling at her to *go, go, go*—and fly toward the prison where she and Sal had barely escaped Cross. She landed, tempest whirling and heart pounding and Elderflower struggling ineffectually in her grip. She almost wished Cross would be here, just so she could release some of this anger, this power thundering inside of her.

But no one was there, just the barest facsimiles of trees and the walls made of ice, smoking in the living world's heat. She let slip some of the storm's power, a fierce gust of wind that pushed open the massive doors of frozen stone, revealing only darkness beyond. She pushed Elderflower toward it and released him, with her hand if not her will. "This is where you get off," she said.

I can help you, Elderflower whispered. *I know things.*

"I know things too," Renai said. "I know you willingly took the side of a goddess of destruction, knowing she was going to damn an innocent boy to a fate worse than death, knowing she intends to bring more harm into a world already full of it. I know you took a woman against her will just because you're stronger than her, and that you intended to steal her power and destroy her utterly. I know that for years you have amassed power on the backs of others, corrupting souls, spying and stealing and lying and blackmailing, and that you have felt no more guilt for any of these than if you had killed a bug." She smiled, and though it felt good on her face, she knew it was terrible.

"Well, now you're the spider and I'm the boot," she said. "And I know you best carry your ass through those doors before I decide to get real nasty about it."

When he was gone and the doors were closed and she was in the air once more, Renai could feel the other side of her tugging at her strings, the compassionate side, the part of her that tried to understand. She knew it was a warning, knew that she had to be careful of how fierce she let the storm inside of her grow. Flying toward the river and the Thrones and her last, desperate hope, she let the tempest build. It hurt, but the pain was nothing she couldn't live with.

Nothing she couldn't endure.

CHAPTER THIRTY-ONE

IF YOU FIND yourself on the edge of the River Styx, hope that your loved ones have placed a coin in your mouth, the obol that is Charon's fee to carry you across. The same is true of Urshanabi, the ferryman on the river Hubur. If the waters of the Vaitarna seem — to your eyes — to be clear, sweet nectar, then rejoice, for you have lived a good life, but if you see a river of blood, know that you must swim across to Naraka to have your sinfulness purged. Give praise to Ojizō-sama, who protects the souls of lost children on the banks of the Sanzu River. Pray that when you meet Manannán mac Lir, he is content to carry you to the Blessed Isles in his boat without sails, that he isn't feeling tricky and wearing his drab coat.

Before we came from the earth we came from the water, and so it is always water that we must cross from this life into the next.

On the floor of the Mississippi, hidden by the depths of muddy water and almost entirely buried beneath centuries of silt, a ship. Some saw a paddle-wheel steamboat, others a deep-keel ocean vessel. To Renai's eyes, it always looked like the car-carrying ferries that used to run back and forth across the river, a wide span of concrete and railings and metal walkways: a floating parking lot. She'd been here before, of course, but even as a psychopomp she hadn't made a habit of it.

Not even Death's emissaries were eager to meet them.

She had to use the ghost word to get down to the ship—even having passed through all six of the previous Gates, she was still in a living body that needed oxygen—but once she'd descended to the river bottom and climbed far enough down into the belly of the ship, the water receded and she could pull back her hood, some barrier set in place to keep the throne room dry providing her with air to breathe. As soon as Renai stepped into the bubble of frigid air deep in the ship, she felt the tempest's power slip away from her. She thought at first it was the anxiety and anticipation pushing away the anger that connected her to the spirit's own rage or some ward the Thrones had put in place to keep hostile powers in check, but after a moment, she realized that it was simply that the storm was a spirit and knew it was in the presence of Death and was afraid.

Me too, she thought to the coiled presence inside of her. *Maybe not for the same reasons, but me too.*

Partly worried that the cold might damage them, and partly because they were cumbersome in the tight spiraling stairwell that led down into the throne room, Renai folded her wings away, though she couldn't seem to rid herself of the rigid, flightless versions even here. She blew warm air into her palms and made her way down the stairs. Eventually, the stairwell opened up into a large vacant space, big as a warehouse and just as sparsely decorated. In the center of the room, a column of water descended from the ceiling, a whirling rush like a tornado that vanished into a gaping hole in the concrete floor. Just on the other side of that watery column stood a pair of huge empty chairs, carved from a single piece of wood. They were black, though it was hard to tell from one moment to another whether they were simply carved from dark wood, or if they were covered in soot, or dried blood, or draped with shadow.

Like death itself, the Thrones were many things all at once.

Renai approached, her heart pounding so hard it was difficult to swallow, her hands clenching into fists no matter how many times she noticed and forced herself to relax. It wasn't just the Thrones themselves that gave her pause, but the ravenous beast that lived at the bottom of that pit, where the Thrones cast any Essence that made it this far but couldn't earn the right to continue on into the Far Lands. The gaping hole at the bottom of the Underworld was the abyss, and the many-named monster that lived there was usually called — in hushed tones — the Devourer. Oblivion.

The vacancy of the Thrones didn't concern her. Death was invisible, after all. But she was surprised that she was the only one here. Had Ramses and Cordelia already made their play? Were they even now being chewed into nothing by the Devourer? Was she already too late?

She reached into the nowhere place for her mirror and turned away from the Thrones, angling the polished stone so that she could see the Thrones' reflection in its surface. In this place, smoke roiled off of her mirror, black as oil and sweet as incense. It took a moment to see the figures seated on the Thrones, their immensity hard to capture, to perceive, especially with her mirror broken and only one handhold to work with. When she saw them, she gasped, the sound quickly swallowed up by the roaring torrent in front of her.

The reflection showed a male god in one seat and a goddess in the other, or one deity that shifted back and forth, as much a congregation as an entity. The man wore thick robes and sandals, held a spear in one hand and a short scepter in the other, his face dominated by a bushy, curled beard, and a withered, puckered hole marked where of one of his eyes should be. A sickly green pallor clung to his skin. The woman wore a long, sleeveless red dress that hugged her body. It was hard to tell whether she had two arms or four, or whether it was shadows or frostbite that stained her legs black. Her cheeks were pale, maybe from the chill of death, maybe from funereal makeup, an animal's skull atop her head like a helmet.

They were Death, and each of them, both of them, all of them, sagged in their chairs with their chins on their chests.

Asleep.

⧗

She'd missed it.

The understanding shifted around inside her like a physical thing, like the sensation in the gut and in the inner ears on a swiftly plummeting elevator, only it wasn't a metal box that moved but the whole of creation. The Thrones were the pivot on which the entire Underworld spun, the power that gave psychopomps like her their authority, the judges who defined the afterlife. They'd exerted a gravitational pull on her thoughts from the beginning. She'd thought they were responsible for her missing memories, for the Gates being locked, for Ramses' disappearance, and that they were the target behind Cordelia's plot. The only thing she hadn't been able to decide was whether the cursed revolver was meant to be an offering to beg a favor, or a weapon turned against the very person of Death.

As it turned out, they'd just been another set of Gatekeepers to be slipped past.

The Final Gate stood between the Thrones: the shape of a door frame carved in the wood, twisting and doubling back on itself like a Möbius strip, or a deep shadow that stretched farther back into a long hallway that was longer than the room that held it, or just a trick of the wood grain, a pattern the mind saw where none really existed. Death was a guide and death was an arbiter of justice and death was a journey but death was also this, the guardian of the Final Gate between Earth and the Worlds to Come. That Gate hung open wide just like the previous six, which meant that whatever Cordelia was planning, wherever she'd sent Ramses St. Cyr, it lay beyond death.

In the Far Lands.

With a grim smile that would have made Salvatore proud, Renai followed.

At first, she was just a woman in a hallway. It felt like a hotel late at night, that weird uniformity, that eerie silence, that aggressively sterile cleanliness. The carpets were a soft ivory that only someone who would never have to clean them would have chosen, the walls a rich dark blue. There were no doors, no light fixtures—though the hallway itself was flooded with illumination—nothing to show that there had ever been anyone else in the hallway but her, and it stretched as far as she could see in either direction, with nothing to show that she had ever been anywhere else than this place.

Maybe she hadn't. Maybe everything she'd known or experienced had just been a dream, one of many she'd had and woken from and had again as she walked down this immense, eternal path from everywhere to nowhere. Or from nowhere to everywhere. Maybe there wasn't a difference between the two.

Sometimes, as she walked, the hallway seemed curved, as if she were constantly about to discover something, anything different.

Sometimes, as she walked, she was certain that the floor was made of cloud and the walls were simply sky and that she was spiraling ever higher, but she never dared reach out to find out for sure.

Sometimes, as she walked, she was certain that she was deep beneath the earth and burrowing deeper, a hollow cave at its center her destination.

Sometimes, as she walked, she felt that she traveled not across miles but through time, through history, wending her way to the only true end of time: its beginning.

Sometimes, as she walked, she was just a woman in a hallway.

And then, without any preamble, rhyme, or reason, the hallway came to an end. She stood before a simple wooden red door. Its color made her think, as she reached for the handle, that this whole thing was some trick of Jude Dubuisson's, that he'd been behind it all along, but then she saw that it was the wrong shade of red. This was more of a fiery orange red. Crepuscular, like the sight of a bright noon sky viewed through the skin and veins of your own closed eyelids. And then she realized that it wasn't *like* that color, it *was* that color, because she wasn't opening a door at all, she was opening her eyes and the light was so bright and pure and clear that all she could see was white.

It didn't hurt, this blinding glare; if anything it soothed her, eased the tiny twinges of pain from her bindings, hushed the storm's whirling, calmed her constant struggle against herself. She waited there, basking in the light, for her eyes to adjust to its intensity. She waited and waited, and eventually she looked down at herself and saw that her eyes had adjusted long ago, that she wasn't blinded so much as there was nothing to see. Just pure, empty white space that stretched into eternity in every direction. She stood on nothing, turned in a circle, and saw that she'd come from nothing, moved a single hesitant step in a direction chosen at random and saw that she moved toward nothing.

The only thing here was what she'd carried with her: her clothes, the medal around her neck, the coin of Fortune and Elderflower's cash in her pockets. She thought about reaching for the mirror or her blade, but the thought of reaching into nowhere from nowhere made her a little nauseated, and the thought of vomiting at her feet only to have her bodily fluids fall away from her forever made her heart do an alarming, anxious flutter in her chest.

She worried at the medal around her neck, closed her eyes, and did her best not to panic. "You think this is intimidating?" she asked the emptiness. She had no idea if anyone had actually heard her, but it felt good to break the silence, so she kept talking. "I been through death and resurrection already.

Endured everything life as a black woman had to throw at me, and an after-life as a collector of souls besides. I've stared down fallen angels and Trick-ster gods, a gang of the undead and a straight-up cockroach monster. I'm here and I'm whole, but it was a damn hard road to get here. So help me or don't. But if I got to do this on my own, whoever you are, you'd best stay the hell out my way."

"If you been through all that, ma'am," drawled a voice from behind her, a voice she thought she recognized, "I figure I'd best go on and lend you a hand."

Renai whirled around and saw a hulking brute of a white man—at least, the skin of his hands and arms and legs were the ruddy, dark beige of a white man who spent almost all of his time in the sun—with the furred head and neck of a brown mongrel dog. He wore a dented, battle-scarred steel breast-plate, a leather skirt, and sandals that were worn down to strips of leather. He had a short, thick-bladed sword on his belt and what looked like a shield strapped to his back. He had the same down-the-road Chalmette accent as the psychopomp who had been her mentor, her friend. Between the voice and the canine features, Renai's eyes misted with tears at the sight of him.

"Salvatore?" she asked, knowing as soon as she spoke his name that she was wrong, that Sal hadn't disappeared but had been destroyed. She'd held what was left of him in her hands.

"Sal-wa-tore-ay," the soldier said, correcting her pronunciation. "But no, ma'am. I got no claim to go callin' myself nobody's savior." He gave her a doggie grin that was so like Sal's that it made her heart ache. "Friend of mine sorta got that particular title all locked up, if you catch my meaning." He stuck out a massive, calloused bear claw of a hand, so like a dog who had "learned to shake" that Renai felt herself grinning in spite of the nagging sus-picion in the back of her mind. She told herself that just because Cordelia had betrayed her, not everyone would.

And then, in her grandmother's voice she heard, *Fool me once, child. Fool me once.* When she reached out to shake the giant's hand, expecting either the limp-fingered soft touch most big men gave her—as if afraid they would overwhelm her delicate feminine bones—or the crushing clutch of men who defined themselves by strength and domination. To her surprise, he gave her a firm, concise tug, like they were equals, and then let go.

"Name's Menas," he said, shifting his considerable weight so that he stood with his legs in a wide, confident stance, "but folks call me Cur." He pointed to his dog muzzle of a face. "This bother you? It causes some folk conniptions, but this nose makes tracking so gosh-darn easy that I leave it on most of the time. That's how I found you." He looked around at the white expanse of nothing around them. "We ain't had nobody come in this way in longer'n I care to say."

The moment he said "gosh-darn," Renai finally accepted that—despite his accent and the dog's head and her almost instantaneous liking of him— whoever Cur really was, he wasn't her Salvatore. "The dog head is fine," Renai said. "Comforting, really. You remind me of someone. And my name is Renaissance, but all my friends call me Renai."

Cur's ears flicked and lay almost flat against his skull. "May I call you Renai, ma'am?"

She laughed and nodded. "Sure can."

"Great!" His doggie grin stretched so wide that his tongue lolled out. Then, all at once, his ears came up, alert, and his expression became some canine emotion she couldn't read. "But now I got to ask you some questions, ma . . . uh, Renai." His voice shifted from amiable, almost apologetic, to stern and commanding so fast that Renai would have thought it a joke if his hand hadn't gone to grip the pommel of his sword with all the practiced ease of a cop's hand gliding immediately to the grip of their gun. "Why did you come this-a-way, instead of going straight to where you belong? And you better tell the truth. I can smell a lie. No foolin' around." He sniffed at the air, a rough, panting sound. "No, wait. You still got a living body, and you brought a coin full of Luck here. That's bad and worse. Are you even supposed to be here?"

"To be honest, I'm not even sure where here *is*," Renai said. "I'm a psychopomp, and I'm trying to find someone. A boy named Ramses St. Cyr."

She told him everything then, or at least all the details she thought he'd need. How Ramses was supposed to die and had made a deal to prolong his life, how he'd taken something important and gotten mixed up with a bad crowd, and how she had to find him before things got so bad he couldn't be helped. She kept it simple and to the point, getting the impression that Cur would get confused if the narrative got too complicated. "So that's my story," she said, hoping that telling the SparkNotes version of events didn't have the same smell as a lie. "Do you think you can help me?"

"I sure wish I could, ma'am," Cur said, his ears drooping and his eyes liquid and sad. "If you had something of his I could catch a scent from, there wouldn't be nowhere I couldn't track him down. But without it"—he shrugged—"I won't be no good to you."

Something about that itched at Renai's brain, at something he'd said earlier. "Wait," she said. "You said you found me because of my scent. Did someone send you to find me?"

"Yeah," he said, wiggling a hand under his breastplate like a man in a suit reaching for something in his coat pocket. He pulled out a thin scroll of paper and held it out to her. It was the piece of paper she'd given Elderflower, the one she'd signed with her true name and sealed with a drop of her blood.

A chill ran down Renai's spine, when she realized the only person who could have given this to Cur.

He continued: "She said I was s'posed to rough you up if you showed up on our side of things. Said you was bad news. But she's mean. You know how some people sound nice, but they're really making fun of you?" Renai nodded to show that she did, indeed, know what that was like. "She's like that. I only came to find you in case you were even worse than she is, but don't worry, I won't kick you out. In fact, I'll help you however I can, just to make her mad. Just 'cause she says something doesn't mean I got to listen. She's not in charge of me."

Renai felt a flicker of hope. "Do you think you could find the woman who gave you this? She's one of the bad ones trying to get my friend in trouble."

Cur reached up and scratched behind an ear. "I could try," he said, "but it would take me a while, and you sound like you're in a hurry." He shrugged an apology. "She's one of the shifty ones," he said. "Always changin' shapes and whatnot. That makes her scent get all tangled up and confusing."

Of course it couldn't be that easy. Renai's mind spun, trying to put together what she suspected Cordelia might be planning, and the little she knew of the Far Lands. She needed help. She needed a guide. She needed, she realized, "one of the shifty ones." "Cur, do you know a god named Hermes?"

"Sure," he said, "what about him?"

"Do you know where I could find him?"

"That I can do, ma'am." He drew his sword—a short, wide blade that looked heavy enough that she'd need two hands to even lift it, its edge as sharp and as polished as Cur was disheveled and worn—and used it to cut a rough doorway in the empty air, one continuous swipe that peeled away and left a gaping hole in the white blankness of this place. She'd have been happy to see anywhere through that hole, but a street corner of downtown New

Orleans was a welcome—if surprising—sight. "We can't," Cur said, "go straight to Olympus, I'm afraid. But I got us as close as I could." He sheathed his sword and held out a hand toward the door in the air.

"After you, ma'am."

Renai knew from the moment she stepped through the doorway that she wasn't in either the living world or the Underworld.

It was definitely New Orleans, the corner of Poydras and St. Charles, according to the blue signs that shared the poles stretching over the street with stoplights and dangling Mardi Gras beads, but no version of the city that she'd ever seen. She could smell it, a sweet, heady fragrance like a magnolia tree after a hard rain, could actually feel it in the air, a tingle of anticipation, like waiting for a parade to start.

This New Orleans was quiet, but not silent. Somewhere a brass band played, or maybe a marching band, something with horns and drums and a swaggering, jubilant beat. The streets were empty of people and traffic, but she heard the droning rumble of a streetcar's engine, the clacking sparks of its contact with the wires overhead. Part of her wanted to wait here for the streetcar to roll by, in case Barren might be in the driver's seat, in case the caduceus's spell had been temporary, but Cur came blundering through the hole in the air and pointed behind her, to the massive office complex called One Shell Square.

"This way," he said.

A massive monolith of limestone and glass, One Shell Square was the tallest building in the city, her first true skyscraper, and for a long time after it was built, the tallest building in the South. Its base took up an entire city block, and it rose fifty stories above the New Orleans streets, towering over the other massive office complexes of downtown. Its top floor was higher than the peak of Mount Driskill, Louisiana's only mountain. Renai had to crane her neck back to see the very top floor, its windows twice the size of all the stories below it.

It hadn't occurred to her until this moment, but she had to admit that it made a certain kind of sense: where else in New Orleans would an Olympian make his home?

She hurried to catch up to Cur, who took the sprawling stone steps that led to the front door three at a time, not showing off or in a rush, just moving at the natural pace of his massive stride. Once inside, she followed him across the gleaming marble floors and glitzy, expensive trappings of any high-dollar office complex: glass and chrome and flat-screens. Broke people, Renai had always thought, were broke in their own unique ways. Money always just looked like money.

Cur led her toward the banks of elevators — each of which only serviced a selection of floors — but continued past them, even the ones that indicated they went from the lobby to floors forty and higher. Instead, he stopped at the far wall, an unadorned span of dark gray marble as reflective as her own mirror. Between one stride and the next, without slowing down at all, Cur drew his sword and aimed its point at the wall. Its tip touched its twin reflected on the marble's surface, and then slid into the stone, smooth as cutting butter.

Renai thought at first that the soldier god was cutting the stone in half, but when she looked closer, saw that he'd simply inserted his blade into a hairline crack so thin it was nearly invisible. Once the sword was buried almost to the hilt, Cur leaned his weight against it, and the wall split open the massive stone slabs, separating with a rumble. He sheathed his sword and put one hand on each, and muscles shifted and bunched in his arms that made something in Renai's belly squirm. Even though he wasn't really her type, that kind of display got a girl wondering just what he looked like when he didn't have a dog's face, whether the rest of him was that tightly built under his armor. She bit her lip and let those thoughts linger while he opened the hidden elevator doors.

Inside, there was only one button, unmarked, which made sense. An elevator like this only went straight to the top.

The doors opened with a soft musical tinkle, like wind chimes. Sunlight came streaming through the doors, a warm glow that carried with it the scent of laurel trees. Renai stepped out of the elevator alone — Cur said he'd stay behind and hold the door for her — and onto a lush green carpet of grass. Trees grew all along the edge of the roof, enough of them to give the impression of a secluded glade, but not enough to block the view of the city stretched out beneath them. This high up, Renai could see the twisting rust-brown meander of the river, the urban sprawl of red brick and gray concrete and sparkling glass, the flat green squares of parks or cemeteries, all of it laid out like the pieces of some giant game.

In the center of the roof stood a brief semi-circle of marble columns, ribbed and decorated and capped in ways that Renai knew had names—thanks to some long-ago history teacher who spent a week on the terms but then later that year skipped over the entirety of the civil rights movement—but didn't remember. The space inside this open-air temple had been paved with loose gravel, which made a pleasant crunching sound beneath her feet as Renai walked inside. Within, Renai found twelve backless chairs, like a shallow capital U made out of stone, a shimmer hanging in the air above each one.

As she approached the farthest one on the left, that shimmer in the air resolved itself into a lyre: a musical instrument about the size and shape of a hunter's bow, but with multiple parallel strings like a harp, instead of one perpendicular one used to nock an arrow. Though Renai had a nice—if untrained—voice, her musical aptitude was limited to being able to keep the beat at a second line. Despite that, the lyre called to her, her fingers twitching with desire to attempt a song on its silver strings. It was a beautiful instrument, a twist of bone or horn engraved with an image of a chariot riding across the sky. Renai realized she had started to reach for it and stuffed her hands in her pockets, instead.

Following the arc of chairs, she discovered a bow made of silver and a quiver of arrows, a statue of an owl wearing a plumed helmet, a short-handled maul and a pair of tongs, a sheaf of wheat that shined like gold, a scepter with a head shaped like the frilled eye of a peacock feather, a thunderbolt, a trident, a wicked spear with a jagged-edged blade, a fringed lacy veil, a wide-bowled chalice—and at the final seat all the way on the right side of the temple, Hermes' caduceus. She reached for it and—as she expected—her fingers passed right through it. It was as convincing an illusion as all the others, though, with depth and detail and a shadow beneath it that shifted as it spun slowly on its axis.

"What are you doing here?" a voice said from behind her.

She turned, and there he was, the god who'd called himself Mason, leaning against one of the columns, hooked nose and light brown skin and fine all the way to the ground. He wore a red plaid suit that had no business looking as good as it did, double-breasted and tailor cut, solid black undershirt and tie, and a pair of red-winged, mirror-polished black shoes. Unlike any Trickster god she'd ever met, he wasn't smiling.

"I was just wondering if this seat was taken," she said, unable to resist.

"Clever," Hermes said, glancing down at his nails as if he found his cuticles more interesting, "but I truly hope you didn't come all this way just for that joke."

"I found your caduceus, May's Son." She enunciated the wordplay in the name he'd given her, Mason, to show that she'd figured out his true identity, realizing only after it left her lips that the whole caduceus thing was probably a better mic drop.

He looked up at her with feigned indifference, which told her that he actually cared very, very much about what he was about to say. "And where might that be?"

"Ramses St. Cyr still has it."

He left his insolent lean against the column and came to stand right in front of her without bothering to cross the space in between, without making a sound on the gravel floor. He was just there and then here, faster than Renai could blink. She flinched, and then hated that she'd reacted at all. "And why, little ker, dear sweet tenebrae, why did you let some mortal child keep what was mine?"

Renai could feel his rage so clearly that it cut away some of the fear, called out a summons for her own storm to come coiling to the surface. Not enough to give her access to its power, but just enough that she could withstand the subtle seductive glamour of his honey-brown eyes. "Didn't have much of a choice," she said. "Which I'll explain, once we renegotiate the terms of our deal."

At that, Hermes did smile, though it wasn't a kind one. "And why, in the name of Zeus' eternally engorged prick, would I go and do a stupid thing like that?"

Renai stretched her arms out to either side, taking in everything around them. "Look where we are. The Far Lands. I got here on my own, trick. You want my help getting your little wand back, you better come correct with a better offer."

Hermes slumped to the side, his shoulder turning and his hips cocked, tilting his head so that he looked at her slantways. "Oh, so you're the big shit now, huh? You workin' on a come-up?"

Renai did not appreciate his tone. God or no, he didn't get to talk to her like that, not when she'd come this far. The tempest rose fully in her now, enough that she could seize its power and let some of it slip free. Lightning crackled in her fist and, yeah, it hurt, the bindings straining as she leaned hard toward the purely destructive half of her, but it was worth it when Hermes stood up straight and took a step back. His eyes—moving so quick she wasn't entirely sure she saw it—flicked over to the thunderbolt on the chair in the middle of the row, the one raised just slightly higher than all the rest.

"I think you have mistaken me," Renai said, "for someone else."

Hermes showed her his palms. His voice, when he spoke, took on a placating mien. "Apologies," he said. "I think you'll agree that we're both a bit caught up in the circumstances. I'm sure we're both in a position to help one another. What is it I can do for you?"

"I need to be able to withstand the caduceus's abilities. I don't stand a chance against Ramses if he can knock me out as soon as he sees me." Up until this moment she'd been hoping that the ghost word would conceal her long enough to get close to Ramses, but if Hermes could make her immune, that would be even better. "Do that for me, and we'll go from there."

He gestured at her with a flick of his fingers. "Okay," he said, "done. Now tell me how the hell this child has had my property in his possession for so long."

Renai lifted an eyebrow at him. "Seriously? That's your best 'fake magic' game?"

Hermes let a reluctant, chagrined smile curl along his lips. "Okay, fine," he said. "I admit it, I didn't do anything. The truth is, there's nothing more I can do for you." Renai felt her hopes sink, and it must have shown on her face, because Hermes held a hand up. "I can't do anything else because the caduceus only works once. It can send you to sleep. It can raise you from the grave. But it can't do both. You're already immune." He nodded in the direction of the elevator. "That big Christ-bearing mook of a bodyguard, too."

Renai's thoughts went immediately to all the Gatekeepers, to the Thrones, who had fallen under the winged staff's spell. "So once it puts you to sleep, you can never wake—"

Hermes was already shaking his head. "No, it can undo what it did, but again, only once. Once you return it to me, I'll go back and reverse whatever pranks this little shit pulled."

"*Pranks?* Have you not been paying attention?"

Hermes licked his lips and took a deep breath before he answered. "With my staff loose in this city during the Hallows, I thought it prudent to be somewhere else for a while. Samhain in Dublin is a real kick in the ass, for the record. I forgot how fun it is to be Amadan Dubh. Why, what's been going on?"

And so Renai told him. About Ramses finding the caduceus and falling to its sleep spell, which allowed the demon possessing him to assume control and take Hermes' staff. How he'd then used it to storm the Gates of the Underworld while he was still alive, putting even Death to sleep with the caduceus's magic, sneaking into the Far Lands and headed who knew where with the staff and the cursed revolver. How all of it was part of some plan by a deity who went by the name of Cordelia.

"*Eris,*" Hermes said, and he made it a curse. "Of course it had to be fucking Eris." When Renai didn't seem suitably impressed, he continued. "You ever hear of the Trojan War? You know how it started?"

"Sure, Helen of Troy. The Greeks were coming to steal her, right?"

Hermes made a twisting motion with his wrist. "Wrong way around. The Greeks went to Troy to get her *back*. See, Paris stole Helen from her husband, King Menelaus, because Aphrodite promised she would be his wife."

Renai kissed her teeth. "They started a war because some king got his ass dumped? White people are fucked *up*."

Hermes chuckled. "Yeah, well, they were Greek, not white, but sure. Anyway, the important part of it is, Aphrodite promised Paris that the most beautiful mortal in the world could be his wife because he was judging a contest to see which of three goddesses deserved a golden apple of immortality. Eris is the one who gave him the apple in the first place, all because she didn't get invited to a wedding." He shook his head, wistful like the destruction of an entire civilization was the kind of shit everyone got into when they were young.

"You seem to know a lot about her," Renai said.

"Who do you think brought Paris the apple?" Hermes shrugged. "I'm just trying to tell you that they called her Discord for a reason. Her whole existence is about getting snubbed or not getting something she wants, and then burning the whole thing down. If you're not careful, this place could be next."

"Why? She not get invited to another wedding?"

"Worse. Eris went by another name back in the day: Echidna. Her lover was a god called Typhon; when he was here in New Orleans, he called himself Mourning."

All the pieces suddenly clicked into place. Mourning had been behind all the conflict with Jude Dubuisson five years ago, the mastermind of the plot where her own death had been collateral damage. She hadn't been around for their final confrontation, but the way she understood it, Jude was the only one who walked away.

"Oh shit," Renai said.

"'Oh shit' is right. Way I hear it, Jude shipped Mourning's ass down to Tartarus. If I was a betting man, I'd say Eris is heading that way to bust lover boy out."

"So what can we do to stop her?"

"*We?*"

"The caduceus is your responsibility, isn't it? That damn god-killing gun, too, now that I think about it. Weren't you supposed to protect it? You're really not going to do anything?"

Hermes held his chin in his hand, an index finger stretched across his lips. Like he was asking for silence while he considered his response. After a moment, he said, "Since you're about to rush off and get yourself killed, I'm going to tell you something I don't tell anybody. There's a reason I got so antsy when that stupid winged stick went missing. It's my fate. My destiny. When I die, it'll be the caduceus that takes me. So no, so sorry, but I won't be breaking into a hell prison built to hold the worst monsters in all of creation to go chasing after a demon armed with a gun that kills gods and the magical artifact prophesied to end me. That will not be how I spend the rest of the Hallows. You have fun, though. Bring me back my caduceus if you survive, and I'll do something nice for you."

Renai turned her back on him, on all his lies and his promises, on his failures and cowardice. "Cur," she shouted, "open a door for us to Tartarus!" Whether that place held no fear for him like it did for Hermes, or whether he just heard the determination in her voice, he did as she asked without hesitation.

It was dusk here, but full night on the other side of the door Cur's blade had cut in the air. Even as far away as she was, she could feel the cold pouring in from the other side.

"You forgot to ask the most important question," Hermes called from behind her.

Much as she wanted to walk away without giving him the satisfaction, she couldn't risk the chance that he might actually have something valuable to say. So she stopped and turned back. "What question is that?"

"How you have immunity from the caduceus forcing you into slumber. Your boy over there fell under my staff's spell when he was a guard dog back in the day. I put him to sleep so Heracles could fulfill a task, and I woke him back up once he was back where he belonged." He smiled then, a feral grin that was both hungry and cruel. He couldn't help being a bastard, Renai knew, no more than Cordelia—Eris—could help destroying everything she touched. It was in their nature. "But when you made that deal with the Thrones to give Jude a second chance, I'm the one they asked to bring you back from the dead."

Renai turned away then, not waiting for him to finish, already knowing what he was going to say. She was through the door and into the cold night of Tartarus before he had a chance to speak, but the knowledge had already wormed its way into her heart.

Ramses couldn't use the caduceus to make her fall asleep, but he could use it to snatch away her resurrection.

CHAPTER THIRTY-TWO

THE NEW ORLEANS on the other side of the doorway was a broken mirror. Litter blew on the cold wind, which carried the hot, rancid shit stink of a backed-up sewer. The nearby interstate roared and roared, a constant drone that never left your ears, even when the wails of sirens or the sharp, intermittent pops of a semi-automatic stole your attention for a moment. She stood in the street, cracked and buckling because the sediment beneath it had washed away, the coastline creeping closer every year. The only illumination—a single buzzing streetlight overhead—flickered on and off, on and off, glittering on the broken safety glass at her feet, probably some poor bastard's car window smashed in. Somewhere a woman screamed, shrill and full volume, impossible to tell whether it was drunken elation or fear, only that it cut off too abruptly to be by choice. Elsewhere, deep voices rose in short guttural consonants, vulgarities or threats or both.

And in front of her, the gravitational core of all this misery, the squat, ugly bulk of Orleans Parish Prison.

Like Olympus at the top of One Shell Square, the Far Land of Tartarus was an eerie reflection of the prison in the living world, an edifice of stone and sharp wire and metal bars. Standing there next to Cur, so uncomfortably sim-

ilar to her memory of standing next to Sal in the Underworld, Renai half expected Cross to show up and accuse them of orchestrating a prison break. It
would be especially fitting because, just like the Oubliette in the Underworld,
the massive doors of Tartarus stood open, the razor-wire-topped fence's gate
swinging back and forth in the wind.

At least she wouldn't have to use the ghost word to get in.

Cur stood next to her, one hand on his sword's hilt and his shield already
clutched in the other. A row of fur along his head and the back of his neck
was standing on end, and he practically vibrated with tension. She wasn't
sure how much of her conversation with Hermes he'd heard, didn't know
how much he knew about what they were facing. But then, the atmosphere
made it pretty obvious. Renai reached out to put her hand on his shoulder,
and then thought better of it. "You okay?" she asked. "This isn't your fight.
I'll understand if you don't want to stay."

"I'm fine," he said. "I said I'd help and I will. I keep my word."

She couldn't tell if Cur meant that to reassure her, or if it was a subtle dig
at something she'd done. *Probably the first one*, she thought, *my dude doesn't
seem to do subtle.* "Okay, then," she said, "let's see who's home."

The corridors of Tartarus were a labyrinth. Worse than the strange, eternal hallway she'd walked through to get to the Far Lands, this place was a
monotony of stone and flickering lights and right angles. She and Cur had
walked for what felt like hours; only the biting chill in the air kept her from
sweating through her stupid lace dress, only Cur's constant assurance that
they weren't going in circles kept her moving forward.

They hadn't found a single door, not one cell, just endless branch after
branch of identical, impossible hallways. At every fork in their path, she'd
asked Cur if he smelled anything. The first two times he'd said he didn't, but
she'd known it wasn't entirely true. The third time he said the only thing he
could smell in this place was filth and death.

She'd stopped asking after that.

After so many split corridors that Renai had lost count, always turning in
the same direction, like she'd heard you were supposed to do in a labyrinth,
Cur stopped and looked down the other path. "What is it?" she asked.

"In that direction. Something"—he paused, as if unsure he should say what he was thinking—"something familiar." He looked back at her, muzzle hanging half-open. "Show me what you're carrying," he said. His voice had taken on that commanding, abrupt tone.

She reached into her pockets—startled at how unwound and unraveled the binding threads on her wrists had gotten—and took out all that was left to her in this or any other world, a single coin that held a human being's Fortune from cradle to grave and what had once been a seeing stone, cracked right in half. "No," he said, pointing to the zippered-closed cell phone pocket that she'd just about forgotten. "What's in there?"

She started to say that it was empty, but even as her mouth formed the words, she realized she was wrong. She unzipped the pocket and took out the little slip of paper that Seth had given her in Pal's way back when all this started, a tiny scroll with Ramses' name written on it. Just like the one Cur had used to track her scent in that white nowhere space at the edge of the Far Lands. Cur sniffed at it, turned back down the corridor and sniffed again, and then, without looking back, said, "Follow me."

She followed.

Cur's stride quickened, and then after a few turns, it turned into a jog. By the time they reached the dead end and the cell door, they were practically running. It only took a moment for Renai to catch her breath, grateful for all those nights she'd spent running mile after mile to burn off the excess Voice pounding away inside her. She still brimmed with power from the centuries of Elderflower's Voice she'd consumed, but she wanted to conserve her energy, knowing she was close to finding Ramses, to putting an end to all of this. Knowing she'd need every scrap of power and will at her disposal to make sure it wasn't her end, as well.

The cell door, an iron gate made entirely of bars, made up most of the wall, and showed only the shadows that hid the depths of the room. The scent of Ramses' name had led Cur here when before they'd found nothing else but bare walls, but something about this still felt off. Why would Ramses be locked in a cell? Had Cordelia betrayed him, too? Forced him to trade places with Mourning? Had they come this far, just to find out that they'd already lost?

Footsteps shuffled in the darkness, a shape moving among the shadows. And then a pair of hands passed through the bars, forearms leaning against them with years, decades, centuries of familiarity. Hands marked with the simple, sketched designs of prison ink, hands stained the rich dark red of deep soil. Hands that Renai recognized.

It wasn't Ramses' scent on the paper that Cur had followed. It was Seth's.

                                    ⧗

Renai only had a few heartbeats of confused, frustrated panic, and then the red-handed god pressed his ugly face against the bars and gave her a gap-toothed grin. "Guess you come to collect your favor, then?"

She lifted an eyebrow. "You don't look like you're in much of a position to help anybody."

He glanced down at the bars of his cage and chuckled. "No, I suppose not," he said. "But appearances can be deceiving."

"Like you appearing to be locked up? Because last I saw, you were free as a bird and playing cards with a bunch of other shady-ass tricks. Where they at, the next cell over?"

Seth shook his head. "I don't know what game you're talking about." He waved that away as if it didn't matter. "But you did help the boy, didn't you? That's why you're here? To tell me it's done, at last?" Seth's demeanor was so trusting, so eager for information that Renai felt off balance. It just didn't make sense. He'd been helping Ramses, which meant he'd been help-ing Cordelia. Why, then, didn't he seem to see her as an adversary? If Corde-lia had needed the caduceus or the cursed gun to release Mourning from Tar-tarus, how had Seth escaped? Why was he back here?

Seth was waiting for an answer, and all she could do was tell the truth and shame the devil. "Actually," she said, "I came here to find him. To stop what-ever he and Cordelia are planning and take his life if I have to."

A complex series of emotions shifted across Seth's ugly features, confu-sion and disappointment and weariness and desperation all at once. "*Stop him?*" he asked, his voice nearly a whisper. "Why would you *stop him?*"

"He's got Hermes' caduceus and a gun that can kill a god. Whatever they're planning can't be good." Cur—standing with his back to them and staring back the way they'd come—growled when she said that, a low, dan-gerous rumble deep in his chest. Obviously some of that had been new infor-mation for him.

"But—" He stopped, his eyes narrowing. "Why would you think he's here? What do you think they're going to do?"

"They're going to release Mourning." Seth dropped his head to the bars with a thump that had to be painful, and let out a low moan. "What? What did I miss?"

He looked up at her with his goat-slitted eyes full of pity. "That's not what's happening at all, Renaissance. Cordelia *is* Mourning."

CHAPTER THIRTY-THREE

MOURNING, SETH TOLD her, was just a name for a fundamental aspect of reality: conflict, strife, discord. When Jude had
sent the part of discord that had been Loki, Raven, and Lucifer to
this place, he'd inadvertently released the part that had been Eris, Inanna,
and Lilith. Cordelia was Mourning's Shadow, his Petwo half, like Cross was
the other half of Legba. The difference between Cross and Legba was that
Cordelia and Mourning worked together, complemented each other even as
they balanced each other.

Strife loved nothing so much as more strife.

When Cordelia had found Seth in his cell, she'd told him what she'd been
planning down through the centuries that she'd been here. She'd heard ru-
mors of a weapon with the power to kill a god, and she wanted to use it to do
what Seth had been unable to do in all his time.

"Which was what?" Renai had asked.

"Kill Apep. The embodiment of evil destruction."

Seth, unlike most of the other gods, had never hidden his identity behind
a false name. Set, pronounced Seth, was the Egyptian god of the chaos of the
deep desert. His job was to protect the barge of the sun as it passed through
the Underworld each night from the giant malevolent serpent Apep, who

wanted to devour it. Without the sun, all life would end. Seth admitted that he'd been wild and destructive as a deity, a god of change and endings, but never, he swore, evil.

"Well," he said, staring down at his hands, "maybe once. I killed my brother. Scattered his pieces across the whole of Egypt." His grin, when it came, was feral and brief, and changed the tone of his voice. "Tossed his dick to some fish in the Nile." He shrugged, grew somber again. "Maybe that was evil. But maybe it's evil to fuck your brother's wife. Maybe we were both wrong, in the end." He shook his head, his weird, elongated ears dangling back and forth. "But that's all water through the reeds. The point is, I know I've done wrong in my life, but the world is different than it used to be. Now you're either orderly and rule-abiding, and thus good, a saint, like your boy there"—he nodded at Cur—"or you're a deviant, a problem, and you're evil. And they stick you here."

Which was why Cordelia wanted to kill Apep. She'd convinced Seth that the reason the world thought they were evil is because when they saw chaos, they saw only the kind of destruction that was the end of the world. Not the kind of destruction that swept away stagnant rules or oppressive regimes. And so he'd agreed to help her. Cordelia had let him out of his cage, and he'd delivered his message to Renai, to ensure that Ramses—or more specifically, the djinn, the creature of holy fire Seth believed was inside of Ramses—would be free to end the cycle of Apep's evil once and for all.

"But you're wrong," Renai said, "you're so, so wrong."

"About what?"

"Cordelia. Ramses. All of it. But that damned gun, most of all."

"I don't understand."

"It doesn't work the way you think it does. It isn't powerful. It doesn't kill gods with bullets. It's *cursed*, so it can never be used. It pulls the sin of anyone who touches it into itself, draining them of the desire to use the weapon at all. When it's touched by a god or a spirit who has perverted their whole reason for being, who has become nothing but evil intent, like a fallen angel, it 'kills' them by drawing their evil into it. I've seen it happen." Even there, standing outside a prison cell that held a chaos god in literal Hell, Renai shuddered at the thought of that night, of being held in a fallen angel's clutches and praying to any god who would listen that Jude Dubuisson's plan would work. "Whatever Cordelia plans to do with that gun, it can't be what she told you. You can't fight evil with more evil."

She was trying to recall the MLK quote about a night devoid of stars when her thoughts were interrupted by the sound of thunder, by a hissing noise that she first thought was rain, but when she realized it was coming from Seth, recognized as the whisper of desert dunes rushing away from an oncoming simoom. Seth stood in the center of his cell, wreathed by lightning and fury, his hands clenched into fists. Her own storm shrank away from the chaos god's tempest. Seth's storm was a chaotic beast, a maelstrom so many orders of magnitude more powerful than the spirit living inside of Renai that it was hard to believe that they served the same purpose, the difference between a hand grenade and an atom bomb.

And she'd gone and pissed him off.

Just when she thought he had built to a crescendo, bracing herself for the explosion that would follow, Seth swallowed it — all of it — with a breath. He opened his goat-slitted eyes, and Renai saw only pain and sorrow and rage reflected back at her. One prison-inked fist reached through the bars of his cell. When he opened it, a single glittering grain of sand rested on his calloused, red-stained palm. "I can't escape this cage on my own," he said. "It was built to hold me. But I can give you my power. My strength. You'll need it to strike down Cordelia."

Renai reached for it, instinctively, hungrily, but when she grasped it, it *hurt*. A line of fire raced across her body, the bindings stretching harder now than ever. Only half of her wanted this power, she realized. The killing half. If she took it, if she accepted that role, then that's all she'd ever be. The kind of bringer of destruction that took lives, that tore down. The other part of her, the Underworld half that retained compassion, that destroyed only to change, that broke down only that which couldn't be repaired, that part of her would die.

But maybe that was a sacrifice she needed to make. Maybe compassion was holding her back, making her weak. If she added Seth's power to her own, she wouldn't be a fractured, pitiful excuse of a psychopomp anymore; she'd be a god.

The moment seemed to stretch out, and though she knew her thoughts were racing, she felt perfectly calm. She thought about Jude and what he'd said godhood was like, and Elderflower, and the things he'd sacrificed for immortality. She tried to imagine what Celeste would tell her in this moment, or Sal, or her mother, or her grandmother. She remembered what it was like to be half of herself, to be a task and not a person. She saw the smile of every god she'd ever met and couldn't be sure a single one of them had actually been happy.

She pulled her hand back, and the pain eased, though it didn't retreat completely. She ached all over and knew that the decision to turn away from Seth's offer had cost her almost as much as embracing it would have. "No," she said. "What I need from you isn't power, it's knowledge. Information."

Seth nodded, sad but not terribly surprised. When he closed his fist over the grain of sand, she couldn't help but wonder if she'd made the right choice. "Apep sleeps at the foot of the eternal tree," he said, since there was only one question left for her to ask. "In the Garden of Eden."

CHAPTER THIRTY-FOUR

CUR LED HER out through the corridors of Tartarus, some magic of the place keeping him from simply cutting a hole to Eden from within its walls. He hadn't said a word since she'd spoken to Seth, and she couldn't tell if it was focus or anger or if he was just the strong, silent type. After a while, though, she couldn't take the uncomfortable silence any longer, and if he was going to betray her, she'd rather he did it now than when she was face-to-face with Cordelia.

"Why are you really helping me?" she asked. "And don't say it's because Cordelia was mean to you. I can smell a lie."

His wide doggie grin was a comfort, and not just because it looked just like Sal's. He hesitated for a moment before answering, not like he was searching for the words, but more like he was embarrassed by the truth. Finally, without breaking his stride, he reached up and tapped his chest, the hollow at the base of his throat. "You've been asking for my help your whole life, ma'am. I'm just finally in the right place to do you some good."

Renai reached up to her own throat, right where he'd indicated, and found the medal her mother had given her, the one her Aunt Celeste had blessed. The medallion that depicted St. Christopher, the patron of travelers, ferrymen, and storms. She smiled, and a comforting warmth filled her that she hadn't felt in a long, long time. She felt protected. Righteous, in the sense that she was following the path that she was meant to be on, that she was fulfilling her purpose. She'd been resurrected five years ago, but this was the first time since her murder that she'd really felt alive.

She'd guided hundreds of souls to their just reward, but this was the first time in what felt like forever that she didn't feel lost.

By the time Renai and Cur made it out of the gates of Tartarus, it was well after midnight, according to her cheap cartoon watch. Even though they were two worlds away from where the thing might have any relevance, by one way of reckoning things, by another, she hadn't ever left New Orleans. Given the way her bindings ached and stung whenever she moved, though, she had a feeling the watch was right: It was the Feast of All Souls. The last day of the Hallows.

And her last chance to set things right.

CHAPTER THIRTY-FIVE

THE WORLD IS a tree. It might be an ash, an oak, a fig, an iroko, a ceiba, or a fantastic many-hued tree that no mortal eyes have seen. Yggdrasil and Ashvattha, the Tree of Life and the Tree of Dawn and the Tree of Humanity.

Vast and eternal, sheltering and nourishing, vulnerable and unmoving and unknowable. Whether we poison its air or nourish its roots, we and our children and our children's children must share it, because in the great wide universe, only this one is ours.

The world is a tree.

Cur cut a hole in the world, and Renai stepped through into pristine, idyllic daylight, surprised at their destination. When Seth had told her that Apep slept beneath an eternal tree in a garden, her first thought had been the famous ancient oak in Audubon Park that locals called the Tree of Life. Instead, Cur had brought her to the traffic circle on Wisner Boulevard, facing the long paved road that led to the New Orleans Museum of Art.

"Are you sure we're in the right place?" she asked.

She had no idea how a dog's face managed to look indignant, but the expression on Cur's face was exactly that. He gestured with his muzzle to look behind her. She turned, expecting to see the racist-ass statue of racist-ass Beauregard on his—in all likelihood—racist-ass horse, but instead, there was an empty stone plinth. She started to ask what she was supposed to be seeing, when she realized that she heard snoring.

On the far side of the pedestal, she found an angel sprawled out on her back in the grass, sleeping the enchanted slumber of the caduceus, a sword with a burning blade lying on the strip of sidewalk next to her outstretched hand.

Guess we're in the right place after all, she thought.

Beside her, Cur said, "After he had expelled the man, the Lord God placed winged angels at the eastern end of the Garden of Eden, along with a fiery whirling sword, to prevent access to the Tree of Life." He pointed toward the road that led into City Park; the columns standing on either side seemed grander than Renai remembered, more like barriers than markers. Like a massive gate that now stood open. "Eden," he said, and then, aiming his finger somewhere deep within the acres and acres of City Park, added, "The Tree of Life."

At first, their journey into and through Eden was exactly as pleasant as a stroll through Paradise ought to be. They walked down a wide, straight path —two lanes of paved road separated by a wide, grassy neutral ground that led straight to the NOMA in the living world—delineated by a springy, resilient moss that stretched through the grassy meadow of the Garden. The branches of fruit-bearing trees hung low with riches, and flowers bloomed in shades of red and orange and purple. Off to her right, a clearing filled with clover led to a lake, its surface rippling in the breeze, its waters so clear and bright that they had to be fresh and pure.

Renai breathed in, taking the heady, perfumed air deep into her lungs, and felt all her muscles relax, limbs loosening and stretching, her wings begging to be unfurled so they could bask in the warmth of the sun. Ahead of them, where the angular and columned entrance to the museum would be in the world of the living, a massive crystal bubble rose over the trees, a divine hothouse or some future civilization's utopian dwelling or something Renai couldn't even imagine, but whatever it was, it was beautiful and grand and perfect. The mossy path led to the structure and around it and past it, and Renai knew, with some sadness, that she wouldn't be going in, and the tree they sought was elsewhere. *Still,* she thought, *this is easier than I thought it would be.*

Though she hadn't said it out loud, she regretted those words as soon as they formed in her head.

The sweet-scented breeze picked up, the temperature cooling and the pressure dropping so fast that Renai's ears popped. Remembering that all she had between her modesty and the world was a lacy white dress, Renai zipped up her jacket, knowing what was coming next. Clouds, dark and thick with rain and already flickering with lightning, rolled in over them like a dark shroud being draped over the globe of the world. The rain came down in one gushing roar, so thick Renai could barely make out the shape of Cur stepping in front of her, his shield at the ready, so loud, she could feel more than hear his snarl as he drew his sword. It was a sweet gesture, and also kind of stupid. What was he going to do, she thought, stab the rain to death? She stretched up on her toes to shout into his ear.

"Get to the Tree!" she yelled. "This is all for nothing if we don't stop her!" Cur didn't question her judgment, didn't argue that she needed protection, didn't even catch her eye to see if she was sure. He just gave her a single curt nod, and then ran off into the deluge.

That confidence filled her, made her feel stronger, more certain of herself than she really was. Which was good, because she'd need all the swagger she could muster if she was going to bluff her way past whatever storm god was up there. The one good thing about this ambush was that it meant that they still had time, because if Cordelia had already done what she'd come here to do, why would she still bother to try and slow them down?

Sure is a good thing I turned down Seth's power, she thought, letting her wings unfurl, bracing herself for the yank of the wind's pull. *I'd hate to be evenly matched or anything.* Her wings filled out with a sharp crack, loud as a gunshot, though she'd angled them into the wind like a knife, cutting its strength so that they didn't tear from the strain, didn't lift her up until she was ready. But despite the sarcastic thoughts she lashed herself with, she turned her face up to the menacing clouds and smiled. *Never let 'em see you sweat,* she heard her mother say, and her grandmother's voice said, *They can only tell you who you is if you believe 'em when they say it,* and Sal told her to *give the fuckers hell, Raines.*

So she reached into the nowhere place for her broken stone blade and shifted her wings and let the winds carry her up into the heart of its fury.

Renai first thought, once the clouds had enveloped her completely, was that the inside of a thundercloud was just like the dark fog that blanketed the Underworld, wet and cold and windy, but strangely familiar. And then lightning streaked past her, a white-hot bar of sizzling threat, and her second thought was: *the fuck it is.*

She reached down for the spirit inside of her, but it wilted away from her, cowed by the display of power surrounding her. She'd gotten used to the idea that the magic living within her was alive, a spirit that was as conscious as Kyrie or psychopomps in their own limited ways. But now she was disappointed to also learn that it was a fucking coward.

A second bolt of lightning flashed by, then a third, each one closer than the last, and then the hail started, a pounding rain of ice pellets that — if they connected with anywhere not protected by the thick leather of her jacket — hit hard enough to bruise. Renai gritted her teeth and climbed higher, fighting the buffeting winds for every inch, more curious about her opponent than truly afraid.

One thing was certain: Whoever it was, they were trying to summon up a goddamn hurricane.

After a few moments that felt like hours, Renai realized she could hear voices on the wind. A man and a woman, speaking in short, sharp syllables, grunting and cursing. Renai couldn't tell if they were fucking or fighting, but whichever it was, it was desperate and real. And then, moving in their direction, she burst out of the cloud cover and rose into the crystalline-clear sky above.

Two of the storm gods from Jude's card game were locked together: the furious-faced woman with multiple arms whirling around her head and the fang-toothed man with the feathered headdress. Her fists struck at him again and again, each blow releasing a peal of thunder. He held a hatchet that glowed incandescent, and lightning flashed every time he hurled it at her.

Renai took one look at them and pushed her knife back into the nowhere place, knowing it would do her no good against them, no matter how sharp an edge it had. Renai had no idea how Cordelia had orchestrated this argument, how she had teased them into conflict in this moment and this place, but Cordelia knew that there was no way Renai could fight them off or broker a peace between them. Not in time.

They broke apart and rushed back at each other, howling with voices like hurricane gales, lashing out with fists and feet and elbows and foreheads and fury. Nothing could stand against that kind of destruction. Nothing could endure that kind of punishment. Nothing could reconcile that much rage.

But Renai had to try.

She reached out to the spirit inside of her, not for its strength, but for its knowledge. She could feel the similarity between her spirit and the hurricane beneath her. That same great whirling fury, the same desire for destruction, and beneath it all, the same pain. Each of these gods — *Tlaloc and Guabancex,* her spirit whispered to her — were bending the storm to their will, pouring in their strength and their magic and forcing it to return that magic in the form of wind and lightning. But in doing so, it was being made to tear itself apart. Its whole existence was this moment, this fleeting eternity of pain and fear and aggression, knowing that when it was of no more use to these gods, it would dissipate into oblivion, and yet it feared and longed for that moment with equal passion.

Renai leaned in to the compassionate side of herself, feeling an alarming looseness to the pull of her bindings, a pain that wasn't the pull against her stitches but of her selves starting to tear apart. As though the constant wavering back and forth between her two selves had loosened her restraints so much that she could weaken them more and more with each strain. She pushed past it, even as she danced on the wind and dodged the hail and the lightning of the storm gods' conflict. She ignored her own pain and her own danger and focused on the quickening hurricane below, on its fragile, infantile mind. Through the spirit inside of her, she reached out to it, asked it why the gods were fighting.

It was the first time in the hurricane's entire existence that someone asked instead of commanded.

It — no, she — hadn't always been a hurricane. Pieces of her had been Elderflower's demons, spirits of the wires sent out to steal bits and scraps of information and secrets, holding them inside of her mind, no matter how badly it burned. Other parts of her had been psychopomps, those quiet, bobbing wisps of light that led the Essences of the newly dead along the path of the Underworld. Before that, she'd been Shadows and shades, the cast-off remnants of a human's regrets and follies, gathered together into a thinking, feeling bundle of magic and locked away in the Oubliette until some higher being called her up. Before that, when the other half of her Essence was asleep, or distracted, or drunk, or careless, she'd been alive.

For a single heartbreaking instant, Renai saw the whole system laid out before her. Humans grew and lived and died in all their wonderful complexity, and then the Underworld split them apart. Into the parts that were deserving and the parts that were made to serve. Gods and psychopomps and magicians and priestesses and alchemists, anyone with the will and the Voice and the desire to command these spirits, they got to bend and twist and break these others through control of a compulsion that was deep and cruel and completely unaware. Masters unburdened with the awareness that they owned slaves; slaves who couldn't even exist without the master's say-so.

She thought about what she'd done to the spirits she'd turned into playing cards, all the Shadows she'd helped her dead cast off, and was nearly sick. It hurt, worse than anything she'd ever felt, to realize how complicit she'd been in this system of torture and domination and pain. Understanding led to rage, a righteous hatred of the centuries upon centuries of this hierarchical bullshit.

And with that, deep within her, Renai's fury and her compassion at last found common ground.

Her two selves joined together in a wholeness that felt impossibly good, unbreakable, and complete. She knew, at last, who she was. Not a taker of lives, nor a forgiver of sins, but a liberator—a breaker of chains. The yarn bindings slipped free of her skin and went twirling away in the wind.

"What do you want to be?" she asked the hurricane. "If you could be any kind of spirit or shade or demon or djinn, what would you choose?"

In that whispering non-voice of the dead, the storm answered. Renai reached out, not to compel, not to control, but to *grant*. She gathered the hurricane in her arms and destroyed the storm utterly, like Grace, the blacksmith at the bottom of the world, shattering the hurricane so that she could make something new. What she did wasn't so different from what the two fighting gods were doing, except where they had to impose their will upon the thoughts and magic of the scraps of spirit to force her to take the form of winds and clouds and lightning, Renai merely had to *ask*. Where the gods had to drag the magic to them, it flowed, willingly toward her. Faster and faster as the hurricane realized that she was keeping her promise.

Nothing she could have said or done would have distracted Tlaloc and Guabancex from their battle, but they certainly noticed when they felt their power dwindling away. They turned on her, then, in that instant—conflict forgotten in the face of the threat to their authority that she represented. Lightning flashed. Wind howled.

And faded away into the pile of ash cupped in Renai's hands.

She didn't know if they understood what was happening, or knew only that she'd done something they hadn't seen before in all their long lives, but they shared a single glance and vanished. Renai hung there in the sky, her wings—also a spirit enslaved to a purpose they hadn't chosen, though not by her—keeping her aloft. She promised them they would have their chance. She gathered the last remnants of the storm, the sky returning to its pristine brightness, the sun's warmth glowing on her skin, pulling it all together, and changing the last gasps of wind into a leather pouch that held the ash that had once been a great and wrathful hurricane. It occurred to her that she'd done almost the same thing, unconsciously, with the remnants of Salvatore's Essence, that otherwise the scraps of his personality would have eventually been gathered into a shade, a Shadow, a slave. She vowed to set him free as well.

They were all going to go free.

CHAPTER THIRTY-SIX

RENAI DESCENDED BACK down into the Garden of Eden both found at last and utterly lost. She'd made peace with who and what she was for the first time in her existence, but had no idea where in the immense, maybe infinite Garden she'd landed.

The mossy path was nowhere in sight. She folded the spirit shaped like wings back into their nowhere place — asking, now, instead of telling — chose a direction at random, and started walking. As she struggled through the beautiful, idyllic underbrush of the Garden, she reached out to the spirits around her, first her wings, then the living magic bound into the shape of her leather jacket, then the thunderstorm that slept in her belly, asking about their lives and deaths and service. The wings and the jacket each thanked her for her concern, but said they'd rather stay as they were than change. Her wings, she learned, had once belonged to Arke, the messenger of the Titans. The tempest, though Renai knew the spirit heard her, had nothing to say.

A dryad, overhearing their conversation and impressed by Renai's compassion for the spirits around her, slipped out of her tree and offered to guide Renai. She followed along in a kind of trance, like a runner's high, balanced between understanding and rage in a way that wasn't truly sustainable but didn't take much effort to maintain, either. It took a while for Renai to reach the path that the dryad promised, and a while longer to reach the huge oak that was the Dueling Oak in the living world. But in truth, it had taken her far longer than she'd thought it would take to get there.

Days and worlds and lives further than she'd ever thought she'd go.

The oak towered and sprawled, its branches in all the heavens and its roots in all the hells. In the shadow of its canopy, Cur lay on his back, one of his eyes bruised and swollen, blood trickling from his mouth, a massive six-legged mare pinning him to the ground with her hooves. Somehow, the black horse was familiar to Renai. On a nearby stone bench, Cordelia sat with one leg draped over the other and her dangling foot kicking, indolent and beautiful and terrible.

She turned at Renai's approach, and a smile danced across her face, so bright that Renai would have sworn it was genuine. "Well, there you are," Cordelia said. "We were beginning to think we'd have to plod on without you, weren't we, dear?"

Her companion didn't reply, didn't smile, as still, as menacing, as *wrong* as any ghoul, his eyes full of fire. In one hand he held an old, ugly revolver. In the other, a short staff engraved with two snakes and capped with a pair of outstretched wings.

Days and worlds and lives further than she'd ever thought it would take her, but Renai had at last found Ramses St. Cyr.

CHAPTER THIRTY-SEVEN

KNOWN AS UKTENA to the Cherokee, a vast horned snake of terrible power who possessed a magical gemstone in his forehead. In the Bible he is merely "the serpent," tempting Eve to take her bite of the forbidden fruit. To the Celts he was Cernunnos, sometimes a snake and sometimes a man, but always with the virile, arresting horns of a ram curling upon his head. The Sumerians named him Ningishzida, the ancient serpent who sometimes wore the head of a man. In ancient Egypt they called him Apep, the gigantic snake who fought each day to devour the sun, to destroy the source of light and life. The Greeks called him Python, coiled and huge in the center of the earth. Known to the Norse as Níðhöggr, the terrible dragon who gnaws constantly at the roots of Yggdrasil, the World Tree.

Horned and immense and malicious and inevitable. The Serpent who will devour the world.

⧗

Renai stood there, hands in the pockets of her leather jacket, toes curling inside her black combat boots, waiting for the axe to fall.

Cordelia had everything she needed. The boy. The gun. The staff. She'd had time alone here, with the Tree and—Renai assumed—the serpent Apep coiled around its roots. She'd waited for Renai. All that time and energy and plotting had gone into this moment. But if Cordelia had restrained herself from putting her plan in motion until Renai got here, it couldn't just be to gloat.

"It was such a struggle waiting for you to get here," Cordelia said, "you know I am not a patient deity."

Damn, Renai thought, *maybe she* did *just want a victory lap.*

Cur struggled beneath the horse's hooves, groaning. "I'm sorry, Renai. I tried."

Cordelia crooked a finger and the mare stomped down on Cur's chest, though she also let out a snort that said she hadn't really wanted to do it. That was interesting. "If he speaks again, crush him," Cordelia said, her polite veneer cracking and revealing something cold and cruel beneath it. Then she smiled and the mask had been replaced. "You know, you were a very difficult little death spirit to manage," she said. "Every time I thought I had you pointed in the right direction, you wandered off somewhere else. It was quite distracting."

"Sorry to be so much trouble," Renai said.

"I didn't say you were trouble, dear. I am a goddess of chaos. I *thrive* on trouble. *You* were a *distraction.*" She gestured, and an emery board appeared in her hand. She began to file away at one of her nails. "I nearly swapped you out for that Magician girl once or twice, and I daresay she would have been more effective in your place, but well, here we are. We must make do with what we have, am I right?" She flicked a finger, like she was halfheartedly pretending to conduct an orchestra, and Ramses—or more accurately, the demon inside of Ramses—raised the gun and pointed it at Renai.

"Wait," Renai said, talking to the demon now, the lost and tortured spirt that possessed Ramses, "just a second." Her hands were in the air, something she didn't remember doing, but that's what you did when someone aimed a gun at you. She moved closer, slow step after slow step, her heart pounding in her chest. "I don't know what she told you about that gun, but it's cursed. It'll draw you into it and trap you in there forever."

The demon laughed. "You think I don't know that?" he said, his condescension incredibly discordant coming out of Ramses' creaky adolescent voice. "I'm *counting* on that. You know the one thing I crave, after centuries of slavery? Oblivion. I'll do whatever it takes to get it." He gestured with the barrel of the gun. "And you can stop right there. Like I don't notice you creeping up on me."

Renai stopped, almost—but probably not quite—close enough to lunge at him. If she could get the demon out of Ramses' body before he pulled the trigger, she might be able to stop this.

But she needed a distraction. She turned to Cordelia. "What's so special about me and Regal? How does shooting us get you what you want?"

Cordelia chuckled. "Do you really think I'm a villain in some penny dreadful? Shall I tell you my whole plan now right as I am about to bring it to fruition?" She tapped the emery board to her lips, pretending to consider. "I think not." When she moved, it was as if she became smoke, diffuse and swift and invulnerable. She re-formed right next to Renai, slipped a hand into her jacket pocket, and danced away, all before Renai realized what she was doing. A half second too late, the black-bladed knife was in Renai's hand. Cordelia raised an eyebrow but smiled. "Let's just say," she said, holding up the coin of Fortune so that Renai could see what she'd taken, "that you both have access to a significant source of this."

Understanding dragged at her with terrible gravity. "Jude," Renai said, "you wanted me to bring Jude here."

Cordelia shrugged, an oh-gosh-you-caught-me smile playing along her lips. "His presence would have been appreciated, but it's no matter. I have what I need. Do it."

Everything happened at once. Renai leaped for the demon, who raised the pistol and yelled, "Bang!" with a smile, expecting, Renai would guess later, for her to flinch. She didn't. Instead, the jacket reacted to protect her, the hood flying up and the magic of the ghost word taking effect without her needing to command it. Renai reached inside Ramses' chest, hands searching for the shadowy substance of the demon, the pain of the revolver's curse shocking her fingers numb and making her clumsy. Her hands closed on something, a tiny, fragile bit of Essence, just as she heard the quick, deafening bark of the revolver. Cur howled, and Cordelia laughed, a delighted, musical sound.

She stood, trying not to look, already knowing she'd been too late.

He lay stretched out on the oak's roots, smoke drifting up from the revolver's muzzle, a small neat hole in one temple, the other side of his head a bloody ruin. The demon was gone, sucked up into the cursed gun just like he wanted. And Ramses was gone, too, just as the Deadline had predicted, from a gunshot wound. The timing had just been a little off.

The noise came out of Renai without warning, a sound of grief, a full-throated anguished wail without words or form or restraint. She knelt at his side and wept for him, cradling the far-too-small bundle of Essence she'd pulled from him, yelling until her throat was raw, a psychopomp keening for the life she'd been unable to save.

Renai allowed herself only a moment for tears, a moment that Cordelia seemed content to watch. Seemed, in fact, to savor. The pain of losing Ramses didn't go away, was far from satisfied, but it receded enough for Renai to function. She stood, cushioning the tiny Essence to her chest with one hand, and Cordelia's smirk brought lightning crackling to her other one. She hadn't had to ask the storm spirit to lend her its power: it came roaring to the surface, eager to lend its aid. "Why?" Renai asked. Her voice was hoarse, the taste of blood in the back of her throat, but she swallowed and spoke again. "Tell me *why*."

Cordelia spread her hands. "Same reason the scorpion stings the frog," she said. "It's my nature."

A single spark, a fraction of the destructive power within her, scorched the earth at Cordelia's feet. "Not good enough." Renai was so full of righteous fury that she felt like the ground quivered with every step she took.

A flash of anger passed across Cordelia's face. "Fine. It's because this world is broken. You know it as well as I do. It's why you tore yourself apart. How can you possibly love this world when it's full to bursting with so much *shit?* You've seen it yourself. Everything about this world, from the way the gods above twist and control the spirits for their own ends, to the monstrous acts these mortals commit on each other again and again and again. Children dying because they don't have clean drinking water, while an entire nation pisses in theirs. The wealth of an entire world clasped in the hands of a few, everyone else fighting over the loose change that manages to slip free. The legions of them who go their whole lives hating everyone who is the slightest bit different. Their skin, their sex, their gender, their love, their faith, their home. As if they don't all look like that"—she pointed at the Essence in Renai's arms—"to us."

"You know I'm right," Cordelia continued. "You're death in a pretty dress, after all. You and me, we're the forest fire that clears away all the dead wood. We're the inevitable end to all things. Destroying this world isn't an evil act, Renai. It's a mercy killing."

Renai took a long, deep breath, and let the lightning slip away from her grip. "You're right," she said. "You're absolutely right." She unzipped her jacket and slid Ramses' Essence inside, where he would be safe.

Cordelia cocked her head to the side, exactly like she would have done when she was an unassuming little brown bird. "Beg pardon?"

"You've convinced me," Renai said. "I was already halfway there. We're on the same team, right? The inevitable end, just like you said. Just wish you'd have given me that speech, like, a week ago."

Cur began to snarl and gnash his jaws, his eyes full of rage and hate. "Traitor!" he yelled. "Fiend!"

Cordelia glanced at him, and then turned narrowed eyes at Renai. "What is his malfunction?"

"He can smell lies," Renai said. "So he knows I'm telling the truth." She bent down and picked up the caduceus, its power throbbing in her hand like a heart. She reached out—with her free hand, with the power of a psychopomp—toward the six-legged horse, recognizing the mare for who she was, begging for her trust. "Drag that idiot outside the east gate," she told the mare, "and kill him." The massive horse kicked Cur's sword away where he wouldn't be able to reach it, grabbed his breastplate in her massive jaws, and dragged him, roaring and spitting insults, out of sight. When they were gone, Renai turned to Cordelia, forced herself to smile, and said, "What's next?"

The chaos goddess studied Renai for a few silent, tense moments. Renai's legs trembled, as she waited to see if her gamble paid off, if her honesty about wanting to tear down the world that the Thrones had built—which had been enough to convince Cur's nose—would be enough for Cordelia to trust her. At last, she smiled, and shook one finger at her in mock rebuke. "I knew you had potential," she said. "Next we summon Apep. He will need a vessel, so we'll use this"—she held up the coin of Fortune she'd stolen from Renai— "and this"—she held out her other hand, waited for Renai to give her the caduceus—"to resurrect the dear departed Ramses St. Cyr with Apep growing inside of him."

"That's it?"

Cordelia's eyes narrowed again. "What do you mean?"

"All this just for one person?"

The chaos goddess smirked. "What were you expecting? A serpent the size of a city? An asteroid plummeting from the heavens? The destruction of an entire world in one screaming, bloody night?" She shook her head, smiling, indulgent. "You still think too much like a mortal, Renaissance. You think the devil is a dragon, a shadow overhead who swoops down and burns your city and flies away with your children in his belly. Or he's the dark whisper in your mind who tells you to kill your neighbor. But the truth is, all he's got to do is tell you that your neighbor is different. That his food smells funny, that he's more successful, or that he wants what you have. Then you do it for him. And when you're done with the devil's work, you invite him into your children's hearts too." She smiled, and the joy in it was the manic glee of a fire leaping from one building to the next. "Today it's this boy in this city, Renaissance, but Apep is already everywhere. It'll be the little things. Trust in those they choose to lead them. Faith in their friends. Compassion for those closest to them, and for those furthest away. A crack here, a break there, all around the edges, until one by one, they're alone and angry and afraid, and it's everyone's fault but their own. They'll leave people to fend for themselves when a hurricane destroys a whole community. They'll send their thoughts and prayers when a concert gets shot up. Or a movie theater. Or a school. They'll elect demagogues and sociopaths and avatars of pure, unfettered greed. And when the flames rise, they'll blame each other."

Cordelia smiled, her tongue caught between her teeth like she couldn't believe she was the one who got to spill the tea. "We won't have to destroy this world, my dear. They'll do it for us."

Renai bit the side of her mouth so she wouldn't scream. The tempest whirled within her, ready for her direction, but desperate to act. It took all of her self-restraint, every ounce of her newfound balance, to keep from un-leashing the storm right in Cordelia's face. After a few breaths, she recovered enough to ask, "So how does this work? Is there a summoning ritual or—"

Cordelia giggled, shoving the heel of her hand against Renai's shoulder. "Oh, don't be foolish," she said. "Did you really think I was going to rely on you coming to your senses? Or that I would tell you the details of my plan if you had one chance of stopping me? The blood of a sacrifice on the roots of the World Tree is all we needed. Apep's already here."

That's when Renai realized that the quivering beneath her feet had been a steady, increasing thing, more noticeable now that she was still and quiet and not filled with the fury of the storm. That her legs hadn't been trembling with fear at all. That the earth itself shook.

The grass beneath the oak split and tore, brown soil thrust up from the earth beneath. Two sharp points broke through first, smooth and glossy and hard instead of the scales Renai had been expecting. Above them, the oak creaked and groaned, shifting because its roots were being displaced, perhaps, or maybe in actual pain.

And then Apep shoved his way into the Garden of Eden.

His scales were pure white, as though sunlight had never touched his flesh, and his flat, broad head was crowned with a pair of thick black horns. His body was about half as thick as Cur's, yet if he rose up from the ground to his full height, he'd be twice as tall. Menace radiated from him like heat from a furnace, and he smelled like incense, like burnt flesh, like sacrifice and spilled blood. It gave Renai an idea, just one chance to do this right.

"I thought he'd be bigger," Renai said.

If the embodiment of chaotic, evil destruction took any offense at her words, he didn't show it, but Cordelia threw back her head and laughed, and that's when Renai made her play.

Everything she'd done and endured since her resurrection had led to this moment: the splitting and reunification of her self, every soul she'd separated from their Shadow, every wrestling match with the destructive impulses of the storm spirit inside her, every glimpse of her family she'd managed to steal using her mirror, every scrap of Voice she'd consumed, every moment she'd wished for a change to this life of hers, even if it was an ending.

But mostly, she remembered that she'd been able to show Cross his Shadow self in a broken piece of polished stone.

She reached into the nowhere place for her knife and for the mirror, pulled them both free at the same time, one in each hand. She brought them together, slow enough that she wouldn't chip the edges but quickly enough that she'd already fitted the two broken halves back together by the time Cordelia asked what she was doing.

For this to have any chance of working, her mirror, like her soul, would have to be whole. It would have to be big enough, strong enough, to show Apep, the most ancient, malevolent being in creation, that there was another way.

But she had no magic that could repair or restore. She was destruction, an embodiment of the inevitable end, an emissary of death, that much of her agreement with Cordelia had been true. She couldn't make so much as re-make, creation through destruction. She just had to hope that—like the two broken pieces of herself—whatever spirit lived in this mirror would want to be reconciled. She could only hope that her will would be enough.

She could only hope.

Renai let slip her winds of destruction, of change. Apep looked down at her, curious, but unconcerned. So beyond her power that he stared right into her mirror without fear. The wind poured out of her in a torrent, a tornado, a hurricane. She thought about every injustice, every indignity she'd endured. Apep and Cordelia had chosen her city for their destruction, and so she gave them every kind of destruction this city had ever known.

The destruction of the lives chewed up and shat out in this city during slavery, the destruction of even their history, the lie that slavery was some-how different here, with their "even free people of color owned slaves," the destruction bred from a society that allowed even one human being to own another.

The destruction of neighborhoods flooded and never rebuilt, torn down to make way for "development," ground beneath the heel of poverty, re-painted with the gloss of gentrification.

The destruction of entire generations of men, churned in the thresher wheel of shitty education, drugs, violence, and incarceration, any worth of their minds or their backs or their blood beaten and dragged from them like grain to fill the pig trough, the chaff that was left thrown into the compost heap to fertilize more meat for the grinder.

The destruction of every woman she'd ever known devoured in little nib-bling bites, of concern for her safety, of telling her how to dress and who to love, and not to get drunk in public, and not to leave her drink unattended, never walk home alone, never smile too much or not enough, never ask for a raise nor seem ungrateful, women who were sluts if they gave it away and who were killed if they didn't, every single inch of their bodies belonging to someone else every day of their lives, bitten and chewed and swallowed.

Renai summoned up every moment that this city had disappointed her, had broken her heart, had threatened her shamed her embarrassed her ig-nored her abused her neglected her hated her destroyed her murdered her, every last one, and she changed them into a fierce, howling wind, into the voice of a hurricane.

And she screamed with that destructive voice a demand that he look into her mirror and *see*, a plea for him to *change*, her magic and her fury and her need lashing against Apep's scales and his horns and his eyes.

She could only hope it would be enough.

His eyes went first. Between one blink and the next, they were red, and then they were blue. After that, the white scales on the top of his head began to flake off, scoured away by the fury of Renai's wind, first one, then a handful, and then a wave down his head and along his coils to the tip of his tail. Where the white scales swept away, the scales beneath were red, dark as fresh blood welling up from the cut, orange as the fire racing across the sky at sunset, yellow as marigolds spread out across a field, green as duckweed spread out thick across the water like a carpet, blue as the Gulf just after a storm, stretching to the horizon, indigo, like the sky at the first breaking light just before dawn, violet as the handprints smeared on cave walls by the first artists.

Renai gave it all of her strength, all the power of the spirit within her, who gave it gladly, sacrificing itself and dwindling away to nothing, not even a hint of a breeze. It felt like days, it felt like less than a second. She gave it her all, her strength abandoning her just as Cordelia hurled some magic in her direction, a golden ripple of force that shattered the obsidian mirror beyond any chance of repair—finger-sized shards scattering everywhere—and hurled her to the ground. She flinched as she landed, expecting hard ground or even harder roots, but her impact was cushioned by something relatively soft.

The fleshy coils of a serpent.

Cordelia stood over her, fists trailing smoke and ruin, breath coming in quick pants. "I am going to enjoy this," she said. Before she got the chance to unleash whatever destruction she intended, the other half of Apep reared up, a diamond embedded in the center of his forehead, rainbow scales glistening down his length, the opposite of Apep in every way.

"Cordelia, meet Damballah Wedo," Renai said, "the loa of creation."

The chaos goddess looked up at him and shrieked, in rage and in threat of violence, her hands full of flames and blades and her eyes eternally dark. She was the embodiment of hate, of order disrupted, the poison in the well, the knife in the dark. She'd killed men and gods and a psychopomp named Salvatore, and she screamed even in the face of pure benevolence.

Damballah laughed.

It wasn't cruel or mocking. It was the laugh of a being who had seen one end of creation to the other and found joy in it. Renai felt a knot within her unkink. Something she hadn't realized she'd been holding on to, something beyond even anger.

Despair, that was the word. Since her resurrection, she'd lived with that knot inside her, the fear that the world got a little bit worse every day. That she'd only been granted a brief reprieve, and worse would come later. When Damballah laughed, that knot slipped loose and vanished.

Renai felt tears rolling down her cheeks and didn't know if they were from gratitude or relief or just pure, unfettered joy.

Cordelia shrank. She curled in on herself, hands into fists, arms over her head, bent at the waist, knees drawn up to her chest. Her golden gown enveloped her, dwindled with her, shifted and changed as she tried to escape. She went, screaming, into irrelevance. When Damballah Wedo spread his great feathered wings and launched into the sky, all that was left of the goddess of Discord was a golden apple lying in the pristine grass of Eden.

PART FOUR

AS ABOVE, SO BELOW

LATE IN THE evening on November 2nd, the Feast of All Souls, a black family gathered in St. Louis No. 1 around a small tomb labeled CROCKER. It was the tomb that would one day hold the ashes of Celeste Dorcet and her sister Rosamonde Raines, and already held — as far as anyone in the Raines family knew — the ashes of Rosa's daughter Renaissance. They'd come because Celeste asked them to, even though there had been bad blood in the family since the untimely death of one of their own. After they'd washed and painted the tomb, laid fresh flowers at its base, they stood there in uncomfortable silence, Celeste constantly checking over her shoulder at the front gate, as if expecting someone else to arrive. Eventually, they were driven indoors by the sudden, gentle downpour that fell from the belly of a winged serpent circling overhead, a being only Celeste would have seen if any of them had looked up. In the spirit of reconciliation, Celeste was invited along to dinner.

Only when she got home would the former Voodoo Queen of New Orleans find the effigy slipped into her purse, a simple thing made of twigs and twine and hair, once bound together with red yarn, now fused together like petrified wood.

The family cleaning the grave never saw the other group gathered together to watch them. Even though the second group—a tall, lanky black man in a dark suit; a short white woman with spiky hair in a *Legend of Zelda* T-shirt and jeans; a dark six-legged horse; a slender Creole man with a wicked grin who wore a stars and moons vest and somehow pulled it off; and a young black woman in a leather jacket with hair as iridescent as a raven's feather —stood close enough to the family to touch them, in truth they were worlds apart.

"So, fuck-face," Regal said to Jude, "tell me again why my girl Sparkles here shouldn't take her shiny new sword and shove it so far up your tight, puckered asshole that you can shave with it?"

Jude laughed, a deep honeyed sound. "Because, Queens, like I said, I helped y'all as much as I could."

"You told us you was hosting a card game that never actually happened," Leon said, patient and disappointed all at once. "Your 'help' was an illusion. A trick."

"Yeah, so I could let Renai steal that little glimpse inside and show her all the creeps she was gonna have to deal with!" Jude said, throwing his hands in the air. "Have y'all forgotten that I'm fucking Trickster now? Hints and misdirection are just how I roll. And, hello? Did we forget that Eris was fuckin' around with people's Petwo halves? Y'all really wanna meet my dark side? I needed to stay out of it." His grin, when it came, was every bit a Trickster's. "But I really did stall the storm gods for as long as I could." He gave a wiggle of his eyebrows to show just how he'd accomplished that feat, which told Renai at least a little about why Tlaloc and Guabancex had been fighting so furiously when she'd met them. "Besides, did you really believe I would let a walking pile of cockroaches into my card room?" He pulled an incredulous face. "Really? I'd have to burn it down and start from scratch."

Regal started to say more, but Renai put a hand on her arm. "Regal, it's fine. If the Fortune God of New Orleans can't admit he was scared, we shouldn't force him. You know how delicate male egos can be."

"Hey, now," Leon said, while Jude just licked the tip of his finger and pretended to mark off a point on an imaginary scoreboard.

"Storm-fucker," Regal said, shaking her head at Jude before turning her back to him, and focusing her attention on Renai. "I can't believe you got a magic sword and I got a magic ring. This Halloween really was the best D and D adventure ever. St. Christopher really wasn't mad you took his sword?"

Renai shrugged. "He was more than happy to give it to me when I told him he should keep the angel's flaming sword. I bet the angel was pretty pissed when they woke up and it was gone, of course, but when you fall asleep on the job, what do you expect?"

"And the revolver? Hermes' staff?" Renai really didn't like the hunger she saw in Regal's eyes. She might make jokes about magic items in role-playing games, but the Magician of New Orleans was no stranger to accumulating power. Renai had told them all about the aftermath of her conflict with Cordelia, how she'd gone to find Cur and Kyrie—the six-legged horse was her former motorcycle's true form—to tell them that she didn't need backup after all. Cur, bless his heart, hadn't realized that her turn to the dark side was a trick—more or less—until Kyrie had picked up the flaming sword by the hilt and shoved it, covered in horse spit, into his hands.

"By the time I went to find the cursed revolver and the caduceus, they were gone," she said. "I guess maybe Damballah took care of them."

Which was a lie, of course. St. Christopher's blade in the hands of a psychopomp could destroy just about anything. She'd cut the revolver in half and buried the pieces on either end of the Garden of Eden, and she'd thrown Cordelia's golden apple into the center of Eden's lake, where she hoped no one would ever find it.

She had her own plans for the caduceus.

"Sounds to me like you done earned yourself a rest," Leon said, nodding at the child's Essence in her hands, "but by the looks of it, you already back on the job."

"This is Ramses St. Cyr," Renai said bobbing the Essence up and down and cooing at him. "He was destined to die before his first birthday. His mother prayed too hard without caring who listened, willing to make a deal with whoever showed. The child lived, locked away in his own mind, while the demon who took his Fortune also took over his life. So in a way, he lived as much of a life as he was ever going to." Renai wasn't sure exactly how Cordelia had gotten Ramses' name into Plumaj's book a second time, but finding out was pretty close to the top of her to-do list.

"So I guess you bringing him to the other side?" Leon asked. He sounded like the idea made him sad.

"No," Renai said, asking Kyrie with a touch to bend down, so she could climb onto her back. "I'm bringing him home."

𝕀

Late that night, Renai stood in the bedroom of her older sister, Claire, while she and her partner slept. The jacket's magic rendered her unseen, unheard, and untouched, yet still she whispered when she asked the spirits she'd assembled there for their permission to unmake them. Once, she'd have tried to force her will on them, and maybe it would have worked, and maybe it wouldn't have, but she'd have felt a knot within her that she never truly acknowledged grow a little bit tighter. Asking, though, made everything flow together like magic.

On the dresser before her, she had the coin of Fortune that she'd been carrying around for days—the one Cordelia had intended to use to resurrect Ramses' corpse with Apep riding inside—wiped clean and free with a little destruction magic; the plump, ripe fig that was almost ten years of Ramses St. Cyr's unused Voice, brimming with magic and sweetness; the leather bag of Salvatore's scraps of Essence, his gruff humor and affinity for art and his loyalty and determination; and the infant Essence of Ramses St. Cyr.

Tears rolled down her cheeks as she unmade them all, her magic always and ever a thing of destruction. As she unmade them, she guided them into their new forms, the coiled braids of Voice and Essence and Fortune that made a living human soul, not Sal or Ramses or the lost spirit or any of them, but some of all of them, with a new chance, a new life. Carrying this delicate, impossible, magical being to her sister, who had the quickened embryo of a new life growing inside of her, waiting for the deity whose job it was to deliver newly forged souls—they weren't all storks, but many of them were —to the inanimate flesh flowering in the womb. She felt the soul take, felt it the moment he went from a might-be to a will-be. And then Renai left them. Alone.

𝕀

In the home of Juliette St. Cyr, she stood over the bed of a woman who hadn't slept more than an hour at a time in days. A woman who had worries in her mind that would only be confirmed when the police found the body of her son in City Park just after dawn. A woman who had years left to live, a road left to walk that wouldn't get any easier. A woman who stared up at the ceiling with anxious, sleepless eyes that only thought they'd run out of tears to shed.

Renai waved the caduceus over Juliette's face and granted the woman the balm of sleep.

From her pocket, Renai took a leather pouch filled with ash, a spirit that had once been a hurricane, a spirit who had asked to become this. Gently unwrapping the silk bonnet that Juliette slept in, Renai dumped the ash into her hair, rubbing it in, massaging it into the grieving woman's scalp. She could feel the spirit entering Juliette's dreams, granting her a vision of the baby growing in Claire Raines's belly, the soul of her own child given a second chance. Then the ash spirit whispered to Juliette about gun violence and support groups and the horrifying statistics that her son had just joined. She wasn't the only mother who had lost a son, the ash spirit told Juliette. Hers wasn't the only family scarred by violence in this city, day after day, hour after hour.

There were groups she could join, the ash whispered. This wasn't a burden she had to carry alone, wasn't a pain she had to endure. She could use it. What could they do, all those grief-stricken, rage-filled mothers, if they spoke with one voice?

Together, in her dreams, Juliette and a spirit of ash began to make plans.

⊠

In Regal Constant's apartment, Renai stood in Regal's bedroom, embarrassed because neither the Magician of New Orleans nor Leon was sleeping. Far from it. Thankfully, Regal had taken off the brass and iron ring before . . . well, before. Renai picked it up from nightstand, slipped it into her pocket, and left.

⊠

Renaissance Raines watched the seconds tick over toward midnight on her cheap cartoon watch, waiting for the Hallows to end. She stood next to Kyrie, at the foot of Canal Street, cemeteries all around them, leaning against the horse-spirit's solid, muscular warmth, hoping her presence would be enough to keep the six-legged horse in the world of the living with her, instead of crossing over into the Underworld with the other spirits and shades and Shadows.

Midnight. A Vietnamese man standing at the streetcar stop vanished as the living world and the Underworld separated. Renai hoped he found his way home, but knew, now, that guiding him there was someone else's job. She felt the worlds pull apart, and for the first time in five years, she stayed whole. Beside her, Kyrie blew out her lips, a sound that she made when she was frustrated, or amused, or bored. Renai was still learning to tell the difference. She patted Kyrie's flank in gratitude; she hadn't commanded the horse-spirit to stay with her, after all. She'd only asked.

She'd already decided she couldn't go back to being a psychopomp. Not the way the Thrones ran things. She couldn't be a part of that system. Couldn't separate Shadow from Essence knowing what was in store for them. She wasn't dead, wasn't exactly alive, wasn't a 'pomp, certainly wasn't a god.

But she wasn't conflicted anymore, either. She hated parts of this city enough to tear down everything that was wrong with it without a moment of nostalgia or hesitation, and she loved it deeply enough to only tear down the parts that deserved it, and only so something better could grow. She didn't know what to call that. Gods could only be one thing, kind or malevolent, creative or destructive, but she was capable of both. Like the two sides of a coin.

She took out Jack Elderflower's brass and iron ring and drew St. Christopher's sword. She pressed the ring to the blade, and—hardly using any pressure at all—used the blade to slice through the Seal of Solomon engraved on the metal. Careful, controlled destruction. *What was the word for that?* she thought. Leon would know; he liked big words as much as she did.

Spirits began to pour from the broken ring like smoke, lost, wounded, desperate things. Ghosts and djinn and shades and Shadows, they were all lost souls to her. They swirled around her, speaking in that whispering non-voice that she'd learned to listen to.

Are you her?

Did you free us?

Are you her?

Can you really send me home?

Are you the one who helps?

"Yes," Renai said, smiling. "I'm her. I'm the one who helps."

When Death comes, he takes everything: ambitions, charity, shared jokes, secrets. All are lost. And when Death comes, she leaves nothing behind: the slant of your smile, the timbre of your voice, the forgiveness you never got to speak aloud, all are gone. Yama and Odin, Orcus and Erlik, Mara and Mictecacihuatl, and the silence of a heart not beating. They are hunters and trappers, they are beasts and they are raptors, and they are scavengers and they are forces of nature. Death stalks us and chases us and waits for us and is always inside of us. Death is a door and a bridge and a guide and a mouth and a transition and an end. It is the one experience everyone and everything must encounter. Microbes and heroes, the ancient oak and the cicada that leaves a husk clinging to its bark, gods and children and cities and ideas and fathers and mothers and countries and stars and me and you. Everything dies and everything ends and that is all.

And yet.

Everywhere Death walks, Life follows. Everything Death takes, Life gives to another.

She is Asase Yaa. Onuava. Demeter. Coatlicue. Phra Mae Thorani. He is Kokopelli. Makemake. Geb. Lono. They plant the seeds in the earth and children in the womb. They gave birth to the gods and to the first mortals and to the cosmos and to the sea. They give their lives to water the earth, to bring plentiful game to hunt, to keep the sun in the sky. They are the sky. They are the sun. They are the buds of new growth in spring, and after a fire, and after a flood, and in the shadow of a failed nuclear reactor. They are everywhere we swore they couldn't be, in the exothermic vents of the deep ocean, in the ones and zeroes of information, in the fossil record of Mars. Death can end a life, or lives, or this life, or every life.

But not *Life*.

Just as Death's promise is always fulfilled, Life's offer is continually extended.

But where Death only ever promises an end, Life offers the hope of a new beginning.

ACKNOWLEDGMENTS

Second books are tough, and this one threatened to tear me in half. What follows is an incomplete list of thanks to all of the family, friends, and kind souls who helped stitch me back together:

To my editor, John Joseph Adams, for his continued enthusiasm for this world, and for guiding me through the depths of the various drafts of this novel. May your steaks always be on swords.

To my copy editor, Erin DeWitt; cover artist, Will Staehle; to Michelle Triant, Hannah Harlow, Dani Spencer, Beth Burleigh Fuller, and everyone else at HMH, for all your tireless work.

To my agent, Seth Fishman, for being able to look forward to the future and focus on the present all at the same time.

To his assistant Jack Gernert, Anna Worrall, Will Roberts, Rebecca Gardner, Ellen Coughtrey, and everyone else at Gernert for their support in getting these words in front of as many eyes and into as many ears as possible.

To Michelle and Bryan Camp Sr., Rose Camp, Bryndon Camp, Bryttany and Keith Wogan, Gerri and Ed Merida, Mary Anne Iles, Abigail and Michael Labit, Becky Merida, and Hal Harries, for being a wonderful, supportive family.

To Bev Marshall, Amanda Boyden, Joseph Boyden, Jim Grimsley, Mary

Rosenblum, Stephen Graham Jones, Connie Willis, George R. R. Martin, Gavin Grant, Kelly Link, and Chuck Palahniuk, for all the writing lessons over the years. I drew on your wisdom over and over again while writing this book.

To Alex Jennings, Alys Arden, Bill Lavender, Bill Loefehlm, Candice Huber, Casey Lefante, Chris Bowes, Danielle Smith, Greg Herren, Henry Griffin, Les Howle, Lish McBride, Nancy Dixon, Neile Graham, Nick Main-ieri, Niko Tesvich, Susan Larson, Tawni Waters, Tracie Tate, and Wayne Rupp, for all the imperceptible and irreplaceable ways you've all left your mark on me and my work.

To the Clarion West class of 2012: Alyc Helms, Blythe Woolston, Brenta Blevins, Carlie St. George, Cory Skerry, Georgina Kamsika, Greg Friis West, Helen Marshall, Henry Lien, Indrapramit Das, James Harper, James Herndon, Kim Neville, Laura Friis West, Huw Evans, Nik Houser, and Sarah Brooks. You're all editorial voices in my head and stitches in my heart.

To Michael Thomas, I wouldn't be able to do any of this without you constantly pushing me to do better. I am, as always, grateful to be your friend.

Finally and always, thank you to my wife, Beth Anne. As hard as this book was on me, I know it was even harder on you. You never give up on me, never let me compromise, never waver in your support or your faith in me. I don't know how you do it, but I'm grateful. Even though this isn't the book you hoped I'd write next, your presence is on every page. Even though I wrote these words alone, you're always with me, and always will be.